RAINEY

THE STORY OF A WOMAN

*For Jeanette and Charles,
With best wishes*

Copyright © 2001 by Lloyd J. Guillory
All rights reserved.
No part of this book may be reproduced, stored in a retrieval system, or transmitted by any means, electronic, mechanical, photocopying, recording, or otherwise, without written permission from the author.

ISBN: 0-75962-126-8

This book is printed on acid free paper.

1stBooks - rev. 05/17/01

INTRODUCTION 1935

Although this novel is a work of pure fiction, it begins in one of the most traumatic times in American history, and to fully understand the crucible in which the life of Rainey Wether was forged, it behooves the reader, especially those too young to have lived through it, to better understand those times by reading the following words which are a simplified and condensed accounting of those turbulent times.

The great depression of the thirties lay heavily upon the land and it remained so from 1930 until the forced expenditures of World War II rescued the nation from its grasp. Many attempts by the Federal government were made, through its many relief programs, to mitigate its hold on the populace, but none of them worked on a permanent basis. There were philosophical differences among the political leaders as to the merit of government intervention. Those of the old guard, the conservatives, felt that aid of any kind only stifled man's incentive to aid himself. Those of the new breed, now referred to as "spend and tax" liberals, believed that it was the role and responsibility of government to come to the aid of its distressed citizens. In retrospect, one must conclude that Franklin D. Roosevelt, who had the misfortune to be President during that difficult period, was the right man for the times.

Regardless, it is not the intent of this introduction to pass judgment on either faction, but merely to reflect the effect of the great depression on nearly all Americans.

The population of this nation at that time was nearly 150,000,000 people. Of that number, somewhere between 13,000,000 and 15,000,000 citizens were unemployed (they were never sure just how many). If the children were taken into consideration, as they must be, and allowing for four children per family (a conservative figure for that period), then it can be assumed that nearly 50,000,000 people were without incomes. Desperate fathers and husbands resorted to any means to feed their families, from selling apples on street corners to stealing. Many unfortunates, who had lived in one home all their lives, now became itinerant and were assigned the unfortunate title of "hoboes". I can remember, as a child of ten at the time, men coming to the kitchen door of our home, asking for left-overs..."Please, Ma'am, I ain't had nuthin' to eat for two days." Those, too proud to beg, had small hand grinders, offering to sharpen knives and scissors for ten cents.

Thousands of banks had failed and the deposits in them were lost since there was no FDIC in those days. Those families who were fortunate enough to have had savings had now lost them. There was distrust of banks and even bankers. There was distrust of government and elected officials. To many, there was even a distrust in God. Many asked: "How can a merciful God allow this to happen to a God-fearing nation whose motto is... IN GOD WE TRUST." Many, especially those of strict fundamental beliefs, felt sure that the country, during the fast living and moral disintegration of the twenties, had, indeed, offended God to the point that he imposed Divine retribution on both the guilty and the innocent. But, since the depression had spread to Europe also, it could be assumed that the entire planet had offended Him.

As if the depression had not caused enough misery, nature added more misery by inflicting on the central part of the country the worst drought in recorded history. The drought years for some strange reason, paralleled the depresssion in the years of 1932 to 1936, inflicting even more hardships on those who suffered the most- the poor. The drought caused the "Dust Bowl" in parts of Arkansas, Texas, Oklahoma, and other states of the region. This period had no better chronicle than John Steinbeck's monumental story of the "Okies" in THE GRAPES OF WRATH.

When one considers the depression and the drouth being imposed on one generation, is it any wonder that people questioned God's mercy. But, it is my belief that the trials and tribulations of the thirties produced the kind of people who were able to rise to the awesome tasks of the forties.

Some parents, unable to care or even feed their offspring, resorted to passing them out to other more fortunate family members, or in some cases, to anyone who would take them in. Families were fragmented and scattered. The more fortunate ones were reunited in later years... some never.

It was into this world that Rainey Wether was born.

Lloyd J. Guillory
Columbia, Missouri
January 1998

CHAPTER ONE

The kerosene lamp on the kitchen table flickered as the two women sat opposite each other. The older woman knocked a roach off the table, saying nothing to the younger one, as if it were so common an occurence that it was not worthy of mention. The younger woman sat with her chin in her hands, her head swaying from side to side in deep misery. She coughed constantly, wiping her mouth with a kitchen wash cloth.

The older woman reached for her daughter's hand: "Cassey, honey, you got to make up yore mind. You got to do somethin' bout that chile. You know you ain't got much time left 'n Ah cain't take care 'o her... not at mah age."

The younger woman continued to shake her head, back and forth: "Ah know, Ma, but it ain't easy to give up yore baby. Rainey is all Ah got to show fer this miserable life 'o mine."

"Iffen ya only knew fer shur who her papa was, but whorin' like you done all yore life... you don't even know that. Iffen ya did, you could send her to her pappy, but..."

The woman looked up at her mother, coughing: "Maybe Ah wasn't nuthin' but a whore, but whorin' kept us alive since Pa died. What else could Ah do? Ah ain't got no edjication. Ah don't know nuthin' 'cepting how to please a man." She shrugged as she continued: "Ah only got one thing they want 'n Ah cain't understand why they'd even want that, seein' as how Ah look. Sometimes, Ah cain't stop coughin' long enough fer them to finish, but they don't seem to care."

The mother nodded her head in agreement: "Thar ain't no 'splainin' men when it comes to that, but thank the good Lord they still wants that. Don't know what we womin' would do iffen they didn't," she chuckled, adding, "but you still ain't settled nuthin' 'bout Rainey, Cassey, you got to make up yore mind."

The daughter sighed deeply: "Ah guess Ah'll have to give her away, Ma... what else kin Ah do? If Ah cain't do any more whorin' 'n you cain't do any more work heer on the farm, what in the world kin we do? We ain't got two dollars between us."

The mother sighed: "And we is way behind in our taxes. They gonna take this place from us... ain't no doubt 'bout that."

The daughter coughed once again: "What 're you gonna do, Ma? It don't matter 'bout me. Ah'm dyin'. Ah ain't got much time left, but you... whar you goin', Ma?"

The old woman dragged deeply on her Picayune cigarette, one of three she had purchased from the general store the day before for one cent apiece: "Ah don't know, Cassey. Mah sista in the next county tole me she'd take me in, but she said she don't want Rainey...

The daughter's head came up sharply: "Why 'd she say that? Rainey is a sweet litt'l girl. She don't cause no trouble."

"No, not now, 'cause she's only five, but when she is older and has tits, then they give trouble... just lak you did."

The daughter seemed offended: "You know that man raped me when she was made... you know that. Ah was only fifteen then."

The older woman shifted in her seat: "That may be true, but he wasn't the fust. You teased that man! You know that... swishing yore butt and stickin' them tits out. Ah tole you what would happen to you if you kept on doin' that 'round them grow'd men... you know Ah tole you that. And you don't know fer shur it was him who made that baby... the way you fooled 'round."

"Pa should'a killed him when he done that to me."

"Knowing yore pa as Ah did, he would have 'ceptin that boy's papa owned the mill whar yore pa and yore brotha worked. They'd both been outa work 'n we was too pore fer that."

"Maybe so, but you shoulda let me give Rainey his name. She deserved that. They had money. Maybe, she'd gotten some of that money when that boy was killed later on."

"Oh, Cassey, that's all in the past. Let's worry 'bout tomorra. What we gonna do with Rainey?"

"Ah guess Ah'll hafta give her to them Fosters the welfare people tole me about... ova in the next county. When Ah ast them welfare people 'bout it... you know... when Ah tole them Ah had to let her go, well, they tole me 'bout them Fosters who is lookin' fer a little girl. They'se willin to take her in."

"Shur 'n you know why. That ole goat wants to git his hands on her. He likes litt'l girls... I heerd from a neighbor."

"Oh, Ma, you don't know that fer shur. That's just gossip."

The old woman walked to the wash tub which served as a sink and dipped the cigarette in the wash water, then tossed it out of the window, asking, "You gonna give her away fer good? You ain't neva gonna take her back? That don't seem natural, Cassey-givin' yore flesh 'n blood away like that..."

"Well, what else kin Ah do? Ah'm dying 'n you're too old to take care of her... you said so yusseff... 'n yore mean ole sister said she don't want her... what else kin Ah do?" And she resumed shaking her head back and forth.

"You do what you think best, Cassey. Ah ain't got no more ideas."

The younger woman coughed into the wash cloth, and holding it back to view its contents, said, "Oh, shit, Ah'm coughin' up blood agin."

The mother ignored the comment, saying, "Cassey, go wake up Rainey 'n tell her what's gonna happen to her, and whar she's goin'. And tell her what to 'spect from that ole billy goat. Tell her to kick him in the balls if he tries to touch her."

The child stirred as she heard the bedroom door open on its squeaky hinges. She rubbed her eyes, smiling, asking, "Mama, do we have anything to eat today... I'm hungry."

The mother managed a weak smile in return. Suppressing a cough, she sat on the edge of the bed. Taking the child's hands in hers, she smoothed her hair: "Rainey, honey, you gotta git up 'n git dressed. You goin' somewhar today."

The child's eyes widened in anticipation. "Whar?"

The mother hesitated, not knowing how to break the news to the child with whom she had not even discussed the possibilities of their parting for good.

"Well, you see, honey, we got troubles in this family 'n we got to do somethin', somethin' else. We cain't take care of you any longer 'n you gonna hafta go live with another family."

The child's eyes widened: "But, Mama, you coming with me, ain't you?"

The mother tried to suppress the tears, but she could not. "No, honey, Ah cain't go with you, but Ah kin visit you eva now 'n then... Ah promise."

Now, it was the child whose eyes were filled with tears. "But, Mama, where am I going? Who's gonna take care of me?"

The mother cleared her throat, coughing into her hand: "Well, you remember that Foster family we met at the firemen's picnic last month... at the old church?", with the child nodding, not sure she remembered at all, "well, you're gonna go live with them fer a while, jus till Ah git on mah feet... you see."

"For how long," she asked, her voice filled with fear.

"We'll, Ah don't know fer shur, but it shouldn't be too long."

The child could no longer suppress her tears, and with her voice shaking and her chin quivering, replied, "But, I don't want to, Mama. Do I have to?"

The mother nodded: "Yes, honey, you hafta. God only knows Ah wish you didn't but... you jus hafta. Now, come on, git up 'n git dressed. Ah'm gonna put yore best dress on you so's you will look so pretty."

As the child stepped down out of bed, she asked, "Do them Fosters have any girls for me to play with?"

The mother thought about it for a while, nodding her head: "Shur, they have a daughter just yore age, 'n three boys older than you."

The child brightened a little: "Does she have toys to play with?"

As she began to comb the child's hair: "Well, ah suppose so, seeing as how they got a litt'l money... least ways... more'n we got."

The child inquired: "How come we so poor, Mama, that you got to give me away?"

The question struck her heart like a driven spike as she groped for an answer. "Well, thar's rich people in this world 'n thars pore people 'n God made us pore."

As she stepped into her best dress: "Why didn't God make us rich?"

The mother shrugged in resignation: "Rainey, honey, thar ain't no rich people in this part of the country... we all pore. Just some more pore than others. With this depression goin' on, the whole country is pore."

"Grandma told me you make good money whorin'. What's whorin', Mama?"

"Ah'm gonna kill yore Grandma some day fer havin' a big mouth 'n tellin' you things like that."

"But, what's whorin'?"

"Well, you see... men pay me money to keep them company when they're lonesome... lonesome fer the company 'o womin."

She nodded, as if she understood, asking, as her mother turned her around to tie her bowstrings, "Well, why cain't you go on whorin' then and I won't have to leave here?"

Once again, tears came to the mother's eyes as she groped for an answer: "Mama is sick, Rainey, honey... real sick, 'n Ah cain't work no more... no kind 'o work."

"But, I'll go to work, Mama. I'll take care of you."

The mother managed a smile: "Ah wish you could, honey... Ah wish you could," and with that she opened a brown paper bag she had brought into the room and tossed the child's meager belongings in the bag.

The grandmother was at the kitchen stove as the child and mother entered the room. Throwing a fresh piece of wood into the old stove, she smiled at her granddaughter, saying, "Rainey, honey, Grandma's got some fritta's all fried up fer you 'n Ah got some syrup fer you to eat with 'em."

The child, forgetting her momentary sadness, brightened at these words, replying, "Oh, boy, do you have some milk, too?"

The old lady saddened: "No, honey, since that damn cow went dry we ain't had no money to have her bred to no bull so we ain't got no milk, not even Pet milk."

The mother of the child gave the grandmother a dirty look: "Mama, Ah tole you before it ain't necessary to go into all them cow 'n bull details with Rainey... she's too young."

"Oh, baloney, Cassey, she ain't too young. She's gotta learn the facts someday 'n the soona the betta," and as she turned back to the stove, "'specil whar she's goin'."

The child's eyes widened, quizzically, but instead of asking what it was all about, she dove into the fritters and syrup.

As the hungry child consumed the fried dough the grandmother turned to her daughter: "Cassey, how you gonna let them Fosters know that Rainey is comin?"

"Oh, I guess Ah'll stop at the store 'n call them on the telephone... what else kin Ah do? Gotta go by the store to ketch the bus anyhow... that's whar it stops."

"That's a long distance call 'n that'l cost money. You got any?"

"Ah got a dollar thirty five 'n that's all Ah got."

"How much you think that bus ride is gonna be?"
"Ah done checked before... it's thirty five cents."
"Well, afta you pay fer the bus 'n the phone call, you ain't gonna have much left fer food. Whatcha gonna do 'bout that?"
"Ah guess I'll go by the mill 'n see if that foreman needs any lovin'. He's always got a little money... not that Ah feel like doin' it," as she suppressed a cough.

The grandmother's eyes widened in anticipation: "How much you gonna charge him?"

She sighed: "Ah tried to git a dollar but he won't pay but fifty cents... so Ah take that. It's betta than nuthin."

As they stood at the front door to the old house with its weathered boards turned to a pinkish-gray patina, the grandmother groaned as she stooped down to kiss the child goodbye. Because of the circumstances of the child's conception, she had failed to accept her as a grandmother normally would. She had loved the child, but with a detached kind of love, as one would love the neighbor's child from across the street, hoping sooner or later that the child would go back to where it came from. But, for the past five years, this detached kind of love was the only kind that the child would ever know. Her mother was not capable of real, deep, warm, motherly love, because she had never experienced it, so she did not know how. On so many occasions, in the performance of her "professional" duties, she had been forced to display "love" so often, that when she got home, as she put it: "Ah 'm all loved out." And the child suffered because of it.

But on this occasion, the day of their parting, the grandmother felt real genuine regret and sorrow in spite of the fact that the child was only going to the next county, and it showed as she hugged and kissed the child goodbye.

"Rainey, honey, grandma's gonna miss her litt'l girl."

The child began to cry: "Ain't you coming to see me?"

"Well, now honey, Ah don't know how Ah can do that. You see, it's a long way from heer to thar 'n Ah cain't walk that far, so... Maybe them Fosters will bring you heer to see me."

The child nodded. suppressing her tears, with the mother taking her hand, saying: "Come on, Rainey, it's time fer that bus to pass ' n we still got to walk to the main road to catch it."

As they walked off the grandmother could be heard yelling: "Remember, Rainey, don't take no crap offen nobody... 'speci'l from no man."

As they started down the dirt path, the child turned to wave to her grandmother one more time, but the old lady had gone into the house. The child turned to her mother: "Ah wanted to wave to grandma, but she's gone already."

The mother took her hand, replying, "It's because she's so sad at you leavin' that she cain't stand it, so she went inside."

Lloyd J. Guillory

They held hands as they walked down the long path to the main road, the county road of Corbin County in southeast Arkansas. There was a shallow open ditch on either side of the path, cut there by the previous owner who had a tractor. When the father of Cassey, Norbert Wether, purchased the place with his World War I's veteran's bonus, he was left too poor to own any mechanical farm equipment, and his ploughing was done with the aid of a sway-backed mule. And then the mule died, and then Norbert Wether had died, and then the only boy in the family was killed in a drunken brawl. The widowed Orella Wether, left with her only daughter, Cassey, managed to eke out a living with the help of a sharecropper neighbor. There was never enough money and when her promiscuous daughter, Cassey, suggested going commercial with her sexual favors, the mother pragmatically replied, "You enjoy doin' it so much, Cassey, you might as well git paid fer it. 'Sides, we could use the money."

When they reached the main road, it formed a junction with a state highway, and there was a general store on one corner, an Esso service station on the other, and a bar on the third. The fourth corner was vacant and on the weed filled lot a FOR SALE sign had been there for several years.

Cassey led the small child up the wooden steps, telling her as she sat her down on the steps, "Now, Rainey, you sit thar 'n wait fer mama whilst Ah call them Fosters to tell them you on yore way. Don't talk to nobody... understand?"

"Yassum," as she petted a coon dog sitting near her.

Cassey, having completed the phone call, went to the store counter, which also served as the bus company's ticket agency, and purchased a ticket to Oglethorpe for one child- a one way ticket. She had argued with the store owner that Rainey was small and should not be charged full fare, which drew this reply: "Her butt may be little, Cassey, but she still takes up one seat. That'll be thirty five cents iffen you don't mind."

Having completed the phone call to the Fosters, and with ticket in hand she made her way to the wooden steps and watched as the child petted the docile hound. Knowing this would be the last chance to tell her what little she could of the situation, for there was so little to tell, she took the child's free hand, patting it: "Rainey, I want you to be a good girl when you get to them Fosters. You remember to say yessum 'n yessuh when they talk to you." She hesitated a moment: "You gonna hafta help them around the house, too."

The child looked surprised: "What do Ah hafta do?"

"Well, you hafta help with the housework... washin, dishes 'n sweepin' and moppin' floors... jus like you did fer grandma."

"Are they gonna whip me when Ah'm bad?"

"Oh, Rainey, we neva whipped you... you know that!"

The child nodded: "Grandma slapped me when Ah didn't listen to her."

"Well, maybe you needed it some times. Grandma slapped me when Ah was little. But, iffen you ain't bad, thar won't be no reason fer them Fosters to whip you, so be good... hear me?"

The child nodded, without serious commitment. "How long do Ah hafta stay with them Fosters. When you comin' to take me back?"

This was the one question Cassey had hoped the child would not ask. She wanted to be truthful with her, but the truth was so painful. She looked away for a moment, suppressing some tears, and then running her fingers through the child's hair, she replied: "Well, as Ah said, Rainey, Ah'm sick... real sick. Ah ain't got no money to go to a real doctor, but them Public Health people told me Ah was real sick." The child looked at her with eyes wide with apprehension, as she continued: "But, you neva know. The good Lord may make me well ag'in and then Ah'll be able to go to Oglethorpe to pick you up and bring you home with me agin." It pained her to lie, as much as she wished it were so.

The child stammered: "But, supposin' the Lord don't make you well... what will happen to me?"

"Oh, let's don't think 'bout that right now, honey. Oh, look, there comes that big bus you're gonna ride on. Won't that be fun?"

The large Greyhound bus stirred a cloud of dust as it came off the blacktopped county road onto the general store's dirt parking area, obscuring its own image until the dust blew away. The dust caused Cassie to cough as she took the child by the hand, holding the clothing bag in the other. The incoming passengers were disembarking with the whites coming off first from the front of the bus and then the blacks from the back.

Cassey took the bus driver by the arm, looking at his name tag. As she made out the name, she brought the child forward, pointing to her: "mista Fred," using his first name only, "this is mah little girl, Rainey, 'n she's gonna ride with you all the way to Oglethorpe. Kin you keep a eye on her," and as she looked around at the passengers, "and make shur she gits thar all right, iffen you know what Ah mean."

"Yessum, you don't hafta worry 'bout her as long as she is on mah bus... but, is someone gonna meet her in Oglethorpe?"

Cassey nodded: "Yessuh, Ah called Mista 'n Miz Foster 'n they said they would meet the ten-thirty bus in Oglethorpe. Is this the ten-thirty bus to Oglethorpe?"

"Yessum, it shur is, and Ah run on time... all the time."

She stooped to hold the child: "Now, Rainey honey, try to remember all Ah said 'n try to be a good litt'l girl 'n not give them Fosters any trouble. It's right nice of them to take you in like this... real nice, so try to show yore 'preciation by helpin' round the house, and..."

The child, now that the moment of truth had arrived, was in a state of complete bewilderment. She had no idea what was really happening to her and though she tried to understand, her little mind could not grasp the reality of it. She was going simply because her mother, whom she trusted, had told her she had to go. To her immature mind, it was a temporary thing. When her mother got well she would come for her. Her mind was not capable of believing anything else, for the alternative was beyond the ability of her mind to grasp.

She led the child onto the bus and showed her to an empty seat, saying, "Now, don't you git out of this seat until the bus driver tells you to in Oglethorpe, and don't talk to no strangers... you heer me! You do what the bus driver tells you to do," and she bent over to kiss the child one more time, and being emotionally incapable of prolonging the parting one more moment she turned and left, making the sign of one more kiss thrown in her direction as she reached the step-down exit from the bus.

The child, really in a state of non-acceptance, slunk down in her seat, bewildered, wiping her tears with her hands. She looked around for comfort, but there was none. The other passengers, engrossed in their own lives and their own problems, paid no attention to the sobbing and lonely little girl.

In the usual departure fashion of country bus drivers, Fred had his air horn emit a loud blast, warning humans and animals that the right of way was his as he stirred up a new dust cloud as he pulled onto the state highway and carried a small and frightened little girl to her new destiny.

The mother watched as the bus disappeared down the road, her vision clouded by tears. She sniffed, wiped her nose with the back of her hand and headed to the mill to see if the foreman was in a romantic mood at this time of the day. She needed the money.

AUTHOR'S NOTE:

To those readers who believe such an event as that related above is unthinkable or improbable, it should be remembered that those were desperate times, being lived by desperate people who awoke each morning intent on surviving through the day- by whatever means. Those were the days before the massive social programs available to indigents in this day and time. Is it anymore unthinkable than a young unmarried mother of today, after giving birth, to assign her newborn to another, never to see it again. To illustrate further, there are bizarre reportings of children taken from their natural parents and court awarded to another couple simply because some well-meaning judge believes it is in the child's best interest, and often, it is. Life was never intended to be fair, and for some it would appear that it is less fair than others. In attempting to understand how God dispenses justice, or fate, I am tempted to agree with the great French writer of the last century, Alexis de Tocqville, who wrote: "Rather than question God's wisdom, I would prefer to question my own understanding."

CHAPTER TWO

The Foster farm in Oglethorpe nestled on 160 acres, half of which was arable and planted in cotton, and the other half covered with Southern Yellow Pine, that fast growing marvel of nature which can produce a mature tree each human generation. Compared to the Wether family the Fosters were relatively well off, in that there was an adequate supply of food, an unmortgaged roof over their heads, decent clothing on their bodies, and a 1929 Model A Ford in the barn. Money was scarce in those depression days, but since it was scarce to nearly all, the family felt no worse off than most of their neighbors. Arvil Foster had married Nell Hamlin when she was eighteen and he was thirty-five. Her family had been concerned about the difference in age, but the family considered him a "catch" since he owned his own 160 acres, left to him by his father who had inherited it from his father who divided his section of land with its 640 acres among his four sons, each receiving his own "quarter section". To his three daughters the old man had left nothing, saying, "They's girls and they'll git married. Thar husbands kin provide fer 'em."

Nell Foster was a sweet tempered woman with a gentle nature and a sweet smile. Now, at the age of thirty-two, she had a matronly spread of which she seemed to be proud, and Arvil shared her pride, because he liked "women with some meat on their bones" as he put it. They could be considered to be fairly well educated people of that period since they had both gone through elementary school before dropping out, because both set of parents felt that, "You don't need no more edjication than that to run a farm."

Arvil Foster was as onery and cantankerous as his wife was sweet and gentle. He was that way because he felt he owed it to society to be that way, having seen his father that way. He had also seen his father slap his mother on many occasions and he felt he owed that type of discipline to his wife, Nell. Nell felt she must have deserved those slaps because he convinced her she did. But in between those abusive moments, there had evidently been enough passion on one or both of their parts to have produced four children- the three oldest being boys of 12, 10, and 8. The youngest child, a girl, was now 6. A glance at the chronological sequence of their children would lead one to assume they procreated every two years, but that was not so. Arvil Foster had a very active libido which was put into use at every opportunity, whether with his wife, or someone else's, for he was a notorious adulterer. But he was also a deacon in the Pine Hill Baptist church and his adulterous ways were either overlooked or not spoken about openly.

Before offering to take in Rainey as a foster child, there were many discussions between Arvil and Nell as to the necessity or wisdom of it. Now convinced she would have no more children, Nell wanted another girl in the house to keep her own daughter, Cora, company, and to help with the housework. Arvil, for his part, felt that there might be some use for the child as she grew older and he grew more adventurous, especially noting the advantages of a lack of biological inhibitions on his part. The thought did occur to Nell, especially after the scandal of a year before when he was implicated, but not tried, in the seduction of the thirteen year old daughter of a sharecropper who worked some of his acreage. The local constabulary felt that the seduction, if true, was part of his entitlement according to the medieval rule of "droit de seigneur". (In medieval times, it was generally agreed that it was the priviledge of the lord of the manor to rid the young daughters of the vassals on the estate of their virginity, and it was referred to in France as "droit de seigneur"- the right of the lord). Of course, the poor sharecropper fathers and mothers did not subscribe to this doctrine, but what is a poor sharecropper to do? Nell Foster felt, deep in her heart, that her husband was as guilty as homemade sin, but what is a poor abused wife to do? She even made some attempt to keep a wary eye on their six year old daughter and one of the main reasons she wanted Rainey to come and live with them is that the two girls would share the same bedroom... and there is safety in numbers.

On the day of Rainey's expected arrival, and having had the event confirmed by Cassey's call of that morning, the family sat at the breakfast table with some members excited, and some not so.

Tom, the older boy, pouted noticeably, exclaiming, "Why do we need another girl to live with us? We got enough with Cora."

"Yeah," added the second oldest, Joe, "we don't need her."

From Bill, the youngest of the three boys: "Oh, it might be fun to have another sister. I hope she can play baseball better'n Cora."

Cora listened to the complaints with typical reticence, for she had long ago learned that she was outnumbered three to one.

Nell, wishing to hear her daughter's feelings, asked, "Cora, honey, how do you feel about Rainey coming to live with us?"

The child looked around the table, shrugged her shoulders, replying, "I guess it will be okay. I'll have someone to play dolls with." She mentally calculated that the odds would now be three to two, and she smiled inwardly, adding, "But I wish she was older than me."

The father, mopping up the remaining grits and eggs in his plate with his bread, took a long swig of coffee and said, "Well, whether you like it or not, she's a comin', so let's go and meet the bus."

Rainey had not moved one iota since the bus had left the general store, but she began to fidget as the forty-five minute bus ride came to an end. She had to go to the bathroom to make number one as it was called in her home. She tried to press her legs together but that did not seem to help. She shuffled her feet, but that didn't help either, and when she could hold it no longer, she let go, and she could feel the warm liquid running under her little bottom. She looked around, embarrassed, frightened, as if there would be someone there to punish her for her indiscretion, but they continued to ignore her. All except the bus driver, Fred, who called out to her after he had brought the bus to a stop: "Come on, Rainey, it's time to get off. Do you know these people, these Fosters who are supposed to meet you here?"

She slowly arose from the seat, looking down at the large wet spot where she had sat. She quickly looked at Fred to see if he had noticed it, but as he remained at the door to the bus waiting for her she was spared the misery of having to explain to him that she could not wait. She ruffled her dress and pulled at her underpants, trying to achieve some comfort from the warm wet liquid, as she replied to Fred, "No, I don't know them people... the Fosters."

"Well, come on, honey, I'll help you find 'em... come on," and he extended his hand to her, which she grasped. As tenuous as their relationship was, it was all she had. The driver saw the family of six waiting nervously nearby, and assuming correctly that they were the group who was supposed to meet her, he inquired, "Are you folks the Fosters?"

The father took charge and came forward, replying, "Yes, I'm Arvil Foster. Is this little girl Rainey Wether?"

"Yessuh, she is, so I guess you're the folks I'm supposed to turn her over to. She is all yours."

Nell Foster come forward holding her daughter, Cora, by the hand. The boys stayed back, not particularly interested in welcoming the newest member of their family, since as far as they were concerned, she was not welcomed.

Nell Foster, sensing the child's timidity and reluctance to come forward, went to her, and bending down as far as her girth would permit, placed her hand on the child's shoulder, saying softly, "Rainey, dear, I'm Mrs. Foster, and you're coming to stay with us for a while, and we are so glad to have you. Come on and meet the rest of the family, especially Cora. Cora, honey, come and meet Rainey."

Rainey held back, driven by fear and embarrassment. The mother sensed that something bothered the child and she repeated, "Come on Rainey, we want to be your friends. What's wrong, honey?"

The mother was now in a squatting position with her eyes almost level with the child's. Rainey looked sheepish, biting her knuckles on her right hand as she stated, louder than she had intended, "Ah pee'd in mah pants on the bus," and she began to cry.

The three boys had heard this and they emitted a raucous laugh as they each pointed a finger at Rainey. The father also joined the boys in a good laugh at the child's expense. The mother gave each a stern look, saying as she brought the child to her bosom, "It ain't funny and stop that laughing, you boys," and turning back to the child, "Rainey, honey, that ain't no sin to do that, especially in your predicament. Don't worry about it. When I get you home, I'll get you washed off... now don't you worry, honey. Now, say hell'o to Cora... Cora, you come and say hell'o to Rainey.

The two girls just stared at each other for a moment, as children of that age will do and with some prodding from her mother Cora finally came forward and stood near Rainey, a slight smile on her face. Rainey, as though it were a painful act, returned a hardly noticeable smile.

Arvil Foster gave the son nearest him a slight push to get him started and told the rest, "Well, come on, we can't stay out here all day... let's get going home."

The mother took Rainey by one hand and her daughter by the other, saying, "Come on girls, let's go and show Rainey her new home. They all piled into the 1929 Ford model A which had, as of that date in 1935, only 13,856 miles, testifying to the pausity with which Arvil Foster drove his pride and joy of an automobile.

During the ride back to the house, Rainey was instructed to sit in the front seat between the father and the mother, with Cora squeezed in along side. The three rambunctious boys, still tittering over Rainey's unfortunate accident sat in the back seat, wispering to one another and pointing towards the front seat. Rainey and Cora exchanged glances at least once a minute, with neither saying a word. Still uncomfortable with her wet bottom, which now began to feel cooler, and with a quite noticeable smell of urine in the air, Rainey felt miserable.

The matter was not helped when the father observed: "Jesus, but that pee is beginning to stink, Nell. Can't you do something about it before we all pass out?", which only made the frightened and insecure child all the more miserable. She bit her lower lip and sank down in her seat.

The Foster home was typical of the rural farm houses of southern Arkansas and northern Louisiana where the summers were more severe than the winters and the homes were built up on brick piers, elevating the house about three feet above the ground. The crawl space under the house was useful for storing old lumber and gave the dogs a place to come in out of the hot sun in the summer months. It also provided a place for the rural kids to learn the facts of life by playing "dirty" out of sight of the wary mother who had learned her facts in the same manner; there or in the barn, depending on the opportunities.

The house had a front porch and a back porch, a central hall which acted as a breezeway in the summer when the front and back doors were opened. A parlor, dining room and kitchen were on one side, with three bedrooms on the other. A small bathroom had been squeezed in between two of the bedrooms as a twentieth century improvement to the late nineteenth century house which had started out with an outhouse near the barn.

The house had clapboard siding on the exterior which had not been painted for well nigh on to twenty-five or thirty years, mainly due to Arvil Foster's parsimonious ways. In response to his wife's pleadings to "please whitewash the house, at least," his reply was, "Having paint on that house ain't gonna make us no more comfortable than we are now. 'Sides, it's planting time and I ain't got time." In the fall, it was, "Sides, it's harvest time and I ain't got time."

Modest though it was, to Rainey it was impressive compared to what she had lived in all her five years. Her home had only two bedrooms; one for the grandmother and the other she shared with her mother. There was no indoor bath or toilet. She had used a chamberpot all her life. Her little bottom had never rested on the seat of a sanitary toilet except on several occasions when her mother had taken her to the restroom at the public health office. She derived great pleasure watching the swirling mass dissapear down the hole with the mere crank of a handle. To her simple little mind, it was a marvel of engineering. When she had inquired of her mother, "But where does it go?" she was told, "Ah don know... in the ground, Ah guess!"

Immediately upon entering the house Nell Foster took Rainey by the hand, saying, "Come on, Rainey, I want to wipe you off with a wash cloth and put some dry drawers on you. Is your clothing in that paper bag you been holding on to so tight?"

The child merely nodded in reply, extending the bag to her. As the mother searched through the meager belongings looking for a pair of underpants, she found only one other pair and those had a hole in them. She shook her head, saying nothing, but thinking to herself..."poor child."

Rainey's stomach was growling from hunger when Nell Foster announced that dinner was ready. As she was led into the dining room, she looked around for the stove and saw none. She had always eaten in the kitchen where the old wood stove was nearby and food could easily be passed from the pot to the table. She was fascinated to see a table all set with china and flatware and serving dishes heaped with food. She felt her mouth watering as she smelled the chicken stew and saw the steaming bowl of rice.

"Rainey, do you like chicken?" inquired the mother. "I hope so because it is our favorite dish. Bill!" grabbing her youngest boy by the arm..."you wait until everybody is seated and we say grace before you reach for the food. Rainey, honey, you sit next to Cora... there, right in that chair. That will always be your place at mealtime."

Arvil Foster rapped on his glass with a knife, and bowing his head, looking around the table and in his most pious mode, intoned the blessing.

Rainey nodded in the affirmative when asked if she liked this or that. As hungry as she was, there was little she did not like at this moment until the spinach greens were offered. she hesitated, wrinkled her nose, shrugged her shoulders, and shook her head. Arvil Foster, seeing that, commanded his wife to put the spinach in her plate: "She'll eat what our kids eat as long as she stays in this house." The boys tittered in delight and even Cora smiled, glad that she would have company in downing the hated vegetable. Rainey mixed the spinach with her chicken stew, held her breath and swallowed. She felt sure in her young mind that she would never get to like that man seated at the head of the table. She was not used to men, having never lived with a man in the house. She had spent her entire life with only two women, her mother and her grandmother.

As bedtime approached some time later and arrangements had to be made to for the family to retire, the mother asked, "Rainey, have you had a bath today?" The child thought about it for a moment, then, shaking her head, replied, "No Ma'am, I bathe every Saturday night in summer time. Is today Saturday?"

The mother smiled: "No, it is not Saturday night, but why don't we have you take a bath tonight, anyway, so you can get on our schedule. You and Cora will bathe together so you might as well get used to that." Rainey became apprehensive. She did not bathe often, but when she did her mother would put warm water in a No. 2 galvanized tub near the stove and she would bathe herself, even though her mother and grandmother would come and go, with one or the other stopping to wash her back. No other person could have fit in the No. 2 tub even if they tried, but when she saw the bathtub and realized that two small people could easily fit into it, she shrugged her shoulders and nodded her head. To her young mind, this was all an adventure to be endured until her mother was well enough to come and take her back. Whatever indignities she had to suffer until then, she made up her mind to endure them... for her mother's sake.

As she and Cora undressed for their baths, they eyed each other from head to toe. One being five and the other six, they were not surprised to see that they were made the same way, and after a final glance, each stepped into the tub, concerned only with the temperature of the water. Rainy, innocent that she was, was simply amazed to learn that the tub not only had running water, but one spigot had hot water coming out of it. As she glanced at the toilet in the same room along with a lavatory, she concluded that the Fosters were indeed rich compared to the Wethers.

As Nell Foster scrubbed the girl's backs, she looked at Rainey, smiled a warm smile, asking, "Rainey, you have such a pretty and unusual name, especially when you put it with your family name. How did you get the name of Rainey?"

The child smiled, relaxed for the first time since leaving her mother's side. "Well, my grandma give me that name the night Ah was born. She tole me that it was a lightnin' and a thunderin' whilst mah Mama was having me 'n she tole mah Mama when it was all ova that they ought to name me Stormy, but mah Mama tole my grandma that she knew a whore named Stormy 'n she didn't like her so mah grandma said she would name me Rainey."

At the sound of the word..."whore"... Nell Foster first looked at her own child for her reaction, which was none, since Cora had obviuolsly never heard the word. Then she looked at Rainey, who had heard the word several times applied to her own mother, and showed no outward sign of surprise that she had said it.

Nell Foster rushed to ensure that the bathroom door was closed, and rushing back to the bathtub in an excited and agitated state, gasped, "Rainey, where did you learn that word?"

The child seemed surprised. "What word?"

Nell Foster looked around to ensure there were no others within listening distance: "The nasty word..."whore"... where did you hear that word?"

The child seemed perplexed: "Mah Grandma tole me mah Mama was one... a whore."

Nell Foster looked towards heaven, crossing herself in the process and looking at her own daughter as if to determine if she had been contaminated by the evil word. "Jesus, God in Heaven, Rainey, surely you misunderstood your Grandma when she told you your Mama was a... a... whore."

As the child continued to wash herself: "No Ma'am, she told me mah Mama made good money whorein'... when she felt good enough to work. She's sick, you know."

"Oh my God!" intoned a shocked Nell Foster, "do you know what that word means, Rainey?"

"No, Ma'am, but Ah ast mah Mama what it meant 'n she told me she gives company to men when they wants the company of a womin'."

And as Cora looked on with complete detachment and non-interest, much to the mother's gratification, she inquired further of Rainey: "And that is all she told you about what she did?"

"Yessum... that's all Ah know 'bout whorin'."

The mother shuddered each time the word was mentioned. She took Rainey's hands in hers, then with her hand on the child's cheek, said, "Rainey, honey, I want you to promise me something with your whole heart and soul, and Cora, honey, I want you to promise this also... that you will never say that word again in this house... never... ever again. Do you promise me that?"

Rainey, not sure what offense she had committed, and Cora, not sure what she was promising, nodded their heads in unison as they looked at each other, as Cora asked, "Mama, did Rainey do something wrong?"

"Oh, no, Cora, honey, Rainey didn't do anything wrong. She just said a word that we don't use in this house. She didn't know it was wrong because," and she hesitated as she patted Rainey's head, "it was used in her home, I guess, but we don't use that word in our home... that's all."

Rainey, somewhat confused but willing to comply with the wishes of this gentle woman she had taken a liking to, merely smiled a weak smile at Cora and her mother... a sheepish smile. She was sure of one thing. She would never mention the word whore in this house again, even if her mama was one.

Nell Foster, after having put the girls to bed, returned to the bathroom, not so much for personal hygiene reasons as to have some time to herself to sort out the shocking revelations of the child's admission that her mother was a whore.

Could this be true. After all, they knew virtually nothing of the Wether family, and being old line fundamental Southern Baptist, the very though of a "nice" girl from a "nice" family selling herself, even to support her daughter and mother... well... it was shocking to say the least. She asked herself: My God, what have we gotten ourselves into taking this child into our home. What else will she say? What else will she do? Will she contaminate my own children? She wished she knew.

But, in another room in that house, the source of the mother's concern was, herself, beginning to experience the trauma that had entered her life that day. It had happened so fast, without any advance notice, that in her young mind the separation from her mother and grandmother was similar to being invited on a picnic for the day, expecting to return to their bosom when the sun set in the west. As she lay in the bed with her new foster sister, Rainey engaged in little girl talk with her... about the farm... the animals... what they would do the next day... But, now, with Cora fast asleep, she lay alone with her thoughts. This was the first night in her entire life that she had not lain in the same bed with her mother. True, on many nights her mother was not in bed when she retired for the night, due to the demands of her work, but almost without exception she would find her mother in bed with her in the morning when she awoke. It was not that Cassey had any moral or physical compunction against "one night stands"; on the contrary, she would have welcomed the money. No, it was due to the lack of discretionary spending money in those depression days which made even a "quickie" a financial undertaking which could strain the budget of a poor farmer boy.

As she lay in bed looking at the ceiling in the darkened room, Rainey finally realized what was happening to her. The uncertainty of the day now gave way to the reality of the moment, even one her five year old mind could evaluate. Her mother had sent her away... to live with strangers... in a strange house... in a strange town. Would her mother ever come to take her back? Would she ever see her mother again? She bit her lower lip as she always did when she was disturbed. Then the lip began to quiver until her whole chin was shaking, and then tears began to roll down her cheek and onto her pillow. She pulled the sheet up to her face and began to cry softly; quietly at first, then loud enough to wake Cora. When Cora asked her what was wrong she could not answer, for the words would not come... just tears. Cora sprang out of bed and ran into her parent's bedroom, the next room down the hall, yelling out to her mother that Rainey was crying. Nell, with motherly compassion rose and went into the children's bedroom with the sounds of her husband's tirade in her ears: "Dammit, Nell, let that brat cry. I told you we were making a mistake taking her in. She'll expect you to go to her every night." But, for once, Nell paid no attention to her irascible husband and continued on her way to the crying child. Upon reaching her she took her in her arms, cuddling her to her breast, saying, "Rainey, honey, what is wrong? Why are you crying? Please tell me what is wrong?"

The child, now sobbing uncontrollably, clung to Nell's arms as if they were her last refuge from life's uncertainties. She continued to cling and to sob, with Nell stroking her hair, trying to reassure her. Then, the sobbing subsided and the small frightened child looked up into the mother's face, managing to form these words between sobs: "I want my mama."

CHAPTER THREE

As the weeks passed by, that first night in a strange bed in a home with complete strangers, was merely a precursor of the nights that followed. The days were bearable due to the mother and daughter's attempt to "make her feel at home". But, she never felt "at home" for she longed for her own home, the only one she had ever known in her young life. It was not much as homes go, but she was not aware of just how humble it was.

But, oh the nights. She cried herself to sleep each and every one of them. Upon hearing her, Cora would reach for her hand, and as they touched, Rainey felt some degree of comfort and the tears would slacken to some extent. Hardly a day went by, however, when she would not ask of Nell Foster: "When is mah mama coming to git me?" The compassionate mother would suppress a tear of her own as she replied: "Soon, honey, I'm sure she will come to see you soon."

In desperation, Nell had even suggested to her husband, Arvil that, perhaps, some Sunday they might drive the 40 miles to the next county to allow Rainey to visit her mother and grandmother. His reply was both cruel and pragmatic. "Now, woman you know Ah ain't gonna waste no gas taking that kid to the next county just to see her mama... money is too tight. 'Sides, Nell, you know that will do more harm than good. She'll jus git lonesomer and lonesomer... you know that. Let well 'nough alone. Ain't it enough that we took her in like the good Christians we are?"

Nell smiled a faint smile. "Perhaps you're right, Arvil. It'll just make her more lonesome, but the poor child..."

This went on for three months, with the young child making some adjustments to her situation. With the flexibility and short retention of young minds she became more and more accustomed to her plight. As much as Cora and her mother attempted to make her feel at home the boys did otherwise as they observed and mocked the father's attitude, thinking that was the way to make their cantankerous father pleased with their actions. They teased and taunted her at every opportunity, from tripping her to pulling her hair when they were out at play, careful not to do so in front of their mother who had taken a protective interest in the child. She knew what the boys were up to, but each time she mentioned it to her husband the reply was the same: "It's a tough world, Nell. That kid is no better than an orphan so she better git used to it. Orphans got it tough." Not wanting to provoke her irrascible husband Nell merely shrugged and turned away, biting her lip and her tongue.

The mother attempted in many covert ways to make the child happy and it did some good. She had even attempted to buy her a doll of her own. She had watched, painfully, as Rainey sat by Cora as she played with her doll, a look of desire on her young face. But, since she had absolutely no money of her own and was dependent on her husband's parsimonious nature for every cent she wanted, she was told, "Now, Nell, Ah agreed to take the kid in... not to make a litt'l princess of her. Money is too tight."

But, Nell had made up her mind, Rainey was to have a doll of her own. She contracted with some ladies in her church to do some sewing for them, to adjust the older children's clothes to fit the younger ones, as they were outgrown. When she had enough money to buy Rainey a simple little doll and two doll dresses, she was excited as she broke the news, in private, to her own daughter. "Oh, Mama, Rainey will be so happy," replied the child. "When can I give it to her... I want to, myself."

"Oh, Cora, wouldn't it be nice to give it to her on a special occasion... like her birthday. Has she ever told you when she was born?"

"No, Ma'am, I asked her and she told me she didn't know fer sure."

"Do you mean to tell me," asked a surprised Nell, "that the poor child doesn't even know when she was born? Go and get her and ask her to come here, Cora. Tell her I want to talk to her."

Holding Cora's hand, Rainey was led into the kitchen as the mother stood at the stove stirring a pot. She was apprehensive each time she was summoned, fearing she had done something wrong, but was relieved when she saw the mother smiling. Nell put the spoon down and taking the two young girls by the hand, led them to the kitchen table. Continuing to hold Rainey's hand as she let go of her daughter's, she asked, "Rainey, do you know when your birthday is? I would like to bake a cake for you so we can have a party... do you know?"

The child, taken completely off guard, furrowed her brow as she tried to remember. "No, Ma'am, Ah ain't sure. I think Ah was born in July... maybe August... Ah ain't sure."

"And you don't know the date of your birth... the day you were born... like Cora was born on March the twenty-fifth."

She shook her head. "No Ma'am. Ah don't remember. Did Ah do something wrong?"

The mother held her to her bosom. "No, honey, you never did anything wrong. I have a little present for you and I thought it would be nice to give it to you on your birthday... if you had a birthday coming up, I mean."

The child's eyes widened. "Does that mean Ah won't git the present 'cause Ah don't know mah birthday?"

"No, honey, it doesn't mean that at all, and turning to her daughter, "Cora, go and get that package I have behind my dresser. You know where I hide things from your father and the boys... bring it here... go ahead. Rainey, you stay here with me 'til Cora gets back... and close your eyes 'til I tell you to open them."

As she placed her hands over her eyes: "Yessum."

Cora, as excited as Rainey, came running back proudly holding the package wrapped in a brown paper bag in front of her.

Lloyd J. Guillory

The mother took the package and turning to Rainey, "Now keep your eyes closed, Rainey, till I tell you to open them. Here, Cora, you give it to her. Now, Rainey, open your eyes."

As she removed her hands from her eyes and saw the doll, simple and modest though it was, her mouth opened and her eyes want wide with excitement. "Ohhh... Miz Nell... a doll. Fer me?" as she held it to her bosom.

"Yes, honey, it's for you... all yours. Now, you and Cora can play house together and you can each be a mama. Won't that be fun?"

Still practically speechless, she nodded. "Yessum."

"And what do you say, Rainey, when someone gives you something?"

She thought for a while. "Ah'm supposed to say thank you."

That night, as she lay in bed with her doll in her arms, along side Cora who had her doll in her arms, she smiled in motherly fashion. It was the first night since her arrival that she did not cry herself to sleep. She was happy. She did not remember her loneliness that night.

When the father and the three boys saw the doll in Rainey's arms at breakfast the next morning, their expressions indicated that they did not share the joy of the females. The older boy, Tom, the leader of the pack, frowned: "Aw, who wants an old doll, anyway... nobody but sissy girls like you and Cora, huh, Joe?" turning to the second oldest.

"Yeah... who wants a sissy doll?"

The youngest, Bill, not wanting to be left out of the male haranguing for fear of being called a sissy, added..."Yeah, who wants a doll?"

The father, taking it all in, grinned at his boys, proudly, and turning to his wife, "Well, Nell, you went and done it. Ah hope you're happy, now."

In a rare moment of defiance, she smiled at him. "Yes, Arvil, I'm happy and so is this little girl. She deserved it and I did it with my own money so you can't complain about it. It ain't your money."

As he rose, motioning to the boys to follow him, "That don't mean Ah cain't complain. You ain't heer'd the last of this. Come on you boys... let's go shoot some blackbirds. Them birds is eatin' all my seed corn."

The Foster farm was a short ways from the town of Oglethorpe, but far enough out to have R.F.D. (Rural Free Delivery) mail, the pride of the U.S. Postal Service in those depression days. Not that mail service was that important to those farm families, for so few of them knew how to read or write. Since most could not write, it was necessary to have the local druggist, or some other literate person, write the letter, and if you were fortunate enough to have received a letter, it might be necessary to have that same literate person read it to you.

And if letters could generate some excitement when received by a rural family, a package could produce even more, bordering on euphoria- especially in the young because it usually meant a mail order had arrived from Sears Roebuck & Co.

Rainey

And so it was when Cora and Rainey had retreived the mail from the mailbox at the road, some distance from the house, and saw the shoe box-sized package in the mailbox. "Oh, boy, Rainey, I bet it is something my mama ordered from the company (she had no idea what company)."

As they ran and skipped to the house, Rainey replied with girlish enthusiasm, although she was sure the package would mean nothing to her, "Ah wonder what it is."

Breathless, they ran into the kitchen to present the package to the mother, with Cora yelling, "Let me open it, Mama! Can I open it?"

On the verge of telling the child, "Yes, you can open it," the mother saw the address in the upper left hand corner of the box which was wrapped in brown paper. It said: Orella Wether, R.F.D. Route #8, c/o Sherman's General Store, Lasonia, Arkansas. The mother did not know the Wether family well at all, but she did know that Orella was the name of the grandmother. A feeling of foreboding came over her, and she quickly took the package from her daughter, saying, "No, Cora, I don't want to open this package. I'm not sure it's for us. It may be a mistake." Knowing her child had not started school yet and barely knew her ABC's, she was sure her lie would not be detected, and Rainey had never attended school, as yet.

"No, you girls go and play. I might have to return this box to the post office and I don't want to wrap it again... now, go play... outside. I'll call you when it's time to eat. Your pa and the boys will be home in a short while... go ahead... go play like good girls."

The girls, somewhat confused, turned to go, shrugging their shoulders as they left, with Cora saying, "I wish I could read."

"Me, too," Rainey added.

Now alone in the kitchen the mother was filled with fore-boding. Why would the grandmother write to them? Why not the mother? She shivered as she removed the wrapping from the box, which was indeed a shoe box. She hesitated as she removed the top from the box. It was an old box which had evidently been used for storage for quite a few years judging from its tattered edges. There was a letter on top, folded in three as if done by a secretary or someone familiar with office practices. As she unfolded the sheet, she observed that the letter had been typed, quite obviously written by a person of more education that she imagined the grandmother had. As she faced the kitchen window to better accomodate the light to the page she adjusted her glasses as she began to read, slowly:

Dear Mr. & Mrs. Foster,

This is Orella Wether writing to you. I am Cassey's gramma, as you might know. I don't write too good so I had Mr. Haslip write this for me. He's the druggist at the drug store. (Note from Mr. Haslip: I wanted to rearrange her words to conform to a more acceptable style, but thought better of it, so I am writing it as she spoke it to me. She is uneducated, but intelligent.) The letter continued: Cassey done gone and died like I figured she would. Poor child, she was sick. We all knew it, but they told me there was nothing they could do for her. Anyhow, I'm grateful for you people taking Rainey in like you did. I don't know what I woulda done if you hadn't. I got rheumatism so bad I can hardly walk to the outhouse. Speaking of Rainey, she is yours now. I give her to you. Please be good to her. She's a good girl. The rest of the stuff in this box is all the papers on Rainey. I guess you know she ain't had no daddy, if you know what I mean. My poor daughter, she fooled around so much, she ain't had no idea who her papa was although she claimed she did. May the good Lord bless her even if she was a sinner. (At this, Nell Foster could only shake her head.) The letter continued: Also in the box is Cassey's jewelery she wanted Rainey to have. It ain't much but it's all she had. Well, that's about all I got to say. I'm going to live with my relatives. This land here where my farm is belongs to me. I will try to have somebody sharecrop it for me until I die and then I will leave it to Rainey. It ain't much but it's all I got. It's 160 acres.

God bless you.

Orella Wether (x) (her mark)

P.S. from me, the druggist. I don't know if this letter will ever be worth anything, but I decided to witness her signature and since I am also a notary, I hereby stamp and notarize this document.

 The mother looked up slowly as she pondered the contents of the worn and dilapidated shoe box, thinking to herself: My God, what a legacy this poor child has. She ran her fingers through the jewelry, all dime store stuff except for one piece. She lifted it up to take a better look at it. It was a cameo locket on a silver chain and the locket itself appeared to be silver. She open the locket and saw small miniature photographs of two women, one on each side. The woman on the left, older than the one on the right, was obviously the grandmother, Cassey's mother, in years past. She seemed to be in her thirties when the photo was made. The photo was not of good quality and had begun to fade somewhat. She might have been a pretty woman at one time, in a different place and under different circumstances. The woman on the right was much younger, twenty perhaps. she was very pretty, Nell thought. she decided that this was Cassey, Rainey's mother. To herself, Nell reasoned that a girl this pretty would be chased by boys as soon as she sprouted, which, as she reasoned further, probably accounted for Cassey's misspent life. Girls like her start out wanting affection, since they had not gotten it at home. Boys had easily convinced her that affection came with a price, which she had reluctantly paid at first, but as time went by, it became more easy and then more lucrative as she settled into the role of an amateur prostitute, for that was all she ever was. She had not even achieved great success at her imposed profession.

Nell Foster sat quietly for a while pondering the future of this child now "given" to her. She had never viewed taking in Rainey as a permanent situation-only for a year or so until her daughter was a little older and better able to handle herself in the male dominated household. Now, what? She knew her husband would not accept this child on a permanent basis, nor was she sure that she wanted to. Her reverie was broken by the sounds of the males in the family coming in to eat followed by the shrill cries of the two girls. She hurriedly closed the box and threw the brown paper wrappings in the garbage can outside the back door. She was able to hide the box in a kitchen cabinet as the family came striding in amid shouts, yells, and teasing of the girls. She turned to greet her family as she resumed stirring the pots on the stove, saying, "All right, you get washed up and come to the table... dinner's ready."

Much to Nell's distress Cora had hardly sat down at the table when she inquired: "What was in the package, Mama?" followed by the father inquiring, "What package? Did my new saw come in from Sears, Nell? "

"No, Arvil, it was not from Sears. It was some church material the Southern Baptist sent me from Nashville." she hated lying to him but she was not ready to disclose any of this material just now. She had to think. Not waiting for a reply, he had dived into the ham hocks and potatoes, just nodding his head as he chewed.

With the family in bed later that night and the deep breathing and snoring of her husband testifying to his sleep, she eased out of the bed and retreated to the kitchen. She snapped on the bare bulb ceiling light overhead and retrieved the shoe box from the cabinet where she had hidden it. She once more took the locket in her hands and looked at the two women whose photographs appeared on either side. She began probing deeper into the bottom of the box. The contents were as meager as she had first discovered. A small ribbon bow, a pair of cheap rings, flashy, but cheap. Then she noticed a folded paper lying on the bottom of the box. It was an envelope with a return address from the Vital Statistic Bureau of the State of Arkansas. It has stamped on its face... IMPORTANT DOCUMENT. Withdrawing the contents she could see it was a birth certificate, the same kind she had received for each of her four children. It was the birth certificate of Rainey Wether, born April 18, 1930. To herself, she thought: At least we now know when the poor child was born. She perused it further and as she had expected the line with the father's name showed: FATHER UNKNOWN. On the lines for godmother and godfather she read names completely unknown to her. She assumed they were either relatives or people the minister had cornered to complete the baptism ceremony, which was not uncommon in those days of fragmented families.

Searching further in the bottom of the box, she found nothing. This was Rainey Wether's entire legacy. She pondered: The only thing of real value is that hard scrabble farm of her grandmother's which she would inherit some day. But, when? How would she ever know about it? Would she lose it for failure to pay taxes on it, so common in those depression days. Nell Foster knew she had no answers for these questions. The only thing the child was left of any value to her at her age was the locket. She debated whether to tell her husband of the land. If she let him read the letter he would discover that for himself, and knowing his greed, he would attempt, by hook or crook, to get his hands on that land. She decided to withhold the letter from him, to merely show him the rest of the contents of the box, saying this was all there was. With that decision made she returned to her bedroom and as she climbed in bed to the raucous snoring of her husband she thought: I still have to tell that poor child her mother is dead. Oh, God, give me strength and wisdom to choose the right words.

After breakfast the next morning she shooed the children off to play and do chores, asking her husband to remain in the kitchen for a talk. "Eva time you want to talk, Nell, it means you want some money. What is it now?"

She poured him a cup of coffee, something she seldom did nowadays, but she wanted to get him in as good a mood as it was possible for him. He accepted the coffee with a curious glance as he waited for his wife to bring up what he was sure would be a request for money, especially after her serving him coffee.

"Arvil, that package that came in yesterday was not from the church. I had to lie to you because I did not want the children to hear what I have to say about the contents." He started to protest about the lie, but she held up her hand, and he, instead, inquired, "What was in the box that is so gol-danged important?"

She hesitated. "Rainey's mama has died... poor soul."

His deeply ingrained religious fervor surfaced. He bowed his head: "Amen... Amen."

The wife continued: "The grandmother had the druggist write the note. She said she gives us the child... to keep."

His head came up sharply, his religious fervor fading into the background: "Now, hold on a damn minute, Nell, Ah ain't neva agreed to keep that child on a permanent basis. You told me you wanted her fer only a year or two. Didn't you say that?"

She nodded. "Yes, Arvil, but I thought Cassey would come and get her after a while, after this miserable depression is over, or until she found herself a husband who would support her, but. ..but... I didn't know she was dying until after the child got here."

"All that don't matter, Nell! Ah'm a man 'o mah word. That kid can stay fer only two years and then she has to go." As he pondered the matter further, "Why, it'll be eight or ten years before she kin be married off 'n Ah ' ll hafta support her until then. She'll neva earn her keep on this farm... she's a girl. Now, iffen she was a boy."

"Girls are as precious to our Lord as boys, Arvil."

He looked at her with incredulity: "Then, Nell, how come the good Lord didn't send his daughter down to save us?"

Without waiting for a reply: "Cause he knowed she couldn't git the job done... that's why!"

The mother ignored the statement as she had so many over the years, adding, "Well, Arvil, since we can keep her for two years and no more, I must start planning for her future."

He looked up: "What future? She ain't got no future, Nell."

"Everyone has a future, Arvil... everyone," and she walked out the kitchen and into the yard where the girls were chasing chickens.

"Cora and Rainey, come here girls, I want to talk to you both," and as they each circled her, grabbing her apron, she walked them to the shade of an old oak tree where the family had a wooden swing hung on rusty chains. She had one child sit on each side and turning to Rainey, took her hands in hers. "Rainey, honey, I have something very important to talk to you about. I wish you were older... so you could better understand what this is all about... but you're not, are you," as she smiled at the perplexed child. She continued: "You know that box that came in yesterday." The child nodded. "Well, I told you girls I was not sure what was in it and I might have to send it back. Well, I now know what was in it, and I don't have to send it back. Rainey, the box was from your grandma Orella..."

The child became interested, her eyes widened. "Was it mah mama's old shoe box?"

The mother nodded, not replying audibly.

The child stood up, her chin quivering. "Mah mama is dead, ain't she?" and she ran off towards the open fields with Cora in pursuit.

CHAPTER FOUR

"Rainey is an orphan! Rainey is an orphan! cried out the oldest boy, Tom, the main tormentor of both Rainey and Cora. This was generally echoed by the two younger boys prodded on by the oldest who had inherited his father's obnoxious and irascible disposition. Since this had been going on for weeks, ever since the shoe box had arrived with its sad message, Rainey now began to take it in stride, not crying each time as she had done at the beginning. Now, a side of her nature which had heretofore never shown up, because it had never had to, began to emerge. She had a latent mean streak in her little body, obviously a genetic trait inherited from the equally mean grandmother, Orella Wether. She now assumed a more defensive posture by mounting a strong offense such as throwing dried cow manure at the boys when they weren't looking. After curing in a hot sun for several weeks, it can become as hard as brick and a full-sized paddy can leave a whelp when directed to the side of the head. Even Cora began to join in the fun since she was taunted by her brothers nearly as much as was Rainey.

Upon complaining to their mother that Rainey had indeed hit them with dried cow dung, and in some cases, some not too dry, they had received little sympathy from the all-knowing mother who had, from the kitchen window, heard the cries of: "Rainey is an orphan." But not until she heard her oldest son cry out one day in a moment of extreme anger as he wiped the fresh cow dung from his face, "Your mama was a whore!", did she decide to take action. For two reasons: she did not want that unacceptable word spoken in her home, especially by her minor children, but even more importantly... Where did they find that out? She had discussed it with her husband and pleaded with him to not tell the boys about it, fairly sure in her mind that they did not know what the term meant, and: "They are too young to know, Arvil."

As they lay in bed that night and her husband turned over to go to sleep, she touched his arm: "Arvil, I have to discuss something with you"

"Aw, cain't it wait til morn'in, Nell. Ah'm tired and sleepy."

"No, it can't, Arvil. This is important."

"Oh, it's always important to you, Nell," as he turned to face her. "What is it?"

She took a deep breath. "This morning, Tom yelled at Rainey, your mama is a whore."

"Well, what's wrong with that? She was!"

She remained calm as she promised herself she would. "What is wrong with it is that I told no one but you about what Cassey was (avoiding the use of the word again) so if the boys know it, then you told them about it."

"So what? They got to know the facts of life someday."

"That is beside the point. I asked you to keep a thing to yourself and you told the boys. Do you think that was the right thing to do?"

"Oh, hell, Nell, don't make a big deal out of this. It ain't important."

"Yes, it is important, Orvil. You are missing the point."

"What point?"

"Do those boys know what whores do?... you know what I mean."

He was silent for a while, then: "Hell, Nell, those boys bin lookin' at chickens and cows doin' it for years. They know what that is all about."

"It's not the same and you know it. What those chickens and cows do they do because their nature tells them to do it. What Cassey did is not what her God tells her to do. You know that the Bible has many references to harlots and it is seldom in a good light."

"That is not true. Our Lord Jesus Christ befriended harlots on some occasions."

"Arvil, I am not in the mood to debate the Bible with you at this time of the night. I want to know if our boys know what a whore does for her money. That is what I want to know," and before he could answer, "and what of Cora, does she know of all this?"

"Cora is your responsibilty, Nell. Them boys is mine. Now go to sleep 'fore Ah lose mah temper."

But, she did not go to sleep. She lay awake for hours pondering the answer to her own question concerning her own daughter..."What does Cora know?" Like most mothers of that generation, they told their daughters only the rudiments of what they had to know about periods and pregnancies, with the age old admonition..."if you keep you legs crossed, nothing can happen." The rest they learned in the barn, under the back porch, or, in the hay loft or back seat of a car. She had never discussed anything with Cora, assuming she was too young. She was aware that, like most farm children, Cora had watched barnyard procreation since she was old enough to walk outside. But, whether she had ever connected the barnyard procreation with human procreation, she really did not know. Cora had never asked and she had never volunteered. Now, in addition to Cora she felt some maternal responsibility for Rainey's education along those lines. Even though Rainey would probably be gone before she reached the age of puberty... still, she ought to know something. As she rolled over to go to sleep, she resolved that she would talk to the girls as soon as possible... maybe tomorrow, or, maybe, the next day. But, she had to do it.

The Fosters owned a stud bull which was used not only to service his milk cow herd, but was rented out to stud for the neighbors who could not justify the keeping and feeding of an ornery bull. The bull was kept in a private pasture out beyond the barn and those cows who required his services were brought out to him and left with him for a period of an hour or so, for he was as dependable as the Old Faithful geyser, and if he happened to miss on one try he would, without fail, connect sooner or later. When the boys were younger Arvil Foster agreed with his wife that they should not be present at these breeding times, mainly so that he would not have to explain something to them that they were too young to understand, anyway. But, as the boys got older, especially Tom who was now 12, and Joe who was now 10, he made no attempt to hide them from the proceedings. Unkown to him, even Bill at 10 had witnessed the act on several occasions. In the older boy, Tom, now approaching puberty, the sight of these beasts in the actual act had begun to have an affect on his growing libido, which was only natural and human, and he began to feel urges in his body that he had not felt previously, urges he could not discuss with anyone, not even his brother, Joe, and certainly not his parents. Upon seeing the bull in action, he could feel in his own body those changes that enabled the bull to perform his deeds in so magnificent a fashion. It was now getting to the point that he had those feelings even when he was not watching a bull in action. All he had to do was think about it, and he did often. Since there were no girls on their farm except Cora and Rainey, he was somewhat restricted in his "age of discovery" period. He had so often heard the minister talk on the subject that he knew he should never think of his sister in that way. But, Rainey was different. She was not kin to him, and he began to eye her in a different light, even to the point of being nice to her. The younger boys were as puzzled as were Rainey and Cora, and the mother, in all her innocence, merely accepted it as part of his growing up and becoming more responsible. He was growing up, all right, but responsibility had nothing to do with it. He just had to see "it". He had seen it on animals and he knew what "it" looked like on them, but he had never seen "it" on a real live female, and he just had to. The urge was there and it could not be denied. He thought about it and thought about it. How could it be done without his getting into big trouble, even from his father. He was behind the barn one day admiring his growing manhood as he so often did these days and he saw the two girls walking towards him, together, as always. He cursed his luck. Those girls were always together. Then, fate smiled on him as he heard his mother call out to Cora. She had failed to pick up her clothes and left them lying on the floor and was being called back to rectify the situation. Cora had turned back, and yelling out to Rainey: "You go on. As soon as I finish I'll meet you behind the barn."

    What an opportunity, he thought... Rainey coming by herself behind the barn where he was already in hiding and in a state of excitement, but as he made ready to exposed himself and had half done so, Rainey, who was nearer than he thought came around the corner, just in time to see his manhood before he hurriedly turned away, half surprised, half embarrassed, as he stamered the age old classic line..."Rainey, I'll show you mine if you show me yours..."

    Rainey, who had gotten all the look she wanted, never having seen one before, blurted out..."Ah don't have to show you mine, Ah done seen yours!" and with that she ran to the house to report the incident to Nell Foster.

Cora, stood nearby, wide-eyed as Rainey told the mother of the entire episode, ending with the graphic description of his organ, that..."he's got one just like a dog."

Nell Foster's hands went to her heart as she intoned: "Oh, my God, I can't believe what I'm hearing. Rainey, are you sure you are not making this up. Tom would never do anything like that... not at his age..."

The child nodded. "Yessum, he showed me his thing... he did, and he ast me to show him mine, too, but I ran away 'cause mah mama tole me to neva show nobody mah bottom."

"Oh, my God... oh, my God!" as she shook her head, wringing her hands. she now knew that the matter she had decided on just a few days ago would now have to be done... without fail. Taking the girls out to the yard, each holding her hand, she headed for the swing under the oak tree. Rainey asked: "Miz Nell, did Ah do something wrong?"

As they hurried along: "No, honey, you didn't do anything wrong... my son did. But," she added, "these things are going to happen in life. Why I remember a little boy exposed himself to me when I was just about your age, but he was only six, but Tom is...". She didn't finish the sentence as they reached the swing. She sat the girls down and arranging her apron as she composed herself, she began: "You girls have seen animals doing it in the yard... chickens, dogs, cats... haven't you?"

The children had seen it, but they were not sure they should admit the foul deed. They looked at each other, then nodded.

"Well, when you see a rooster chasing a hen around, and then, and then... well, he mounts her. Do you know what they are doing?"

Cora looked down at the ground, embarrassed, but Rainey proudly spoke, "Yessum, Ah know... they're making baby chickens. Mah grandma tole me so... she did," as she nodded for emphasis.

Nell, somewhat embarrassed, herself, nodded, asking: "But, do you really know what is happening?"

Once again, it was the wordly Rainey who replied: "No ma'am, I don't understand how you kin make baby chickens by that rooster doing that to that hen. Ah thought baby chickens came from chicken eggs... not doing that."

Nell could not suppress a grin, realizing her job would be a lot more difficult than she had thought. "Well, you see girls, hens will lay eggs without that rooster doing that to them, but the eggs are not fertile."

The two girls looked at each other with Cora asking: "What does that mean... that word... fertile?"

Nell took a deep breath. She was now into it and she might as well go all the way. "Well, you see, in all animals and humans there are eggs provided by the female and the male has to fertilize the eggs. That is why you see the mating of female cows with bulls and hens with roosters. The males are fertilizing the eggs in the female Do you understand so far?"

The girls, not sure they understood, nodded, with Rainey asking, "Do the females like it?"

Nell's hands went to her cheeks as they flushed. "What do you mean, Rainey?"

Rainey took a deep breath. "Well, Ah see them hens running all ova the yard trying to git away from them roosters. They cain't like it too much."

Nell looked away for a moment. She had no reply for the child that would not have gone far beyond what she intended, and she was happy when her daughter asked, "Do Rainey and me have eggs in us?"

She knew she had gone beyond her own knowledge area, so she replied, "Well, when you are older, yes, but you are now too young to... to... have eggs."

Cora looked at her mother. "Do you have eggs in you?"

"Well, yes, of course, Cora. All grown women have eggs in their bodies," as she began to perspire although there was a cool breeze blowing.

Cora persisted. "Did I come from an egg?"

Nell knew where this was leading, but what could she do. "Yes, you came from an egg in my body."

"How did it get fertilized," persisted Cora, now completely entranced by this conversation.

Nell could be heard to groan. She shrugged her shoulders, looking off in space as if asking for Divine guidance, but none was forthcoming as she looked at her daughter. "As I explained to you about all animals and humans, a male has to fertilize the egg."

"But, who fertilized yours, Mama?"

Nearly reaching her limits of endurance, she replied, more brusque than she had intended, "For God's sake, cora, your father fertilized my egg. Who do you think?"

Cora's eyes widened. "You mean you and Papa do it... like the hens and the roosters?"

"For God's sake, Cora, all adults do it. That's how babies are made. That is what I'm trying to explain to you and Rainey, but you are not supposed to do it until you are married."

Cora, now interested, persisted. "Animals don't get married, do they... I mean... not for keeps... just as long as it takes."

Nell capitulated: "No, Cora, animals do not get married. Marriage is a sacrament instituted by God just for humans. You do not do it until you do it with your husband. That is what I have been trying to tell you girls. You don't show your private parts to anyone and, you do not look at the private parts of anyone... do you understand?"

Rainey, having never lived in a house with a male, had never given the matter much thought. She had heard her outspoken grandma say to Cassey on many occasions, "If you only knew who Rainey's father was," but that meant nothing of substance to her, but she now was getting the picture of what her mother did for a living. She pondered the matter for a while as Cora interrogated her mother some more, then, she tugged at Nell's sleeve: "Miz Nell, is that what mah mama did that was wrong. She let those men see her bottom, 'n they was not her husband?"

Nell Foster hated to reply, but she had to: "Yes, I think that is what she did, Rainey, but don't judge her too harshly, honey, your family was poor and your mama did what she had to do to make a living."

The child got up and began to walk away, murmuring more to herself than the others: "Ah ain't neva gonna let no man see mah bottom... no siree."

Relations were strained between the sexes in the Foster family after the organ exposure episode. Nell, quite naturally, informed her husband of the matter, and Arvil, also quite naturally, found great amusement in the thing. "Hell, Nell, why're you so worked up on that boy trying to become a man? It's only natural for him to git worked up at his age..."

She did not let him finish, for she, too, was worked up in a different manner, as she lashed out at him..."But, Arvil, that child is only five and a half... so young... so innocent."

"She ain't too young and innocent to throw those cow chips at the boys 'n some 'o them ain't even cured yet."

"They deserve it! They tease her all the time."

The husband stood near her chair, looking down at his wife: "Ah coulda tole you this was gonna happen, Nell. We made a mistake taking that kid in 'n the soona she is gone... the betta."

She looked up, uncertain of her position in the matter: "But, you promised she could stay for two years... you promised. It's not fair to her to make her leave. Where would she go?"

As he walked out the kitchen door, he paused: "Ah tole you she could stay fer two years 'n Ah'm a man 'o mah word. She kin! But, you betta start lookin' fer someplace to send her when her time is up."

From that time on a schism developed between the males and females of the Foster residence. Joe, having been exposed, both literally and figuratively as a provocateur, now hated Rainey and vowed revenge of some kind. The other two boys, taking their lead from the father also developed a cold and hostile attitude towards the innocent child who had invaded their lives. The females formed a buffer between the boys and Rainey. For the next two years, girls played only with girls and boys played only with boys. At the dinner table, which was really their only time of contact, relations were strained and conversation between the sexes took place only when food needed to be passed.

Lloyd J. Guillory

In September the three boys and Cora began to go to the county school several miles from their home. They left early to catch the bus that stopped on the main road and would not get home until late afternoon. Rainey, still only five and a half, would not start school until the following year. She and Nell Foster were home alone for nearly all the day. They became close, almost like mother and daughter. Nell Foster had both pity and love for the child, but she decided her attachment to Rainey had to be kept in check, for she knew she was not hers to keep. She knew her husband would be uncompromising in his insistence that the child leave at the agreed time of two years.

Nell began to work with the child, to improve her English, gently correcting her grammar errors, trying to smooth and polish her rough-hewn demeanor which she had acquired from her rough-hewn grandma, the main role model she had been exposed to.

Unconsciously, the young and impressionable child began to form an opinion of the adversarial relationship between the sexes that was to stay with her all her life. We tend to be molded by what we see and hear around us in our formative years and all she ever saw and heard was the strained and awkward relationship between Nell Foster and her irascible husband and the complete polarization of the sexes in that household. In her young mind, based on what she had seen and experienced in her nearly six years on this planet, and it would be enforced to a greater degree as she grew older, men were just no damn good and the only reason that any female needed one was to fertilize her eggs.

CHAPTER FIVE

1937

As the two year period came to an end, Nell Foster began to worry anew. She had asked her husband to extend the time for Rainey to stay with her, but he was adamant- she had to leave. Even though he had reluctantly agreed to the initial offer to take her in, at his wife's request, he never developed any warm feelings for the child. It is doubtful that he would have developed warm feelings for any child since he had never experienced the feel of true warmth, even with his own wife and their female child. Cora Foster would remember him, later in life, as an abusive father incapable of true love. Even the boys, so anxious to please him as children to the point of subjugating their true feelings to conform to what they thought he wanted them to be, as they grew older, finally came to admit: "He was a mean old bastard."

Nell, in desperation, began to ask families who lived in the area if they would take the child in. But, Arvil Foster had spread the word throughout that part of the county that Rainey Wether was a "bad kid... come from bad blood... her ma was a whore! And worse, she is a bastard chile. What kin ya 'spect?" And to the fundamentally religious old line Southern Baptist, the sins of the parents were, indeed, visited upon the child. If she had had leprosy she would not have been any less welcomed into the homes of that area.

But, Nell persisted, especially among the women in her church group, appealing to their motherly instincts. "What if she was yours, Matilda? Could you turn her out like a puppy and drop her off in a pasture... could you?" Matilda, wiping a tear from her eye, for she had been orphaned as a child, shook her head "No, Nell, Ah couldn't do that," and as she pondered the problem further, "Ah got a sister in Basil... ova near Pine Bluff. Ah'm gonna go to see her next week. She's mah older sister and a kindly soul... I'll see what she says."

It took a lot of pleading and a lot of tears but the sister agreed to take her in..."fer a while."

Nell dreaded telling Rainey that she had to move to a strange place, once again, and the child, when told, merely looked down at the floor and nodded. She was now seven years old and the last two years had convinced her that she was really not a valuable commodity to any farm family. She was a girl and all girls of her age were good for was to do house chores and eat. She had had only one year of schooling and could barely make out words when she tried to read from her McGuffey's reader. When Nell had told Arvil of her slow learning, his reply was: "She's dumb, Nell. Look what she comes from." But, when the time came to physically transfer the child to her new home, Arvil gladly volunteered to drive the thirty-five miles to take her there. "It's worth the gas, Nell, to be rid 'o her." They had decided not to take their children with them, leaving them with a nearby neighbor who was having a picnic.

When Nell Foster first saw the house to which she would surrender this child, her heart sank. She had believed that if this woman was willing to take her in she was, at least, as well off as the Fosters, but to her dismay, this was not so. As they drove off the main road and turned onto the dirt driveway she could make out a cabin made of pine logs, with old rusty corrugated iron roofing, and for an addition a discarded school bus had been shoved up against one wall and used as additional space. Nell bit her lip and looked at her husband who had a smile on his face as he perused the place.

"Well now, Nell, ain't this a pretty place fer Rainey to come to. She'll be right at home heah," as he looked down at the child and grinned. Nell merely squeezed the child's hand, saying nothing.

An old woman came out of the house wiping her hands on her apron as she came forward. She was grossly overweight and had not a tooth in her mouth. Her grey hair was stringy and she wore no shoes. Nell went forward to greet her with: "Howdy, Ma'am, I'm Nell Foster and I was looking for Matilda Steven's sister, Anna."

The woman smiled a toothless grin. "Ah'm Anna... Matilda's sister. She done told me you was comin', 'n my, my, this must be Rainey... ain't you a pretty little thing," as she patted the child on the head, with Rainey recoiling at her touch. Nell was shocked into disbelief. She expected a woman of perhaps forty, at the most, but this woman appeared to be sixty or even older, Then, to add to her shock, an even older man came stumbling out of the cabin, apparently drunk since he was still waving a wine bottle in his hand. The woman turned to him: "Now, Papa, Ah told you to stay inside til Ah came back in... now, you go ahead 'n do what Ah tole you to." Turning back to Nell and Arvil, adding, "Papa is feeling poorly today. Ah tole him to stay in the house, but he's got a hard head 'n, he ain't all right up heah all the time, iffen you know what Ah mean."

Nell, trying to show compassion, replied, "I'm sorry to hear that your father is ill..." but she did not get to finish as the woman laughed, "Lawdy, he ain't mah real papa... he's mah ole man."

Nell's hands went to her cheek; embarrassed, she said, "Oh, I'm sorry about the mistake."

The woman laughed a hearty laugh: "You ain't half as sorry as Ah am. Ah'm married to the old fool," and she giggled as she said to no one in particular as she added: "Iffen you folks want to come in Ah'll put on some coffee 'n we ' ll git to know each other."

As Nell was about to agree, for she wanted to see the inside of the house, feeling that if the outside were any indication, she would be placing Rainey in a hovel, but Arvil intervened, sayin, "Now, that's right friendly of you, Ma'am, but we ain't got time," and taking Nell by the arm, "we got to go."

Nell, filled with apprehension and despair, patted the child on the head, and bending down to her level, kissed her warmly and hugged her tightly, saying in her ear, "try to be brave, Rainey, and be a good girl. I'm sure this will be only for a little while until I can find you something else... somewhere."

The child nodded, saying nothing. Once again, she was in a state of complete bewilderment as to her predicament. Since she had never known any kind of stable environment in her young life, she felt this was the way it was. This is how people lived, especially little girls who had no mama or papa to care or them.

As Nell and Arvil Foster drove off, they said nothing for a while, then Nell broke the silence. "Arvil, I have never felt so dejected in all my life. I have never hated anything so much in all my born days as leaving that child in that home with that couple, and you made me do it. I'll never forgive you for that," and she began to sob. He pulled off the road and put the car in neutral, then, swung his hand full force, striking her on the side of the face, snapping her head back. He put his forefinger in her face, sneering at her. "Woman, don't you eva talk to me that 'away agin. Iffen you do, you'll git worse than that," and he put the car in gear and drove off.

Nell, wiping her tears as she rubbed the stinging face, looked out the car window and swore to God, "I'd leave him if I had someplace to go with my kids. I swear it."

Rainey watched as the car drove off, feeling that the only life she had known for the past two years had gone with them, and once again, she was to live with complete strangers, people she did not know and from what she could see, she would not take a liking to.

Rainey stood there with a paper bag holding her clothing in one hand and the shoe box with her legacy in the other. To her the shoe box was all that was left of her mother and though its contents were meager, in her mind it was a thing of value. The old woman came towards her, extending her hand, smiling her toothless smile, "Come on, Rainey, honey, come into the house and I'll give you some milk and cookies. The old man, still weaving and still standing, merely grunted and turned to go back inside, the wine bottle still in his hand.

As she entered the shack Rainey looked about her with fear and apprehension. She had not expected much but it was far less than she had expected, compared to the Foster home, it was indeed a hovel. The furniture was decrepit and worn, the walls were stained with water leaks, and there was dust everywhere. Even her grandmother's house, humble though it was, was better than this. She swallowed hard and bit her lip and suppressed a tear as the old woman repeated, "Come on, honey, sit down at the table and I'll pour you some milk. These cookies might be a little stale... but they'll do. Now, you just put yore things right there on the chair," as she motioned to the child's clothing bag and shoe box.

Rainey complied as she continued to look around. The old man sank into his worn old rocker, belching as he did, and taking another swig from his wine bottle, "Anna, this wine is 'bout gone... you got a'nutha one?"

"No, Ah ain't you ole bastard... Ah tole you to make that one last... not to make a pig 'o yoresef. Now, what ' ll we do fer tonight? You betta go 'n check the junkyard to see iffen you kin find something to sell. You ain't bin outa the house in a week. How you 'spect us to live?"

He looked at her through bleary, bloodshot eyes: "Ah 'spec us to live lak we always done."

"Yeh, sure, beggin our kids fer money... beggin the grocer fer more credit... beggin... beggin... beggin. That's how we live."

"You ain't got no right to talk. You takin' that kid in. That's one more mouth to feed. She ain't big 'nough to earn her keep. Ah ' ll bet she cain't even milk a cow 'o slop the hogs," and turning to Rainey, "kin you, li'1 girl?"

As she munched on the stale cookies, she nodded, replying, "I kin milk a cow, but not too good. I pull an them tits but the milk don't always come out. Some cows is just stubborn."

He belched. "Ah tole you Anna... she ain't gonna be good fer nuthin'."

The old lady groaned as she sat at the kitchen table. "You don't pay no mind to that ole drunk, Rainey, honey. He talked the same way to our kids. 'Reckon that's why they all packed up and left... all five 'o then."

"Where did they go?" she asked, always interested in why people leave and where they went, since that seemed to be a way of life in those depression years.

"Well, let's see. The three girls all got married by the time they was fifteen. All 'ceptin Harvella, she ain't exactly married, but she got hersef a man."

"Is she a whore?" asked Rainey in all innocence.

The woman was deeply offended. "No, she ain't no whore. She ain't had 'nough sense to be a whore. Whores git paid... she give it away," but she did have 'nough sense to give it to the same man, so he took up with her... moved her into his house on the farm ova in Tuckerville. How you know 'bout whores? You too young to know 'bout them."

"Mah mama was one!" she exclaimed rather proudly.

"Oh, yeh, Ah heered that from mah little sista, Matilda.

Rainey begin to count on her fingers. "You said you had five kids. What happened to the two boys?"

"The woman drew herself up proudly. "Them two boys is both in the C.C.C. (The Civilian Conservation Corps- started by Franklin Roosevelt to put millions of young men to work). You know 'bout the C.C.C.?"

She shook her head: "Uh... uh."

"Well, they pay them boys thirty dollars a month 'n they got to send twenty-five home to their mamas and papas. That is all we got to live on, 'cepting when that ole goat," as she nodded to the now sleeping old derelict in the chair, "goes out and sells some junk to the junk dealer."

"Where does he get the junk?" Rainey asked with some interest.

She laughed. "Anyplace he kin find it or steal it," and as she took the empty milk glass away from the child, "come on and Ah ' ll show you whar you gonna sleep. You kin put yore things in that old dresser ova thar 'n that's yore bed," pointing to an old army cot in the corner. "We had beds when the kids was with us, but," and she sighed, "we sold them when they left. "That-a-way, they cain't came back to visit us too often."

"Why did you take me in?" Rainey asked with the increasing practicality and pragmatism forced on her by her itinerant life.

The old women lit a Picayune cigarette, blowing the smoke up at the ceiling as she pondered a reply. "Wal, mah sista Matilda told me you needed a place to go 'n Ah felt it was mah Christian duty to take you in... fer a while." As she looked around the hovel..."Course, Ah kin use some help in this place. Thar's some things you kin do to help out... to make yore keep."

Rainey looked around. "What do I have to do?"

"Nuthin more'n Ah would 'spect from mah own three girls when they was heer. You kin help me clean this place up. You kin wash the dishes. You kin help milk that old cow 'n you kin slop the hogs... when we got slop. You're seven years old, Rainey. You're old 'nough to work 'round the house."

She nodded. Even though Nell Foster had insisted on the girls doing some work around the house, it was more to train them than a matter of necessity. As to the milking of the cows, that was done more out of curiosity and fun, especially when she and Cora found out, from the boys, that a teat could be aimed and milk could be squirted for several feet, which it often was... in someone's eyes.

"Speaking of work, Rainey, you kin start in by cleaning them dishes in the sink. They ain't bin cleaned far a few days 'n when you git through with that you kin take that ole broom in the corner and sweep out this place. Iffen that ole goat," and she motioned to the sleeping man in the rocker, "don't wake up, jus sweep 'round him, Maybe the dust'l choke him to death 'n put him outa his misery" and she chuckled.

That evening, as she had finished all the work the old woman had pointed out to her, she sat, tired and disgusted. The old man had gone to the general store a mile or so away and bought another bottle of cheap wine and now they both began to take alternate swigs from it. She sat and watched them. She had never seen the drinking of alcoholic beverages before. Her grandmother had no money to waste on liquor. Her mother, in spite of her other faults, could not stand the taste of it, and the Fosters had a religious disdain for the "devil's brew". She sat and watched as they drank and ignored her. Except for saying, "pass the bottle", they ignored each other. An old radio in the corner had an Amos 'n Andy program on it, but the inebriated pair had no interest in it, and neither did she. The Fosters had had radio, but listened only to the weather and politicians explaining the depression away, promising that the "worst was over and good times lay ahead".

    She sat in the old chair, her legs under her and her hands folded in her lap. Even at her tender age, she had enough perception to understand that this would be a tenure of misery. The old lady had told her after she had finished the day's work what was expected of her the next day. It would mean working from daylight to dusk. There would be no young children for her to play with, really no one of her age to even see. The hovel of a house was located off to itself, a good half mile from the county road. No one would even come to see them... or her. Her young mind began to ponder her future with these derelicts of humanity, and even at her tender age she could understand that her future with them would be nothing short of miserable. And what of her schooling? The old woman had made no mention of it, and there was no doubt in her mind that it was not to be part of her life. If there was one thing she had learned from the talks with Nell Foster, it was the value of education. She remembered the words: "Women don't count for much in this world, Rainey, not in the minds of the men. We are meant only to have their babies and provide them comfort when they want or need it. I think you know what I mean since we have had our talks. The only women who have been able to break those bonds are women who have gone out and gotten an education. Learn to do something, Rainey... to be able to earn your own living so you will not have to depend on any man to support you." The words had impressed her at the time since she clearly remembered her mother's situation. She had only one thing to offer a man and when that was gone, she had nothing. She remembered her grandmother's "hard luck" was all time-framed from the time "poor Norbet died". When her husband died the farm had died with him. She remembered and the words burned in her.

    She sat and watched as the couple drank themselves into a stupor. Eventually the head of each went back on the chair and couch they occupied. Their mouths opened and the snoring began. It was not a pretty sight to witness, especially to her who had never seen such a sight before, in spite of her deprived existence. She got up and picked up the kerosene lamp which was the only source of lighting in the unelectrified cabin. She went to her room, opened the drawer where she had stored her clothing bag and shoe box. She gathered them up, and going to the cot, she removed the old smelly wool blanket from it and tip-toed past the sleeping couple. She went out to the front porch and looked around. It was a warm night with no breeze blowing and she knew she could sleep outside without being too cold. She went out towards the barn but the chickens, their slumber disturbed, began to cackle loudly. She knew she had made a mistake in coming near them. Now, the cows began to move about and the hogs became restless. She quickly exited the barn. There was a lean-to on the south side of the barn which covered several bales of hay and she climbed in there and spread her blanket, trying to make herself comfortable as she lay her head on a clump of straw. Sleep did not come easily or quickly. She was filled with foreboding. She knew she had to leave this place and go somewhere... anywhere. But where? She knew absolutely nothing about the countryside and she was only seven years old. She knew she was not physically or mentally capable of taking care of herself, but she didn't care tonight. She made up her mind. She would leave this place... for good.

She had a restless night. It was dark with no sign of a moon but she could tell by the chickens becoming restless that dawn was approaching and she wanted to leave this place before the drunken couple stirred. She wrapped her belongings in the blanket and made a knapsack of it. She realized that she was stealing the blanket and she had never stolen anything before in her life, but she rationalized that it would be payment for the hard work she had done. She headed out towards the county road, a half mile away, stumbling many times on the unfamiliar dirt path. As she reached the road she looked in both directions. She had no idea in which direction to head, so she relied on an age old method of determining direction. She spit in her hand and slapped it with the other and the direction of her spit determined which way she would head out. She had walked for nearly an hour in almost total darkness without seeing even one vehicle, and then, a pair of headlights appeared on the horizon. They moved up and down and sideways as the vehicle, whatever it was, bumped along on the gravel road. She had no idea who or what it was that was coming, but in her desperation she was determined to ask it or them for a ride. As the vehicle came near the headlights began to light the roadway. She edged out into the middle of the road and waved her one free hand from side to side. The vehicle came to a halt and she could see it was an old truck loaded with pine logs. A man alighted from the cab and came around to where he could see her in the headlights. He removed his cap from his head and chuckled, more to himself than to her as he perused her up and down. He came closer. "Lawdy, lawdy, you ain't nuthin but a chile. What you doin' out heer litt'l girl? All by yursef... whar you goin' chile?" he asked in a friendly voice.

She gathered up her resolve, answering in a voice more fearful than confident, "Ah'm running away... Ah need a ride."

"You runnin' away? Whar you runnin' to and what you runnin' from?"

"Ah'm runnin' away from these mean people who beat me all the time." She had never lied before but she was desperate and she felt her plight would be received with more compassion if her situation were enhanced with some pathos.

He scratched his head, replacing his cap: "Well, whar you want to go? You ain't nuthin' but a chile. You cain't go 'round the country by yozesef, chile!" he said with some degree of fear and apprehension as he looked around to see if anyone was coming in either direction.

She said with increasing bravado, "Ah don't know where Ah'm going but Ah'm just going. Will you give me a ride... please?"

"Wal, Ah ain't gonna leave you out heer by yoresef, that's fer shur. You climb up in that cab 'n Ah'll figga out what to do with you when we gits goin'... go 'head... climb up."

With some help from him, she was eventually seated in the truck cab, delighted to be off the road and with someone who, so far, seemed to be a friendly man. She felt relieved but still unsure of where she would tell him she wanted to go.

He put the old truck in gear and resumed his travel in the same direction, stealing a glance at his passenger from time to time, trying to collect his own thoughts as to what to do with the child. "What's yore name, chile?" Thinking that maybe he had heard of her family and could return her there.

"My name is Rainey."

He looked at her. "Rainey? Rainey... what?"

"Rainey Wether."

He laughed. "You joshin' me chile? You mean to tell me yore name is Rainey Wether? You joshin' me... ain't you?"

She shook her head. "No, my name is really Rainey Wether."

"Whar you live, girl?"

She shrugged her shoulders. "Ah don't live nowhere."

"Evabody lives somewhar... you gotta have a family... somewhar."

"Ah ain't. Ah ' m an orphan. Ah ain't got nobody."

He thought about it for a while. "But, you got to come from somewhar... you ain't dropped outta the sky!"

"When mah mama died Ah went to live with a family... then, they didn't want me no more and they give me to another family, and they was mean to me 'n Ah'm running away."

Near tears, the man asked, "But, what you gonna do? Whar you gonna go?"

"Can Ah live with you?"

He was shocked. "No, chile, you cain't live with me. Ah got too many kids, nah. Ah got eight kids to feed."

The dawn had arrived and enough light had entered the cab so that she could see him more clearly. She squinted her eyes as she leaned forward to get a better look at his face. She had a surprised look as she exclaimed: "You a nigga, ain't you?"

He chuckled, now, for he had believed she had noticed that when he first stopped for her and stood in the headlights, as he replied, "Ah shur am. Bin one all mah life, too. Ah guess Ah ' ll be one til Ah die. Why, ain't you neva seen a colored person 'afore?"

"Well, shur, Ah seen plenty of them, but Ah ain't neva talked to one before."

"You ain't skeer'd 'o me, is you?"

"You gonna hurt me?" as she drew away from him.

"No, chile, Ah ain't gonna hurt you, but a colored man kin git in a lot 'o trouble runnin' around the country wit a litt'l white girl... you know that?"

"Why? 'Cause you a nigga?"

"Yeah, 'cause Ah'm a nigga!... that's why! And, Rainey, Ah got to tell you, it ain't nice to go 'round calling colored folks niggas. We don't like it."

"Ah didn't mean no harm."

He chuckled. "Ah know that, but don't do it no more... okay?"

"Okay, Ah won't... Ah swear. Where you gonna take me?"

"Ah don know, chile. Ah'm thinkin' right nah," and as he turned to look at her, "the only place Ah kin think of is mah house, but mah wife ain't gonna be happy 'bout this... that's fer sure."

"She doesn't like kids?"

"She betta like 'em. We got a bunch 'o them, but Ah don't believe she wants anymore 'n 'specil not a white one."

"Would she like it better if Ah was a colored kid?"

He chuckled once again: "She'd like it a lot betta... that's fer sure. Rainey, don't you know how it is 'tween colored and white folks?"

In innocence she said, "No, Ah don't know nuthin about that."

Lloyd J. Guillory

CHAPTER SIX

"Rufus... you crazy? Bringing a litt'l white girl home with you... you crazy'" an exasperated wife yelled at the hapless husband as he attempted to explain his actions in bringing Rainey to their home.

"What you 'spect me to do wif her? Leave her alone on the road in the dark? You tell me, womin!"

"That's 'nutha thing, Rufus! You know what they do to colored men who pick up white girls on the road? They'd lynch you so fast you wouldn't know what happened. Then, what'd me and those kids do without you... you tell me."

Rainey stood nearby during this tirade, near tears, and once again experiencing the hard fact that she was not wanted or welcomed. The eight black children, ranging in age from six months to twelve also stood nearby staring at the white child thrust into their midst. They had never seen a white child in their home before and as their parents argued, they merely stared in wonderment.

"What you gonna do with her? She cain't stay heer in this house!"

"Oh womin, Ah ain't neva 'tended fer her to stay heer. Ah just brought her heer 'cause Ah didn't know what else to do with her... that's all. Ah got a load 'o logs Ah got to git to the mill 'fore seven when that cuttin' crew gits thar. Ah gots to go! Cain't she stay heer til Ah git home tonight?"

The wife looked up at heaven in desperation. "What else kin we do nah she's heer, but Ah'm tellin' you... she got to go 'fore tonight. Ah don't want her in this house tonight. 'Sides, we ain't got no place fer her to sleep."

As he made for the front door he looked back once more. "You look afta her today... Ah'll think 'o somptin 'fore night."

The mother went to Rainey and looked down. As she viewed the frightened and bewildered child motherly compassion came over her as she took her by the hand. "Come heer, chile. You shaking and shiv'rin. Don't you be afeerd. We ain't gonna hurt you," and turning to her oldest, "Magnolia, don't stand there lak a bump on a log... go make some grits so we kin feed this bunch 'n her too. Poor litt'l thing. You hongry, honey? Ah know you is 'cause litt'l kids is always hongry. You go 'n sit down at that table 'n Clarissa gonna give you somep'n to eat."

"You, Rufus, Jr., you make room fer her at the table... go on."

The children, not accustomed to a white child in their midst, continued to stare even as they took their seats at the table. Rainey sat as she was directed between two of the black children, and the children continued to look at each other, saying nothing.

After a hearty breakfast of grits, fritters, and coffee milk, Rainey felt a lot better. She went to a chair and still clutching her knapsack with its meager contents she merely sat and stared at her surroundings and the people in it. A little girl near her age sat next to her, asking, "What yore name?"

Rainey, hesitant at first, replied, "Mah name is Rainey. What's yours?"

"Mine is Dahlia. How old is you?"

"Ah 'm seven... going on eight... how 'bout you?"

The child shrugged her shoulders and looked at her mother with the mother exclaiming: "Dahlia, you six... you know dat," and turning to her oldest, "Magnolia, go change that baby's diapa 'n make shur you rinse it out lak Ah show'd you. Ah know he's dirty. Ah kin smell it," and turning to the others, speaking to no one in particular, "nah, you chilluns go out 'n play 'n take Rainey wif you 'n you make her feel at home... you heer me," and under her breath, "till we figga what to do wif her."

Seeing her oldest returning with the baby, she continued: "Magnolia, you git riddy to take that washin' 'n ironin' to Miz Powell's house. She gonna pay you fer this week 'n last week too 'n don't you lose that money 'neitha."

"But, Mama, it's a mile to Miz Powell's house!"

"You think Ah don't know dat. Ah done walked it 'nough. Nah, you go git ready. We needs dat money."

The Miz Powell referred to was an elderly woman who lived in a small town near Pine Bluff. She was a widow who had turned her home into a boarding house for female school teachers who taught at the nearby elementary and high school. Her daughter, Martha, was one of the teachers who taught there and lived with her. The other two teachers, Annie Raymond and Bertha Krautte, all spinsters, lived there also. In addition to providing the elder Mrs. Powell with some additional income the women also provided support to each other, for each one, at some previous time in her life, for various reasons, had been treated badly by a man, rejected for another woman. Typical of the women of those times who sat by and waited patiently, and sometimes not so, for the man to take the lead, they mistakenly believed that those lost loves were the only loves in their lives and they vowed to resent all men for the rest of their days. Now approaching middle age and having abandoned all hopes of connubial bliss, they relished their spinsterhood and took pride in their virginal state, whether actual or not, imagined and self-imposed.

The mother, Cornelia Powell, was of a genteel background and good family-an educated and cultured family who had migrated from the east to the wild and relatively uncivilized Arkansas during the early part of the century. Her husband, an accountant by trade, had been transferred by his lumber company to set up and keep the books on the new mill in southeastern Arkansas. During his lifetime they had led a comfortable lifestyle in their two story frame house on the outskirts of the small town whose main source of employment was the lumber mill. The town's fortune rose and fell with the lumber market. The depression would have had dire effect on the area had not the federal government placed

Lloyd J. Guillory

sizeable orders for lumber to supply the construction program of the Civilian Conservation Corps.

The husband and father, Orion Powell, died of tuberculosis in the early thirties and the loss of his income had its effect on the family. Only the daughter's meager income as a teacher and the equally meager rental income from the other two female teachers kept the family from going into their savings, which were also meager, and as the mother continued to explain: "We are keeping that for a rainy day," as if the depression did not qualify for such a circumstance.

As to the three teachers, they had all met when they attended the Sophie Newcomb college for girls in New Orleans, and with their teaching certificates in hand after graduation had accompanied Martha Powell back to her home in southeastern Arkansas to teach the children they described in private moments as "those Arkansas hillbillies" even though the term would have been more appropriate some two hundred miles to the north where the true Ozark "hillbillies" actually lived.

As the tired little colored girl arrived at the Powell home after her mile long walk, she wiped the sweat from her brow and shifted the load of washed and ironed clothes from one shoulder to the other. She labored up the high back steps and knocked on the door. The colored house maid, still affordable to the Powells because of her three dollar a week salary, went to the door to let the child in. "Magnolia," she intoned, "you be shur you clean yore feet 'fore you come in. Ah just mopped dis heer kitchen."

"Yassum," replied the tired child as she placed the clean clothing on the kitchen table.

"Ah tole you 'fore chile not to put no clothes on da tabl'l."

"Yassum," as she moved them to a chair and turned to leave for the same mile-long walk back home as the mistress of the house entered the kitchen and seeing the child and the clothing remarked, "Why, Magnolia, I didn't know your mother would let you come here alone. You must be getting to be a big girl."

The child looked pleased, a bright smile on her face, showing a set of glistening white teeth. "Yassum," she replied proudly, "Ah gitt'in big. Ah done start'd bleedin' lak big girls."

The older woman nearly choked as the child mentioned that natural development of nature which was never mentioned except between mother and daughter in those days. "Well now, Magnolia, we don't discuss things like that with strangers," as she turned to the colored maid for concurrence. The colored maid shook her head, intoning, "Ah declare Miz Powell, Ah don know what dis world is comin' to wif childrun talking lak that... Ah sho don't," as she resumed her work.

Cornelia Powell motioned the child to a chair. "Why don't you sit at the table, Magnolia, and I will give you some milk and cookies. Would you like that? You look so hot and tired after that long walk."

The child, having tasted cookies at the Powell house, before, as she accompanied her mother to deliver the clothes, and remembering that Mrs. Powell's cookies were fresh and the milk was cold, nodded, smiling her bright smile. "Yassum," as she hurried to the chair.

After watching the child take her first bite, Cornelia Powell smiled at her and in an attempt to make conversation, asked:

"And what is happening at your house these days? Is everything all right? How is you mother feeling?"

The child continued to eat as she replied, "She feelin' all right, but," and she hesitated..."we got 'citement at de house."

The older woman's eyebrows went up, and thinking it would be an announcement of yet another pregnancy asked, "Excitement, what kind of excitement?"

"We got a litt ' l white gal mah papa found on de road."

Her eyes widened as she asked, "A little white girl. Your papa found a little white girl on the road? Did I understand you correctly, Magnolia?"

"Yassum," as she nodded, adding no more details.

The older womans's hands went to her throat. "Was she alive or dead?"

"Oh, she 'live. She seven years old, she tole us."

"Oh, my God. What was she doing on the road by herself?"

As she continued to chew. "She runnin' away... she say."

"Running away... from whom... from where?"

The child merely shrugged her shoulders with Cornelia Powell asking, "Is the child still at your house?"

"Yassum."

"Has your papa notified the authorities?"

Not knowing the meaning of the word authorities, the child merely shrugged again. She had finished her snack and feeling her welcome was over she rose to leave, but the older woman placed a hand on her shoulder. "Wait, Magnolia, I am going to drive you home. I want to see what this is all about. Your papa could get himself in big trouble with a white girl in his house."

The child nodded. "Dat what mah mama say, too."

"Come on. You wait until I back the car out of the garage and I will drive you home. You go and wait over by that pine tree in the back yard."

As she went out the door, thankful that she would be spared the long walk back home, she smiled inwardly.

As the 1930 Studebaker came into view and came to a stop, the child proceeded to open the door to the back seat, having seen colored people in the back seat being chauffeured around by white women all her life. "No, Magrnolia, you sit up front with me. I don't believe in all that foolishness... come on... up here with me. That's a good girl."

As she traversed the dirt road leading to the Jackson cabin Cornelia Powell shook her head in disbelief. She was no staunch white supremist, and while she did believe in the separation of the races, she felt great compassion for the colored people of the south and felt that more could and should be done to improve their lot. That was before the onslaught of the great depression. Now, she had compassion for the poor whites as well.

As she made her way up the old wooden steps to the cabin, Clarissa Jackson, having seen her come up the drive, and feeling sure that something was wrong, had the children stay inside as she went out on the rickety porch. "Oh, Miz Powell," as she nervously wiped her hands on her apron, "did that chile do somethin' wrong? Ah bet she dropped those clothes..."

"No, Clarissa, Magnolia has not done anything wrong, but... she did tell me that Rufus had picked up a white child on the road and I..."

The colored woman's eyes widened with fear. "Yassum, dat Rufus done picked dat chile up... but she aw 'right. He ain't know'd what else to do wif huh. We ain't done nothin' wrong... is we?"

She patted the anxious woman on the arm. "No, Clarissa, you and Rufus have done nothing wrong... but, I'm afraid if you keep her in this house... there could be trouble."

"Yassum, Ah tole Rufus dat... Ah sho did! But, he had to go to work. He say he ain't got time to do nuthin' 'bout her."

The white woman smiled. "I know... I know. He did the right thing at the time, but now, I think I better take her with me before you do get into trouble. May I see the child?"

Opening the rickety screen door: "Yassum she right heah. Rainey... come heah chile. Dere's a white lady come to git you."

Rainey appeared, as usual, uncertain, afraid, not knowing what was to happen to her, her hand in her mouth- her eyes wide with fear.

Extending her hand and smiling warmly, the older woman placed her hand on the child's shoulder. "Come here, my dear, I want to talk to you. I want to be your friend... come on."

The child came forward reluctantly, for as she had done in the past, she felt more secure with those with whom she had been the longest, even if only for several hours, but she came and stood by the white woman, feeling some rapport with one of her own kind.

"I understand your name is Rainey... is that so?"

She bit her lip nervously. "Yessum."

The older woman stroked her hair, smiling at her, as she continued, "And your last name. Do you know it?"

She nodded: "Yessum."

Cornelia Powell smiled at the child's reticence. "Then, what is your last name?"

"Mah name is Rainey Wether," as she looked down at the floor waiting for the effect her name seemed to have on all people.

"Rainey Wether? Is that your real name, child?" she asked, slightly amused.

The child nodded. The colored children had all crowded around to witness the inquisition, but their mother, as usual, directed her remarks to her oldest. "Magnolia, you take dem chilllun out in de yard whilst Miz Powell talks to dis white chile... go on... rat nah!"

As the colored children marched out with the older ones prodding the younger ones, the white woman continued, "Rainey, my dear, where do you come from? Where are your parents?"

So, for the next few minutes the perplexed child recounted the last two years of her life as she perceived or remembered it. Both women, white and colored, sat in amazement as they heard of her itinerant life since her mother "gave" her away.

The white woman, obviously moved by the child's plight, turned to the colored woman. "Clarissa, I have got to take this child from you before this thing goes any further. The last thing I want is for you and Rufus to get into trouble for what is really a humanitarian act. You know how Sheriff Poulter is."

The colored woman, not knowing what the word humanitarian meant, got the essence of the remark, replying, "Yassum, dat's what Ah tole Rufus... we gon git in trouble wif dat chile."

"Clarissa, I will take this child to the authorities to determine what to do with her. I will tell them some white people... a white couple... found her along side of the road and brought her to me, knowing me as they do. It is against my Baptist religion to speak a lie, but I am sure God will forgive me... under the circumstances. Is that all right with you?"

Greatly relieved to be rid of this problem, the colored woman replied quickly... very quickly, "Oh, Yassum, dat de best thing to do, Yassum!"

Looking back to the child, the white woman asked, "Rainey, my dear, do you have any luggage?"

Not knowing the word luggage, she returned a blank stare and shrugged her shoulders as Clarissa spoke up. "She just got a bag wid huh clothes 'n auh ole shoe box... dat's all. Ah'll go git dem... rat nah."

With Rainey now ensconced in the front seat with her wordly belongings, and a relieved Clarissa, with her brood in tow, waving goodbye (and good riddance) the Studebaker started down the dirt path to the county road. The child sat quietly, saying nothing, once again believing that this move, like all the previous ones, would not bode well for her, but she had gotten used to being bounced around. She now felt that this was the way her life was destined to be until she could take command of it herself.

As the car moved down the highway at her top speed of thirty-five miles per hour, Cornelia Powell pondered her course of action. Of course, she reasoned, the child would have to be turned over to the authorities, but which one. Money was so tight that no one was anxious to take on another mouth to feed and a body to clothe. There were orphanages, she knew that, and she had heard what she considered horror stories of the way the children were treated who were unfortunate enough to be sent there. She vowed to avoid that, if possible. She drove to the county courthouse and taking the child by the hand went in to see what was available. The first person she ran into was the last one she wanted to see- Sheriff Alvin Poulter, a true red-neck if ever there was one. His attitude on the racial problem was..."we ain't got none! Soon as one 'o them causes me some trouble... well, he's gone by sundown, 'n they knows it, too."

Tipping his cowboy hat (his trademark although he had never sat a horse), he bowed from the waist: "Goodmornin', Miz Powell, you just as pretty as a honeysuckle blossom in the sunshine. And how's that pretty daughter 'o yourn?"

Ignoring both vacuous compliments she stood with the child at her side, asking with complete authority (the mode she always used in addressing the sheriff- she had long ago found out that he was intimidated by any white woman who stared him down, especially when he was certain he was dealing with superior education and intelligence), "sheriff, this child was found on the side of the road... hitching a ride... I believe it is called..."

He interrupted her. "Found... found? who found her?"

She gave him a perturbed look. "That is not important, now. We can discuss that later. The important thing is, what shall we do with her at this time. This child is only seven years old. She is a minor. She needs the protection of the county, or the state, or whoever does these things."

He removed his hat and scratched his head. This seemed to aid his thinking processes. "Now, Miz Powell, Ah don rightly know what to do with her. There's so many 'o them kids runnin' 'round the countryside nowadays... Ah jus don know. That man from the orphanage, he tole me not to send him no more. He says he ain't go no room fo more."

"What about the churches?"

"Same thing. They say they got all they kin handle, too."

"Then, what shall we do with her?" Rainey had heard all this and she began to sob quietly, her fist going to her mouth.

"Well, Miz Powell, all Ah kin do is keep her heer at the jail 'til we figga out what to do."

The woman became indignant, and placing her hand on the child's shoulder as if to protect her. "I should say you will not keep this child in a jail. Have you lost your mind?"

He was now really intimidated as he shuffled his feet. "Well, Ma'am, Ah'm jus trying to help... that's all."

She took the child by the hand, saying, "Come on, Rainey," and turning to the bewildered sheriff as she walked off in a huff, "I'll take this poor child to my home until we can find some place to take her in. Good day, Sheriff!"

She regretted her impulsive move all the way home with neither she nor Rainey saying anything. The child looked out the window, shaking her head from side to side. The older woman watched her and she was filled with compassion. Her thoughts went out to the country as a whole. To herself: My God, what has this society of ours come to when people are forced to give their children away. Where are the relatives? Where are the friends? Are things so bad in this country that we must forsake our children. Thank God my daughter is raised and has no children of her own, although I do miss not having grandchildren.

As they neared the large two story Victorian house which the Powell family called home, with all its filigreed porches and gables, Rainey's head turned to view the imposing residence. To her young mind, so long accustomed to humble or modest abodes, this seemed to be a castle. She turned to Cornelia Powell. "Is this where you live?"

She smiled at the child. "Yes, this is our home. My husband built this for us when we first moved here from Charleston many years ago."

"Where's Charleston?"

She sighed. "Charleston is a beautiful city in South Carolina." She sighed again. "I wish we were still there. My family is from there?"

"Do you have a mama and papa?"

"Well, not anymore, dear. My parents are dead."

"My mama is dead too. Ah wish Ah had a mama."

She looked at the child with compassion. "I know, dear. I wish you had, too, but life is not always fair to people. These things happen."

The child looked at her. "Why do they always happen to me?"

Cornelia Powell nearly had to suppress a tear and she was happy to change the subject with: "We're here, Rainey. Come on in and see where we live. Don't forget to bring your two packages."

She had parked the car in the side porte cochere which the family always used during the day. Her daughter and her two teacher friends depended on the Studebaker for their transportation to and from school and for all other purposes. But, when nightime arrived, the Studebaker was lodged in its garage some distance from the house, safe from the elements. The Powell family knew, that in their now modest circumstances, the Studebaker would be the last car to be purchased for quite some time.

The older woman took the child by the hand as they climbed the steps leading from the porte cochere to the serving pantry which separated the kitchen from the dining room. With eyes wide in anticipation, Rainey looked in all directions, viewing what she perceived to be a palace, with complete awe.

As the colored maid came forward to greet them, Rainey was perplexed as she saw the dark woman. She had never known people who had a maid and the presence of the black woman made her wonder... what is she doing in this white house?

"Tessie, this is Rainey Wether, the little girl you heard Magnolia Jackson discuss earlier. She will be spending the night with us. Is that maid's room in good shape far her to sleep in?" In their more prosperous times, when the father was still alive and his generous income from the mill allowed it, the Powells had a live-in maid. As he had told his beloved wife at the time, "Cornelia, my dear, I took you away from your genteel lifestyle and brought you out here to this primitive place, the least I can do is provide you with a maid."

The day maid, Tessie, replied as she gave Rainey the once over, "Yassum, all Ah need to do is put some fresh sheets on tha bed. I cleaned the room yestiday."

"Very well, would you put her things in the room... on the bureau next to the bed. I'll take her to the kitchen and give her some cookies and milk... would you like that, Rainey?"

She nodded. She was beginning to like this kindly lady and she definitely liked this large house, as she continued to puruse her surroundings as they made their way to the kitchen.

As the child sat at the table and began to slowly eat her snack the older woman continued to talk to her. "My daughter, Martha, will be home soon. She is a school teacher," and as an after thought, "and her two friends who live with us are also school teachers... and I used to be one, so you see, Rainey, we are a house full of school teachers."

The child merely nodded, chewing as she did.

The older woman continued. "School will begin in two weeks and they are having meetings at the school. Another teacher picked them up today and I was able to have the car. Thank goodness for that, because if I hadn't, I never could have gone to get you," and she sighed as she looked at the child, "I don't know what would have happened to you if I hadn't..."

The child, perplexed, interrupted her discourse: "But, they threated me good."

"I know, dear, but that is not what I was referring to. I know you are too young to understand but the way things are in this country, especially here in the south, a white child should not be found in the house of a negro family."

"Why? "

She shrugged her shoulders. "Well, that is just the way things are, Rainey, but don't you be concerned about that. I promise you that nothing will happen to the Jackson family. I still have that much influence around here, especially with that ignoramus of a sheriff. Now, when you are finished with your snack I will show you where you will sleep tonight, and you can wash up if you want."

"Where will Ah sleep tomorrow night?"

The older woman clasped her hands in front of her. "I really don't know yet, my dear, but don't you fret about that. You will not be turned loose on the street, I assure you," as she smiled and patted the child's head as she directed her to the maid's room.

CHAPTER SEVEN

The three school teachers arrived later in the afternoon, having completed a series of pre-opening school meetings. They were all chatting at the same time as they came into the kitchen, and seeing Cornelia Powell sitting at the table talking to a young girl, ceased their talking as they slowly came forward.

"Well, Mother, I see you have found a young friend to keep you company this afternoon," observed her own daughter, Martha. "Who is this pretty child?"

As the other two teachers, Annie Raymond and Bertha Krautte, just as curious because a young child was seldom seen in that house of females, crowded around the table, Cornelia patted Rainey on the head, replying, "This is Rainey Wether. Rainey, this lady," pointing to her daughter, "is my daughter, Martha, and this lady is Miss Annie Raymond," and turning to the last, "and this one is Miss Bertha Krautte. They are the teachers I told you about."

Rainey smiled, faintly. She had been introduced to very few people in her lifetime and did not know how to act.

Martha Powell inquired, "Where does she come from, Mother?"

As the women each backed out a chair to sit down, the mother related the history of the child as best she could. There were no interruptions during the entire discourse. The three teachers sat there with their mouths noticeably opened, with Martha inquiring, "But, what will you do with her?" in rather hushed tones, hoping the child would not hear.

"I don't know, Martha, at least, I don't know at this time. She will sleep with us tonight and tomorrow I will attempt to find out if we can..." and she chose her words carefully for the child's sake..."see if we can place her somewhere."

Martha looked at the child with a mixture of compassion and curiosity. She had seen many such cases in the past several years in her school- children who were in her class one day and gone the next- where, she usually never knew.

As the other two teachers became more curious, Annie Raymond asked: "You said, Mrs. Powell, that her name is Rainey Wether? Did I understand you correctly?" she asked, smiling.

The mother nodded in concurrence. "That is what she says. I am not sure how her last name is spelled, but you must admit," as she smiled at the child, "that is a name to remember without much difficulty."

Martha turned to the girl. "Rainey, dear, how do you spell your last name?"

She looked embarrassed as she shrugged her shoulders, answering meekly, "I don't know."

An audible groan could be heard from all three teachers, with Martha inquiring, "How old are you?"

Rainey, finally hearing a question she could answer, proudly replied, "I'm almost eight."

Before she could catch herself, Bertha Krautte, in her teacher mode, asked, "And you cannot spell your name?"

All the other women regretted the question, not wanting to embarrassed the child, but it was out. Rainey, somewhat embarrassed herself, merely shook her head.

Cornelia Powell intervened. "I think we have asked enough questions of this young lady for the time being. Let us all make her feel at home for now," and turning to the child, "Rainey, I noticed that you carried two packages and a doll with you. May I asked what is in them? Do you have any clothes?"

"Yessum, I got some clothes in that paper bag."

"And in the shoebox... what is in there, may I ask?"

"That's what mah mana left me."

Cornelia Powell's eyebrows raised. "Oh, may I see it?"

As she rose to fetch the box, the child replied, "Yessum, Ah'll go and git it."

The three teachers winced at her countrified use of the English language.

Having returned with the box, Rainey took a seat next to the mother and proudly displayed the shoe box's contents. The women were visibly disappointed. They expected much more as they anticipated her mother's legacy, but the birth certificate and locket did catch their attention. After commenting on the locket and remarking over the small photographs, the women watched as the mother read the birth certificate. She looked at the others, explaining: "Yes, her name is definitely Rainey Wether, spelled W-E-T-H-E-R. Isn't that unique?" intoned the mother as she looked at the others, "and her birthday is April 1930," and turning to the child, "so you will be eight next April, Rainey... did you know that?"

She answered proudly, "Yessum, Ah know when mah birthday is."

The mother rose, saying to no one in particular, "So, ladies, that is the history of Miss Rainey Wether. Now, I suggest we discontinue these inquiries and make her feel at home for tonight."

As Rainey lay in bed that night she realized that this was the first time in her entire life that she would be sleeping alone, both in the bed and in the room. She clutched the doll Nell Foster had given her, the only thing she had been allowed to take with her from the Foster Home, along with some extra underwear and two dresses which Cora had outgrown. She looked around the room. There was a light on the night table- an electric light. The room was not as luxurious as the family bedrooms on the upper floor, but to Rainey it seemed so. She cuddled her doll and after what could only be described as a traumatic day, she finally fell asleep.

Cornelia Powell decided the next morning that she would not take Rainey with her as she made the rounds of the agencies to see who would take the child in. She asked Rainey if she minded staying with Tessie for a while so she could do some shopping. The truth was she did not want the child around as she asked, or begged if necessary, for someone to take her in, even if only on a temporary basis, until permanent arrangements could be made.

She made the rounds of the agencies in and around the small town, few though they were. She found several who would take her in for a week, then, she would have to leave to make room for others. The churches were already overburdened with more than they could handle. In some cases, people knew of people who would take here in, but upon more detailed examination, it was discovered that the arrangement was to be to the benefit of the foster home, not to the child. Cornelia Powell, in all probability due to her own privileged upbringing, could not accept the rudimentary offerings made for the child. She wanted better, whether justified or not. She considered a hovel no improvement in the child's position. She was looking, quite unrealistically, for a good functional family with adequate circumstances, the kind she would want her own daughter to be housed in if it were necessary. It was this unpragmatic and unrealistic attitude which doomed her mission of that day to failure. She arrived home that afternoon, quite tired and even more discouraged. She had made absolutely no progress that she could accept. There was no one to tell her her expectations were too high, so she felt she was justified in her position.

As they sat around the supper table that night, the women talked in hushed tones as Rainey ate with her usual gusto, only occasionally looking at whichever woman was talking, for she knew they were discussing her future. After supper, the women retired to the parlor, as they always did each evening with each woman pursuing her own interest, be it reading or knitting, but they were always occupied with their own thoughts, seldom breaking the silence except to make some important point or observation. The others, usually, merely nodded in assent unless the comment required a rebuttle, for they were three strong-willed women, as teachers are prone to be. For seven or eight hours a day in the classroom, their pronouncements and comments were hardly ever challenged and that tone carried over to their personal lives.

Rainey was given some books to look at, mostly children's books the women had brought home from the school that day. She sat in a large chair in the corner of the spacious parlor, looking at the books without much interest, and from time to time, looking at the women.

It was Martha who finally asked: "Rainey, dear, have you ever been to school?"

The child gave a description of her very limited time in school after living with the Fosters. Four sets of eyebrows were raised as the women listened. Martha, having heard what she really expected to hear, was silently aghast, and they all exchanged covert glances as Martha continued to question the child. When they got around to questions about her family, her mother... her father... the child searched for answers. She had already come to the conclusion after the episode with Nell Foster that she would never again proclaim that her mother was a whore, for it was not well received. She replied that she hardly remembered anything about her immediate family with, "Ah was too young. Ah don't remember." The women accepted this and the questioning ceased for a while. During the school months the women usually retired to their respective rooms at nine to perform their nightly toiletries so they could be in bed, ready to sleep, at ten – a regimen they followed religiously.

At nine o'clock, Cornelia Powell rose and said to Rainey: "Come, Rainey, dear, it is time you went to bed. Little girls require so much more sleep than us adults. Come on…I'll see you to bed." Her real intent was to see that the child performed her required toiletries. These were disciplined women, and if one was to live among them…"Well, one must conform."

Upon her return to the parlor nearly a half-hour later, it was obvious to Cornelia that the women had been in deep discussion. They were all grouped together on the couch and the nearby chairs, something they never did when each had retired to her own part of the room. Seeing them, she smiled and asked, "And what are you three conspiring about, may I ask?"

It was only her daughter, Martha, who felt she had the right to inform her of the discussion. The other two, although rent paying boarders, still felt they were outsiders in some matters, especially those pertaining to hearth and home.

"We have been discussing Rainey, Mother. What is to happen to that poor child? Where will she go? What is to become of her?"

Cornelia Powell, her sixty-five years beginning to show on her, eased herself into a chair. "I spent the entire day, as I have already explained to you and the others, attempting to find someone who would take her in. Oh God, what horrible times we live in these days, with one-fourth of the work force without jobs, millions of people without any source of income. What is to become of them? Of this nation?"

"And you found nothing? No one?" the daughter persisted.

The mother sighed deeply. "It would be an inaccuracy to say that I found nothing. I found several…"

"But, I don't understand," interrupted the daughter, "you told us you found nothing."

She sighed again, holding her hands up as if in prayer. "I guess I should have said I found nothing that I considered acceptable for the child."

"Perhaps," replied the daughter with school teacher pragmatism, "your standards are too high…

"Perhaps," interrupted the mother, "but they are my standards, Martha. I have so much difficulty in accepting these present conditions in this country. Could these times have been avoided? Are the Republicans to blame? I think it was that Mr. Hoover. That is what happens when a Republican is elected president. (Her old South democratic beliefs still beat strongly in her bosom) I hope that Mr. Roosevelt will do better I'm sure he will…at least he is trying."

"Oh, Mother, this is not the time to discuss politics. We are trying to solve Rainey's immediate problem. Where will she go?" She glanced around the room at her cohorts for they had already hatched a scheme. It would bear repeating that these three school teachers, all spinsters, all spurned or rejected by the one true loves in their lives, now lived a lonely existence. The daytime hours, usually spent in the company of many other human beings were tolerable, but oh the nights. Each dreaded those lonely unspoken nights in that parlor, with only Cornelia Powell to remember the touch of a man, the feel of a close embrace, the experience of spent passion. The other three could only imagine. They longed for some change in their lives and they now viewed this young child as, at least, some semblance of love and excitement. She was to be to them like a large doll they could play with, to mother, to dress, to teach the facts of life... to love, for there was a vacuum in their lives that needed filling. They had decided among themselves that they wanted this child in their midst. Not only was it their Christian duty, but she could fulfill a long dominant and long dormant maternal feeling to mother something.

The mother shrugged her shoulders, then slumped in her chair. "Well, Martha, if you and Annie and Bertha have any ideas, I would be more than glad to listen to them. What shall we do with her?"

Martha rose and went to her mother's chair, kneeling at her feet as she had done so many times as a young girl when she had wanted something special. Taking her mother's hands, also as she had done as a little girl, she looked deeply in her eyes. "Well, Mother," she replied nervously, "we think it might be a good idea if we kept her... here... in this house with us."

The mother sat up, her hands went to her cheek. "Stay with us? What on earth do you mean? For how long? I would have no objection to a month or so, but..."

The daughter shook her head. "No, Mother, that is not what we have in mind. Don't you believe that this poor child has been kicked around enough. She has never had any stability in her entire life and it shows in her. She has a scared look in her eyes... she is never sure of what to say for fear of offending someone. She never knows on what pillow or in what bed she will place her little head at night." Tears now began to flow in the daughter's eyes, and upon seeing that, the mother's eyes filled as the daughter continued. "What will it cost us, except a little love which all of us have bursting at the seams," as she turned to the others, all nodding with filled eyes. "She won't eat enough to make any difference in our food bills. And look at this big house we have, which was built by a loving husband to accomodate a large family which nature did not provide for you and him." At the sound of those words, the mother emitted a groan, replying, "But, that was not my fault, Martha, we tried... oh, how I wanted to present you with a sister or brother/ but..."

"I know, Mother... I know... but perhaps fate is now trying to correct what nature did not provide."

"Oh, Martha, do you really think this is a good idea?" as she looked at the other women, too.

It was Annie Raymond, drying tears on her sleeve who spoke up: "Mrs. Powell', I don't make but seventy-five dollars a month but I will contribute five dollars a month to Rainey's unkeep."

"Me, too, Mrs. Powell...I will, too," added Bertha Krautte, moving her overweight torso to the edge of the chair.

"See, Mother," intoned Martha as she rose with aching knees from her awkward position, "Rainey will not be any financial burden on us. And just think, we are all teachers in this house. We can teach her to speak properly, to dress properly...to make a little lady out of her...oh, Mother, please say you agree."

The mother was silent for a long time as she pondered the pros and cons of what the younger women wanted. "Have you thought this all the way through. What will eventually become of her? Are you three prepared to make a permanent commitment to this child?"

"Mother, you are over dramatizing. This does not have to be a lifetime commitment...only until she grows up. When she is old enough to take care of herself, she can do as she pleases."

The mother, older, wiser, more experienced in the vagaries of life, asked, "Will you be willing to let her go when that time comes?"

"Well," replied the daughter, looking at the others, "it would not be any different if she were our own daughter, would it?"

The mother looked at all three women. "Yes, there is a major difference. She will have three mothers, and that brings up another thing..."

"What?" asked a nervous Martha.

"What of the legality of this thing. We are not talking about bringing a puppy into this house," said the mother. "We are talking about a human being. We can't just take her. She is not ours to take. She has got to belong to someone, in spite of what she says. She has got to have a family somewhere. Everyone does, you know. It is not possible to come into this world without coming from two people who came from two people..."

The daughter nodded. "Of course you're right, Mother, we cannot just take her. We have got to have this looked into, but who will do that...the sheriff..."

The mother stiffened. "Certainly not! I don't want that ignoramus having anything to do with this..."

"Who then?"

Bertha spoke up. "I have a brother in Hot Springs who is a lawyer. I could ask him to look into this. He will not charge us much...I don't think. I can contact him if you wish."

The mother nodded. "That is a good idea. We have got to do this legally. I don't want this to come back to haunt us."

Martha smiled at her mother. "Then, you agree?"

Now tired, sleepy, and emotionally drained, the mother nodded, "Yes, if we can do it legally. How do we even know the child wants us to take her in…"

"Don't worry about that, Mother, just wait until I show her the doll room."

Pleased with themselves and happy that their introspective lives might now assume some degree of excitement the three school teachers rose and retired to their own chambers.

Each of the three school teachers, as they placed their heads on their pillows that night, imagined what effect the child's coming into their lives would have on each. They led boring and uneventful lives, especially when away from school, so it did not take much to convince them that it would be an exciting adventure which they looked forward to. But, the problem would be that each had her own agenda for the child. They each knew, or felt they knew, what was best for the young girl, based on what was lacking in their own lives. But, each arose the next morning, exited, anxious to inform Rainey of the wonderful news about her future and the change it would make in her life.

After explaining their intent and their offer to her, they waited for what they expected to be a joyous acceptance, but the child merely looked at them, quisically. "Well, Rainey, what do you think of that? You will live with us in this house for some time to come… you will be our little girl. What do you think of that?" asked an enthusiastic Martha as the others grouped around waiting for her equally enthusiastic response.

The child merely shrugged her shoulders, giving them all a quisical look. She simply did not understand what they meant, and even if she did, based on her past moves with other families, it produced nothing but eventual disappointment.

Martha persisted. "Aren't you excited about that?"

The mother intervened. "Perhaps, Martha, Rainey has not had time to fully digest the news. Let's give her some time to sort things out," and lowering her voice, "why don't we show her her new room when she is finished with breakfast. We will let her stay in the doll room. Is that all right with you? I don't think the maid's room downstairs is a suitable room for a young lady to call her very own room… do you?" smiling as she spoke. Martha swallowed hard. The doll room had always been her room, the room in which, as a child, she had retreated to dream her dreams, to imagine the day when her knight would come and take her away. She had retreated to it when she wanted to shut the world out. Her father had spoiled her as an only daughter can be spoiled by an over indulgent father. He had gotten into the habit of giving her a different doll on every occasion he could justify it: birthdays- Christmas- Easter- Halloween, no matter which. She had placed all these dolls in this room on every horizontal surface which could hold one, and she continued to view this as her inner sanctum until she reached adulthood. Now, forty-two years old, a confirmed spinster, whose dreams had vanished like bubbles blown into the air in a stiff breeze, the room had now taken over a different ambience for her in her present age. Gone were the hopes and aspirations of a young girl, replaced by the resignation of a middle-aged woman.

She replied to her mother after some hesitation: "Why, of course, Mother, the doll room, indeed, shall be her room," and extending her hand to the child, "come, Rainey, would you like to see your new room... your very own room?"

The child finally showed some interest. She rose and gave her hand to the daughter. The others, for some reason they probably could not explain if pressed to do so, stayed behind and allowed Martha to share this moment alone with Rainey. Rainey had never been upstairs, as yet. In fact, she had never been in a two story home. She stared as they climbed the oak stair with its stained glass window at the middle landing. The light coming through the stained glass played on the walls and to her this was a thing to behold. Martha, still holding her hand led her to one of the five bedrooms on the second floor. She led the child to the door, saying, "Now, close your eyes, Rainey, and don't open them until I say so. Go on...close them."

Suspicious as ever, she reluctantly closed them as the older woman led her into the room. She stopped just inside the door. "Now, Rainey, open your eyes."

The child opened them slowly as if she feared what she would find. As she looked around the beautiful room with its dozens of dolls in all places, the beautiful drapes with matching bedspread, the beautiful antique furnishings, the four poster bed with a canopy of matching material. Her mouth opened and she sucked air through her mouth as she tightened her grip on the woman's hands. "Oh, Miz Martha...it's so pretty. Ah ain't neva seen anything like this in mah whole life...I sure ain't."

The woman squatted down to her level. "And this is your room, Rainey, for as long as you live in this house."

She shook her head. "Oh, Miz Martha, Ah can't live in a room like this...Ah jus couldn't."

"But, why, dear...why?"

"Ah jus don't deserve it. Ah ain't neva had nuthin like this."

"Well, you do now, and Rainey, you do deserve it," and as her eyes filled with tears, "I don't know any little girl who deserves this room more than you do."

The child continued to stare, looking in all directions. Her fears and suspicions had vanished. She could not believe what was happening to her, and it would be some time before she came to realize what they had offered her.

The years Rainey Wether would spend in this house would be some of the most stable she would know. She would become a young lady under this roof, and true to their intent, these four women would treat her as if she were their doll. She was pampered, yes, but with complete restraint, for these were pragmatic and disciplined women. Yet, with all the advantages the home offered, it was not a well-rounded functional one. It would remain a house of females, and now with Rainey, there were five females and no males. She would not develop a normal perception of how a male fitted into the life of a female because, except for the mother, who died the year after Rainey arrived, these three spinsters did not know, nor did they want to. Men seldom if ever came to the house, other than delivery or repair men. Rainey entered puberty without much fanfare and only a minimum of instruction as to what was happening to her young body. She got most of the details from the other girls at school, some of it factual, and some not so.

As to her relations with the opposite sex while in high school, she was not encouraged to pursue her own natural feelings. When she attempted to discuss this boy, or that boy, with her three "mothers", each in turn would tell her what was wrong with that boy or his family. She became perplexed and on some occasions, completely frustrated. She would ask one or all of them: "Aren't there any decent boys in this world?" They usually looked at each other, then..."not too many!" She had never been alone with a boy on a date, with the explanation: "Dating at your age, Rainey, is just asking for trouble. Boys only want one thing from girls like you, and after they've gotten that, " and they turned away embarrassed as they continued, "they cast you aside," then, they would occasionly add, "I should know!" But, they never told her why.

As she entered her senior year in the small school, she could look back on her accomplishments in the Powell house and under the tutelage of the three teachers: Her English and her vocabulary were exceptional for a girl of her age. She had been taught how to dress properly, without "sexual provocation." As they had explained it to her, although she yearned to dress that way as she watched the eyes of the boys as they perused the girls who did. She was now 5'-7" tall, thin of build, but well rounded, with straight blond hair and pale blue eyes. She had been voted one of the ten prettiest girls in school, and the boys longed to date her... and she longed to be dated. They did allow her to go to school dances. They took her there as they chaperoned the dances in the school gym, and they took her home when the music stopped.

But, now, the nation was at war and the boys were gone...some forever.

CHAPTER EIGHT

Rainey had always liked this boy, Douglas Walker, ever since her early high school days, and he liked her, too. But, the three strict and celibate school teachers who had guided her life for the past eight years had never allowed her to show her affection for the boy, not overtly anyway. The couple had to confine their show of affections to classroom glances, corridor conversations, and in more daring moments, hand holding on or near the school grounds, always out of sight of the three guardians of her morals. Once, behind the gymnasium, between two azalea bushes, they had even kissed, ever so lightly on the lips. She had blushed and turned away and he quickly put his hands in his pockets as young boys are compelled to do on such occasions. But other than these stolen moments their love was unrequited. She had hinted to her main custodian, Martha Powell, on several occasions that she found Doug Walker quite attractive and "a nice boy". Martha had sniffed at that: "They are all nice boys, Rainey, when they want something, and they will remain nice until they get it, then..."

"But", she complained, "are they all like that?"

She pondered the question for a moment, then, "Yes, I'm afraid so."

"Then, how do girls eventually get married and live happily and raise children and...?"

She squared her shoulders as if in defiance. "If you look around you, Rainey, most marriages are miserable. The women are mistreated and abused by those brutes they are married to"

She was perplexed. "But, your mother always spoke of your father in loving terms. She loved him, didn't she?"

Having been backed into a corner, Martha Powell thought for a moment. "My father was an exeption. He was a loving and considerate husband and father. My mother adored him until the day he died. I, too, adored him."

"Aren't there more man out there like him?"

"Of course there are, Rainey! I am merely trying to spare you the heartache I endured in my love life..."

She had never in all their discussions about the opposite sex ever heard Martha Powell refer to her love life. She had fleetingly implied that she had been wronged, but never supplied the details.

"Miss Martha, were you ever in love?"

She took on a pained expression as she groped for an answer. Except for her mother, she had never discussed her "betrayal" with anyone else, not even her two cohorts, Annie Raymond and Bertha Krautte. Finally, she looked the young girl in the eye, then she rose and walked to the window, looking out with her arms folded against her boson, she spoke slowly and softly: "Painful though this is to discuss with anyone, even after so many years... how many years has it

Lloyd J. Guillory

been?- twenty, almost, it still hurts. I guess it always will. I was a student at Sophie Newcomb in New Orleans and he was a senior at Tulane University. The campuses are near each other. We had been dating for nearly two years and we were in love. At least, I was," and she returned to her chair near the girl as she continued, "and he told me he loved me more than anything in the world, and I believed him."

Rainey drew her legs up under her. She had never in all the eight years she had lived with this woman seen her show any pure and unadulterated emotion and warmth. As the older woman paused in her thoughts, Rainey asked, "But what happened?"

She took in a deep breath. "As time went on, we became more intimate in our necking, as they call it these days. He wanted much more than I was willing to give him... my upbringing had been so strict... my religion so ingrained in me. I fought him off... gently, but firmly, and it made him angry... more and more so." She rose once again as if the retelling of the story, even after so many years, was still painful.

Rainey, impatient..."but what happened?"

"It got to the point that I either had to agree to become intimate with him," and she turned away in embarrassment, "or I would lose him. He told me there were other girls not so prudish as I..." She paused again..."so I made the mistake so many young women have made throughout the ages; I sumitted to his insistent advances..."

Without thinking, Rainey exclaimed, "You mean you did it with him?"

She was deeply pained at this revelation as if she had not known of it previously. She looked down at the floor. "Yes, Rainey, I did it!"

Rainey's hands went to her cheeks. It was not the revelation which shocked her. She had friends in school who "did it" on a regular basis, but this was Miss Martha, that bastion of morality, that paragon of virtue. People like her never "did it" with anyone.

The older woman looked remorseful. "Is that so shocking to you, Rainey, to learn that Martha Powell once did it?"

She nodded, truthfully: "Yes Ma'am, it is."

"I'm human, too, Rainey, I have feelings like any other person, any other woman. Is that so difficult for you to believe?"

She did not reply to the question, but asked one of her own. "What happened after that? Why didn't you get married? He said he loved you, didn't he?"

She gave a shrug and a smirk. "Apparently, there was someone else he loved more than me. He sent me flowers the next morning and told me what," and she paused for the word, "a delightful night it was, and that he would be leaving for the east coast within a few days and would probably not be seeing me again, what with final exams and all, but that I should remember that I would always be in his thoughts," and she sobbed on those words as she shook her head, back and forth.

"Jesus... what a louse!"

She shrugged and practically snorted. "I could not agree with you more."

"But, didn't you ever meet anyone else... someone who could love you always?"

She spoke without rancor, but with some degree of defiance. "I never gave any other man a chance to get that near to me. I lost all faith in men. They only want one thing from a woman," and turning to the girl, "what do you think I have been trying to impress upon you all these years, Rainey? You cannot trust a man... not in matters of the heart."

"But, surely... there must be some out there who..."

She rose, intending to signify that the conversation was over. "I guess there are, but, try to find one, and one more thing, Rainey; I have never discussed this matter with anyone other than my mother, not even with Annie Raymond and Bertha Krautte. I hope you will respect this confidence with totality. I beg of you."

She nodded. "But, Miss Martha, many girls have done what you have done, and many girls have been disappointed in love, but..."

As she paused at the door: "Oh, yes, I left out one very important detail which I was not going to share with you, but..." and she raised her hands as if in desperation, "I became pregnant from that one experience and I had an abortion to save my mother and father the trauma of having a bastard child," and with that, she was gone.

Rainey sat alone in the room for a long time. These words weighed heavily on her for many reasons. She thought of her mother and her profession. She thought of her own conception and murky though it was, she knew she could not even have the satisfaction of knowing she was a "love child". No, she was the result of a violent act according to her mother's conversations with her grandmother, and though they thought she was too young to notice or remember, she did. Martha Powell's words bore heavily into her brain because she had considered for quite some time to defy her friend and mentor's words and to engage in a more intimate relationship with Doug Walker. Only his induction into the marine corps in the fall of 1944 prevented that. He was older than she by two years, and knowing full well he would be drafted when he reached his eighteenth birthday, and succumbing to the glamorous promises of glory and service to his country shown on the Marine posters of the period, he enlisted. He had completed basic training at Camp Pendleton near San Diego and was now in a more advanced training detachment engaged in combat tactics. He was being trained to go overseas, to take part in the closing battles of World War Two.

He had written her letters expressing his love for her, and since no one else had ever "loved" her before, she easily succumbed to his words. She loved him, too, as she understood the emotion. His letters, after having been read and re-read, were tucked away in her shoe box along with her other treasured valuables. When she mentioned his name or his latest reports on his military career to the three teachers, they merely nodded, with Martha's admonition..."remember what I told you, Rainey."

His most recent letter caused quite a stir in her emotions.

He was coming home on leave, his last leave before being sent overseas. She was now a senior in the eleven grade educational system of the period. Her grades had been exemplary due to the constant tutoring of her three "mothers" who had access to her each and every night, whether she wanted it or needed their help. But, since the arrival of his letter telling her he was coming home and once more, and more strongly, professing his love for her, she could not concentrate on her school work.

She shared this feeling with the three women who feigned some interest in the young man's coming home, if for no other reason than it was the patriotic thing to feel that way And when he finally appeared at his old school in full Marine dress uniform, both teachers and students were impressed and marveled at the change in his demeanor. Before, he was not too careful of his personal appearance. His hair had been long and stringy as his family conserved their meager finances and avoided his going to the barber. His clothing had been mostly hand-me-downs from two older brothers. His stature was not exactly erect at all times. He had somewhat of a slouch. But, he had nice regular features, blue eyes and light hair, and a slim build which had slimmed even more after several months in the Marine Corps. Most girls in school had considered him "cute", but with the blurred vision of one in love, Rainey had considered. him handsome, and now- ramrod straight, with his dress hat perfectly horizontal to the ground, his, white gloves tucked in his Sam Brown belt, his trousers with a razor sharp crease, his square-jawed glance, he was, to Rainey, a sight to make a girl gasp for breath... and he was hers.

The principal, as he had always done when one of his former students appeared at the school, introduced him to the full student body as they congregated in the school gym that day, for patriotism still permeated all levels of American life at that time, even more so since the defeat of Germany and the impending defeat of the people who had plunged this nation into war with their attack on Pearl Harbor- the Japanese.

The younger boys, too young to serve as yet, still with pimples and fuzz on their faces, looked on in envy, anxiously awaiting their day. The girls, so young and so impressionable, looked on with their own libidinous thoughts, even those "going steady" with others. To Rainey, he was a Greek God, descended from Olympus, and now reposed within her reach. She could hardly wait for the school to be dismissed so she could have him for her own. She knew the three teachers with whom she rode to and from school each day would be waiting for her at dismissal time. She had to be alone with him – she just had to. In her mind, she was no longer a little girl- no, she was a woman and she wanted to be with her man.

He came up to her after the other students had had their chance at him. He stood a little more relaxed since he was not on review. The nearness of him made chills go up and down her spine. She knew that this was a love reaction. This is how females were supposed to feel when near the one they love. For him, his long-pent up desires of basic training came to the fore and he sweated slightly under the arm pits. He could feel it and he hoped it didn't show on his face. They stood there, awkwardly, for each was as green as grass in their dealings with the opposite sex. They would glance at each other and then, as if embarrassed, look away. They were doing this, now and then touching hands, then breaking away when Martha Powell came towards then. Rainey hurriedly let his hand go and moved six inches further away from him as if to ensure her chastity. Martha Powell noticed her reaction and she was overcome with compassion. In spite of her misgivings about the union, she could not deny them their moments together, if for no other reason than patriotism. After all, the principal had announced that "this brave young man, the cream of the youth of this country, was headed for the South Pacific."

She smiled as she came forward and taking her ward by the hand, said, "Rainey, perhaps Douglas would like to come to our home for supper tonight," and turning to the young marine, "would you, Douglas?" and as an afterthought..."would that be all right with your parents?"

He stammered. His marine demeanor rattled by the unexpected invitation. True, Martha Powell had taught him during his school years, but she had never exhibited any degree of affection towards him. He looked at Rainey whose heart was now pounding with excitement, for the invitation startled her too. He looked from one to the other, then, "Yessum, Ah'd like that," and looking at his loved one, "if Rainey don't mind." (Martha Powell observed that the Marine Corps, in spite of their magnificent training, had not improved his country speech).

Rainey, with an expression somewhere between desire and blushing, replied, "Oh... I'd like that... if you really want to, Douglas." She usually called him, Doug, but for the sake of propriety she formalized his name.

"Then," intoned the older woman, feeling someone had to finalize these arrangements, "it is all settled. We can ride you home with us now, Douglas, but if you have to go home first to tell your parents, I guess you'll have to find some way to get to our house. You do know where it is..."

"Oh, yessum, Ah know where it is. Ah'll go home and tell mah ma and pa and then Ah'll have mah brother drop me off in the pickup truck. He got himself a truck with the money he makes as a lumber grader at the sawmill," he said with pride.

"Then, we'll expect you any time before supper. Come on Rainey, we have things to do, my dear." With one last longing look, they parted.

The young marine, accustomed to a farm kitchen table prior to his going into the service and then the mess hall clamor of the Marine Corps, was not well versed in table etiquette. The profusion of silverware mystified him and he watched Rainey for guidance. (Her eight years with the educated women in a cultural atmosphere had naturally put a hone on her manners as it did her speech and dress). She sensed his shortcomings and she viewed them with compassion, for she, too, had had those same shortcomings before her metamorphosis. It made her love him all the more as she deliberately accentuated her choice of untensils as she guided him with her eyes.

After the supper, as she attempted to help remove the dishes from the table, Martha Powell surprised her, again, with, "Why don't you and Douglas go into the parlor and listen to the radio, or since the evening is so warm, you might want to go out and sit on the swing." Although surprised by this suggestion, Rainey felt she loved Martha Powell more at that moment than she ever had in the past eight years. She jumped at the suggestion, but with these parting words, "Are you sure you don't want me to help?"

"No, dear, you go on," and she added with somewhat of a sob in her voice, "time is so precious these days." Rainey was not sure she understood the comment but taking him by the hand, she led him out to the backyard swing. During the past eight years, the old swing had become an important part of her life. When weather permitted, this was where she spent most of her hours alone, trying to get away from the sometime stifling atmosphere of having three people tell her what to do. It was on this swing that she dreamed her dreams... her fantasies. Life had never given her much, as yet, so all she had to look forward to was the future. She did not like her past.

Not sure of himself, the boy made no attempt to sit close to her, but, with a glance at the house to make sure no one could see them, she sat close to him. He smiled and looked away, but he took her hand as his gaze returned to her. With an unsteady and unsure voice, "Rainey, we ain't got much time. Ah'm leaving in three days..."

She was startled. "Three days! You just got home, Doug!"

"Ah know, but my leave was only fer two weeks and it took three days to get here on the train and it will take at least three days to get back. That don't leave too many days here. And if we get back late... well, it's a Court Martial for sure!"

Her hands went to her face. "Oh, Doug..."

A little braver, now, and a little more desperate, he put his arm around her neck. (He had lost his virginity in the brothels of San Diego and now considered himself a man of the world) as he pulled her close. "Rainey... Ah love you."

She went to him willingly, but as yet unsure as she glanced at the house. "Oh, Doug, I love you, too. Do you really love me? For real?" as she pondered Martha

Powell's admonition. She knew what he wanted and she knew the situation fitted Martha Powell's sad experience precisely as she pulled away just a little. "How do I know you really love me?"

"Cause Ah say so, Rainey... Geez... what does it take to convince you?"

She twisted her hands nervously. "I don't know. I just want to be sure... that's all," and she once more glanced at the house.

He, too, looked at the house and sensing her concern, said with some resentment. "It's those old hens in the house, ain't it? You can't let yourself go as long as they're around. Ain't that it? Tell the truth, Rainey."

"Well, I don't know... I guess so, I owe them so much..."

"Look, honey (he had never called her that before and it gave her a sense of intimacy) you don't owe those old girls anything. They ain't nothing but a bunch of dried up old maids, anyhow. Everybody in school knows that... all the kids say that. Ain't you heard it?"

She resented his criticism of the three women but did not want to press the issue as she replied, "Oh, Doug, what can we do? If you leave here in three days, how do I know I'll ever see you again? Maybe, you might even get ki...", but she caught herself and she could have cut her tongue out, as she held him close, her hands in his hair, "Oh, I'm so sorry. It slipped out. I'm so sorry... I didn't mean to say it, but..."

He drew back with a hurt look. "Well, you ain't just whis'ling Dixie, believe me. The scuttlebutt in the camp is that they're getting ready to invade Okinawa and we're gonna be part of the invasion first wave.

"Oh, Doug," and she held him close.

He seized the moment as he began to grope and fondle her. She had never been groped and fondled in her life and she did not readily accept it, as much as she wanted to. She nervously looked at the house over his shoulder. She pushed him away with, "Not here, Doug..."

Frustrated, he retorted, "Then, dammit, where? Ah swear, Rainey, Ah cain't wait much longer. You driving me crazy Ah want you so bad."

"You think I don't want you too... but, not here, and besides, I'm afraid."

"Afraid of what? Ah ain't gonna hurt you... I swear."

She now stood up, nervously looking at the house, and as she did, the voice of Martha Powell could be heard. "Rainey, dear... I think it is time you and Douglas came in. We'll drive him home... come on in."

He sat there, panting, frustrated. "Rainey, we ain't neva gona be able to do it as long as them old hens are around. You betta make up your mind what you want to do. Ah'm leaving here in a few days and I may never come back, if you know what Ah mean."

"I know, Doug. I have to think. I promise you, I'll think about us and what we can do. I promise," as she let go of his hand and headed back to the house.

Lloyd J. Guillory

    Later that night, she lay in bed in an agitated state of mind. She reviewed her options. She was a senior in high school and was scheduled to graduate in June. She had been a ward, so to speak, of these three women for the past eight years, and she surely owed them some loyalty. She was an orphan with no family of her own, as far as she knew. She also knew that as long as she lived in this house with these three women, she would never have a life of her own, not unless it was on their terms. But, she was only fifteen, a minor in every state in the union. She was full figured, though, and could pass for eighteen, she thought. And she was in love for the first time in her life and that bothered her. If she had lived in a home with a real mother who had had the usual experience of having fallen in love a dozen or so times, each time thinking it was the real thing, that mother could have counseled her that one never knows if it is the real thing until it has run its course for a period or years... many years in some cases. She was confused. She often thought of her mother and the life she had led... so short... so tragic- the plaything of men. There was no other way to look at it. No man, as far as she knew, had ever whispered one word of true affection to her mother. She had probably never had a man say to her, with complete sincerity..."I love you, Cassey." All she had ever heard were the grunts and groans of animal passion being satisfied. She cried as she thought of her mother. She vowed never to be any man's plaything. There had to be more. But what? What could Doug Walker offer her? As much as she disliked thinking about it, she also mentally pictured his uncertain future. What if she did give in to him at this time when his future was so uncertain. Was it love... or patriotism? She wasn't sure. She had heard so many stories of young girls who had done the same thing, right in her school, and never saw the boys again- at least, never alive or single.

    As she tried to resolve the matter in her mind so she could go to sleep, the words of Martha Powell burned in her brain, "They will say or do anything, Rainey, to get what they want."

CHAPTER NINE

The time was at hand for Doug Walker to return to San Diego and shipment overseas. It was March, 1945, and the war in the Pacific was entering its final phase. It was not a matter of if our nation would win the conflict but when and at what final price. The young couple still had to struggle for each and every moment they spent together, and they were few.

Rainey knew that the boy's invitation to supper at the Powell house was a one time thing, motivated more by patriotism on the part of Martha Powell than an inclination to afford the young couple time together. Martha had not changed her position one iota towards the affair: "You are too young, Rainey, and he is not the man for you. He has no future as far as I can see. He was a poor student in school and he is only a private in the Marine Corps- hardly a good prospect, and besides, as I've said repeatedly, you are too young to even think about being in love."

"How old is old enough to be in love, then?"

"When you are old enough to know... really know."

That answer, of course, did nothing to change or lessen her feelings, the feelings she believed were "love".

Having no other opportunities to meet alone other than at school, since the three teachers drove her to school each morning when they went, and drove her home each evening when they finished for the day, the young couple stole their moments as they could. He had even given up wearing his beloved uniform so as not to attract undue attention and he spent all his free time at the school. They met at recess, they met in the corridors, they met behind the gym and under the old wooden bleachers which formed the seating for both baseball and football. All they could do under the circumstances was talk, hold hands and talk.

"Rainey, Ah'm leaving here day after next and Ah want you to come to San Diego with me. I want to marry you."

"Oh, Doug, I can't marry you. I'm too young to marry anyone at my age and even so..."

"That ain't true iffen they give you permission... if they sign. Ah know that!"

She could not stifle a laugh. "You don't believe she will sign for me, do you? She is not even in favor of my seeing you."

He snorted, "That old bitch..."

Anger rose in her as she came to the defense of her benefactor. "Don't you dare call her that! I won't stand for it."

"Aw, Ah didn't really mean that, but, Rainey, Ah'm tellin' you, you gonna hafta choose between me and her. Ah don't see no otha way."

She pondered her situation for a moment. "If I decided to go to San Diego with you, what is going to happen to me after you ship overseas? What will I do then?"

He had obviously given this some previous thinking as he replied without hesitation, "Ah got this friend 'o mine, he's married and he got this trailer where his wife lives. He said that when we ship overseas you kin stay with his wife. You girls can take care of each otha till we git back."

"Is she really his wife?"

"Hell, ah don't know, Rainey; he says she is. She's from Louisiana, from Oak Grove. That ain't too far from here. You girls will have a lot in common."

"And what'll we live on?"

"Whal, she works as a waitress in a diner. She makes some money 'n Ah' ll have my pay sent to you," and he hesitated for a moment, "ceptin some of it Ah got to send to mah mama."

She said nothing for a while as she pondered the situations and running out of time and patience as he heard the bell ring, he asked, "Whal, what's it gonna be, Rainey? Are you comin' with me or not?"

She turned away to return to class. "I have to think about it, Doug, I just don't know for sure right now."

As she walked off, he nearly yelled, "Whal, you betta make up your mind fast, Rainey... you ain't got much time. I'm catchin' a train in Pine Bluff tomorra night. You won't heer from me no more, eitha." He made it sound like a threat.

That night, she asked Martha Powell if she could speak to her in private, after the other two teachers had gone to bed. The older woman felt sure she knew what the young girl wanted to talk about and she was not anxious to discuss the matter, but she had no idea how far reaching the conversation would go. She reluctantly replied, "Why of course, Rainey, you can always talk to me when you need to... you know that."

Rainey, nervous, hesitant, sat in a chair with her legs apart, a position the prudish school teacher had admonished her for on so many occasions, but this time it went without comment as the two women settled in their chairs. Starting in a low voice, Rainey recounted the events of the past few days, telling her of his insistant demands that she prove her love for him, with the older woman nodding, knowingly, for she derived some satisfaction that her warnings had come true, and as the young girl paused to further gather her thoughts, the older woman replied with some degree of relish, "Well, Rainey, didn't I tell you so? Didn't I tell you that this was how it is with young boys?" and not waiting for a reply, "I certainly hope you informed him that you were not that type of girl... you did, didn't you?"

"Oh, we haven't done anything... if you know what I mean. I couldn't do that... even with him."

She nearly snorted. "I certainly hope so."

"But, but, you see, Miss Martha, he is leaving here tomorrow night. He's taking a train back to San Diego..."

Relieved that the young man was leaving town, she mitigated her feelings with: "Well, Rainey, these things have to end some time. He must go on with his life and you with yours..."

She could delay it no longer. "But, he wants me to go to San Diego with him..."

The older woman nearly rose out of her chair. Her head jerked back as she stared at the young girl. "What does he mean, he wants you to go to San Diego with him? As what? His mistress? What else could it be? You are too young to be married, so there is no other interpretation to put on the thing."

"He asked me to marry him..."

She could not stifle a laugh. "Marry him? Are you insane, Rainey? Fifteen year old girls cannot be married. At least, there is some sanity in these laws of ours!"

"But, he says that if you sign..."

"Me sign! Do you really believe, child, that I would even consider sanctioning such a foolish and impractical union? Do you really believe, Rainey, that I care so little for you that I would throw you away to this... this... country bumpkin," was as generous a term she could come up with in her excited state.

She pressed on, now fully agitated at even the thought of it. "And even if I were willing to sign, which I am not, I could not do so. Even though I have mothered and cared for you these past eight years, Rainey, you do not belong to me- not legally. When my mother, God rest her soul, insisted that we take you in only if it were legal, we had an attorney look into your status. Your mother and your grandmother were both dead by then and we could find no relatives other than the ones your grandmother had gone to live with. (She had never told the girl of these circumstances so this was all news to her) There are some second cousins living there, but when we attempted to get them to sign you over to us, they would not sign anything, and all they would say is, you can have her.

"So, you see, we have only had what the attorneys would call a de facto adoption of you. You don't really legally belong to me, Rainey. I can't sign as your parent or your guardian-not legally, and believe me, my dear, I would not if I could," and she rose to leave, feeling she had made her position perfectly clear and she had no more to add.

Rainey shook her head. "Then, nothing has changed. I still don't belong to anyone."

The older woman started to refute the assertion, but instead, she went to the young girl, and stroking her hair with affection, said, "I suggest you go to bed and get some sleep and that you put this young man out of your mind and out of your life. I have plans for you after graduation, Rainey. I want you to attend the university... to become something... to make something of your life. I have promises of a scholarship to the University of Arkansas for you. That is how much I care for you," and bending, she kissed her on the head. "Goodnight, Rainey."

Without looking up, she replied softly. "Goodnight, Miss Martha." She continued to sit for a long time, and then, sighing as she rose, for she had not resolved her problems- at least, not in her troubled mind, she went to bed.

Sleep did not come as she tossed and turned. She knew if she was to have any future with Douglas Walker she would have to go with him. He was typical of the backwoods young men she had come to know in that locale. They were stubborn to the point of stupidity. They had instilled in them, by birth and family association, that there was no middle ground, no room for compromise. "You eitha with me or you agin me!" was their doctrine. The young man felt that there was only one way to culminate this love affair. She had to become his woman. The legal aspect of it was a secondary consideration, to be resolved in time... if ever. As to the moral aspect, what is immoral about true love, he would have asserted, if not in those exact terms, something similar.

She reviewed her life with these three women these past eight years. They had cared for her, mothered her, given her the nearest thing to a secure home she had ever had in her fifteen years, yet, it was a confining type of love. They lived narrow lives, and in spite of their educations, they lived in a tight little world. They never traveled. At first, they blamed it on the war. Travel was restricted, but not forbidden. They had made no attempt to go even so far as Little Rock, barely a hundred miles away. They had taken her to Hot Springs one weekend and to have heard them talk, it was equivalent to a trip to Paris. She had appreciated what they had done for her, but with a feeling she would express again and again throughout her life..."there must be more."

She mentally compared her two choices as she lay there. If she remained in this house, there was security- a place to call home- three women who loved her and would care for her as long as she needed them. And what of her future if she remained here. Martha's offer of college had never been mentioned before. She had never even considered college. Most children of that generation never did, especially the girls. If any family were willing to make such a financial sacrifice, it would certainly not be wasted on a girl who was expected to marry as a way of earning a living. She felt she was fortunate to complete high school. It was as much as she had hoped for. As to her future, she would get a job in a store or a factory (women had now been accepted in the work force, due to the demands of war), or, if she were lucky, a course in a business school so she could become a secretary- her ultimate goal.

Her other choice running off-with Douglas Walker. What else could you call it? She was now convinced she could not legally marry him, even if she chose to. But, the mention of San Diego had aroused her interest since it was almost everyone's dream, male or female, those reared in those depression days just past,

Rainey

to go to California- that Golden Land where dreams come true, simply because Hollywood had told them so.

She thought of living there, even in a trailer if she had to-the adventure, the excitement, the challenge. These things seemed to her more exciting than the alternative. She was leaning towards that choice as she finally succumbed to sleep. She would make up her mind by morning. She had to. This was her last day to make a decision- if she were going with Doug Walker.

The next morning was a Saturday and the teachers usually slept late on that day in contrast to their six o'clock rising on week days. As if in premonition of what was to come, Martha Powell had a restless night. The conversation with Rainey the night before had disturbed her more than she allowed it to show, disciplined as she was. She awoke early and going down the hall towards the doll room, Rainey's room, she could hear the young girl stirring. This disturbed her because Rainey, too, usually stayed abed on Saturdays. She silently made her way downstairs and into the kitchen. The old colored maid, Tessie, up in years, still worked for them six days a week, and would make an appearance around eight.

She had no sooner sat down to have her first cup of coffee when a tousled headed and sleepy Rainey appeared in her pajamas and robe. The older woman gave her a motherly look. "Rainey, dear, you look as though you did not sleep well. Were you ill?" She felt sure she knew the problem but avoided direct reference to it, preferring the young girl to lead the way.

Rainey slumped in a chair, placing her head on her arms on the table top. "No, I didn't sleep well. I tossed and turned all night."

"Oh, do you have problems? Anything I can help with?" She knew what her problem was. She felt sure, down deep in her heart that Rainey would only make one decision and that would be the sensible one of telling that young man goodbye this day and going on with her life... trying to forget him.

The young girl raised her head and twisting her hands on the table as she replied, "Miss Martha, I've decided to go to San Diego with Doug," and she looked away, not able to look her benefactor in the eyes.

The older woman was jolted in her chair, but she immediately took hold of her emotions as she had done all her life, especially in dealing with wayward students at school. She looked at the girl, calmly. "I see. And this is your final decision, Rainey?"

Without looking at her directly. "Yes, Ma'am. I gave it a lot of thought last night."

"That is quite obvious, by the way you look."

The young girl's hand went to her hair, trying to arrange it. "I know this will not make you happy, Miss Martha, or Miss Annie," and she added laboriously, "or Miss Bertha, but it's my life. I've got to live it as I see fit... isn't it?" she asked not quite certain of her position.

"Yes, Rainey, it is your life, and you are quite correct that each person has the right to live it as they see fit," and she could not help adding, "even if they are misguided."

The young girl nodded without replying.

The older woman, so much wiser in the way of the world, gave the matter some thought, then: "Rainey, is this all about sex? Did you make your decision on what your hormones are demanding of you... is that it?"

The young girl was surprised at the frankness of the question. Although they had lived together for eight years, their relationship had never been intimate. Sex was never discussed except in those terms required to convince her of the evil of it.

"What do you mean?"

"I mean, Rainey, were you driven to this foolish decision by an overwhelming desire to have sex with this boy? That is what I mean."

"Well... no... we've never done it. I told you that before," she replied defensively.

"I know. Is that the problem? Are you driven by an insatiable desire to do it, is what I mean. Or, is he pressuring you to do so, and if you don't... you will lose him? Did he say that.

"Well, he said if I don't go to San Diego with him, it's all over. I'll never see him again."

She shook her head. "Oh, my God, that sounds familiar to me, even after twenty years. Rainey, don't you remember what I told you the other night? I have been through this, and you remember what happened to me... a pregnancy... an abortion... a broken heart... don't you remember any of it?"

She nodded. "Yes, Ma'am, I remember it all..."

She interrupted her, "And you still intend to fall for this crap!"

Rainey was truly shocked. She had never heard a word of profanity ever issued from those lips. She could not look the older woman in the eyes as she said, "My mind is made up. I'm going with him. It's not the end of the world! If it doesn't work out, I'll come back and go to college like you want me to..."

The older woman's head shot back and her eyes became ablazed as she glared at the young girl. "Oh, no, little girl! You will do no such thing. Rainey, if you go to California with that boy, you are no longer welcomed in this house. Don't think you can run in and out of here as your libidinous cravings are satisfied with one yokel after another... oh..No!"

Martha Powell did not intend to make her declaration as harsh as she did, but it was out, and the spoken word is indelible. It can never be retrieved. She looked at the young girl, waiting for her reaction. Rainey rose, pulling her chair back, trying to suppress her sobs as she was finally able to form a reply to this brutal assault. "Then, I guess I'll leave as soon as I can pack," and turning to the older woman, "I want to thank you, Miss Martha, for all you've done for me these past eight years. I really appreciate it. And please thank Miss Annie and Miss Bertha for me, too," and on the verge of profuse tears, she rushed from the room.

She ran up to her room and a tear fell on each and every tread on the stairs. She was shattered. She had never expected this verbal onslaught. She fully expected to be welcomed back if her venture did not work out. She had never imagined this expulsion would happen, not in her wildest moments.

She had acquired a hand-me-down suitcase from Annie Raymond after that trip to Hot Springs and she began to pack as she wiped tears away. The first thing she put in the luggage was the old shoe box with her legacy. She realized years ago that she should have thrown it away, but it was all she had of her previous life, scant though it was, she still treasured it.

She paused at the bottom of the stairs as she made some attempt to tell the three women goodbye. Martha Powell had now aroused the entire household with the traumatic news of Rainey's decision and impending departure. The other two, Annie Raymond and Bertha Krautte, not being privy to all the conversations, were confused. How could this have happened... and so fast. Martha had replied: "I'll explain it to you later."

The three teachers, along with Tessie, stood in the foyer, suppressing sobs as they all hugged. It was a sad moment. Perhaps it had gotten out of hand and all parties would regret it before the sun set that day, but for the time being, it was done.

So as not to convey any impression of encouragement to the young girl, the teachers made no offer to take her to meet Douglas Walker, who lived some distance from their home. Instead, she went to the phone under Martha's Powell's harsh stare, telling the boy of her decision and asking if he could come and pick her up. She felt the sooner she left the house the better for all concerned. She sat on the front porch awaiting his arrival. She felt she was no longer a welcomed member of the family and that pained her deeply.

She felt relieved as she saw the pickup truck come into sight. He did not alight as he parked the truck in the driveway, merely blowing the horn and waiting for her to come forward, suitcase in hand, tears flowing, uncertain, scared, and somewhat apprehensive.

He smiled as she climbed in the passenger side, saying nothing, as she glanced not at him, but back at the home she had shared with these three women for the past eight years. It would prove to be some of the most stable years in her turbulent life.

It should be noted here that in this uncertain world, people often come to a fork in the road of life, a fork which will take them on completely different paths. Depending on which path is taken determines how our lives will evolve. Some people, whether by luck or skill, seem blessed in being able to make the right choice. Others, whether by lack of wisdom, or lack of luck, seem always to make the wrong choice at the wrong time. Call it fate, or what you will, but it does seem to be. Rainey Wether seems to be one of those unfortunate ones.

CHAPTER TEN

As Douglas Walker hung up the telephone after hearing from Rainey that she would accompany him to San Diego, he was elated as if he had scored a victory of sorts, for he had. He had come to the realization in the past few days that if he were ever to have her in any intimate relationship it would have to be some place other than in this small community where she was constantly monitored by the three school teachers. He truly believed, in his own inexperience and immaturity, that he was in love. Since he had never been before, he had no reference plane from which to judge. His mother, more experienced, more pragmatic, and a bride of the depression years, practically snorted when he told her he was in love. "Love... love... boy, you don't even know what love is. It ain't love you got, it's hot pants. Maybe you need to have a talk with your older brother, Lenny, and let him tell you the cure for what you got, and it ain't marriage. And 'nutha thing, you cain't marry that little girl, nohow, she's only fifteen, ain't that so?"

He could not look her in the eye. "Yessum, but we kin jump the broom like you 'n Pa did. Ain't that right?"

"Nah, that ain't the whole picture, Doug," as she wiped her hands on her kitchen towel, "you know we had owah marriage made legal by that Justice 'o tha Peace."

"Then, how come me 'n Rainey cain't do the same?"

She chuckled. "Maybe, you kin, iffen you kin find a J.P who is willin' to break the law. He might say the words ova you, but it ain't gonna be legal 'cause she is too young," and as she took a deep breath, "but you go ahead 'n take her to Californee iffen she is crazy 'nuff to go," and she could not look her youngest in the eye as she added, "Ah reckun a young boy like you, goin' whar you goin', whal, you got a right to some pleasure 'fore you go, but don't you go gittin' that little girl pregnant 'n sending her back home to me to raise yore little snotty nose kid... no sirree! Ah done raised 'nuff with you three boys. Ah don't need no more," and looking out the kitchen window, "Ah see yore brotha, Lenny, coming home now to take you and Rainey to the train." Looking back at him. "Whar you gonna git tha money to buy her ticket? You tole me you ain't got 'nuf for you 'n her both."

He gave her a desperate look. "Lenny tole me he'd loan me the money, but," and he shook his head, "he said he wanted four percent intr'st. That ain't right, Ma, we brothas. That ain't no way to treat a brother goin' ova seas. Iffen he wasn't 4F, his ass ' d be in the service like mine 'n he wouldn't be home makin' all that money..."

She turned on him. "Now, listen to me, boy! You know Lenny got his laig crush 'd at tha mill. That's why he's class' fied as 4F. He ain't no coward."

"Aw, Ah didn't mean nuthin' by it, Ma. You know that."

"You ain't had no business sayin' it then," and turning to the door as her son entered, "Hell'o Lenny. You want some coffee 'fore you two leave." Lenny was her main source of income and there was no doubt where her heart lay.

"No, Ma, we ain't got time. We got to go 'n pick up Rainey at the Powells 'n git to the train on time. Come on, Doug, you ready?"

"Yeah, Ah guess so," as he rose.

Lenny, turning to him and bringing him to face the mother, said, "We got to git one thing straight, Doug, 'fore Ah lend you the hundr'id dollahs," and placing his forefinger in the younger brother's chest, "Ma, Ah want you to heer this. The only way Ah'll lend him tha money is iffen he pays me back with four percent intri'st and," and he looked embarrassed as he added, "iffen he gits kilt in tha war, Ma, you will pay me back from his G.I. insurance policy..."

The mother gave him a stern look, "Now, Lenny, Ah don't want to heer that kinda talk... 'bout Doug gittin' kilt. That ain't nuthin' to talk 'bout at a time like this."

"Ah ain't meant him no harm, Ma, but business is business. That's a lot 'o money 'n you know Ah'm plannin' to git married mahself. Ah cain't afford to give him a hundr'id dollars."

Doug went to his mother. "It's all right with me, Ma. Iffen Ah die, give him tha damn money... Ah don't care."

The mother, not wanting to point out that if he did die, it would be her money, not his, and wanting to bring the gory conversation to an end, added, "Don't worry, Lenny! You'll git yore money back... one way 'o nutha."

With tearful goodbyes and hugs and promises to "be careful, Doug," they were off.

Even in the closing days of the war, travel had not changed or improved since the middle of the twenties. Trains were still propelled by steam and the fuel of choice was coal. A three day ride from Arkansas to California could be a trip from hell, especially in those pre-air conditioned days when windows had to be left open. Between other sweaty and smelley bodies and the coal impregnated smoke billowing in through the open windows, Rainey was not happy as the train made its way out west.

Since she had never been more than a hundred miles from home, the trip had offered her some expectancy of excitement, but it soom faded when the first night approached. There were Pullman coaches on the train, but she and Doug were not fortunate enough to have one. It had strained all his finances to merely buy the two tickets, much less allow for the luxury of a compartment with bunks and a private toilet. When she had time to evaluate the situation, she looked at him meekly, asking in a plaintive voice, "But, where will we sleep?"

He looked around the car, packed with service men or their families and their dependents. (Since the war was coming to an end, there seemed to be more people on the move than during the war, for several reasons) He gave her an exasperated look. "Look around you, Rainey Whar'd you think we gonna sleep?" and before she could reply, "We gonna sleep settin' up in these heer seats... that's whar."

She started to protest, but refrained, not wanting to start an argument in front of dozens of strangers. but, she had to know this. "But, how about a bathroom? Where do we go when we have to go... you know?"

"Thar's a toilet room on one of these coaches, but Ah ain't shur whar it is. We'll find it. You got to go now?"

Embarrassed; she had never lived with a man in the house since coming to live with the Powells and had no experience in sharing a toilet with one of them, much less dozens of strangers, but she replied, "No, I don't have to go... not yet."

There was a dining car on the train, but having had experience with their outrageously high prices (in his estimation) on the trip home, he had strongly advised that they buy some luncheon meat, a loaf of bread and some soda pop to tide them over between the big meals. In her eight years with the Powells, she had had absolutely no experience with money. The three women had bought her what she needed when she needed it. As far as discretionary money was concerned, it was seldon seen by her.

After their unappetizing meal, they settled down for the night as soon as the darkness allowed some degree of privacy. He suggested to her that she put her head on his shoulder so she could sleep. She hesitated for a moment, looking around the coach to see how many people were watching. When she became convinced that no one was., she did as she suggested. In time, as she became uncomfortable in that position, she shifted her body, and as she did, he placed his arm around her neck, and he began to whisper intimate things to her, things he had never said before, due mostly to lack of opportunity, but now, he felt he was entitled to his due. He began to grope and fondle her. She sat up, embarrassed, as she removed his hands, whispering in his ear, "Not here, Doug, for God's sake... can't you wait until we get to California?"

He whispered back. "That's all Ah bin doin is waitin' and more waitin'! Ah 'm tard 'o waitin', Rainey."

She drew away, replying louder than she intended, "Well, you're going to wait a while longer, believe me! If you think I am going to do it in front of all these people, you are crazy.!"

"Aw, Ah don't expect you to do it. Ah jus wanta play... that's all."

She was exasperated as she exclaimed, "Then, play with yourself! You are not going to play with me in public."

An older woman in the seat back of them chimed in, "You tell him, honey... you tell him," and she giggled.

Rainey raised her forefinger, pointing it at him, whispering, "You see what I mean. We have no privacy on this train. Now go to sleep, Doug."

She thought she heard him say, "Oh, shit!" but she was not sure. She turned her back to him, placing her head on her suitcase which she had retrieved from under the seat. She had to spurn his advances for the three nights they were on the train. But, whether it was done because of her prudish and moral teachings in the house with the three school teachers, or, the admonition of her long departed grandmother still ringing in her ears, "Don't take no crap from no man," we shall never know for sure, but spurn him she did. He was furious, of course, and he ranted and raved, demanding what he considered were his rights. She was adamant and persistant, placating him with her hand on his cheek. "Be patient, Doug... be patient, please."

Arriving in San Diego, they were forced to take a bus to the small trailer court on the outskirts of the bustling military dominated city on the Pacific. He had informed her, previously, that she would be staying with the wife of one of his Marine buddies, who was also scheduled to be shipped overseas when he was. She was nervous knowing she, once more, had to live with a stranger. "What's her name, Doug?"

"Verlie."

"Verlie, what?"

"Ah don't know. What difference does it make?"

"Well, I'd at least like to know her name if I'm going to live with her. What are the financial arrangements? Do you pay her for me to live with her?"

"How kin Ah pay her, Rainey? Ah ain't gonna be here!"

"Well, does she expect to be paid?"

"Whal, shur, you ain't 'spectin' to free load, are you?"

As they neared the trailer, she stopped short. "I don't know what to expect. You haven't told me anything about this."

He shrugged. "Thar ain't much to know. You'll jus be bunkin' out here when you ain't workin'..."

"Working? Am I suppose to work?"

"What'd you 'spect, Rainey? You gonna sit on your butt all day 'n do nuthin'?"

She shook her head. "No, I guess not, but I don't know what to do. Work where?"

"Verlie said she'd find you somethin' to do. Jobs ain't scarce in this town. It's a boom town, what with the war 'n all."

As they approached the trailer, the front door swung open and a couple appeared, a marine in his fatigues and a green T-shirt. He was short and stocky, with bulging muscles. He had the typical Corps crew cut. His complexion was swarthy due to his Italian heritage. The young woman looked older than Rainey had expected. She had dyed red hair, a too-tight blouse showing ample breasts, a short skirt, and was puffing on a cigarette.

The man extended his hand. "Doug, ole buddy, it's good to see you again," and turning to Rainey, "and this must be Rainey," and turning back to him, "She sure looks young to me. Are you sure you ain't robbing the cradle?" He gave Rainey a bone-crushing hand shake which pained her considerably.

The woman came forward, putting her arm around Rainey. "Rainey, honey, I'm so glad to meet you. You know I'm from Oak Grove. That ain't too far from where you live, you know."

Rainey forced a smile. "I'm happy to meet you, too, Verlie, and I don't think I got his name," as she pointed to the man.

"Oh, that's Mario. Mario Cullotta... pure Dago, through and through, I guess you can tell," as she poked him in the ribs.

He pushed her to one side. "Ah'll Dago you, you Cajun hick."

"I ain't no Cajun, I told you. Why I got a Cajun cousin who lives in Lafayette who calls people who live in North Louisiana, Yankees."

"Ah don't want to hear all that crap, Verlie, and neither do Doug and Rainey," and turning to his guests, "Come on and Ah'll show you where you'll be bunking."

"Yeah," exclaimed Doug, "Ah want to see the play pen."

Rainey turned to him. "What play pen? Do they have children?"

The other three laughed at her. She was embarrassed as Verlie whispered in her ear, "That's what these apes call the bed... a play pen... get it?"

Further embarrassed at her naivete', Rainey smiled, saying, "Oh, I should have guessed."

Supper was at the drive in. They had gone in Mario's car far enough from the base to get away from the 3.2 beer served on all military bases. It was Mario who suggested, "Let's go and get some real stuff. Ah can't stand that cow pee they call beer on the base."

Doug yelled out. "You said it, buddy, let's go git some real stuff," and as they climbed in the back seat of the old 1939 Plymouth coupe, Doug placed his arm around Rainey and pulled her close. She allowed herself to be held. She knew she had run out of excuses and time. She could not help thinking as he held her close how he had changed since she had known him in high school. This was not the same young man she had wanted to give her heart to. He had changed, and not for the better.

During the meal, the men drank beer almost constantly. She was amazed once again. She had never seen Doug drink very much before. Perhaps, she thought, it was because he lacked the opportunity back home in that strong Baptist community where drinking was frowned upon, as much by the congregation as the ministers who railed against it from the pulpit. He was getting tipsy, she could tell, and the more he did so, the more raucous and obscene his speech. He even tried to fondle her in the drive-in after seeing Mario indulge himself with Verlie, who accepted it as a usual thing. Try as she might, she felt she was not ready for this... not yet. Was she being prudish, she wondered? Is this the way it was supposed to be in the real world? She didn't know. She had had no experience. She resigned herself to some minimal amount of fondling, but pushing his hand away when he strayed too far. He sensed it, telling her in a loud voice, "You betta have a beer, Rainey, you got to loosen up, honey. We gonna have us some fun tonight... wheweee!"

After they returned to the trailer Mario said to Verlie, "Get us some beer outta the fridge, baby, we gonna have us a few more before we turn in. We got to get up at five to report for duty on the base by seven, so come on, folks, let's have one more for the road."

Doug yawned, stretching his arms. "No, Mario, ole buddy, me 'n mah gal had a hard day. We gonna turn in nah iffen you don't mind," as he gave Rainey a lascivious grin and Mario a poke in the ribs.

Mario, returning his grin, "Ah know what you mean ole buddy. Have fun. Me and Verlie promise not to listen at the door," as he emitted a loud laugh, with Verlie winking at Rainey.

He had undressed as soon as he entered the room, throwing his clothes in all directions, leaving on only his shorts, which also were G.I. olive drab. She sat in a chair for a moment, deciding how to broach the subject, so delicate a matter. "Doug, aren't you going to take a bath? We've been on that train for three days and it was so hot and dirty. Don't you want a bath?"

"Geez, Rainey, Ah wiped myself off when Ah was in the bathroom. Come on, git undressed 'n hop into this bed. Ah ain't waitin' no longa. Ah mean it. Ah'm gonna git it one way or 'nuther."

She rose. "I am going to bathe first, no matter what you say," and going over to the bed and speaking in hushed tones, "Doug, do you have any of those things with you?"

He sat up. "What things?"

She was embarrassed. "You know, those rubber things to keep me from getting pregnant."

"Hell no, Ah ain't got none. We don't need them things, Rainey. We almost married. 'Side, it's like washing yore feet with yore socks on. Ah don't want none of them things tonight."

She rose from sitting on the bed. All her innate senses, her grandmother's stubbornness, her pragmatic teachings at the hands of those school teachers came to the fore. She looked him in the eye. "Doug, if you don't use those things, you will not do it with me, I swear! I won't do it... I won't. I mean it," and she went to the far side of the tiny bedroom, as if the distance enforced her position.

"Aw shit, Rainey, Ah knew you'd come up with some crap like this," he said, loudly, with slurred speech. "Ah guess you know if Ah want to, Ah kin take it whether you want to or not. It's mah right, you know," as he rose from the bed. She looked around her, grabbing the first thing her hands felt, a heavy vase made of cheap glass. She raised it high. "Don't you try it, Doug. I will not be taken against my will. I am not yours to do with as you please. I demand respect."

He looked into her glaring eyes. He knew she meant what she said. He had not played it smart. He relented. "Aw, come on, baby, this is suppose to be our honeymoon. Don't ruin it."

She relented too. "I don't want to ruin it. All I want is for you to use some protection. If you think I am going to take the chance of getting pregnant when you are going overseas and I may never see you again, and we are not married, and I have no family to fall back on," and she began to cry, "if you think I am that foolish, then you don't really know me..."

"But, baby, Ah ain't got no rubbers. Ah ain't had time to think about them."

She tried to salvage this disaster of a "wedding night" for which she had dreamed so long. "What about Mario? Does he have any?"

He rose from the bed. "Hell, Ah dunno. Ah'll go 'n ask him," and going out in only his shorts, he soon returned with a broad smile on his face, as he waved a three pack in the air. "Look what Ah got, baby."

She didn't know whether to be happy or not. She now knew that all her options had run out. She rose, and heading for the bathroom, replied' "I wont be long."

For years, now, ever since she had reached puberty and found out what brides did on their wedding night, she had fantasies about those magic moments she had envisioned. She had dreamed of her prince charming, the man she had chosen to spend the rest of her life with, holding her close, whispering those special words for her ears alone, holding her in close embrace as their love was consumated in fiery passion. Such are dreams made of. But, on this night, it was not to be. She would remember this night, later, in more reflective moments as more of a brutal assault on her person, without regard to her needs or her feelings, but only his own. She could not respond and he could not have cared less. Since he was reared on a farm and his education along those lines had been in the observation of watching animals in the process of procreation, he evidently felt that this was the way it was supposed to be.

In spite of his over abundance of alcohol induced by too many beers, he was able to exhaust his supply of the three pack before he was ready to leave in the early morning. She paid enough attention to ensure that, but other than that observation, she merely lay there without emotions, other than regret and humiliation.

She was asleep when he left in the morning, and as she awoke to an empty bed, she felt relieved, but only for a moment. As she tried to rise to go to the bathroom, she could feel pain in her groin. She was sore, but more so in spirit than in body. She had to smile as she thought of her talk with Nell Foster, so many years ago, sitting in the barn yard after the talk on the facts of life. 'Them hens can't like it too much the way them roosters got to chase them around.' This morning, she felt like a barnyard hen. She wondered if this was the way it was going to be. She had not enjoyed the night one iota. She said to herself. 'There's got to be more to it than this or the world would have run out of people a long time ago.'

Verlie had already left for work by the time she appeared in the living room-kitchen area of the trailer. She saw a note on the kitchen counter.

Sorry I didn't see you before I left for work. Make yourself at home. I'll see you tonight.

Verlie

She made herself a cup of coffee. She had never really developed a liking for the stuff, but she needed something to clear her mind. She was not only sore, she was disgusted as well. The night was such a disappointment to her that she was repelled by the thought of another one later that day. She knew down deep in her heart that with the insatiable appetite of his youth, Doug would once again claim his due by ravishing her in his animalistic fashion. She might be green and inexperienced but she knew enough to know how boys were. Some of the more experienced girls in her class had told her of the incessant demands made on them by their boyfriends.

As she sat on the living area couch, she pulled her legs up under her, her favorite position for meditating. She tasted the coffee. She didn't like the taste. Perhaps a little more sugar would help, and she rose to add some. She looked out the windows on both sides. Another trailer was on each side, less than ten feet away. She felt hemmed in, not only by the closeness of the trailers, but by her circumstances. She could not help but call to mind, again, how Doug had changed. She was amazed how crude and insensitive he had been last night. He cared nothing for her, only for his own animal cravings, and he would certainly expect the same this night, too. She had never felt so alone in her life, not since that first night in the Foster home when she cried herself to sleep. Once again, she began to cry as she considered her predictament. Here she was in a strange place, thousands of miles from home, with absolutely no money of her own, brought there by a man she now realized she did not know and really could not love- not the way she understood love.

She knew she had to make up her mind what to do. She could not... would not... allow him to assault her this night as he had done on the previous one. She had to find a way out. She went to Verlie's and Mario's bedroom, and with a guilty conscience began to rummage in Verlie's personal things. With a sigh of relief, she found what she wanted as she picked up the box of Kotex. She would explain to Verlie later, but for now, she had to convince Doug that her period had begun.

"What? You done started yore period? This ain't no time fer you to have a damn period. Ah'm leavin' fer overseas in two days 'n you start a damn period... shit!" he had nearly screamed at her and through the thin trailer walls. Verlie exchanged smiles with Mario.

She tried to look contrite. "Well, I am sorry, but I'm sure you realize that I have no control over that. I can't help it."

"Shit, if this ain't the pits," and he stalked out of the room in a huff, yelling to Mario, "let's go out fer a beer. Ah got the red ass so bad Ah could spit."

Mario smiled at Verlie who gave him a shrug, and picking up the car keys off the counter, said, "Come on, buddy."

As they drove off to the sound of screeching tires, Rainey came out of the bedroom and saw a smiling Verlie sitting on the couch smoking her usual cigarette.

"I guess you heard, huh," she said meekly to Verlie as she joined her on the couch.

Verlie let out a large cloud of smoke as she patted Rainey's hand. "Just between us girls, honey, I've used the same excuse many times. Sometimes, a girl just has to," and she added after a pause, "with those apes."

"Verlie, I have to confess to you that I'm lying. I'm not having my period. I had to think of something. I cannot bear to go through tonight what I went through last night. And, oh, I borrowed your box of Kotex... I had to."

She took a long drag, inhaling deeply, as she removed a piece of loose tobacco from her lips. She regarded Rainey for a long time as the unfortunate girl sat with her hands clasped in her lap.

Finally exhaling the smoke, Verlie gave her a sympathetic look: "Rainey, how old are you?"

She started to say eighteen, but she could not lie to this woman, the only thread of companship she had. She replied meekly, "Fifteen."

"Jesus! What the hell are you doing out here with that country yokel... a pretty little thing like you? You should be home in school."

"I don't have a home... not a real home... with a mama and a daddy. I wish I had," and the tears began to flow.

Sensing that she needed to get it all out, Verlie ran a hand through her hair, then finally patting her hand, "Want to tell me what it's all about. How did you get yourself in this mess?"

So, for the better part of an hour she told Verlie of her life... her unfortunate life... her foolish choice of Douglas Walker over the stability of the Powell home.

She exhaled more smoke. "You made a big mistake, honey, leaving the security those three teachers offered compared to what that hick could offer you. What made you do it, not that I haven't done some dumb things in my time, but this is major?"

Lloyd J. Guillory

She wiped a tear with her blouse. She sighed. "I guess I just wanted someone to love me... for myself."

"Didn't those women love you?"

"Oh, I guess so, but you know what I mean... real love."

She grunted. "Rainey, honey, I wouldn't know real love if it looked me in the face. You don't think I love Mario, do you. Oh, I guess I have warm feelings for him, but real love, not hardly. I'm still looking for it, too. Most women I know are."

"How old are you, Verlie?"

"Me, I'm twenty-three going on forty."

"What do you mean by that?"

"I mean that the calendar says I am twenty-three but my face and experience say that I am forty. I've got a lot of mileage on me, Rainey. I've done some things I'm not too proud of," and as she shrugged, "a girl has to survive in this world by one means or another. It's a man's world out there."

She wanted to ask what she had done that she was ashamed of, but she felt she had no right.

Verlie looked at her. "Rainey, why don't you take the next train back to Arkansas and those three teachers? That is my advice to you, honey."

"They won't take me back. Miss Martha told me if I left with Doug, she would not take me back."

"Whew, Rainey, baby, that leaves you between the rock and the hard place, believe me. What you gonna do?"

Raising her hands in desperation. "I don't know."

"Well, the good news is those two apes will be going overseas in two days and the bad news is they take their pay checks with them."

"Doug promised me he would have his pay assigned to me while he is gone..."

She practically snorted. "He can't do that, honey. You ain't his wife. He either lied to you or he's dumber than I think he is.

She became terrified. "But, what'll I do for money? I don't have a dollar to my name!"

"Well, with your face and your figure, I can think of a lot of ways for you to make a buck, but at fifteen, you're nothing but jail bait to any man who is interested in you, legal or otherwise."

Her hands went to her cheeks. "You're not suggesting that I... "

"No, honey, I'm not. We're just talking. Oh, I hear the apes coming back from their drinking. You may have a fight on your hands to maintain your chastity tonight, but if you need any help, just call me. I'm an old hand at handling men in a bad mood."

Doug was in a surly mood as they retired to the bedroom. He said very little as he threw himself in bed. She returned from the bathroom in her pajamas and robe, making every attempt to refrain from any provocative gestures. He got up and taking his to towel and clean shorts, said, "Ah'm gonna take a bath. We'll have to talk when Ah git back."

She sat up in bed, waiting for what she was sure would be a confrontation. She attempted to read a Life magazine, but she could not pay attention to the pages. He returned from the bathroom and standing by her side of the bed. "Ah guess the situation is the same with you as it was when Ah left." It was more of a statement than a question.

She faced him squarely. "If you mean am I still having my period... for God's sake, Douglas, sometimes that lasts for a week. Of course, I'm still having it."

"Shit, what am Ah supposed to do?"

"About what?"

"You know damn well 'bout what! Ah'm gittin' ready to git on that damn troop ship and head overseas. An won't be seein' nuthin but gook women fer months 'n you ask me what! What the hell do you think Ah mean?"

"I am truly sorry but we can't do it now"

As he sat on the bed. "Cain't we jus play a little?"

"No, you'll just get excited and then we'll have trouble."

"You mean you'll have trouble... not me!"

She got out of the bed and taking a cover with her. "I think I had better sleep on the couch in the living room. It would be better for all concerned if I..."

"Oh, shit. .go 'head. Ah don't give a damn. Ah'm sorry Ah eva brought you out heer. You ain't no fun."

As she left the room in tears, she made her way to the living room. She was glad to see that Verlie and Mario had gone to bed. She needed to be alone. As she curled up on the couch, trying to arrange the covers, she sobbed to herself. Under her breath, she exclaimed. "Fun... fun! That is all he brought me out here for... fun? Is that all I'm good for? Fun?"

She pounded the sofa pillow with her fist. "Oh, my God, what have I gotten myself into? What is going to happen to me?"

CHAPTER ELEVEN

Verlie tip-toed her way about the trailer the next morning as she viewed Rainey still asleep on the couch. The two men, as usual, had left the trailer quite early in order to reach the base by seven o'clock and roll call time. She put on a cup of coffee and the perking of the pot woke the sleeping girl. She bolted up, not sure of where she was and seeing the other woman quickly looked around to see if the men were there.

Virlie, sensing her uneasiness, smiled at her. "No, don't worry about the two apes, Rainey, they're gone already. Sorry if my noise woke you up. Did you get any sleep at all?"

As she sat up, rubbing her eyes, she replied, "Some, but not too much."

Coming to the chair opposite the couch, Verlie smiled at the younger girl. "Why'd you hafta sleep on the couch? Was the fight that bad?"

"No, not really," and she hesitated to tell all the facts, "but I felt it would be a lot easier if he didn't see me. You know how they are when they want to..."

She shrugged. "Tell me about it. They're like little boys. Rainey, they don't like to be told no. Just like spoiled brats."

Rainey looked at the clock on the wall table next to the couch. "Aren't you going to work today?"

"No, I have the day off. I need to do some things," and rising and heading toward the kitchen, "do you want a cup of coffee?"

She shook her head. "No, thank you. I can't seem to develop a taste for the stuff."

Verlie smiled as she walked back with a full cup. "Well, you see, honey, some things in this world just have to be cultivated before you can enjoy them," and she gave Rainey a knowing glance.

Rainey nodded. She knew what the older woman meant. Looking like a little child, she looked up. "Verlie, can we talk? You know, I've never in my life had a woman I could talk to, you know...really talk...girl talk."

"You couldn't talk to those old maid school teachers, could you?"

"No, not about intimate things...girl-to-girl talk."

"What about the girls at school? That's where I learned most of the things I know," and she giggled, "until I started my own educational program." Then, turning serious, "What do you want to know, honey? If I can't answer it, then it's probably too dirty for you to be asking about it."

"Well, I don't really know how to put this, but...do you enjoy doing it...you know what I mean?"

She shook a cigarette out of her pack, lit up, and took a deep drag. "Well, sometimes I do and sometimes I don't. It depends on my moods and the man.

Some men know what they are doing, Rainey, and some don't. When they don't, its no fun, not for the woman. Why? Don't you like doing it?"

"I didn't enjoy it the other night. It was horrible."

The older woman digested that remark. "Rainey, was the other night your first time?"

She lowered her head, embarrassed. "Yes."

"Do you mean to tell me you came out here with him as a virgin?"

She nodded. "Yes."

"Oh, my God, Rainey. Where did you get your training as a girl... as a woman. Didn't anyone ever tell you anything?"

She shook her head. "Not much. The three school teachers only told me what to expect when I started my periods... that's all."

The older woman sat amazed as she continued to look at the young girl, then: "No wonder you hated the other night. What a recipe for disaster! An insensitive man and an unknowing and inexperienced girl... my God!"

"But, what am I to do? I feel I owe him something..."

Verlie's eyes nearly blazed. "What do you owe him? You are not his wife. He brought you out here for only one thing, girl. You'd been better off if you had given in to him back in Arkansas. It night have saved you a long trip and some heartbreak. At least, you'd know what it was like with him."

"Would it be better with some other man? For me, that is?"

"I can't answer that, Rainey. That is one thing every woman has to discover for herself. That can come in time. Right now, you have to decide what you're gonna do with Douglas Walker. That boy is getting on a boat tomorrow and going God knows where and whether he ever comes back, or not, only God knows that, too."

She nodded. "I know. I've thought about it."

"Rainey, do you love him?"

She sighed. "I don't know. I thought I did, but the boy I thought I loved is not the boy who is here in San Diego. He is different."

She smiled. "It's the Marine Corps, honey. They can turn any nice kid into a killer if you give a good drill sergeant six weeks. They become animals. They have to in order to survive where they're going."

"Do you really think it's the Corps? Will he go back to normal when he gets out?"

"I doubt it. I've never seen one improve after a few years in the Corps."

"Verlie," she hesitated, "I don't know if I should ask you this, but... how many times have you been in love?"

She shrugged, blowing out some smoke. "Hell, Rainey, I don't know if I've ever been in love. I thought I was in love about a dozen times, but," and she raised her hands, "I guess I wasn't."

"Don't you love Mario... even a little?"

"Mario was a refuge to me. The last guy I thought I loved dumped me here in San Diego. It seems he had another wife back home he forgot to tell me about. I was broke, disgusted, and lonely. Mario came to the restaurant where I worked. He had a good line of bullshit... most Italian men do, and he was a good lover... most Italian men are, but they make lousy husbands. So, don't ever marry an Italian... just live with them until the thrill wears off."

"I don't know if I'll ever like to do it. That is what is bothering me right now."

Varlie laughed. "Rainey, baby, when you meet the right man, he will ring your chimes until you think you are in a cathedral."

"Then, I don't think Doug Walker is that man. Oh, Verlie, what shall I do? I owe him something."

She got up, grinding her cigarette in the ash tray and then throwing it in the sink. Turning back to Rainey, "If your conscience hurts you and you think you owe him something, pay him back the way women have paid men back since the dawn of time- screw him before he gets on that transport."

"If I do it under those conditions, I would feel like a prostitute."

"Just close your eyes and pretend you're with someone else like Clark Gable or Tyrone Power... now there's a hunk."

She didn't hear those words because when she mentioned the word-prostitute- it burned in her. Her eventual revulsion at the profession her mother had turned to had made her swear that she could never do it unless she loved a man, no matter the consequences. Now, that she discovered she did not love Douglas Walker... really love him ..then, she felt like a harlot when she submitted to him. That was her problem. And now, in a fit of compassion, she felt she owed him something, and a more experienced woman had suggested the only means one had at hand to repay him was in the time honored fashion. But, was it right? Wasn't she prostituting her ideals? Was it any different?

On their last evening in port the two couples had agreed to have a night on the town, as far as their limited budget could be stretched. She had worried about money all day long. She had inquired of him. "Doug, I have no money of my own. Are you going to leave me any? What if I need to buy something? I can't expect to have Verlie support me. It's not right. Can't you spare something?"

He seemed contrite. "Whal, Ah guess you right. But, iffen I keep ten dollars fer the party tonight, then, Ah only got ten dollars left, but, you can have it. Ah kin always borra some money from the guys on the boat fer cigarettes. Since there ain't no whores on board, Ah don't need no money fer that," he joked. She had not appreciated the joke and she told him so.

"Whal, what the hell do you 'spect? Ah got to git mine somewhar since you always got somepin wrong with you," he taunted.

She placed her arm on his as she lowered her voice. "That is something I wanted to tell you. I think it is almost over. I think we can do it tonight... if you want to."

And so it was done. She fullfilled her "wifely" obligations under duress. She tried, thinking, perhaps if she went into the act with the right attitude, it might help. She was searching for something for herself, but she failed to find it. Nothing had changed except the pain. There was less physical pain but more emotional pain... much more, but Doug was happy as he spent his last night with her. It made no difference to him.

The huge transport with its support ships dominated the navy wharves as the time for departure had arrived. The docks were crowded with both civilians and military. The band played patriotic songs, flags waved, kisses were exchanged as the wives, mothers, and girl friends told their loved ones goodbye.

Doug and Rainey were part of the crowd. So were Verlie and Mario. Verlie shed real tears. Her tough demeanor was diluted as she hugged him tight. It might not have been a marriage made in heaven, but it was all she had at the time. Rainey, still utterly confused about her true feelings for Doug, managed to show some affection... genuine affection. He held her close, the memory of the last night still burning in him, for to him, as with most men, there is no such thing as bad sex, only good and better.

"Rainey, baby, jus tell me one thing! Ah got to know you're gonna be true to me while Ah'm gone... tell me."

She looked him in the eye. "Doug, I swear, there is not another man on the face of this earth that I want." It came out easier than she expected, and it was the gospel truth.

He seemed satisfied with that answer. "That's all Ah wanted to heer, baby. Bye... Ah love you, Rainey."

She waved, smiling, but made no reply.

* * *

The invasion of Okinawa took place on Easter Sunday, 1 April, 1945. Fifty thousand U.S. troops stormed ashore expecting fierce resistance as they attempted to take this 75 mile long island within fighter plane range of the Japanese homeland. But, the resistance did not materialize as it had on the islands farther to the south during the Pacific war. The Japanese had changed their strategy. They had lost one Pacific Island after the other as the victorious U.S. forces fought their way from the beacheads accompanied by superior naval and air forces. The new strategy was to form a defense line farther inland where they were in complete control for the time being and which had not been part of the pre-invasion bombardment.

By six o'clock of the invasion day, four divisions had been placed ashore and formed a beachhead eight miles wide and three miles deep. Resistance had been next to nothing. It seemed too easy, and some commanders envisioned a quick and easy victory, but they were wrong. After encountering some 100,000

Japanese troops further inland, it took a vicious three months of hand to hand fighting to finally take the island. The cost was high, resulting in 12,000 American dead and 35,000 wounded. The Japanese lost better than 100,000 of their troops.

Resistance was much more fierce on the southern portion of the long, narrow island. The northern half was taken much more easily as the 6th Marine Division made its way north. Doug Walker and Mario Culotta were members of the 6th Marine.

After fighting its way to the horn which occurs on the northwest coast, the Marines stormed ashore on Ie Shima, a small island just three miles off the horn. Ie Shima was a small island, just over five miles long and two miles wide, but it had an excellent airstrip. It was like a carrier deck with 100 foot high cliffs on each end of the airstrip, but it was a good airfield and the Air Force wanted in badly.

Just as had happened on the main island, the resistance was low, and the Marines felt, once again, that they had an easy conquest, but history repeated itself. As they moved from the beachhead towards the airstrip, they met with increased resistance. There were no trees to speak of on the alkaline looking terrain but there were short bushes. Mario and Doug, still close buddies, made their way up an embankment. As Mario stumbled in a hole nearly three feet deep, made by an incoming shell, he fell to the bottom head first. That saved his life, for as Doug stuck his carbine butt in the hole, saying, "Grab on to this, buddy, and Ah' ll pull you out. Come on... hurry, Ah heer shootin' on that rid...

He never finished the sentence as a sniper bullet tore off the top of his head, splattering his brains all over his buddy. Mario gasped as he saw his friend's fate, and then, he vomited at the sight he was forced to see, and then, he cried. It was the 27th of April, 1945, the last day of combat on Ie Shima. Douglas Walker's combat career had lasted 27 days, longer than most. In the case of some of the first to exit a landing craft on the Normandy beachhead, those who were killed the minute the gate dropped, their combat careers lasted less than a minute.

* * *

Since Rainey was not the legal beneficiary in the official records of Private Douglas T. Walker, she was not notified of his death. If it had not been listed in the town paper, complete with his high school yearbook photo, she might never have known.

Martha Powell, seeing the news item, suppressed a tear. After all, he had died in the service of his country, no matter her personal feelings about the young man. She had resented him for what he "did" to Rainey. Martha felt he had ruined her life, a life she had molded for eight years, and there was some justification in her position. She had debated whether or not to send the article to

Rainey, but then, she erroneously concluded that, "surely, the Government will notify her as his survivor, and besides," she added in explaining the matter to her cohorts, "I really don't have her address."

No, it was left to Lenny Walker, the most astute member of the family, and the most responsible, who would notify Rainey. She received the news badly. No matter whether she truly loved him or not, they had meant something to each other, and she had shared her body with him, a matter she considered sacred at this stage of her life. She cried long and hard as Verlie tried to comfort her with the usual platitudes. She felt confident when she intoned this one: "Sometimes, Rainey, God causes things to happen which we don't understand, but, sometimes, it is for the best."

She looked up. "How can this be the best for Doug?"

"I didn't mean him, honey. I meant for you."

The two girls were somber the days following the notice of the young marine's death, but Verlie, through economic necessity had to go to work. The small monthly stipend sent to her by the Marine Corps from Mario's pay was not sufficient to allow her to lay around doing nothing and her job as a waitress in the restaurant helped to supplement it to the extent that she was able to survive. Rainey, for the first few days, sat home alone in the trailer, moping for the most part, feeling that life, once again, had treated her unfairly. True, she was ambivalent about her love for the dead marine. She questioned, now, whether she had loved him at all. Perhaps, Martha Powell was right. Like so many young girls her age, she had confused her libidinous cravings for love, an entirely different emotion, and as she thought of her unsatisfactory experience on those two nights, she was even more confused.

Verlie allowed her the luxury of staying home doing nothing for a few days as she played out the part of a bereaved "widow", but the pragmatic and far wiser older woman knew that it was time to bring this to an end. Over tuna salad sandwiches one evening, later in the week, Verlie watched as Rainey chewed without enthusiasm, drinking her Coke more than she ate.

"Rainey, what do you intend to do? Are you going back to Arkansas?"

She laid her sandwich down, shrugging as she sipped her Coke. "I don't have anyone to go back home to. I told you... I don't have a home and I don't have a family."

Searching for a solution, Verlie took another bite, and chewing while she talked, "Are you sure those school teachers won't take you back? My God, Rainey, they mothered you for eight years. They must have some warm feelings for you... some love."

She sighed. "Oh, I guess Miss Martha loved me in her way, but I made her angry when I ran off with doug. She felt I let her down after all she did for me..."

"Hell, honey, you did," interrupted Verlie. "I would have been pissed off with you myself. Let's face it, Rainey, that ain't the smartest thing you ever did."

She placed her hands in her lap. "I know! Maybe, I'm just not too bright," and she looked up at the other woman for expected concurrence.

Verlie smiled in return. "There's nothing wrong with your brains, honey, but there is a lot wrong with your training. What was your mother like? Do you remember anything about her?"

She hesitated for a long time. She had vowed not to divulge to anyone, again, what her mother had done with her life. Now that she was older she felt more kindly towards her mother and grandmother. She attributed her mother's "fall" to the times, to the awful depression which gripped the country at that time. She blamed her grandmother for acceptance and acquiescence, and even encouragement of the choice. But in more somber and reflective moments she reasoned that many other young women, faced with the same dilemma, did not resort to the sale of their bodies to attempt to survive. No, her mother had embraced prostitution too easily and willingly.

As she mulled over these thoughts, she looked at Verlie with saddened eyes. "My mother was a whore, Verlie, until the day she died and my grandmother did nothing to discourage her."

Verlie gasped. "My God, Rainey, you poor thing. No wonder you have had a screwed up life. How did she die? How old was she... your mother, I mean?"

She shrugged her shoulders, taking another swig of the Coke. "I don't know for sure, I think she was in her early twenties," and she suppressed a sob. "I can remember her coughing in a towel and saying she had coughed up blood. I guess she had tuberculosis, or something."

"Holy shit," as she shook her head, "ain't life a real bitch, though?"

"I can't say it's been much fun," and looking like a little girl to the older woman, "is it always going to be this ways"

"Oh, no, honey! You have to get control of your life... to make something of yourself. You have to find the right man, someone you can really love, get married and have children..."

"But, no one will want me now... after what I've been through with Doug. I'm not a virgin any more..."

Verlie could not suppress a howl. "Geez, Rainey, don't be stupid! Do you really think those two or three times you did it has ruined you for any other man?"

"Well, yes, men don't want soiled goods... do they?"

"Hell, honey, don't be dumb! They won't know you're soiled goods unless you tell then so, and don't ever be that dumb."

"But, isn't that deception?"

"You bet your sweet ass it is, and you had better get good at deception, sweetheart. Those bastards will try to deceive you every chance they get. It's a way of life with them."

She sat there for a while, digesting these thought, then: "Verlie, what are you going to do? Are you going to stay here in San Diego until Mario comes home? Didn't you tell me he wrote that he would have to stay overseas at least a year until he had enough points to come home?"

"Uh, huh, that's right. He won't be home for a year, at least."

"Where's he from?"

"His family lives in San Francisco. They have a little money. They're in the produce business... typical dago operation," she smiled.

"If they have money, did you ever think of going to them? After all, they're your in-laws."

"Humph! I'd be about as welcome as a fart in a crowded elevator."

Rainey shook her head at Verlie's salty language. In spite of her disfunctional background, Rainey had not been exposed to much profanity since she left her salty grandmother. The Fosters never used any profanity to speak of, and to the three school teachers, it was anathema. As Martha Powell had described it in one of her many instructional dialogues, "Profanity is the language of the uncultured in society, it is a poor excuse for an inadequate vocabulary to express one's thoughts."

"You sure do cuss a lot, Verlie."

"I'm sorry if I upset your delicate senses, honey, but sometimes it's the only way I can really express myself to where I'm satisfied with what I said," and turning to the young woman as she rose, "look, Rainey, I've got to go to work. Why don't you come with me and watch what I do. You might like it, and who knows, that gorilla I work for might be tempted to hire you when he sees that cute little face and shapely butt..."

"Oh, Verlie, I hope if he decides to hire me, it won't be because of that."

She grunted. "Rainey, honey, you got a lot to learn, and you are lucky you got me to teach you instead of those three lesbian school teachers you been living with."

Rainey was truly shocked. "Lesbians? Surely, you don't think those women were... were... like that?"

She turned, giving her a surprised look. "I'm surprised you haven't figured that one out after eight years. Rainey, honey, when three women in the prime of life are willing to live without a man for twenty years, there is something fishy going on, believe me. I'll bet my left tit that they were knocking on each other's doors at night... huh?"

She recoiled at the thought which had never entered her mind. "I don't know. I never thought about it."

As she disappeared in her bedroom, "Well, think about it."

As Rainey rose to go to her bedroom to dress, she shook her head. "My God, Miss Martha, Miss Annie, Miss Bertha... my God! I can't believe it.! What can I believe in in this world?"

Rainey spent the entire day at work with Verlie after she had explained to the owner of the restaurant, Max Steiner, that she had just lost her "boyfriend" on Okinawa and needed cheering up. Max, a compassionate and patriotic old line Jewish grandfather had replied, "Well, okay, but make sure she keeps out of the way. I don't want her to interfere with the customers. This is a business, you know, and I run it like a business."

"Oh, don't worry, Max, the poor kid is too upset to cause any trouble. She'll just sit in that booth by the kitchen door-you know the one no one wants to sit in-and sip Cokes all day."

The old Jew grunted. "Well, okay, and Verlie, if the kid is tight for money, well, she can have three Cokes on the house, but not more than three for the day."

She patted him on the cheek and walked off. Max watched her go. He thought Verlie had the second best looking rear in the place, second only to his wife, Thalia, who outweighed Verlie by at least thirty or forty pounds, but Max liked her that way.

Rainey watched with fascination at the goings and comings of the customers, the smell of all the food, some good and some not so. She listened with interest to the repartee of Verlie and the other waitresses as they fended off the crude remarks and suggestions of the customers, most of whom were military personnel. She estimated that Verlie had had at least twelve to fifteen propositions that day, as well as had most of the other waitresses. One man offered to leave his wife for one weekend with Verlie. Verlie had retorted. "Honey, you'd better stay with what'cha got. You couldn't handle this and I'd hate to be responsible for your death at so early an age."

Rainey was apalled. She had never heard conversation like this. She came to the realization that she had a lot to learn, and who better to teach her than Verlie.

At supper in the trailer that night (Verlie had told Rainey that she never ate at the restaurant where she worked. "Hell, I don't mind serving that crap, but I won't eat it.") she asked Rainey..."well, what did you think of it... the restaurant, I mean."

She smiled. "I liked it. I wish Max would give me a job. I need to work somewhere, Verlie. I can't go on sponging off you. It's not right."

Verlie patted her shoulder. "No, it's not right and I won't put up with it forever, but until you find something, I don't mind."

"You've been a real friend, Verlie, my best."

She grunted. "Hell, that ain't no compliment, Rainey! I'm the only friend you've got."

"Well, with one like you, I don't need anymore."

"Aw, that's sweet, honey, and changing the subject, are you really interested in working in the restaurant?"

"Well, sure. Where else can I work... at my age..."

Verlie looked worried. "Oh, yeah, your age. I'm afraid that's going to be a problem. Do you have a birth certificate with you? I guess not, huh?"

"Oh, yes, I do. It's in my shoe box. Want to see it?"

"I don't think it will have any good news, but lets see it."

Returning, breathlessly, with her beat up old shoe box, she first pulled out the silver locket and showed it to Verlie.

"Oh, this is pretty, Rainey, Why don't you ever wear it?"

"I don't know. I guess I was saving it for a special occasion - or something."

As Verlie opened the locket and saw the two women, "Let me guess... your mama and grandma."

Rainey could not suppress a tear. "Uh, huh."

"Your mama was a pretty woman. You resemble her. What did your daddy look like?"

She looked away, the tears now flowing. "I don't know who he was. I'm not sure my mama knew."

The older woman was truly contrite. Taking the younger one and holding her close, "I'm truly sorry, Rainey, I didn't mean to pry... me and my big mouth."

Raising her head and sighing, she sniffed. "It's okay. I'm used to it by now. I'm a nobody with no family and I better get used to it, huh?"

"No, honey, everybody is somebody! You better get used to telling yourself that or you will end up a real nobody. I don't want to hear you say that, again, okay?"

She sniffed again, wiping her eyes and nose on a paper napkin with one hand while she continued to dig in the shoe box with the other. She felt the birth certificate and then she felt something else under it. She brought both pieces of paper out, and gave the birth certificate to Verlie to read. She looked surprised as she saw the other envelope. It was beginning to turn yellow with age. She saw the address to Nell Foster and the return address from Orella Wether, her grandmother. She never knew the envelope was in the bottom of the box. Evidentally, she surmised, Nell Foster had put it there. As Verlie reviewed the birth certificate, saying, "Hell, just as I thought, this won't help us, honey, you are fifteen like you said. That could be a problem... what's that in your hand, more official stuff?"

Rainey had completed the letter which she had never read before in her life. Strange, she thought, why didn't Nell Foster ever tell me of this, and she handed it to Verlie to read. After a moment, she turned to Rainey: "I'm no lawyer, honey, and I'm not even sure of what I'm saying, but you might own 160 acres of land in Arkansas. Did you know that?"

"No, I didn't even know it was in the box. I never saw that letter before."

"But why didn't that woman, Mrs. Foster, tell you about this?"

"I don't know. I can only guess because I was five when I went to live with her she felt I was too young to understand, and I would have been..."

"And you never looked in the box since then?"

"Well, sure, many times, but it was at the absolute bottom under the birth certificate and I just never found it. I never had any reason to look at the birth certificate after I read it one time. It only brings back bad memories to me, especially the line which states that my father is "unkown," and she once again suppressed a sob.

Patting her hand, "I know, honey, don't dwell on it. There is nothing that you can do to change that at this stage of the game, but what are you going to do about that land in Arkansas?"

"Nothing! I probably lost that land a long time ago. My grandma died a few years later... I know that, so the land went to somebody... not me."

"Those relatives she went to live with, you know them?"

She shook her head. "I don't even know their name. I can barely remember her telling my mama that she was going to live with her sister in the next county... funny how some things stay with you and others don't, huh?"

"Yeah... funny about that, but Rainey, don't you think you ought to look into this. It sight mean somenting."

She shrugged. "It takes money to look into things, Verlie. I'm living on your charity. Where would I get the money to look into this?"

Verlie shook her head."Hell, I don't know, honey. If I had it to spare I would lend it to you, but... I don't!"

She folded the letter, replacing it in the box. "It'd probably be a waste of time, anyway. Don't you have to pay taxes on land every year? I haven't paid any... for sure."

"Yeah, I guess you're right. Say, let me see that birth certificate one more time."

Opening it, she looked at the birth date- 1930. "Rainey, we have to change your birth date. You will never get a job being fifteen. Nobody will hire you at that age."

"But, you can't change a birth certificate. That's against the law... isn't it?"

"What law? Whose law? Arkansas or California? You really think anyone is going to go back to Arkansas to check on your birth certificate... hell no!"

"But, how can you do that? It is typed on there."

"That's right, and if it can be typed one time, it can be typed over again," and she smiled, "if we can find some way to erase the old letters."

"But, assuming we can do it... how old do you want to make me?"

Verlie looked her up and down, then, pulling her to her feet and walking around her two times, saying, "With your tits and your ass, you can pass for eighteen, and that is what we will make of you. How does it feel to be eighteen, Rainey? Feel any different now that you are a woman... a real woman?"

"Verlie, I feel scared about doing this. That is how I feel."

"Rainey, look at me, girl. You say you can't go back to Arkansas and you wouldn't if you could... right? And you're really only fifteen and can't get a job... right? And other than you selling that beautiful little body of yours like your mama did, there is nothing else you can do... right?"

She merely nodded her head, saying nothing.

"And other than me, you don't have a friend in the world you can count on... right?"

Once again, she nodded her head, suppressing a sob.

"Then, Rainey, honey, listen to mama Verlie for once."

CHAPTER TWELVE

"What makes you think she'll do it, Verlie? People are not too anxious to alter an official document, do you think?"

"She'll do it for me! I saved her marriage for her. She owes me a big one and she knows it."

Rainey's eyes widened. "You saved her marriages How could you do that?"

"She failed to return home one night after some fooling around with another man. Her husband was ready to kill her- he is a Marine sergeant and he would do it- but, she told him she had spent the night at my house when it was too late to drive home. He was on duty at the base and she couldn't reach him by phone, so it was my word that saved her. She finally convinced him that was the case and when I went to see him, I lied through my teeth for her. Believe me, she owes me."

"Who is she? What's her name?"

"Her name is Gertrude Olsen, a Swede from Minnesota."

"Does she have a typewiter?"

"Uh, huh, she is a secretary to a captain on the base. She's been fooling around with him, too."

"My God, is anyone on that base faithful to anyone?"

"Not hardly! It's been a long hard war, Rainey, and people get all screwed up in war time. War is not pretty on the home front, as well as for the boys in the fox holes."

"Where will we meet her?"

"She comes in the restaurant to eat now and then. That's how we met."

Curious, Rainey asked, "Why does she play around so much, with other men, I mean, if she is married?"

"Well, she is stacked, if you know what I mean, and a natural blonde with long legs. The men just won't let her alone, and I guess she likes it."

Wistfully, "I wonder if I'll ever like it that much?"

Verlie smiled. "Don't worry, some man will drive you out of your mind some day, Rainey, you'll see," and turning the Plymouth into a parking space, added, "I see her Chevvie convertible, so she's here."

Gertrude Olsen was seated in a booth having a sandwich and coffee. She waved to the two women as they entered. After introductions, Verlie, in characteristic fashion, got right down to business. Taking Rainey's birth certificate out of the envelope, she showed it to Gertrude, telling her, "It's like I said over the phone, Gertie, this poor girl can't go to work at her age. She needs to alter this thing," and as the woman perused the document, added, "what the hell, it's an Arkansas document and I can't believe anyone will question the thing here in San Diego."

Gertrude eyed Rainey with typical female thoroughness, looking especially at her bosom. "No, I think she could pass for eighteen with her build. Is this all you want... a change of birthdate?"

Verlie looked at Rainey, saying, "I guess so, huh?"

Rainey looked sheepishly at Verlie and then at Gertrude.

"Would it be much more difficult to make a change on this line?" and she pointed to the FATHER- "unknown" line.

Verlie looked at Gertrude as she read the line, and waited as she looked with compassion at Rainey. No explanation was necessary to this wordly older woman. Turning to Rainey and lowering her voice: "What do you want me to put there, honey?"

She had evidentally given the matter some previous thought. "Well, my grandfather's name was Norbet Wether. If you put him as the father, the names will match and no one living can ever complain that we stole their name."

Verlie smiled, patting her on the back. "I'm proud of you, Rainey, you're learning, honey," and turning to Gertrude: "Any problems as far as you can see?"

She looked at the type closely, shaking her head. "No, it was typed on an old Royal. We have several in our office, so matching the type will be no problem."

"And the erasures... how can you hide them so they won't be too obvious in case someone looks at it closely?"

Gertrude gave them a knowing look.' "I'll use a carbon paper when I re-type it. It always makes smudges and hides the erasures."

Verlie patted Gertrude's hand. "I'll bet you've done this before, you conniving female," and she smiled.

Gertrude grinned and grunted. "If you only knew how many times and for whom! I doctored more passes for more officers and enlisted men than I can remember."

Poor naive little Rainey looked surprised. "And it doesn't bother you?"

Gertrude giggled. "Rainey, honey, the only thing that bothers me is when I'm two weeks late for my period and my husband has been on maneuvers for three months. Now, that is something to worry me," and she rose. "Gotta go. I'll have this for you tomorrow, Verlie."

She touched the woman's hands. "Thanks, Gertrude. We'll be even after this."

"Don't be too sure, sweetie. I may need you again real soon. I've just met the most gorgeous man I've ever met in my entire life. I'm working on him now... maybe soon... who knows?" and she waved goodbye as she went out the door.

Rainey watched her leave with eyebrows raised as she turned to Verlie. "Gee, she is something, isn't she?"

Verlie giggled. "That's what the guys tell me."

Max Steiner took the birth certificate in hand as Verlie handed it to him, with Rainey standing by nervously. He turned, saying, "I've got to get my glasses. Thalia, sweetie, did you see my glasses?"

"Oh hell, Max," protested Verlie, "you don't need to put glasses on to read a date. Look, there it is, big as day... 1927. That's her birthday... 1927, which means she is eighteen years old. For God's sake, look at her. She is stacked. Do you think a girl can get this way in fewer than eighteen years. No, God doesn't work that fast Max. It takes a long time to produce something like Rainey."

Max had always considered himself a connoisseur of beautiful women even though he had never been unfaithful to Thalia in all their forty years of marriage. Some men are doers and some are talkers. Max was a talker. He felt that Verlie's challenging remarks had given him the right to peruse Rainey in great depth, which he did, to her embarrassment. Then he grinned. "Yeh," he said with some degree of lasciviousness, "yeh, she is stacked pretty good."

"Well, does she get the job or not?"

He became serious as only an old line Jewish business man can. "I'm willing to try her for a week." He raised his hands. "If she woiks out, okay, and if she don't... well," and turning towards the cash register where Thalia held sway, "Thalia, we'll need some uniforms for... for... what did you say your name was, sweetheart?"

*   *   *

Martha Powell watched through the long living room windows as the sheriff's car came up her driveway. She had inherited her mother's complete disdain for Sheriff Alvin Poulter and she did not look forward to any visit from him for any reason. He knocked on the front door with his fist instead of using the beautiful brass knocker her father had so proudly installed after the completion of the house. That further irritated her as she had Tessie answer the door, preferring not to give him the satisfaction of speaking to her, personally.

He did not remove his hat for Tessie as he would have done for a white woman. After all, any good southern sheriff had his standards in those days. Tessie, as were most colored people of that period, had no love for any law enforcement person, for they always meant bad news in some form or other.

"Yassuh?"

"Tessie, is Miz Martha home?"

"Yassuh, she home," without moving.

"Well, Tessie, would you be so kind as to ask Miz Martha to come to the door?"

Nodding, without further word, and turning to get her mistress, he shook his head as she walked away, muttering something to himself.

Rainey

She appeared at the door, holding it partially open. "Yes, Sheriff Poulter? What can I do for you?"

He now removed his hat, holding it in his hands. "Miz Powell, Ah was wond'ring iffen you knew whar Ah kin find Rainey. You rememba that litt'l gal you raised fer so long..."

She cut him off. "Of course, I remember Rainey. Do you think me senile to have forgotten her so soon?"

Defensively, "Oh, no Ma'am, Ah ain't meant that... Ah jus..."

"Why do you want Rainey? Has she done something wrong?"

"Oh, no Ma'am! At least, not as fer as Ah know. No, Ma'am, this heer lawyer from Pine Bluff... he come lookin' fer her. Ast me to try to locate her... that's all."

She was intrigued. Why would a lawyer from Pine Bluff want to locate the girl? "What did he want with her? Did he say?"

"Well, as Ah recall, it had to do with some land her grandma left her."

"Land... land? Rainey never spoke to me of any land. Are you sure?"

"No, Ma'am, Ah ain't shur. All Ah know is he wants to locate her 'n Ah knew iffen anybody in this heer county knew whar she was, it'd be you, Miz Powell."

She gave him an imperious look. "Well, you are wrong, Sheriff! I have no idea where she is."

"You ain't got no hint a 'tall?"

She was inclined to tell him no, but the matter had caught her fancy. After some thought. "You might try that Walker household. She left town with Douglas Walker some time ago. I think they went to California."

"Walker... Walker?" as if he were sniffing the air on a bird scent. "What Walkers is that?"

"You remember that boy who was killed in the invasion of Okinawa? It was in the paper."

He scratched his head. "Oh, yessum, Ah 'memba now. They live out on Route 36... don't they?"

"I wouldn't know. Is there anything else, Sheriff?"

Bowing from the waist. "Oh, no Ma'am," and as he prepared to thank her for her time, the door closed in his face. He walked out to his pickup muttering..."damn bitch. No wonder she is still 'a ole maid. Who'd want to live with that?"

* * *

As the weeks went by Rainey became accustomed to her new routine and it was so different from the life she had led before, she was fascinated by even so menial a job. It was the first time in her life she had ever made any money, or, had any to spend. She was parsimonious, too. She guarded her every penny as if it were her last. Verlie laughed at her. "Rainey, that stuff was made to spend," which brought the reply, "When you've been as poor as I've been in my lifetime, you don't ever want to get that way again... that's why."

As to the men who came to the restaurant, she began to learn what to do with them, what to say, and how to say it. She had a good teacher. Verlie had more miles on her twenty-three year old body than most her age. Verlie had instructed her on how to hassle tips. "Rainey, you got to make them think that they are the only important customers you got in the place. Smile at them, honey. It don't cost nothing, and it makes the boys excited... and generous," she quipped.

"But, what if they get the wrong idea?"

"So what? Just don't promise them anything!"

"But, they are always asking me out," and she partly blushed, "and they don't hide the fact of what they expect, either."

She giggled. "Most of them don't," and then she thought about her remark for a while, adding, "but there is one other type, Rainey, and they are the most dangerous... even for me."

Her eyebrows went up. Ever eager to learn, "What type is that?"

Verlie lit up a cigarette, settling down in her chair for a real deep "mother-daughter" talk with the younger girl. As Rainey leaned forward, for she felt this was something important.

"Well," said Verlie as she continued, "you know I always told you that it was easy to tell what the men wanted 'cause they all want the same thing."

"Uh, huh..."

"Well, that's not completely true," and she took a deep drag. "There are some men out there who are so smooth, so charming, so smart, so desireable, that the average woman doesn't stand a chance of resisting them," and as she exhaled, "not even me. They can fool me, too."

"You mean... you've met some?"

She nodded. "Just once. Oh, he played me cool. He let me believe he had no interest in me whatsoever, and all the time plotting and thinking, thinking and plotting, on just how to get me in bed."

Rainey was nearly falling out of her chair. "Well, did he? I mean, did you?"

"Hell, I guess I did. He had me just about to go crazy with desire for him, and you know how he did it. I figured it out later..."

Her eyes widened. "How... how?"

She exhaled first, speaking through squinting eyes. "He made me believe he had no interest in me at all. It nearly drove me crazy. After him teasing me that way, letting me believe he was interested, and then..."

"What?"

"He pretended he had lost interest in me. I couldn't stand it. I made a play for him like you wouldn't believe. I threw myself at him."

"Did it work?"

Rainey

She giggled. "Well, hell yes, he got what he had wanted all along and I got what I wanted. We both ended up happy and... satisfied."

"But, you said that was a dangerous type. What is so dangerous about that?

"Well... well... you see. He had me believing he wasn't interested and all the time... oh, hell, you have to go through it, Rainey, to understand what I mean."

"Was it fun?"

"Rainey, honey, it was the best. Of all the times, that was the best."

Confused. "But, what became of him? Why didn't you stay with him? Why did you let him go?"

"Oh, I forgot to tell you. He was married. They always are."

"Always!"

"Always! Remember that! Nothing that desireable is ever running around loose... never!"

She wrapped her arms around her legs as she drew them up on the chair, lowering her chin on her knees. "I wonder if I will ever meet that kind of man."

"You better hope you don't, honey. You'll just end up with a broken heart."

"Does it have to be that way?"

"Of course, it does! Think about it. He is already married, successful, with a big house, a big car, and several kids, all with braces."

"But, I don't understand. Why is it that only that kind of man fits the description you gave. Can't a single man be all those things? Someone eligible?"

"No, he can't! How long does it take a man to become successful and accumulate a lot of money? Believe me, honey, unless he inherits it from his daddy, he will take ten or twenty years, or more."

"But, that doesn't mean I won't find one like that who's still single and eligible."

"Rainey, you live in a dream world. If a man that handsome, that successful, that wealthy, can withstand ten or twenty years of avoiding the beautiful, smart, and predatory females of this world, then, sweetheart, you don't want him, because there is something really wrong with him. Why, do you know that there are expensive girl's finishing schools in this country that specialize in teaching girls how to trap men like that," and before Rainey could answer, she added, "what chance do you think girls like you and me have with men like that? None! Oh, sure, they will be happy to share a night or weekend with us, but that is all they want."

"Does it have to be like that?"

"Trust me. I've been there!"

She gave her a wistful look and said nothing more for a while.

Verlie, sensing the girl's preoccupation with her own thoughts, asked, "What are you thinking about?"

She shrugged her shoulders. "Oh, I was just thinking about you and Mario. Do you miss him?"

"Well, Rainey, what a dumb question! Of course, I miss him. He is my husband, isn't he?"

"Have you heard from him lately?"

Lighting another cigarette and inhaling deeply, "Uh, huh, I just got a letter from him. He has been assigned to the guard unit at General MacArthur's headquarters in Tokyo. He says the headquarters are in the Imperial Hotel, He says it was designed by a famous American architect named Frank Lloyd Wright. Did you ever hear of him?"

"No, I never did."

"Me, neither, but, anyway, Mario said he might be coming home sooner than he thought. They have lowered the point system again, so, maybe..."

"I bet that will make you happy, huh?"

"Oh, I'll be glad to see the big ape again, but I'm sure you've guessed by now that this marriage was not made in heaven. As I told you before, he was a refuge for me. I needed a man to take care of me and he needed a woman to take care of him. It's as simple as that."

She gave Verlie a sheepish look. "Do you think he has been faithful to you in Japan?"

She laughed. "Hell, no. That man couldn't be faithful if his life depended on it. He writes and tells me about him and his buddies visiting the Geisha houses. He had the nerve to tell me that Japanese women know how to please a man better than American women."

She looked amazed. "And that doesn't bother you?"

"What?"

"His being unfaithful to you?"

She gave the younger girl a discerning look. "Rainey, you don't think I've been faithful to him, do you?"

She looked embarrassed. "No, that is what I've been getting to. I know you've been seeing other men. I don't know if you're doing it or not... you know what I mean, but..."

Verlie smiled. "Then, let me put your mind at ease. Hell, yes, I've been doing it. Do you think I am willing to go without it for a year? You've got to be kidding! Maybe you can live in your virginal state, but I am not willing to. I've asked you time and time, again, to let me fix you up with some nice young kid, but, no, you have some misplaced idea of morality that I don't understand. Just because you had a sour experience your first time around doesn't mean it will always be that way. Hell, Doug Walker was a green hillbilly kid who didn't know anything. There are men out there who do."

"I am just not ready. I now realize that I was too young when I left Arkansas with Doug. I made a big mistake. I don't want to make another one with some other boy."

"Hell, Rainey, I ain't talking marriage, honey, I'm just talking good times... and a little excitement, if you know what I mean."

She seemed reflective. "Maybe, later. Give me a little more time. Remember, I'm only sixteen..."

Verlie laughed. "Really? How come your birth certificate says you're nineteen?"

Rainey gave her a sheepish look. "You know why."

Verlie rose, yawning. "I'm going to take a nap. I've got a date tonight with a real hunk and I need my rest," and turning to the young girl, "are you sure you don't want him to bring a friend for you?"

"No, thank you. I'm going to the movies tonight with Lenora from the restaurant. We're going to see Clark Gable and Greer Garson in something or other."

"Humph... sounds like fun," with some sarcasm, then turning to her, "do you have any idea what time you will come home?"

"I don't know... why?"

"Well, my date and I might just be in the bedroom when you get home, so don't make any attempt to come in to talk to me." She giggled. "I'll be busy."

"Oh... I understand. I'll be quiet."

Verlie gave her a mischievous grin. "It's not your noise I'm worried about. It's ours."

As she watched her friend go into her bedroom, Rainey became reflective. She was leading a lonely life without any male companionship, she knew that. But, her ill-fated attempt at happiness with Doug Walker had ended in disaster. Not only had she lost her virginity, she had lost her self respect to some extent. She had been too easy a conquest for him, and she vowed not to repeat it with some service man on a weekend leave looking for a good time.

As she lay in bed later that night, she thought of Verlie who could so easily give in to her cravings with a man she hardly knew. But, on further reflection, maybe that was the best way in her case. Still being married to Mario, she could not afford to became involved in a serious and long lasting relationship. No, if she were going to do it, her way was the best way- the most practical way. She clutched her pillow, embracing it as if it were a lover, and it was in this manner that she finally fell to sleep sometime later.

She had no idea what time it was when she first heard the noise of two people in the living area of the trailer. She could hear the tinkling of ice in glasses, the muffled sounds of talking, some of it cooing and some of it laughter. She lay awake, embarrassed that she could hear them. She rolled over, trying to go to sleep so as not to hear, but sleep eluded her.

Finally, she heard Verlie say in a husky voice, "Come on, it's getting late. We're just wasting time," and then, she heard the bedroom door closed shut. In short time, she could hear the muffled sounds of people moving around, the

Lloyd J. Guillory

creaking of the bed, the moans and groans of passions being satisfied. She buried her head in the pillow. She felt she was invading their privacy, but it was more than that. The sounds of the amorous couple aroused in her emotions she had been trying to suppress for the past year. She longed to be held... to be loved, and for the first time in months, she cried herself to sleep.

CHAPTER THIRTEEN

Rainey awoke with a start as she remembered the sounds of the night before. She raised her head to hear better, to determine if the amorous couple were still at it. She heard nothing, and thinking they were probably still asleep, she eased out of bed. The trailer had only one bathroom and fearing that perhaps the strange man might be using it, she tip-toed to her bedroom door and listened. She heard nothing. She quietly opened her door and seeing the bathroom door open, she made her way towards it.

She reluctantly entered the kitchen to make coffee, fearing that the perking pot would awaken the couple, but before she could worry further, a sleepy Verlie appeared coming out of her bedroom. She made her way to the kitchen table and flopped in a chair, placing her head on her hands, saying nothing.

Rainey waited a while, then, feeling she had to say something, meekly said, "Morning, Verlie," and her gaze went to the bedroom door as if she expected to see the man emerge.

Verlie saw her look in that direction. "If you're lookin' for him... he's gone," and lifting her head, "I had to get him out before daylight, what with that old inquisitive hen living next door just ten feet away. That's all I need is for her to know what is going on," and she yawned. "God, but I'm tired and sleepy. That guy is an animal! I thought he'd never wear out."

Rainey, now completely embarrassed, said nothing in reply as she mentally pictured the goings on.

Verlie continued. "I hope we didn't keep you awake. I asked him to be quieter, but..." and she shook her head.

Defensively, Rainey shook her own head. "Oh, no, I didn't hear a thing," she lied, and she rose to get some coffee, asking Verlie..."can I pour you a cup?"

Without looking up, "Please," and getting up to go to the bathroom, "I've got to tinkle. I'll be back."

Yelling out, Rainey asked, "Are you going to work today?"

She stopped at the bathroom door. "Hell, yes, I can't afford to miss a day's work because of last night," adding..."now, if I charged for it, that would be different. I could afford to stay home," and she went into the bathroom.

The remark pained Rainey as she thought of her mother and her tragic, short, and misspent life. She rose and went to her bedroom to dress for work.

As the two women drove the hilly road down to the restaurant, neither said very much. Verlie was reliving her amorous moments with her new lover and Rainey was deep in thought about Verlie's unfaithfulness to her husband who was overseas. After a while, she turned to Verlie. "Are you going to see him, again?" It was a fair question because Verlie seldomed saw them again, believing that familiarity bred contempt and trouble.

Lloyd J. Guillory

Without taking her eyes off the road. "Hell, yes! I've been looking for someone like him for months. I'm not through with him, yet," and turning to the young girl, "he's what you need right now in your life, Rainey... someone who can teach you to appreciate what you have and what to do with it."

She was embarrassed. She turned away, saying nothing, but thinking very hard. Seeing she did not want to discuss the matter, Verlie began to hum a tune as she drove on, smiling from time to time as she looked at Rainey.

Max was waiting for them as they entered. He appeared nervous as he approached the two women, clearing his throat. Thalia was immediately behind him as she generally was. He went up to Rainey, looking around to ensure that none of the customers were listening. "Rainey, this came for you after you left work yesterday. It's a registered letter... from Arkansas. I signed for it. The postman said he ain't going way up in those hills to that trailer park to find you since you girls both get your mail here at the restaurant..."

She became apprehensive as she looked at the letter. "A registered letter from Arkansas. Who would write me a registered letter?"

Max pointed to the envelope. "Well, I ain't opened it, Rainey, if that is what you think, but look, it's from a lawyer down there," and getting serious, he touched her arm. "You ain't in no trouble with the law down there, are you? I don't want no trouble."

Verlie, impatient as ever. "Hell, Rainey, the only way you're gonna find out what it says is to open it... go on... it ain't gonna bite you."

Max closed in. "I got a registered letter once. They ain't never good news. That bastard told me he was gonna sue me. I don't like registered letters, especially from a lawyer."

Rainey looked at the return address. It was from Justin P. Holstead, Attorney at Law. She nervously tore it open as Verlie, Max and Thalia looked over her shoulder. Max moved Verlie. aside so he could read it himself as he adjusted his glasses.

Dear Miss Wether:

I am writing to you on behalf of a Mr. Otis Hotard, who is a land man for some company. It concerns the 160 acres of land left to you by your maternal grandmother, Orella Wether, or, at least, it was her intent to leave you the land. The title is very cloudy at this time and it will take some legal action to clear it.

I do not want to go into detail by means of this letter. It is too complicated, I am merely, now, attempting to make contact with you. I am requesting that you get in touch with me as soon as possible. It is my understanding that this gentlemen, or the company he represents is prepared to purchase this land from you if the title can be cleared.

I will await your reply.

Sincerely,

Justin P. Holstead, Attorney-at-law

No one said anything for a while, but finally, Max, who could smell the faint odor of money a long way off touched her arm. "Rainey, sweetheart, do you know about this? How much land did he say your grandma left you? This could mean money for you."

Verlie pressed in. "Oh, Rainey, honey, maybe this is the break you've been waiting for... geez... honey. What ' cha gonna do about it?"

She looked bewildered. "I don't know what to do," and turning to her employer, "what should I do, Max?"

He placed a fatherly arm around her, leading her to a booth for she looked pale and weak. "I don't know what to tell you what to do until I know more about it. Tell me all you know."

So, she related the contents of the letter she had found on the bottom of the old shoe box, a letter she had paid scant attention to all these years, believing that the hard scrabble 160 acres which had brought her family nothing but misery, would bring her the same thing. She had never perceived it as a thing of value.

Max listened attentively, then, "bring the letter to me so I can read it for myself. You're so young, sweetheart, old Max wants to make sure you ain't cheated out of nothing. You know you can't trust anybody anymore since the war. The country has gone to pot," and Thalia nodded in agreement.

It was too difficult for Rainey to concentrate on her job that day. She made so many mistakes with so many orders, that a solicitous and understanding Max finally said, "Rainey, sweetheart, take the rest of the day off before you ruin my business. Go home and get the letter. It will give you something to do and get you out of here before I lose all my customers."

She nodded, knowing he was right. "But, I can't go home without Verlie. She has the car. I don't have one."

Max nodded with understanding. "But, you can drive, can't you?

"Yes," she hesitated in replying.

"Well, then, you take my car and go... go. Thalia, sweetheart, give Rainey the keys to the car. No, not the Cadillac, Thalia, the keys to the pickup truck."

As Max perused the letter later in the day, he considered its contents for a while. "Now, Rainey, I ain't no lawyer, but this is not too binding a document as far as I can tell. Your grandma should have gone to a real good lawyer, preferably a good Jewish lawyer, and had a real will drawn up..."

"But," replied Rainey in a quivering voice, "there is no doubt she wanted me to have the land. There was no one else to get it."

He gave her a discerning look. "That may be true, but who has had the land since that time. How long has it been? Over ten years? Somebody had to pay taxes on the land all this time or you would have lost it by now."

She shook her head. She simply did not know.

"But," continued Max, "that land man must have some reason to believe you have some claim on the land. He would not be wasting his time on you if he didn't think so," and touching the young bewildered girl on the arm, "Rainey, sweetheart, you have got to go to Arkansas to look into this."

She became despondent. "I don't have any money to go to Arkansas. I have no place to live when I get there."

He considered the matter for a while, for Max was not the easiest man in the world to separate from his money, but after a while, he reluctantly said, "Well, perhaps I could lend you some travel money... for a while," and he nearly choked on the words.

She became more enthusiastic and her eyes lit up. "But, do you really think I should go? It's a long way."

He nodded. "Yes, sweetheart, I think you should go."

"Well, okay, but I insist on paying you back... with interest."

He smiled. "I insist on it, too... with interest."

She wrote the attorney that she would go to Arkansas as soon as she could make travel arrangements. She was not too anxious to return to the place of her birth and early childhood. It held no pleasant memories for her. On the contrary, she concluded, in retrospect, she had not been happy while there.

Verlie was truly excited with what she perceived to be good news for her young friend. "Just think, Rainey, you might own 160 acres of land..."

She grunted. "I don't get too excited about that. If my grandma had to talk my mama into becoming a whore in order to survive there, what the hell makes you think it is something valuable for me?" (She had begun to season her language with a little salt, due to Verlie's influence on her)

"Well, I don't really know. But, if that man is interested in buying it from you, he must have some reason to think it is valuable. Perhaps, he represents some farmers who want to farm on it."

She shrugged. "I wish them good luck if that is what they want to do with it. My family damn near starved to death on the place."

"But, that was years ago, honey. Things have changed since then."

Pragmatically, she replied. "Dirt is still dirt."

"Oh, well, you'll know more about it when you get down there."

Wistfully, "I wish you were coming with me. I'm scared, Verlie."

She patted her hand. "Now, Rainey, honey, Mama Verlie has taught you a lot in the past year. Why, you're getting' to be as mean and ornery as I am... you're even beginning to cuss like me."

She blushed. "I know! Like you say, sometimes there just isn't any other way to make a point."

"True... true," Verlie smiled in reply. "I have a date tonight, Rainey. I just wanted to tell you in advance in case you want to make some plans of your own," and turning with eyes ablaze, "say, why don't we celebrate your good fortune? Why don't you let me have Bruce get you a date for tonight? Come on, we'll make it a foursome... what do you say?"

Rainey shook her head "You know if Bruce the animal gets me a date, that boy will expect the same thing that Bruce does."

She gave her a demure look. "Is that so bad? Maybe, that is what you need, Rainey... some good lovin' for a change."

She gave it a lot of thought. She was half-way tempted to say yes. She knew she would probably have to cuddle her pillow and cry herself to sleep again that night, but she shook her head. "No, not tonight. Maybe when I get back from Arkansas."

As Verlie rose to go back to work, she replied. "Suit yourself, honey, but if I need help with the animal tonight, I'm going to send him into your bedroom."

Rainey grinned. "You do that!"

She had returned to the restaurant to discuss her leaving with Max, to iron out the details. He had not given her the money as yet, telling her he preferred to keep it on interest until the last minute. Thalia came over to see what was going on, but stopped to answer the ringing phone.

Hard of hearing and refusing to wear any type of hearing aid, she practically yelled into the mouthpiece..."WHO? VERLIE? NO, SHE AIN"T HERE ! WHO IS THIS? MARIO? IS THAT REALLY YOU, MARIO? WHO? RAINEY? YES, SHE'S HERE... RAINEY, SWEETHEART, IT'S MARIO. HE WANTS TO TALK TO YOU."

Surprised beyond belief, she slowly walled to the phone, and wispering to Thalia..."Did you say, Mario? Verlie's husband, Mario?"

Handing her the receiver. "He's the only Mario I know."

She tried to collect her wits. She stuttered into the speaker: "Mario? I thought you were in Japan. What are you doing here? Where are you?"

"I got to come home early. I'll tell you all about it later. Where's Verlie? I called the trailer. She ain't there!"

She felt her heart come into her mouth as she nearly choked a reply..."Verlie? She took the day off, said she didn't feel well." Thalia listening nearby, raised her eyebrows. She was accustomed to her waitresses lying to their dates and or boyfriends, but this was a husband.

"Well, where is she? Is she at home or not?"

She shook with fear. "I guess so, Mario. I'm not sure," as her brain raced. Where was Verlie? She had said she had a date with Bruce that night. My God, she thought. I've got to call her... to try to find her. But, where? I don't know where they were going!

Mario continued as she grasped for answers: "I want to go to the trailer to clean up so I can be ready for Verlie when she comes home. I've been on a damn cargo plane for 36 hours and I smell like a goat. Do you have the car or does she have it?"

She replied, nervously. "No, I have it."

A moment of silence. "Well, if you have the car, how did she get home?"

"Well... well, I told you, she didn't feel well, so... so, a girl from the restaurant drove her home... or somewhere..."

"What the hell do you mean... somewhere?"

"I don't know, Mario. I don't know where she is." She felt the thing was getting out of hand. She knew that the hot-blooded Italian had a ferocious temper and she wanted no part of it.

He persisted. "Rainey, I need transportation. Can you come to the base to pick me up?"

Frightened, she replied, "Well, I don't know if Max will let me go. We're kinda busy right now..."

"Bullshit, Rainey! It's three o'clock in the afternoon. That place is dead at this time. Do you think I'm stupid? Are you coming to pick me up or not?"

Desperate for answers and not having any, she meekly replied, "Yes, I'm coming, Mario. I'll be there in about thirty minutes."

"Thirty minutes? Why so long? Oh, hell, come on! I'll be waiting for you by the north gate so you won't have to come on the base. See you." The phone clicked dead.

She made one last attempt to call Verlie at every place she could think of, but no luck. "She just left," she was told.

After a hasty and perfunctory greeting to the marine who was anxious to get home to his beloved, he rode in silence for a while, looking out at the parched hills leading out of the base as they climbed towards the trailer park community.

He looked over at Rainey. "How long has she been sick?"

"Oh, just today. She came down with a bug, I guess..."

He shook his head, muttering mostly to himself. "She picked a hell of a time to get sick with me coming hone after a year of being overseas without it. She picked a hell of a time."

Had Rainey not been privy to other information, she might have felt sorry for him. He was quiet for a while, then, "I haven't had a chance to talk to you about Doug. Rainey. You know I was there when he got it..."

She nearly shouted. "Not now, Mario... please! I don't want to hear about it... please!"

"Geez, I'm sorry. I thought you..."

"Well, I don't. I want to forget it."

He muttered in a low breath. "Ain't that the shits? A poor slob gets his brains blown out fightin' for his country and what does his woman say," and he mocked her..."I don't want to hear about it. What a crock!"

She started to reply, but instead, she looked at him with tears in her eyes. He did not like to see any woman cry, so he turned to look at the Pacific, so calm and so blue, below them. "Okay... okay... I'm sorry," and he rearranged the two duffle bags at his side, as if to give him something to do.

Rainey became more apprehensive as she neared the trailer court. Mario had become quiet, saying nothing after their heated exchange about Doug. Her brain was racing, trying to find some way to keep him away from the trailer until she could ascertain if Verlie was there, or not. She smiled at him. "Are you hungry? I know you've been travelling for a long time and since Verlie is not home, well, we could stop for something to eat if you want."

"Nah! I had a bite while I was waiting for you to pick me up."

"Oh, okay, it was just a suggestion."

She turned onto the main road leading into the trailer court and became even more apprehensive as she turned off into the side road which led to their trailer. Mario sat up, staring towards his trailer. Her heart sank as she saw the car there, Bruce's Chevrolet. Her breath began to quicken as she looked at Mario's face to judge his reaction.

As he continued to look in that direction. "I see a strange car in the parking space. I wonder if she has company."

Desperate for diversion, Rainey replied, "Maybe, that's the girl who drove her back."

As he took hold of his two duffel bags to alight. "Maybe."

Rainey, now certain that Verlie and Bruce were in the trailer, could hardly breathe as she followed Mario up the walk. He opened the front door and seeing no one in the living area, placed his finger on his lip. "Shooo... be quiet. Maybe, she's asleep. We'll just sneak in so we don't wake her up."

Rainey nodded, too panicky to even speak as she looked around. The fact that the couple was not in the living area was even nore ominous to her. If they were not there, then, they were in the bedroom.

As Mario made his way forward, he could hear muffled sounds coming from the bedroom. Ever the cautious marine, he once again signalled to Rainey to be quiet. He quietly went to the bedroom wall, placing his ear against the thin door. As Rainey watched his face contort, she knew he had instantly sized up the situation, and quite correctly. He slowly and quietly cracked open the bedroom door to confirm his suspicions. The amorous couple, locked in embrace amid sounds of moans and groans, heard nothing. Rainey watched in absolute horror as Mario turned away from the scene, his face red with rage. He walked back into the living room and made his way to his duffle bags lying on the floor. He bent over and extracted a .45 caliber service revolver, and wrapping it in a pillow from the couch, turned back to the bedroom. Rainey watched in horror, saying in choked tones, "Oh, no, Mario, for God's sake... no!"

He brushed her aside, putting his forefinger in her face, whispering, "You be quiet or I'll kill you, too."

She gasped audibly, but he once again cautioned her to be quiet as he tip-toed to the bedroom door and without slowing up burst into the room. This caused Verlie to look up and with a look of stark terror on her face, had only time enough to scream out..."No, Mario... no! Please..." Two muffled shots rang out from the pillow encased gun and then all was quiet as the man's head fell on Verlie's face. The bullet had entered her face, just under the chin, blowing the top of her head off, splattering the wall behind the bed. His wound had entered the back of his head, blowing his face off. Mario walked calmly to the bed. He had no idea who this man was he had just killed and he was curious. He grabbed his hair in order to raise the head, but seeing a face now without recognizable features, he let in drop in disgust, and speaking to his dead wife as if she could hear: "Well, Verlie, baby... I hope it was worth it!" and he staggered back, grabbing the bedroom door for support. Walking almost as would a drunk man, he made his way back to the living area. His rage had now subsided and reality began to set in. He was now conscious of the horror of what he had done. He made his way to the couch with the gun still in his hand, but hanging loosely at his side, and fell back on the cushions. He looked at Rainey as she lay on the floor in a fetal position, her hand in her mouth, sobbing hysterically now. She looked up at Mario, fearful that he would now kill her. She was the only witness to his crime. She recoiled- eyes ablaze with horror and fear as she continued to look up at him. Ignoring her, he arose and stood for a moment, thinking. He walked to each side of the trailer, looking out the windows, assessing the reaction of the trailer park. He saw no one moving. He was grateful that it was still before five, the time at which most of the working class people who lived in the trailer park would return home. He sat near the distraught girl for a while. He was still breathing hard, the adrenalin still flowing in profusion. He continued to look at her as she lay there whimpering and sobbing, shaking. His brain was racing. He had not planned on this and he had no plan of action, but trained as a killer, he did not panic. These were not the first humans he had killed, he thought... and they deserved it.

He reached down and took Rainey by the wrist, so tight that she winced in pain. She was certain that he would now kill her since she was a witness to his crime. He pulled at her wrist, saying, "Rainey, I want you to listen to me. I just killed two people and I wouldn't hesitate to kill you too if you don't do what I say."

She only whimpered in reply as she sat up due to his pulling on her arm. He put his finger in her face for emphasis. "Now, you listen to me, girl. This is how it's gonna be. You and I are the only two people who know what happened to this couple. That means if someone else finds out about it, then, it is you who spilled the beans."

She tried to say something, but the words would not come out. He continued. "I've made up my mind what we're gonna do... you and me, so you listen to me. We're gonna set here until tonight... after all the people in this trailer court are asleep and then, we're gonna burn this place." He heard her moan. "Yes, we're gonna burn this trailer and that deceiving bitch of a woman and her lover with it."

"This time, she moaned audibly, shaking her head as if to signify... NO.

He nodded. "Oh, yes, we are, and you're gonna help me do it so if they ever catch me", you will be named as a co-conspirator. A partner in crime. I'll say that you and I were lovers and you helped me get rid of your competition."

She shook her head in protest. "On, yes, baby, that is the way it's gonna be! Now, you go and pack all your clothes. You are going on a trip... far away from San Diego and you are never coming back. Do you understand me? Now, you go and pack before I lose my temper."

Fearful of her life, she rose and went into the bedroom, sobbing and shaking her head as she went. Mario went to the fridge and opened a beer. As he took his first swig, he stood at the bedroom door looking at the two corpses, shaking his head. It had all happened so fast that he, too, found it hard to believe. An hour before he had imagined his reunion with his wife and looked forward to a night of wild love making, and now, he looked at a cold, blood splattered body. He walked closer to the bed for one last look at a woman he had loved, but turned away, revulsed.

He returned to the living room and sat waiting for Rainey to come out. Fearing she might try to escape through a window, he went and opened the bedroom door. She was sitting on the bed, crying, her head shaking in total disbelief. He went to the bed and slapped her face, not hard, but hard enough to startle her. "I told you to get packed. Now, dammit, do it." She nodded and resumed her packing.

In a few minutes, she wandered back to the living room. Slightly more composed, now, she stood before him. Mustering up more courage than she really had, she asked, "What are you going to do with me, Mario?"

Without looking up. "I told you you're gonna take a trip."

"Who with? Are you taking me with you?"

"Oh, no, baby! The last thing I want is for you to be seen with me. They're gonna be lookin' for you and me. They gonna swear that you and I had a thing going and that's why we killed them."

She started to protest that his position had no logic, but one look in his eyes discouraged her from trying to point out logic to him. She sobbed. "I was going to leave for Arkansas in a day or so, anyway."

"You were? Well, now that is great news. Does anyone here in San Diego know about that?"

Lloyd J. Guillory

She nodded. "Yes, Max does... and Thalia, too. He was going to lend me the money to go."

His brain was racing fast. "You don't need Max's money, now. I don't want you talking to Max any more."

"But, I can't leave town without his money. I need to get the money from him for the trip."

"No, you don't! I told you I don't want you to talk to anyone any more. I've got money. I drew my discharge pay at the base. I'll give you enough money to get to Arkansas..."

"But, I'll need some living money. I don't have family there any more."

He reached in his pocket, and peeling off some bills and counting them, he said, "Here's two hundred. That ought to get you to Arkansas in style."

She reluctantly accepted the money, knowing she really had no choice. She did not want to see Max either. She could not have faced him, anyway, without breaking down. "But, what'll I tell Max? He'll be curious why I changed my mind."

"Call him on that phone. Tell him you've had a change of plans and you're leaving tonight... go on... call him."

She dialed the number and between sobs exclaimed to the solicitous old Jew why she had changed her mind. He listened and detected her sobs. "Why are you crying, sweetheart? Tell old Max."

She hated to lie to him. "I've had a death in my family back there and I have to leave right away. They don't want to keep the body too long."

"Oh, I'm so sorry to hear that, but where did you get the money?"

"They sent it to me."

"Oh, I see. Well, good luck, and if you ever need a job, come see old Max. You're a good kid."

She sobbed at that. "Thanks Max. I'll miss you."

CHAPTER FOURTEEN

Having made the telephone call as instructed, Rainey once again sat on the floor with her head on arms folded under it. Her mind could not accept the events of the past few minutes. It had all happened so fast. She had difficulty in believing that her friend Verlie was dead. She made an attempt to rise, with Mario's head snapping up. "Where're you going?"

"I have to go to the bathroom. I want to get some aspirin. My head is about to split..."

"Oh... well... okay, but don't you try nothing funny like trying to get out the bathroom window. I ain't no fool, you know."

As she made her way to the bath which was in a narrow hall opposite the bedroom in which Verlie lay dead, she inched her way towards the open door. Peeking in and seeing the dead couple lying in their mortal embrace, she gagged, and her hands went to her mouth as she raced to the bathroom. Mario could hear her vomiting sounds as she bent over the toilet and emptied her insides, competely revulsed by the gory sight she had witnessed. He merely shook his head.

After she had completed her vomiting, she sat on the toilet, attempting to gather her thoughts. She knew this whole matter was insane, but it had happened, and nothing she could do would change it one bit. Verlie, her one true friend the past year was gone. Although she had not approved of Verlie's affair with Bruce- she had never met him in person- still, he was a human being and now he was gone. She sat, shaking her head, as it rested in her hands which in turn rested on her knees. Mario, feeling she was taking too long in the bathroom, opened the door without knocking, and seeing the girl sitting on the toilet, said, "Oh, excuse me. I just wanted to see how you were doing."

She gave him a stare which implied more bravery than she really possessed. "Would you please get out of here and close that door!" He meekly complied.

When she returned to the living area she was pale and weak. She flopped in a chair as she watched him go to the fridge for another beer- his third. As he popped it open, he asked, "Do you know if there are any candles in this place?"

She looked surprised and already in distrust of his irrational mind, replied, "What do you want to do with candles?"

He burped some beer gas as he said. "I don't have to explain to you what the hell I want with them. Do you have any?"

She nodded towards the kitchen. "Verlie..." and she stopped for a while, continuing..."there are some in that kitchen drawer. The lights are always going out, so..." She did not finish, wondering why she bothered to explain to him.

He rose and retrieved two candles from the drawer. One had been partially burned and was only about four inches long. The other was new and was its full length of ten inches. He took it and placed it in his shirt pocket. He went to the waste basket and retrieved yesterday's newspaper. He extracted most of it and laid it on the kitchen counter. He then proceeded to light the candle and let some hot wax drop on the paper until it was high enough to form a base to hold up the candle once it cooled. Satisfied, he left it on the counter and returned to his place on the couch. Rainey had watched all this, saying nothing although she assumed he was making a torch in order to burn the trailer as he had threatened.

She began to become a little more sure of herself, seeing that he had calmed down from his irrational high during the murders. She looked at him and with her voice still quivering a little, softly said. "You know you'll never get away with this, Mario. They'll know you did it... especially when they find out you just got home from overseas."

He smiled at her. "Oh, no, baby, they'll never hang this one on old Mario," and taking another swig, continued, "You're right about one thing. They're gonna think I did it, but you don't know the Marine Corps, Rainey, honey. You know the motto-Semper Fidelis- you know what that means- always faithful..."

She looked at him with disdain. "And what the hell does that have to do with this," pointing to the bedroom.

He smiled again. "Always faithful means how us marines feel about one another. I can produce at least twelve marine buddies who will swear on their mother's graves that I never left that base while this thing happened. We were having a poker game and I won all this money," and he extracted a roll from his pocket and waved it at her.

She pondered his statements for a moment and she knew he was right. She knew enough about marines to know that they would die for one another, much less lie. She regarded him with eyes filled with hatred. "And what about me? What is going to happen to me?"

He lowered his bottle of beer and thought about the question. "Well, Rainey, after you get on that bus and head for Arkansas, they ain't even gonna worry about you. Besides, your friends Max and Thalia will gladly testify in your behalf and convince the police that you had nothing to do with this mess."

She contemplated that for a moment. "Then, who did it? They'll want to know, won't they?"

"Nobody did it to them. They did it to themselves," and he half giggled. She felt he was getting a little drunk

"I'm afraid I don't follow you."

"It's simple. They got themselves drunk and fell asleep after all that strenuous exercising they were doing. Hell, everybody knows that Verlie smoked like a smokestack. She fell asleep in bed with a lighted cigarette in her hand."

"You think they'll believe that?"

"When I get through, they will," and he got up to go to the kitchen cabinet where he knew they used to keep their liquor. Reaching in, he extracted a bottle of Seagram Seven. "Aha," he said cheerily, "just what I was looking for. We now have all we need to convince them," and looking at his watch, he returned to the living room. He returned to the couch and she still sat on the floor.

"What time is it?" she asked.

"It's nearly seven. Most all these people have come home and there still ain't nobody poking around. I guess they didn't hear the noise after all," and he smiled.

"How long do we have to stay here? This place gives me the creeps. I can't stand it much longer."

As he brought the beer to his lips, "Aw, Rainey, baby, you got to learn to relax. Come on here and sit with ole Mario... come on, baby."

Sensing his intentions, she repelled at the notion. "I'll stay where I am if you don't mind."

His demeanor changed. His mouth became twisted with anger as he replied, "But, I do mind, damn you. I said for you to come and sit by me," and he patted the couch seat next to him. "Come on, baby, we got a few hours to kill and I'm getting in the mood. It's been a long time since I've done it with an American gal. All I've been looking at for the past year is some squint-eyed gals... come on."

Now fully convinced of his intentions, she was sickened at even the thought of it. She said to him in a matter of fact manner, "You don't seriously believe that I would even consider that with you... and at a time like this... after what you've just done... are you crazy?"

She had said the wrong words to this still enraged man. He grabbed her by the wrist and dragging her to her feet, said, "Come on! You get into that bedroom and take your clothes off. I'll show you what you've been missing, Rainey, baby... come on," and he yanked on her arm. She pulled back, her face showing both hate and surprise. She had not expected this, especially after what he had done. She had expected some remorse... some words of regret, but not this.

He let go of her arm, and with a look of anger and rage, he pointed his finger at her with one hand and reaching for his gun with the other, he said in a quiet tone. "Now, you listen to me, girl, we can do this one of two ways- the easy way or the hard way. Which do you prefer?"

She looked at the gun in his right hand. She had no reason to believe that he would not use it again. She now reasoned that he was driven by a mixture of forces- drunkeness and desire, and an attempt to punish Verlie for her unfaithfulness. How better to punish her than with her best friend?

She tried, once again, to muster up some courage as she held back. "You'll never get away with this, Mario. I swear I'll charge you with rape if you force me to do this."

He laughed at her, relaxing his grip on her wrist for a while. "Rainey, honey, think about it for a while. Who you gonna complain to? The police? After what you just participated in? Aw, come on, girl, be realistic. The police are the last people in this world you want to talk to."

She considered his works carefully. She knew he was right. She could complain to no one about this if he chose to do it. She had no recourse, but, yet, she could not surrender to him that easily. She just couldn't. She tried one more tactic. She would appeal to him from a strictly feminine standpoint, assuming he had any chivalry. Looking up at him with pleading eyes. "Mario, I'm having my period. We can't do it, now."

He smirked. "Rainey, you think I give a damn about that," and he pulled her up by her arm. "Now, listen, girl, I'm through talking to you. You get yourself in that bedroom and take your clothes off," and as he shoved her forward, adding, "and I mean right now."

She looked around for help as if it were forthcoming, and seeing none, she walked to the bedroom, sobbing as she went. She stood at the side of the bed for a moment, doing nothing. He had come along side her. "I said to take your clothes off, Rainey," and he slapped her across the face. The tears began to flow as she began to disrobe herself. As he began to remove his own clothing, his earlier words came back to her, "I've been on a damn cargo plane for 36 hours and I smell like a goat." His words were confirmed and his odor repulsed her even more. He eyed her with relish as she exposed her young and shapely body to him. He leered at her and she felt humiliated to the depths of her being. She tried not to look at his naked body but he forced her to do so. He shoved her down on the bed and for the next two hours she was forced, once more, to participate in an act which she had not wanted, had not encouraged nor had she responded to any way. She just lay there, humiliated and disgusted that the one thing in this world she had looked forward to during all her formative years, a thing which she had always imagined would be beautiful and rewarding, was an act of complete degradation and abuse.

His animal passions having bean satisfied, he rolled over on his back, and with a final act of insult, intoned, "Rainey, that has got to be the worst piece I've ever had in my whole life. Doug was right! He said it was lousy, too, but I figured he was too young to know better.."

She ignored his insult. She looked at him with unadulterated hatred, saying quietly, "If I had the gun in my hand, I would gladly kill you right now, you son-of-bitch."

"Well, you ain't got the gun, so get out of bed and get dressed. The party is over. I hope you enjoyed it."

She was only too glad to be able to replace her clothing, but as she began to dress, she realized that she felt dirty. His body odors were still on her and she felt like she might be ill. She had to take a bath, and she gathered up her clothing and headed for the bathroom in a naked condition.

He sat up in bed. "And where the hell do you think you're going?"

She was adamant. "I'm going to take a bath. I want to get your stinky smell off me. I wish I could wash my insides, too, down deep."

He laughed as he rose and began to put his clothes on. "Whew, I always figured you had a temper. Too bad all that spunk didn't show up between the sheets," and he laughed again.

She spent as much time in the shower as she felt she could. The small water heater began to pour forth cool water, after having its supply exhausted. She had washed off odor and sweat and tears. She wondered if she would ever feel clean again.

Finally, she dried off and dressed and meekly returned to the living area. He was sitting having another beer. She could not look at him. Never, she thought, had she hated another human being so much. And once again, she considered the plight of females in that male dominated society. She was resentful in every fiber of her being. She had been violated, once again, and there was nothing she could do about it- absolutely nothing! She was beginning to develop a deep hatred for the male of the species which would stay with her for a long time.

After returning to the living room there was an awkward silence between the two as they sat apart, saying nothing. As time went on, Mario attempted conversation several times with small talk, but he received no answer from the highly agitated and angry young woman he had just assaulted. She, from time to time, gave him looks of utter contempt, but that was all.

Mario looked at his watch, and rising from the couch, went to the kitchen area to retrieve the candle, newspapers and the bottle of wiskey. As he went into the hallway towards the bedroom, she could hear him say, "Hell, it's time to go to work and finish this mess."

She could hear the splashing of the liquor as he poured it over the two bodies and the surrounding bed area, and the sound of the bottle as he let if fall to the floor. Curious, she rose and tip-toed to the bedroom, careful not to look at the two unfortunate souls lying in the bed. She watched as he placed the thick wad of newspapers on the floor near the bed. He then lit the candle and melted some fresh wax which he allowed to drip in the old and now cold recess. When he was satisfied that the candle was firmly supported in its melted wax socket, he gave the room one last look and rose. She quickly departed, not wanting him to see her standing there. She had taken her seat on the chair next to the couch when he hurriedly came into the room. Picking up his two duffel bags and giving the room one last look, he pointed to her packed bags and said, "Let's get the hell out of here... now! Come on!" and he motioned to the door.

As they approached the car, his and Verlie's, he stopped and looked around the trailer park. He saw no one in sight or moving about. He opened the passenger door and shoved an unwilling and not too cooperative Rainey in the seat. She saw no reason to give any serious resistance. She realized getting away from that death scene was as much to her advantage as his. He hurriedly got behind the wheel and with as little noise as possible backed out of the parking area and onto the main exit road. When he reached the county road which would take him to San Diego, he turned instead into a secondary road which climbed to an even higher hill. Rainey noticed the change, and any change from the routine made her nervous. "Why are you going this way?" she demanded.

Without looking at her, he replied, "Because I want to get on that high ridge so I can see if that damn trailer burns like I want it to."

"And what if it doesn't?"

"Then, I'll go back and try again. That baby has got to burn, and burn good. I want them two to be cremated beyond recognition."

"So, that's your game, huh? You want the bodies burned so bad they won't know who they are?"

"Oh, I'm sure they'll figure out one of them is Verlie, but that other poor slob," and turning to look at her,..."who was he?"

She hesitated to reply at first. "His name was Bruce. That's all I know. I never met him."

"Then, how the hell did Verlie know him?"

She shook her head, not really wanting to tell him anything. "I... he... he... was a traveling salesman. He came into the restaurant from time to time. That is how she met him."

He grunted. "The poor bastard should have kept on travelling."

When he reached the highest part of the ridge, he turned the car around so he could look down on the trailer park. He picked out his trailer and he sat and waited.

She looked also and with some reservations, asking, "How can you be so sure that someone won't see the fire and call the fire department and they will come and put it out and discover the bodies before they burn?"

"Because, there ain't a fire fighting unit closer than ten miles from here, and that's a volunteer bunch. By the time they get a crew assembled, that baby will be an inferno." He had no sooner finished the words when he excitedly exclaimed. "Look, there's a bright light. Hot damn... it took!"

As the fire began to engulf the trailer, he could see some people move around in the area. Evidently, he reasoned, the neighbors now knew it was on fire. He squinted as he saw them begin to move about like ants. "Look, those poor bastards are trying to put it out with buckets of water, but oh baby, look at her burn. Trailers are nothing but fire traps. They'll never put it out. That's why I used to give Verlie hell about smoking in bed..." but he let the comment die as Rainey gave him a dirty look.

"Geez," he exclaimed, "that trailer next to ours is beginning to burn," and then, "why the trailers on both sides are burning. Whew, Rainey, baby, we got ourselves a real weenie roast, now!"

She looked away with contempt. "Don't say we! I have nothing to do with this."

He gave her an ominous look. "That depends, sweetheart, on how good you keep that cute little mouth of your shut. You understand what I'm saying?"

She looked away. "Yes, I think I understand very well."

He turned the key in the ignition. "Well, there ain't no use in watching this show any more... they're good and gone," and with that he made his way back to the main road and towards town. Turning to her, he asked. "Where do you want me to drop you off, the train station or the bus station."

She had not had time to think about it, but now she did. The awful train ride she and Doug had taken on the way out burned in her memory and she had no desire to repeat it. "I'll go by bus."

As he drove up to the busy bus station, so active with military personnel going and coming, he placed his hand on her arm. She pulled away. "Don't you touch me, you bastard," and now feeling safe with all the people milling about, "you've had all the fun you will ever have with me..."

He interrupted her, and in a more docile tone, "I just want to tell you I'm sorry, Rainey... about the rape... I had no right to do that... I just went nuts... that's all... I'm sorry'"

She gave him a contemptuous look. "Gee, that really makes me feel better," and then, less contemptuous and more realistically, "Mario, what if I get pregnant from this?"

He gave the matter some thought. "How can you get pregnant? You told me you were having your period."

"I lied. I'm not. I could get pregnant, you know."

He shrugged and grinned. "Well, if you do, be sure to send me a postcard. I always wanted kids," and he laughed aloud.

Now, more disgusted than ever and with only one desire, and that was to get out of his sight, she grabbed her bag and started to get out. He caught her arm. She didn't even turn to look at him, but she heard. "Remember, keep your damn mouth shut about this and nothing will happen to you. If you don't, you're up to your ass in trouble... understand?"

She nodded and hurriedly left his presence.

Although not known for his intellectual brilliance, Mario had, indeed, painted an accurate scenario of the entire matter to Rainey. The police had, after a careful evaluation of the case, made him their prime suspect and he was brought in for questioning. He was immediately released when an entire platoon of fellow marines swore that he was in their presence the entire afternoon and that night. He could not possibly have committed the crime. And when the neighbors had been questioned, it was ascertained that another white female had lived in the trailer with the deceased. What of her? When the police interrogated her employer, Max Steiner and his devoted wife, Thalia, they reported that the young woman had informed them that she was leaving to attend a funeral back in

Arkansas. The bus station had confirmed that a ticket was, indeed, bought by someone fitting her description, and, yes, she had departed the city that night.

There was another body found in the fire ravaged trailer, the body of a white male, approximately thirty to thirty-five years old. Identification was impossible. He was not a military man, they knew that. The military kept good records and they had no one missing. It was true as Rainey had reported. He was a traveling salesman. He had a wife and two children in a town in northern California. She had reported her husband missing some two weeks after his demise, but it was never proved that he was that man. Only his dental records could have proved that, and they could find none.

The fire that night had burned a total of five trailers. No one else had burned to death, but there were many minor injuries inflicted on poor souls trying to extinguish the blaze in their own trailer.

The police, both military and civilian, closed this perplexing mystery with the same conclusion. Yes, two people had died under mysterious circumstances. It was obvious that they were not man and wife. It was obvious that they had been drinking heavily because three empty and burned whiskey bottles were found. The woman was known to be a heavy smoker, and it was possible that she had fallen asleep with a lighted cigarette in her hand. The husband, a prime supect in the case, had an airtight alibi. The missing girl, Rainey Wether, also had an alibi, vouched for by two pillars of the community, Max and Thalia Steiner. When the police reached the conclusion that they would never get the true story, and they could care less, the file was closed. After all, the great war had been over for over a year and the country had more important things to tend to.

CHAPTER FIFTEEN

As the Greyhound bus left the bright lights of downtown San Diego, it headed northeast until it could intersect with U S. 90, the Old Spanish Trail, as it was known since the days when Spanish Conquistadors used the route as their Camino Real (the Royal Road) from Florida to California.

Still seething from the trauma of the rape and still shaking her head in disbelief at the happenings of the past several hours, Rainey found a seat next to the windows on the bus crowded with young servicemen going home. She looked out at the black sky, her eyes moist as she attempted to deal with the irrevocable facts. Even though she found it hard to believe it had happened, she could not escape the reality of it. She had witnessed the murders and had lived the rape. Once again, she had endured an experience caused solely by the violent nature of the male of the species. Both the murders and the rape, she reasoned, were acts of violence by a man out of control of his senses. Were all men possessed of a dark side? If so, then they could never be trusted. As the bus climbed the hills to the west, she became chilled and she folded her arms about her and tried to sleep.

The seat next to her was occupied by a young sailor, so young that his face was covered by fuzz more so than beard, and he had not advanced, as yet, past the pimple stage. He had smiled at Rainey as he moved into his seat. She had given him a blank look and turned her head away to look at the dark nothingness of the outside.

Attempting to be sociable, he had taken a pack of chewing gum from his jacket, and with some hesitation had offered her some. "Gum?"

She turned her head from him back to the window with, "No, thank you, I just want to be left alone."

Bewildered and embarrassed, the young sailor swallowed hard, saying nothing in reply. His buddy next to him snickered at his failure.

The bus trip was no more comfortable than the train, she reasoned, after four nights of attempting to sleep sitting up with the raucous talk and laughter of the other passengers, especially the young servicemen going home after being mustered out and returning to civilian life. It was a tired, sleepy, and disheveled young girl who finally got off the bus in Pine Bluff, Arkansas some four and a half days after leaving San Diego. Since the attorney's return address had shown that town as his location, she felt it was logical to start with him and go from there. Where? She had no idea.

She looked around, not knowing what to do or where to go. It was six o'clock in the evening. She knew he would not be in his office this late and she really didn't want to see him that day. She really didn't want to see anyone. All she wanted was to sleep... forever. She went to the ticket window and inquired of a reasonable hotel within walking distance of the station.

"Ain't none 'o them reasonable, young lady," said the old ticketmaster. "Since the war's ended, everything is goin' up and up, but... if you're willing to walk to the Alamo Plaza motel abut five blocks down the street, they got nice rooms at a good price."

She nodded with a pained expression. "Thank you," and taking her bag in hand, set out for the motel. She felt she had never enjoyed a bath so much in all her life as she soaked in the warm water for nearly an hour, and then, catching herself dozing off in the tub, stumbled to the bed... hungry and exhausted.

As she lay on her back, attempting to achieve sleep, she smiled at her unfortunate circumstances, saying almost audibly, "Well, Rainey, baby, you are back in Arkansas where you started out," and in mimic of her earlier speech, "you ain't made much progress."

She had no difficulty in finding the office of the attorney, Justin P. Holstead. It was an ancient office which had had little done to it in the past half century. The woodwork had been stained in a dark color and the profusion of it made the interior dark and gloomy. After she had told the secretary/receptionist who she was and the information had been relayed to her employer, he strode out of his office, smiling a friendly smile. He was over sixty, bald, rotund, and badly in need of braces when he was younger.

"Miss Wether, I am so glad you were able to come here to meet with me. Did you have a nice trip?"

"No, I'm afraid I did not. That was a miserable bus ride."

"Oh, I'm so sorry to hear that. May I offer you some coffee and doughnuts? I have them every morning," and patting his stomach, "I guess that's why I have this."

Extending his hand towards his office, he continued..."Wether, Wether, I can't say I've ever heard of your family."

Taking a chair, she managed a smile. "I doubt that anyone has. We are distinguished only by our lack of accomplishments."

He was surprised that someone so young would be so cynical, and fingering his gold watch chain as he took his chair, "I won't waste any time with this, Miss Wether. I have a court appearance in an hour," and picking a file from the side of his desk, he continued. "What this is all about is," and he perused the file, trying to reacquaint himself with the facts, "a Mr. Otis Hotard came in to see me about this. He apparently is a land man with a company whose name he did not care to divulge at the time. But, anyway, he expressed some interest in purchasing your land if the title can be cured..."

She made a frown. "What do you mean... cured?"

He cleared his throat. "Well, your grandmother never formalized her bequest to you. It was only in the form of this letter which she had this druggist write for her..."

Rainey looked at him, amazed. "How could you possibly know about that letter. I thought I was the only one who had a copy of it."

He shook his head. "No, that is not true. The druggist is still alive, incidentally, and we have talked to him. He says he made two carbon copies of the document. He gave one to your grandmother and he kept one in his files. The fact that he notarized the document adds some strength to your case. Your grandmother gave her copy to the cousins. That is how they know of her intentions. That is not exactly a properly drawn will," and he chuckled, "as you might imagine."

She gave him a puzzled look. "What cousins?"

He look surprised. "Why, I assumed you were aware that you have cousins over in Bradley county... second cousins, I believe."

As she shook her head, saying nothing, he added, "They are the children of your grandmother's sister," and seeing her confused look, "are you not aware that your grandmother Orella Wether went to live with a sister about the time you were sent to live with some family... by the name of Foster, I believe."

She nodded. "I was so young... only five, but yes, I do remember my grandma saying she had to go and live with a sister," and smiling, "so I have cousins. I thought I had no family."

"Well, I think they're your second cousins. As a matter of fact, if it were not for the fact that your cousin kept up with the taxes all these years, you would have lost the land by prescription..."

She squinted. "Prescription? What's that?"

"In simple terms. When a person, other than the owner, lives on a piece of property for ten years, and it is this person who pays the taxes instead of the real owner, then that person can become the legal owner with a court decision after proving that he had, indeed, been the de facto owner all these years by occupying and paying taxes."

She rose to go. "Then, I guess the property beongs to my second cousin, whoever he is..."

"No, no, that is not so, my dear. He apparently paid the taxes in the name of your grandmother, Orella, and she is apparently the proper owner to this day, or was."

Ever cynical, now, she asked, "Why would he do that?"

"Well, from what he has told us, your grandmother made a verbal deal with him," and he laughed, "which is not uncommon among these rural and poorly educated folks."

Curious, she asked, "What deal?"

"Your grandmother must have been a shrewed old gal, and she evidently felt very strongly that this land belonged to you after she was gone." He brushed a fly away from his nose as he sipped his now cold coffee. "She told him he could farm the land and keep all the proceeds... if he paid the taxes on the land each year in her name. She insisted that he pay the taxes with a check made out to Orella Wether as her rental income from his sharecropping."

"But, my grandma died shortly thereafter."

"Yes, we know that, and that is where the problem lies. There was no probate... nothing in writing, but your cousin is apparently a very honest man. He insists on honoring your grandmother's intentions. He says the land is yours."

She breathed deeply. "An honest man! I can't believe what I am hearing."

The old attorney looked confused at her declaration. "I'm afraid I don't understand your comment about honest men. Why, my dear, there are..."

She cut him off, smiling. "It's a long story. What do I have to do now and what will this cost?" and looking embarrassed as she looked him in the eye, "Mr. Holstead, I have no money at all... just a few dollars in my purse for room and board while I'm here. I am practically destitute."

He cleared his throat. "Yes, I understand. Well, of course, there are some expenses to be sure. If you want me to cure this ownership, I will have to spend some time on it, but" and he gave her a fatherly smile, "I assure you, my dear, I will make every attempt to keep the cost down. I understand your predicament."

"But, I have no money at all for this."

"Well, if we can clear the title, this gentleman is prepared to write you a check, immediately."

"Why does he want this land?"

The attorney hesitated, trying to decide in his own mind if he had a conflict of interest. "How long have you been gone, my dear? In California, I mean?"

"Over a year."

"I see. Then, you are not aware that oil has been discovered in this part of Arkansas."

She breathed deeply. So that was it. Oil. She remained calm, outwardly, but her heart began to beat a little faster, as she gave him a discerning look. "Is this thing a secret around here?"

"What do you mean? What thing?"

"This oil thing? Does everyone know about it?"

"Well, of course, it is public knowledge around here."

"Is there oil on the property?"

He laughed. "I'm afraid I can't tell you that! I don't know, nor does anyone else until they drill on the land."

She gave the matter some thought. "Is there oil on the land around the property?"

He gave her a paternal look. "I don't know. I'm not in the oil business, and if I were you, I wouldn't get too excited about this unless the title can be cleared. I would not want you to get your hopes up just yet."

She gave the matters some thought. "Would you be willing to base your fee on whether or not I'll make any money on the land sale."

He smiled. "Why don't we talk to the land man, first, and see what he has in mind before we talk about a deal between you and me."

"Will it cost me any money to talk to him?"

He laughed. "No, my dear, he is not an attorney! He talks for nothing."

She could be heard to say, "Thank God, someone does."

Otis Hotard, the land man, grinned at her through tobacco stained teeth as he extended his hand in greeting as the attorney introduced them. "Well, now, Rainey, I'm right glad to finally meet you." She developed an instant dislike for him. He smiled too much, and she had found out that people who smile too much usually had something to hide. He was short, fat, and bald. His beer gut hung over his belt which had a large silver buckle with a buck deer design on it.

She nodded, quickly withdrawing her hand. His hand was hot and sweaty and his touch made her recoil. He continued to grin, as he talked in her face, another habit he had that she objected to. "Well, Ah guess, Rainey, the lawyer heer," and he nodded at the attorney, "has told you Ah 'm intarested in buying that property of you'rn... if we kin clear the title."

She nodded. "Yes, he's told me about it," and avoiding his stare, "what do you want to do with the land?"

He grinned more broadly. "Whal, nah, Ah don't believe Ah need to tell you that. This is strickly a business deal. I write you a check far the land 'n then it's mine to do with as Ah see," and turning to the attorney, "ain't that so, counselor?"

The attorney responded, "That is true, unless the usage was made a condition of the sale."

The land man gave the attorney a dirty look. "Whal, nah, there ain't no use in complicatin' this thing with that kinda talk, counselor."

He had held up his hand as he said that and she could not help but notice the huge diamond ring on his pinkie finger, but she also noticed, with the naked eye, that it was full of carbon spots- obviously a cheap and flashy stone, used to impress the uninitiated.

Turning to Rainey and attempting to intimidate her because of her age. "Nah, litt'l girl, you eitha want to sell me this land or you don't. It's as simple as that. What'll it be?"

She gave him a look older than her age. "I can't sell you the land, as yet. Mr. Holstead has informed me that I don't legally own it."

"Whal, nah, that's true, but we think we kin clear that up real fast. All it takes is fer a judge to sign a litt'l piece of paper," and he snapped his fingers, "then, it's done." Turning to the attorney, "Ain't that so?"

The attorney evidently had no more affection for this man than did Rainey. He replied. "It's not quite that simple."

The man gave them both a wide grin. "Whal, counselor, that's why God invented lawyers, ain't it? When are we gonna git started on this thing? Ah'm in a hurry to move. Ah got otha deals cookin' you know."

Standing to indicate the meeting was over, the attorney responded, "I need to have more conversation with my client," and turning to Rainey, "that is... if she is my client."

Alone in his office after the land man's departure, he regarded Rainey in detail for the first time. He had not realized she was so young even though she presented a much older impression, especially in her talk and demeanor. He asked, "How old are you Miss... may I call you Rainey... it's so awkward to be so formal," and after a nod from her, he waited for her answer.

She was shocked by the question. She had assumed when they doctored her birth certificate in San Diego that she would never have to account for it back in Arkansas, and now, the moment had arrived. She nervously reached in her purse and offered him the birth certificate.

He perused the document and gave her an amused and knowing look. "Rainey, I guess you know we have already looked up your age in the Department of Vital Statistics. In Arkansas, you are sixteen, not nineteen as this document says you are," and giving her a friendly smile, "perhaps you'd better tell me about this. I have to know."

She gave him a sheepish look and then told him the truth of how it came about. He laughed. "I can understand you had no other choice in California, but I'm sure you understand that you broke the law out there when you did that."

She shuddered as he said the words, 'You broke the law out there.' The last thing she needed or wanted was to resurrect anything that would cause her to explain anymore about California than she had to. She broke out in a nervous sweat and her hands begin to shake.

He noticed her concern and feeling she was scared of having doctored the birth certificate, he smiled at her, saying, "Now, don't fret about this. Since you are not in California now, it will do no harm, but I'm sure you realize that we will have to go by the Arkansas one... the official one in this state."

She nodded meekly as he continued, "Which means you are a minor at this time, which further complicates the matter. Minors cannot do business in any state, Rainey. That will require some more remedial work."

She was dejected. She could see it all going out the window. She now envisioned the whole deal blowing up in her face and she would receive no money which meant she was back home, broke and homeless. She began to sweat once again. "What can I do? Just between you and me, I need to sell that land really bad. I need the money," and shaking her head, "I need it desperately. The money I have won't last too much longer," and she looked at him like the little girl she really was. "What'll I do?"

Rainey

He looked at her with fatherly compassion. "You have no one here you can turn to... no family? How about your cousins in the next county?"

She gave him a desperate look. "I don't even know them."

He nodded. "Let me think about it for a while. Do you have enough money for a few days?"

She nodded. "Only for a few... perhaps a week or so."

He rose, and putting his arm around her waist in a fatherly fashion, "Try not to worry about it too much until you have to. Let me see what I can do... that is... if you are my client."

She smiled at him. "You are if you don't expect to be paid for sure."

He smiled back, and thinking of his own granddaughter her age, so secure in a stable family, in contrast to this young woman before him who, in actuality, really belonged to no one, he was filled with compassion for her. "Our profession expects us to do a certain amount of pro bono work from time to time, to try to convince the public that we attorneys do have a heart, after all, and if I've ever seen a case for pro bono, this is it.

She gave him a quisical look "Pro... what? What does that mean?"

"It means we work for nothing, for the public good."

She gave him a warm smile. "I like that."

Leading her to the door of his office, "You go on back to the motel and try not to worry about this. Let me see what I can do with it."

She placed her hand on his arm. "I really appreciate what you are doing. I have no one else to turn to."

He patted her arm, smiling and nodding.

She returned to the motel and decided to splurge on a good meal, something she had not had in days. On her long bus ride, she satisfied her hunger with hot dogs and hamburgers in an attempt to save her limited cash.

As she settled in a booth, the waitress came up with a menu and the glass of water, walking off, saying, "I'll give you a minute to decide..."

Rainey suppressed a tear and a sob as she watched the waitress walk off. she was in her forties, at least. She had seen better days. she had waitressed for so long that she had the waitress waddle from those countless trips back and forth. She wore tennis shoes. One had a hole in the toe. Rainey felt sorry for her. She felt sorry for all women who were chained to menial tasks in the male dominated society. She thought, hell, you never see a man waiting on people. No, it's always a poor woman. She remembered the restaurant where she and Verlie had had their happy days, few though they were. She thought of Verlie, and her heart ached. She thought of Max and Thalia. She was deep in reverie when the old waitress returned, asking, "Made up yore mind, honey?"

She sniffed back a wet nose, wiping it with her napkin. "Uh, huh, I'm ready. Is it too late for breakfast?"

Lloyd J. Guillory

The waitress looked up at the old Regulator clock on the wall. "No, not yet. You just made it. What'll it be?"

"Well, I want three eggs sunny side up, a bowl of grits, three slices of toast, and a large glass of ice cold milk."

"Don't you want any coffee?"

She thought about it for a moment. "Ah, what the hell! Bring the coffee, too."

As she wiped her mouth on the paper napkin, she looked at the bill. "Whew... seventy-six cents with tax. My money won't last too long doing this too often." She started to leave the waitress a ten cents tip, but as she smiled in reflection, she laid a quarter on the table, saying to herself: There's no telling what kind of life she leads. Probably supporting some no good man who beats the hell out of her every time he gets a chance, and then, an hour later, assaulting her in bed, telling her how much he loves her. As she walked out the restaurant, she had to pass the table of four typical red-neck types who oggled her as she went by. She kept her eyes straight ahead, even when she could hear as she went by..."Hummm, look at that! That'd make a hound dog break his leash... that's fer shur!"

CHAPTER SIXTEEN

Rainey was nervous as she hung up the phone after being called to the desk in the motel. Her room had no phone. She had waited three days for the old attorney to call her, thinking after a while that, in spite of his kindly offer to help, he had followed the course of most men and not really meant it. The conversation had been short: "Rainey, I need to talk to you. Can you come to the office this afternoon... about three?" And that was all. In her already dejected state of mind, she felt his tone had been abrupt. She felt sure he could not have good news for her. Her money was running out. She was worried.

But, he smiled as he came out of his inner office to greet her. "I'm glad you could come. Come in, my dear. We need to talk, and I'll bring you up to date."

She said nothing as she fell into the offered chair, but finally: "I thought after not hearing from you for three days that you had given up on me. I was beginning to make plans. I can't hold out much longer... money-wise, I mean."

He smiled. "No... no, Rainey. I'm not going to give up on you, but this is a very complicated matter, much more so than I let on to you at our first meeting."

She frowned. "Were you just trying to spare my feelings? Is it a lost cause?"

"No, not a lost cause, but a complicated one," and returning to his chair, "You see, there are two thorny issues here," and holding up one finger, "As I told you before, your grandmother's will is not really a will at all, not even in Arkansas," he grinned. And holding up the second finger, "Then, there is the matter of your age. You are a minor in every state of the union, and minors cannot conduct business for themselves."

"Then," she said with dejection, "I guess it's a lost cause. Nothing can change my age at this stage."

"Yes, that is true, but the law makes allowances for even that contingency."

"But how? I don't understand."

He looked at her with paternal compassion. "Here is what has to be done to straighten out this mess your dear grandmother has made of your legacy," and he became serious. "First, we must locate and talk to your cousin over in Bradley County-the one who has paid the taxes all these years."

He noticed her quisical look as she asked, "Do we know how to find him?"

"Oh, yes, we know where he is."

"So, I have a second cousin, huh?" she asked, surprised that she had any family.

He shook his head. "No, he is not your second cousin as I originally thought. Technically, he is your first cousin, once removed, as the genealogist like to say. You see, he is the son of your grandmother's sister, the one she went to live with."

She grinned as she remembered, young though she was, that this was the same woman who had not wanted her to come also. She could not resist saying, "Oh, that one- the one who did not want me to come with my grandmother..."

His eyebrows raised. "Are you telling me she refused to take you in? Why? Do you know?"

She smiled, thinking if she knew him better she would use the same language her grandmother used, but she felt embarrassed to be so explicit. "She said that girls give too much trouble when they begin to sprout," and she placed her hands in front of her well rounded breasts.

The old attorney, the proud father of three daughters, coughed, and smiled. "Yes, I know what she meant, but really..."

She shrugged. "What difference does it make now? You were saying.."

He tried to regain his line of thought. "Well, to cure this minor thing, I must have a guardian appointed for you and your cousin seems to be the most likely candidate," and looking at her, "or is there someone else you might think of."

She thought of Martha Powell, and she came close to suggesting her, but she gave it more thought. She was not sure how the older woman would feel towards her now.

He sensed her mental searching. "Well, is there someone else?"

She shook her head. "No, my cousin, once removed," and she smiled at the expression, "will do just fine. Is he willing? Will this cost him money?"

"Oh, I think he will be willing. He seems hell bent, if you will pardon the expression, on your having the land. He says it is yours because that is what his Aunt Orella wanted, and as to the money... no! All it will cost him is a little time, that's all. You see he is grateful to your grandmother, his Aunt Orella as he refers to her, for allowing him to sharecrop that land all these years. He made a meager living, but he raised his family on that land."

"But, won't he resent losing the land to farm on?"

"Not really. His mother has died and he now has that land."

She moved to the edge of her chair. "Well, that will cure one of the problems. What of the other one?"

He sighed deeply. "That one, my dear, is much more complicated. In essence, your grandmother's letter to Mrs. Foster is no will at all. A will is a properly drawn legal document, with certain concise language, properly witnessed by at least two people. It should really be done by an attorney."

She grunted. "My poor grandmother didn't have five dollars at any one time, much less a lawyer's fee," and as she shrugged her shoulders: "Jesus, they gave me away because they couldn't care for me any longer," and tears came into her eyes, which made her angry.

He nodded. "I know, my dear, I know, and that is why I am determined to see that this land becomes yours"

"Well... how?"

"This will take some complicated legal footwork, but I've been at this for forty years, and I know a few tricks."

She waited for him to go on.

"Since there is no will, your grandmother died intestate. That is the legal definition of one who dies without a will, and only a probate court can clear up that deficiency."

Seeing her curious look, he continued, "We will have to open probate on your grandmother's bequest, and it will have to go before a probate judge. He will make the final determination, and if he agrees, he has the power to issue a decree and award the land to you with a clear title," and catching himself, he added, "I should have said he will award the land to your guardian."

Knowing how her luck had run in the past: "But, will the judge be willing to do that, do you think?"

In all seriousness, he replied, "I am sure you realize that these matters are decided strictly on their legal merits. He will have his law clerks carefully research the law books, and then they will attempt to find similar cases already decided in years past, and then, he will weigh these matters in great depth, and then and only then, will he render a decision."

"But, do you think he will do it?"

He smiled. "He's my wife's cousin, my dear, and I am godfather to one of his daughters."

She could not suppress a grin, but he saw it and added, "Oh, yes, before You bask in your expected success, there is one thing you need to know..."

She knew it. She sensed it. It was too good to be true.

"What?"

"Well, even though we might legally cure the minor problem, you are still a minor in the eyes of the law. The money cannot be given to you- at least, not by the court."

"But... who will get the money?" she asked in a state of desperation. Her finances were getting critical, and she informed him, "I can't wait too much longer."

He became serious. "I know, Rainey and that will be a problem," and he was sad as he intoned, "I feel that I am doing my share for you with this legal work. I cannot, as much as I would like to, solve your immediate financial problems. I'm afraid, my dear, you will have to find some way to support yourself for a while. This is not going to happen overnight."

Embarrassed that he thought she might be hinting for help, she shook her head. "Oh, no, Mr. Holstead! Please don't misunderstand me. I was not even suggesting that you... Oh, God, please don't believe that..."

He smiled. "I know, and forgive me if I gave you that impression. The point I was trying to make was that this will take some time. You will not be getting this money, even if we are successful, for quite some time."

She looked frightened. "How long, do you think?"

"You had better think in terms of months... not weeks, my dear."

Her hands went to her cheeks. "And that land man... will he be willing to wait that long?"

He grinned. "That depends on how bad he wants the land."

She sighed. "I hope somebody wants it. I need to sell that land."

He raised his forefinger. "Rainey, I feel I must give you some more advice, which is not exactly legal advice, but you are so young and inexperienced..."

She thought: If only you knew what I have been through in my sixteen years, but she asked..."what?"

"It has been my experience that deals made in too much of a hurry usually end up a bad deal for the person who was in the hurry."

This comment burned in her. She remembered her quick and irrational agreement to go with Douglas Walker, an agreement that ended in a disaster. She swallowed hard.

"Are you telling me not to accept the first offer?"

He searched for the right words. "No, I'm telling you to be careful... that's all. I know what this land sale means to you and I don't want to see it go bad."

She rose, nodding, "I know what you mean. I've already made some horrendous mistakes in my life. I don't need anymore." and going behind his desk, but not willing to become too near. Her wariness of men extended even to this kindly gentleman, but she felt she had to do something. She hesitated. "I'm so grateful to you for all you're doing for me. I don't know how to repay you..."

He was of the old school. Familiarity between the sexes was confined to family and anything else was considered in bad taste. She had wanted to hug him... she really did, but as he extended his hand, she took it warmly, and placed her left hand over their joined hands to show some extra affection. He smiled, saying, "All I want, Rainey, is for you to improve your life and find some happiness. Based on what I know, you've had a rough time so far."

She wanted to say more, but her eyes watered. She smiled and turned to leave.

He followed her to the door. "I'll call you at the motel to keep you informed."

She stopped. "I may have to move to cheaper quarters. I don't think I can afford to stay at the motel for months. Are there some boarding houses nearby?"

He thought for a moment. "I'm sure there are, but I couldn't tell you where. Why don't you ask my secretary on the way out? That woman is a storehouse of information. If she can't locate a nice boarding house for you... then, it doesn't exist."

As she walked back to the motel, she examined her options, which were few. She had to find a job, but where? Doing what? She smiled as she realized that the only work she had any experience in was waitressing. She thought of Verlie and her eyes clouded with tears. She tried to hide them from people she was passing on the sidewalk, but it was difficult. When she got to the motel, instead of going directly in, she decided to go in the restaurant next door for a cup of coffee. As she neared the front entrance, she smiled as she saw the sign. WAITRESS WANTED. She shook her head as she removed the sign from the door, and sighing deeply, walked in. To herself: Rainey, baby, you've come a long way! She put on her warmest smile as the manager came towards her, grinning, looking at the sign in her hand.

There was something about him she didn't like. She wasn't sure what it was. The way he looked her up and down, pausing a moment as his eyes passed over her breasts, but she quickly told herself- cool it girl, you need the job.

"Well, miss, I guess you're interested in the job seeing as how you took the sign down... right?"

She forced a warm smile. "Yes, I'd like to talk to you abut it." She took her first good look at him. He was tall, about six feet, nice build, dark hair, brown eyes. His hair was combed straight back, without a part. It was heavily pommaded. Not a strand was out of place. He had a good set of white teeth. Some girls would have considered him handsome, but she didn't care for him at first glance. She was not sure what it was.

He waved his arm around the entire place. "This is all of it. It ain't the greatest place in the world, but we like it," and raising an eyebrow, "hey, didn't I see you eating in here the other morning?"

She nodded. "Yes. I was just coming in to get a cup of coffee and I saw your sign. Do you need a waitress?"

"Yes, we do. Have you had any experience at waitressing?"

"Uh, huh. I worked as a waitress at a restaurant in California for about a year..."

"California, huh? what on earth ever made you leave God's country to come to this place?"

"It's a long story. You wouldn't be interested."

"Are you interested in the job?"

"I might be. How much do you pay?"

He shrugged his shoulders as if embarrassed to say: "we pay twenty dollars a week plus tips."

"Plus tips isn't pay. The tips are what we hustle. Twenty dollars isn't much money for a week's work. How long is a shift?"

"A regular shift is eight hours."

"And what else do I have to do besides wait on customers?"

He gave her a quisical look. "What do you mean?"

"I just want to be sure what is expected of me, that's all."

"Well, we don't like our waitresses sitting around doing nothing when business is slow."

"What do you like your waitresses to do when business is slow?"

Lloyd J. Guillory

Her demanding tone was beginning to irritate him, but he liked her looks, and... who knows? "Well, we like them to keep busy filling salt and pepper shakers, polishing the silver, folding napkins... things like that. Are you interested, or not?"

"Uh, huh, I'm interested. How many girls are working here now?"

Nodding his head towards the counter, "Well, there's Mabel over there. She works the day shift, mostly, and then there's Laverne. She works the night shift."

"What shift will I work":"

"You'll work a split shift, helping these two girls out during the busy hours. We open at seven in the morning and close at ten at night. This is a small business. We try to keep our overhead down."

"Okay, I'm willing to give it a try if you are."

He extended his hand. "Welcome to the Pine Cone Cafe. I'm Bob Acker, the manager."

She reluctantly offered her hand. She still didn't like him, but she needed a job. "When do I start?"

"Right away if you can. What's your name?"

"Rainey Wether."

He grinned. "You kidding me? Rainey Weather... like the weather?"

"Not quite. W-e-t-h-e-r."

"Oh! Well, for one thing, Rainey, no one will ever forget your name. That's for sure." Nodding towards the cash register, "Why don't you go over and talk to Mabel. She's been here since day one. She knows the ropes. When she has time, ask her to show you around... the kitchen... the store room. Oh yeah, she will also get you some uniforms. We like our girls to dress alike."

Remembering Mabel's hole in the toe, she inquired, "Does that include shoes?"

He shook his head. "Hell no! Shoes are by you," and he walked off.

Mabel smiled as she saw her coming. "Hi! I remember you from the other day. You left me a quarter tip. I figured you for a big spender. What the hell are you doing asking for a job in this place?"

"I used to do some waitressing in California. I just got over generous the other day. That is not the real me," she grinned. "Bob said you'd show me around the place when you had time and would get me some uniforms, too."

She grunted. "He's too lazy to come in outa the rain. He coulda done all them things his self, but, no, he's got to play the big shot manager."

"You don't seem to like him too much, Mabel. What's wrong?"

She groaned as she came down off the high stool. "Aw, don't pay any attention to me, sweetie. I'm just gittin too old for this crap. My disposition is gittin' bad. Ah guess that's why Ah don't git tips like Ah used to."

"If you don't mind my asking, Mabel, how much do you average a week in tips?"

The older woman looked her up and down. "You cain't go by what Ah average. Them men don't want to tip me less'in thar wives make them, but," and she again looked her up and down, "with your face and figure, well, you might git as much as ten, maybe even fifteen dollars a week."

Rainey smiled. "I hope so. Do you have time to show me around, now?"

"It's as good a time as any," and they began the tour of the small cafe. When Mabel opened the door to the store room, Rainey could not help but notice the army cot in the corner, behind a high storage bin. The cot had sheets on it. The sheets were rumpled as if no one had made any attempt to rearrange them after their use.

She touched Mabel's arm, and pointing to the cot, "Why would you need a cot in a restaurant storeroom?"

The old waitress grunted. "Hummph! You don't! He says he keeps it thar for them days when his girls are feeling poorly."

"You act as though you don't believe him, Mabel."

"Did you say your name was Rainey?"

"Uh, huh."

"Whal, Rainey, if you work the night shift with Laverne, make shur you don't let him git you in the storeroom alone."

She gasped. "You mean... he'll try something?"

She walked to the storeroom door, closing it, and turning to the young girl. "Listen to me, girl. He's a louse. He's got a sweet litt'l wife and two cute kids at home, but you see, he's one of them guys that believes he's Gawd's gift to women. He feels like he's doing us an injustice if he don't do it to us."

"You mean... you... he...?"

She laughed. "No, not me, honey. Look at me. Ah've produced seven kids in my lifetime. My stomach is half way down to my knees. My tits are sagging. My teeth are gittin bad. I'm gittin wrinkled and gray. No, he ain't intarested in the likes of me. He likes young stuff. He corners poor Laverne in heer every chance he gits, though. She told me so."

"But, why does she stay?"

"Hell, that stupid girl thinks she's in love with him. My Gawd... love. What the hell is that? If Ah ever saw it, Ah damn shur didn't recognize it," and turning to Rainey, "Ah guess we'd betta git back before he gits us both in heer and locks the door," and she laughed.

Rainey spent the rest of the day performing her duties in an easy and practiced manner due to her previous experience, but every time she had a chance to observe her new employer, she did, and now, she liked him even less than before she had gotten the rundown from Mabel. She was anxious to meet Laverne, but she was not anxious to work the night shift.

A call from the lawyer's office got her excited. She had to schedule the meeting with him when she was off on the split shift. She was breathing hard as

Lloyd J. Guillory

she climbed the stairs to his second story office. When she was ushered into his private office there was another man sitting by the attorney's desk. Both men rose as she entered. The attorney came forward with his usual warm smile, taking her hand, asking, "Have you moved to a new place, as yet?"

"Yes, I found a nice rooming house, not too far from where I work..."

"Work? You've already found a job? Fine... fine. I'm glad to hear that you have made arrangements," and seeing her glance at the stranger from time to time, he grinned, "Rainey, I have a surprise for you. I'd like you to meet your cousin, Elmer Ritter. Elmer, this is your long lost cousin, Rainey."

For a while, they both stood there, smiling, saying nothing, then, she moved towards him, uncertain, but with a warm feeling coming over her, she reached for him with both arms. "Well, I guess we ought to hug, or something, Cousin Elmer," and she went into his arms. He was a typical rural country type of that period, in ill-fitting clothes. He was about forty-four years old. He had been too old for the great war but he had sent two sons to it, and only one came back. He was of medium height, slightly bald, with clear blue eyes typical of her mother's family. He released her, somewhat uncertain as to what he should do or say next, but finally, "whal, I'm mighty glad to meet up with you, Rainey," and he took a brightly colored bandana from his rear pocket and wiped his eyes, unashamedly as he continued, "why, Aunt Orella used to talk 'bout you all the time. She said you was the prettiest litt'l thing she eva saw, and she was right, too."

Rainey, overcome with emotion, for she felt she would never meet another member of her family, embraced him again as her tears began to flow. It was a touching scene and the old attorney stood by, smiling, watching it with pure pleasure, but after a moment, he cleared his throat. "Rainey, you and Elmer can catch up on all the news after our meeting. We have business to discuss," and he waved them to seats and began to shuffle papers on his desk. Picking up several of them, and turning to the girl, "I am happy to report that Elmer, here, has agreed to become your legal guardian." She reached for her cousin's hand and took it. It was the first time in weeks that she was willing, to feel the flesh of a male... any male. She smiled at him, and he returned it. Two of his molars were missing, she noticed.

The attorney continued. "I've begun the paperwork on opening probate on your grandmother's bequest," and turning to Elmer, continued, "the fact that Elmer is not only not contesting the matter, but, on the contrary, insisting that you and you alone be the heir to this property has helped in this matter. I've had preliminary talks with the judge," and he smiled at Rainey, "you remember I told you about him." She grinned "Well, he indicated that if all the i's were dotted and the t's were crossed, that he could see no serious impediments to this arrangement"

She sniffed. "Does that mean that I will get the land in my name?"

Rainey

The lawyer smiled. "No, it means you will get the land in your cousin's name, your guardian cousin," as he smiled at Elmer.

Elmer became serious, and turning to the girl, "Rainey, Ah want you to know that this land is your'n," and pausing for a moment to gather his words, "cause that's the way Aunt Orella wanted it," and setting his jaw and raising his forefinger, "and that's tha way it's gonna be."

She squeezed his hand. "I appreciate it, too."

The judge allowed them time for this tender moment, then: "Rainey, that land man, Otis Hotard, has been bugging me with this thing. Now that he has had some assurance that this thing will go off, he wants to talk to you about the money."

Her eyes lit up "Oh, I want to talk to him, too," and turning back to Elmer, asked, "Cousin Elmer, do you know about this land man wanting to buy the property?"

"Uh, huh, Mr. Holstead done tole me everything."

"Is it alright with you?"

He shifted in his chair. "Whal, nah, Rainey, Ah done tole you the land is your'n. You do with it what you want."

"But, you've been farming on it. I know that. You will lose that income. That is what I mean..."

He nodded, knowingly. "Ah 'preciate that, but Ah guess Mr. Holstead don told you that mah mama jus died," and he lowered his head as if in silent prayer, and he continued, "Mama left me ova 300 acres." He shook his head. "Ah couldn't take care 'o both them places iffen Ah tried... no siree. You sell that land with a clear conscience," and leaning over to her as if to whisper in her ear, "just 'tween you 'n me, Rainey, that land ain't no good fer nuthin," and he looked at the lawyer, "ceptin maybe iffen thar's oil unda it."

The lawyer said nothing for a while, thinking the matter over, then turning to the girl, "Rainey, you will have to make a big decision fairly soon."

She looked up, eyes wide. "What decision?"

"You don't know much about the oil business, I'm fairly sure. That man will make you two offers on that land," and she moved to the edge of her chair so as to hear better. He continued: "He will offer to buy the land outright. If he does that, then, anything and everything on that land, and under it, will belong to him and his company, including oil."

"And the other?" she asked softly.

"He will offer you a mineral lease. That gives his company the exclusive right to explore for oil, and if they do find it, it is customary that you as the owner will receive what is known as royalty on all the oil that is produced from under the property. That usually amounts to a one-eight share after expenses are subtracted."

"What expenses?"

"Well, there are considerable expenses involved in the production of a well."

She thought for a moment. "And who keeps track of these expenses?"

He smiled, surprised at her knowledge and her cynicism. He fingered his gold chain. "The operating company keeps the books."

"Then, I get what they say I am due... right?"

He nodded "That's right."

"But, if I sell the land outright, all the money is mine. I know exactly what I'm getting up front... right?"

"Yes, but I hope you realize that you might be trading a comparatively small amount of money up front for a potentially large amount of money, if you are willing to risk and wait."

She turned to her cousin. He raised his hands in despair. "Ah don't know nuthin about the oil business, Rainey."

She turned back to the attorney. "Will you advise me as to what to do?"

He hesitated. "I will advise you, Rainey, based on my limited knowledge of the oil business. If we had the money, we could hire geologists, petroleum engineers, and other experts to consult and advise you, but those people cost a lot of money."

She looked helpless as she shook her head. "I guess you know that is not possible."

He nodded. "I know, unfortunately," and standing, "why don't you and Elmer go and have a cup of coffee and get acquainted."

She avoided the cafe where she worked when she and Elmer decided to have lunch and talk family talk. There was little they had in common. They were no better acquainted than total strangers but in time honored fashion, the old adage that blood is thicker than water came to the fore. Since he had never seen his first cousin, Cassey, he looked at Rainey for some family trait, but other than the light blue eyes, he could find none.

She talked for over an hour without stopping as she related the story of her life, omitting, naturally, the traumatic events that brought her back to Arkansas.

Elmer wiped his eyes with his bandana. He looked down at the floor for a moment, avoiding her eyes, then he looked directly into them. "You know, Rainey, Ah ain't too proud 'bout mah mama not taking you in when Aunt Orella came to live with us. That jus weren't right. Ah don know why mama done it. She weren't no mean person, but... well... you see, she had trouble with one of mah sisters... she got hersef in trouble... 'n that's tha reason, Ah guess"

Rainey shrugged. "I guess it ran in the family, Elmer."

Not sure he understood, he agreed. "Uh, huh, Ah guess so." He munched his food for a while. He was not sure he wanted to say this, but: "You know, Rainey, Ah know you don had a rough time in this world," and he shook his head, "that gal-dang depression was rough on poor folks, but. Ah want you to know that iffen you want to, you can come live with me and the missus... on the farm. You won't have a lot 'o money, but you ain't neva gonna starve, neitha."

She fought back tears. She knew this offer came from the heart, and she appreciated it, but in the micro-second that it takes the human brain to process something, she remembered her early days with her mother and grandmother, then, the only slightly better days with the Fosters, and then the comfortable but stringent life with the three school teachers. Her mind rebelled at the thought of more days in the hard scrabble life of rural Arkansas.

She placed her hand on his and with all the sincerity she could muster, she replied softly, "Elmer, I appreciate with all my heart and soul your kind offer, but... to be frank with you, I am not in love with this state or this part of it. I want to go somewhere else. I want to start a new life," and she sniffed as she searched for words, "that will be better than what I've had so far. There's got to be more."

He nodded, saying only, "Ah understand, Rainey," and after a pause, "Whar you gonna go?"

"I don't know, That's why I want that money so badly. I need it desperately to start a new life. I want to finish my education, maybe go to a business school so I can get a decent job and not have to serve other people." she looked off into air for a moment. "I'd like people to serve me for a change."

CHAPTER SEVENTEEN

Rainey was highly impressed when she had first met Laverne Sutter as she joined her on the night shift. She was a British girl, a war bride, who had met her soldier husband in the British equivalent of the USO. (The USO was an organization which provided social and recreational facilities for the military during the great war). Believing that America was truly the land of opportunity, Laverne, so anxious to leave behind the stratified social life of her native land, entered into a loveless marriage which afforded her a passport to her husband's country. But accompanying her husband to the rural area of Arkansas, she found no more social uplifting than she had left behind in England. She was sorely disappointed and her marriage suffered for it. In time it completely disintegrated until she felt divorce was the only solution.

She was what one can only describe as a fully matured female in the prime of life. She was twenty-eight, five feet eight, with naturally red hair and green eyes- a magnificent example of her Irish heritage. She was what the more cultured would refer to as voluptuous and what the less erudite pool hall types would call... well stacked. So impressed was she with her own figure that she suffered the torture of waitressing in high heels, feeling that the pain was worth the enhancement which higher heels gave the female form. As she explained it to Rainey, "they lift your butt up. Why even women with short, squatty legs look great in heels, and for gals like you and me with long legs, why, it drives the men nuts." Rainey agreed, and for the first time in her life, she bought a pair of high-heeled shoes and she staggered around in them for a few days, until she got the hang of it. She soon realized as she looked back at the guys as they persued her walking away, it was worth the pain. In addition, Laverne spoke with a clipped British accent which the locals perceived as a foreign tongue, but which Rainey greatly admired. Laverne really had too many favorable physical attributes than were required to be a waitress at the Pine Cone Cafe. She deserved better, she thought. Unfortunately, she had everything but brains.

And, she also had an affinity for American men. She found them so much warmer than the cold and stiff British men she had known. She confused warmth with horny, and although she never learned to distinguish between the two, she didn't mind. It was in this light that she had somewhat reluctantly entered into an adulterous affair with her boss, Bob Acker, who, as previously disclosed by Mabel, had a sweet wife and two adorable children. He should have been content with that, but, also as previously disclosed by Mabel, he felt that his manly charms, which he believed, down deep in his heart, he possessed in copious amounts, should be spread around to the females of this planet.

Laverne had not tried to hide her relationship with her boss from her fellow employees or the general public. No, on the contrary, she wore it on her sleeve, so to speak, as a talisman of her own prowess in attracting the male of the species. But, there was more. He had, during those moments when passion replaces common sense, and with coercive prompting from her, promised Laverne that he would leave his wife and children and make her the second Mrs. Robert Acker, Jr. She believed him.

When Laverne first met Rainey, she was upset. She viewed this young and attractive girl as a potential threat to her relationship with her boss, for she knew him for the scoundrel that he was. But, after a few discussions with Rainey and a longer and more incisive look at the young girl, she concluded with typical European female pragmatism: "She is only a girl... not a real woman," and the sense of threat diminished.

Laverne, like Verlie, was a heavy smoker. Rainey, as she had so many times before in her life, made a decision that was wrong and would eventually come back to haunt her. She began to smoke. She felt it would add some sophistication to her demeanor, if that time would ever arrive when she cared about what men thought of her. If only she had been aware of the genetic deficiency that ran through the distaff side of her family. Her grandmother had died of acute emphysema from her lifelong habit of smoking Picayune cigarettes and her poor unfortunate mother had died of tuberculosis. Had Rainey known these things, being an intelligent girl, she might have altered her course, but she did not.

When business was slow, she and Laverne sat on the bar stools at the counter and Rainey coughed and choked her way through learning to inhale... the ultimate goal of all smokers. Coming from rural Arkansas as she did, and having a deep dislike for the country dialect she had come to hate, Rainey began to emummulate the clipped delivery of her British friend. She began to strike hard on her consonants, something unheard of in the deep south, and soon, the patrons who knew her before felt she was "puttin on airs", and those who had just met her truly believed there were two British girls working in the restaurant. She was proud and happy when she was accused of being British.

She and Laverne became close friends... not warm like her relationship with Verlie. She didn't want that kind of close friendship again- the sharing of any and all secrets. It had hurt too much, and she believed to some extent, might have contributed to Verlie's untimely death and her own resulting rape by the enraged Mario. No, she was content to keep Laverne at arm's length. But, she too, even from a female's point of view, considered Laverne "a real woman," and in her more private moments, those when she was alone, she secretly yearned to be more like her.

Rainey, now maturing into a grown woman from her little girl status, was beginning to have those feelings that grown women get. The rape, only a few months ago, was still fresh in her mind, and she still viewed all men as potential rapists under the right conditions. She had subconsciously feared that she might get pregnant from the rape and that worry lay heavily on her mind. That day, some weeks later, when she first felt her stomach cramps, she at first winced, and then, realizing what was really happening, for the first time in her life, actually enjoyed looking forward to that menstrual period.

She, in response to her natural cravings and desires, started thinking of accepting Laverne's offer to "fix her up" with a date, so the four could go out together. Rainey, when this suggestion was first made, looked up surprised. "You mean, go out with you and Bob?"

Laverne laughed. "Go out with me and Bob? Are you crazy, Rainey. Bob and I can't go out. He's married," and taking a deep drag on her cigarette, "why the hell do you think that cot is in the storeroom?" she asked without shame.

"Then, you mean you go out with other men?"

Exhaling, "Hell, yes, do you think I'm a nun, for Christ's sake?"

Rainey shrugged. "No, but I thought you and he had an understanding..."

"Oh, that! Hell, Rainey, do you expect me to sit around and wait on him... geez? I'd dry up and blow away."

"Does he know you date other men?"

She rubbed her cigarette out. "Hell, no! What he doesn't know doesn't hurt him." She paused for a moment. "Now, don't get me wrong. I'm no tramp. If I were married to him, real and proper, why, then, of course, I'd be faithful."

Rainey hated to ask. "Does he go out with other women?"

Laverne laughed. "Well, he goes out with his wife. She's another woman as far as I am concerned."

"That's not what I meant..."

"I know what you mean, luv. Of course the unfaithful bastard goes out with any female he can. I wouldn't trust him with a sheep in estrus, Rainey."

"But," she stammered, "you want to marry him?"

She extracted another cigarette from her jeweled pouch, and pounding the end, she sighed. "Yes, I know it is insane, but is there any sanity to love... really?"

Rainey, still trying in her young mind to sort out this emotion called "love", gave her a puzzled look, responding, "That's what I'm trying to find out."

It was almost closing time. The old Regulator clock on the wall behind the cash register showed 9:38. Bob Acker had, for the past hour or so, pranced around like a bantam rooster. Rainey had begun to recognize that trait in men when they had romance on their mind. She thought of her days on the Foster farm when the roosters in that same frame of mind would sashay around the hens, spreading out their flight feathers in a courting display, and then, they made their move. She smiled as she remembered the evasive action of the hens- her question to Nell Foster..."do the hens like it? Why do they try to run away?"

At exactly 9:45, Bob, combing his hair as he came forwards said to Laverne. "Did that shipment of canned peaches come in today?"

"Without looking up, she replied, still filing her nails. "Yes, Bob," (hitting hard on the B) they came in."

"Well, I can't find them. Would you come in the storeroom and show me where they are?"

She gave Rainey a sheepish look as she got up. "Yes, I'll be there in a minute," and she headed for the Ladies Restroom.

Rainey had not witnessed one of these liasons at close hand before. She was amazed at the openess of it, especially so when Bob, heading for the storeroom, called out to her. "Rainey, this may take a few minutes. Can you take care of the place for a while?"

She nodded. Even though the cooks and dishwashers had gone already, she still marveled at their lack of shame. Surely, she thought, he knows that I know. Does he think me stupid? Laverne knows that I know, so she doesn't care. Mabel knows and she doesn't care. Rainey shrugged and shook her head. The only one who doesn't know and would care is that sweet little wife at home changing diapers and wiping snotty noses, trying to get two kids ready for bed.

Laverne did not walk past Rainey as she came out of the rest room and walked to the storeroom. She had her head down as if she were ashamed of what she was about to do. She arranged her skirt and her blouse as she went through the door and quietly closed it as Rainey heard him say, "What the hell took you so long? We're wasting time," and then the door closed.

Rainey waited a moment or two, then, she could resist no longer. She looked around the empty restaurant. There was not a soul in sight. She walked to the front door and pulled down the shade after turning the CLOSED sign to the outside. She tip-toed to the storeroom door. She knew she shouldn't, but she was trying in her own mind, to establish some kind of pattern between the sexes. She was determined to find out for herself-what do people talk about when they are doing it? People in love? She remembered the awful time with Doug Walker. He didn't talk... not at all. Not one word of endearment, not one tender word. She had to know. Was this how it was?

She placed her head against the thin door. She expected to hear the sounds of passion, but instead, she heard the sounds of protest. She missed some of the words whispered through tightly held lips, more in anger than passion:

"No, I'm not in the mood...

"I don't give a damn about your..."

"I said don't touch me!"

"What the hell's wrong with you?"

"I'm tired of your lies."

"What lies?"

"You're never going to leave your wife..."

"I told you I needed time..."

"Six months is enough time for you to...

"But, the kids need tonsillectomies. I can't..."
"Bullshit!"
"Come on, baby, don't be that way...
"I said don't touch me..."
"Aw, come on..."
"I'm leaving! You and the restaurant..."

Rainey hurried back to her seat at the register, ashamed at her actions, but in another sense, she was glad she had heard it for her sake and Laverne's. It was time for the affair to end, she felt. Trouble was brewing.

Laverne came up to her, disheveled and distraught, arranging her dress and her hair, and before she could say anything, he came storming out of the storeroom, and seeing the two girls there, put his head down and walked to the door. "Lock up!"

Laverne nervously lit a cigarette, shaking the match more than she had to, as if she were trying to kill it. "I guess you heard, huh?"

Rainey gave her an embarrassed look. "I couldn't help it. I tried not to hear," she lied.

"Oh, what the hell do I care! It's all over and I'm glad."

Rainey placed a hand on hers. "I'm glad, too... for your sake."

Still nervous and distraught. "Shit, let's get out of here. I need a drink. Are you coming with me? Please."

Laverne said little as they walked out into the night. She was still fuming over the encounter, still puffing on her cigarette. She guided Rainey around the corner with her arm in hers. "Let's go to the Pastime Bar and get a drink. I need a damn drink."

Rainey hesitated, stopping their progress. "Don't you have to be eighteen to go into that bar?"

Laverne looked surprised. "Well, hell yes, but aren't you nineteen? Bob said you told him so."

Rainey was embarrassed. "No, I'm really seventeen, but I have this birth certificate which says I'm nineteen," and she pulled the document from her purse. She had gotten in the habit of carrying it around. Since the attorney told her it made no difference to him, legally, she saw no harm in flashing it in non-legal situations if she had to.

Laverne resumed their progress. "Hell, come on."

As they entered the popular watering hole, filled mostly with red-necks and pool hall types, for the more erudite went to the country club, they saw the deputy sheriff at the door. Most country bars in that post-war period hired off duty deputy sheriffs to keep law and order among the still wild service men who had come back home with all the bad habits learned in the service. Fights were frequent, usually over women.

As Laverne brushed past him, she smiled at him. She knew him and he knew her for she was a regular patron. He started to turn his attention to other couples when he spied Rainey. He grabbed her arm, pulling her back. "Oh, wait a minute little girl. I know how old Laverne is, but you look a little young. Let me see your driver's license, honey."

Now calm and confident, for she had secured a driver's license in California with her doctored birth certificate, she produced the document and offered it to him. He squinted as he perused it in the dim and smoky light. He smiled at her as he handed it back, saying, "Have fun ladies," and waved them in.

Laverne pulled Rainey aside. "Geez, Rainey, I just thought of something. I could be charged with contributing to the delinquency of a minor if you got into trouble."

"Do you want to leave?"

Heading for the bar, "Hell no! Just stick by me. Let me handle the boys... okay?"

Glad to let her do just that, Rainey nodded. They sat at a table towards the back of the room, trying to be inconspicuous as they ordered drinks. Laverne asked, "What do you feel like drinking?"

Rainey, who had never had anything stronger than beer, replied, "What are you going to have?"

"I want my usual- scotch and water."

She asked timidly, "Do you think I would like that?"

Laverne shook her head. "Hell, luv, I don't know. Try one and find out. I'll drink it if you don't like it."

Rainey nodded at the waitress. "Okay, I'll have that, too."

After drinks were served, she tasted it, and made an awful face. "Uhggg. That's terrible! How can you drink that stuff?"

Laverne smiled. "You have to cultivate a taste for it. I luv the stuff. Why don't you try a bourbon and seven up. It's a little sweeter. You might like that better."

Once again, she nodded towards the waitress. Rainey was determined to try drinking hard liquor. She wanted to spread her wings, although she would not have said so in so many words. If the truth were known, the exchange she had just overheard between Laverne and Bob had triggered something in her. She had become aroused at the mental picture of what she had expected them to do, and she was disappointed when it didn't happen, even though she felt it was best for Laverne. Still, emotions are strange things. They surface sometimes even when they have not been consciously summoned to do so. She had been aroused to the point that Laverne's invitation to join her for a drink was well received even though she had never had a night on the town. The few beers she had had with the late Douglas Walker would certainly not qualify for that. No, she wanted to see how grownups lived. She decided it was time, and she tingled a little as she watched the couples in the bar, those who had already paired off, and the body language and eye contact of those still maneuvering for position. She watched as the women, those with considerable experience, used body language to catch or hold some man's attention. A well placed hand here, a toss of the head in the right direction, a mouth pursed in a sensual pout, eyes dreamily promising more later, if things went well.

The men played the game, too. A macho demeanor, a soft word of endearment, whether sincere or not made little difference. Women wanted to hear them. More drinks in girls who had already exceeded their limits. Each man had his own style which had served him well in the past, or, had been recently revised to correct past failures.

Rainey sat looking and was fascinated. She had not seen this side of life in her deprived youth, and it appealed to her. She still preferred to watch than to participate, but she was enthralled by what she saw. The music started. It was a juke box type of bar, not being wealthy enough to afford its own band, but the clientele could not have cared less. The couples went to the dance floor and gyrated in different styles and modes, but they embraced... closely. Rainey noticed that. She had stiffly attempted dancing at her school dances, and every time some boy had moved in closer, as the brave ones are prone to do, as she looked over his shoulder, she could see the stiffed lip grimace of Martha Powell and the other chaperones. She would automatically move away from the disappointed boy. But, now, there were no champerones. These were adults engaged in the game of boy-girl relationships. Some were just having fun and you could tell them. They jitterbugged every dance, not caring if they ever touched bellies or not. The other types, the ones who were more serious and more aroused, danced the slow ones. Their bellies not only touched, their bodies were held in close embrace, and Rainey observed that the women seemed to enjoy it as much as the men did. Her mind went back to her observation concerning hens and roosters. These hens were not making any attempt to escape, she reasoned. They were enjoying the game.

Laverne was asked to dance by a handsome young man. With propriety, she was heard to ask, "Do I know you?"

"No," he replied, "but I bin lookin at you fer a long time, and I'd like to know you."

"What's your name?"

"Sidney."

She got up and took his hand. "My name is Laverne," and winking at Rainey, "now, we know each other."

Rainey watched as Laverne danced to Glenn Miller's STRING OF PEARLS. She had difficulty in dancing with her high heels. She stopped and removed them, and coming to the table, handed them to Rainey. "Hold these, luv. God, but he can dance," and taking her partner by the hand, she continued in her bare feet.

She returned to the table sweating and breathing hard. Dropping in her seat and looking at Rainey, "aren't you going to dance?"

"I don't know how to dance... at least, not well."

"Hell, luv, who cares. If you jitterbug to that music, no one can tell if you can dance or not. Just move your butt to the beat of the music."

"I don't think I'd like to jitterbug. I like slow music."

Laverne wiped her brow with a napkin. "Hell, whatever turns you on, luv," and she watched as a young and nervous boy came to the table, looking at Rainey. They both looked up at him as he stood there for a while, trying to get his courage up.

Laverne smiled at him. She knew she was out of his class, and she looked at Rainey. He finally said to Rainey, "Ah know you don't know me, but, well, Ah bin lookin at you fer a while. Would you like to dance."

Laverne smiled at Rainey, waiting for her reaction, which came shortly. "I don't know how to dance very well."

"Shucks," he intoned, shifting his weight from one foot to the other, "Ah don't neitha."

Laverne nodded to Rainey. "Go on. Dance with him. He looks safe to me."

Rainey hesitated, then rose. He took her hand as they went to the dance floor. She started to remove her hand, but realized that would have been silly. She had to hold his hand to dance with him. As they faced each other, he grinned at her and she smiled at him. He raised his left hand and she raised her right as she remembered to from her school dances. He put his arm around her waist and she slowly put her left hand on his shoulder, careful not to place it behind his neck. She had watched the more experienced girls playing with the back of the boy's necks and she did not want to do that with him. He held her loose, careful not to touch her body with his. It is, of course, nearly impossible for two bad dancers to follow each other in this fashion, and it went badly for a while. He stepped on her feet and she stepped on his. After several apologies, Rainey made a decision, but she had to explain it to him so he would not get the wrong idea. She gave him a sheepish look as she said, softly and uncertain, "I can't follow you if we dance this far apart," and having made that brazen observation, she moved in a little closer. He responded in kind, and he smiled. Her arm went a little more around his neck, and he responded a little more.

The band was playing Doris Day singing SENTIMENTAL JOURNEY and the slow beat was made for them. Eventually, their heads came together, brow to brow, and a warm feeling came over the two. Rainey, for the first time in a long time, was aware of a warm glow somewhere in her makeup. Some of it was due to the bourbon and seven up, but not all of it. Some of it was chemistry- boy girl chemistry, which she had not experienced before. She liked it.

When the music ended, he asked, "Wanta dance anutha one?"

She pondered that, then, "No, I guess I'd better be getting back," and she looked at Laverne who was smiling.

As she took her seat, he bowed and said, "Thank you so much for tha dance... uh... uh... Ah don't know yore name."

"My name is Rainey."

"Rainey? Rainey what?"

She smiled. "Just Rainey."

Disappointed, he said, "Oh, mine is Tom."

She nodded and smiled. He walked off.

Laverne turned to Rainey. "Now, that didn't hurt much, did it?"

She said sheepishly, "No, I enjoyed it."

Laverne gave her a devilish look. "If you think that is fun..." but she decided not to finish it. Instead, "Well, I feel better already. If you weren't with me, I'd take one of these studs home with me tonight, but, I guess I'd better get you home. I've got to get up tomorrow and find a new job."

Rainey looked surprised. "Are you really quitting?"

"Hell, yes! I don't have a future with him. He only wants one thing from me, and he can get that anywhere these days, so I have nothing to offer him," and turning to Rainey, smiling, "you can have him if you want him."

"I don't want anything to do with him."

"Smart girl! Keep it that way."

As she lay in her bed alone that night, Rainey's emotions were still in an unsettled mood. She had tasted life as the others live it, and though the taste was minuscule, she had enjoyed it. She knew that the young boy, although near her age, was not what she really wanted or needed. He had lit the flame of desire in her, even in so amateurish a manner. Her mind played with one fantasy after another, of older and more experienced men she knew were out there. Verlie had told her so and Laverne was living proof of it. She caressed her pillow as she had done so often in the past few years, but tonight, that was not enough. She hesitated for a long while, for it was against what she had been taught, and even though it had happened before, each time she had felt dirty and ashamed. But, tonight, try as she might to talk herself out of it, as she generally did, her desires were not to be denied. She began to explore her own body, the whole time imagining that she was in the arms of a lover and the soft endearing terms she had always longed for, the same endearing terms her mother had probably never heard, she whispered to herself, and then, when desire could no longer be denied, she did what women without men have done since time began, and satiated, she went to sleep.

CHAPTER EIGHTEEN

Rainey was not anxious to report for work the next day. She knew Laverne was not coming back and she would be on the night shift alone with him. As she neared the front door the WAITRESS WANTED sign was up again. She and Mabel exchanged perfunctory greetings in the presence of Bob Acker who could not look either woman in the eye. But, when Mabel joined her in the storeroom to change uniforms, she came near enough to Rainey to whisper. "Well, it finally happened, huh? Laverne finally got smart and dumped the bastard."

Not really wanting to talk about it, Rainey merely nodded, saying, "Uh, huh."

Mabel nodded to the cot behind the bins. "Ah guess that thing won't git used fer a while... huh?" It was more an interrogatory than a statement as she searched Rainey's eyes for a response.

Rainey sensed what she meant. "Not if he plans on using it with me."

As Mabel walked out the room, she looked back. "Ah hope you got more sense than that, honey," and she was gone.

It was awkward that night with Bob Acker. He knew she knew and she knew he knew she knew. His eyes avoided direct contact when at all possible. He did have a question about the storeroom but he was only too glad to accept a verbal reply from her as she said, "It's on the third shelf, about two feet from the wall, next to the cooking oil. You can't miss it."

Nervous for news from the attorney, she called him. "Rainey, I know you are anxious to complete this matter, but, as I told you before, it takes time. Be patient, my dear. It will happen. I went fishing with my wife's cousin last Saturday. He says he is waiting on the papers."

Disappointed, she nodded as if he could see her. "I know. I don't want to bother you, but..."

"Yes, I know. Be patient."

It was more than a week since Laverne had left. Bob Acker had been a perfect gentleman all that time. But, on this, the tenth day, he made his first move. It was nothing at all, really, he just made sure that their hands touched as she handed him a bill. At first, she thought nothing of it. These things do happen, but, it happened two more times that same day. When she looked at him to judge his reaction, he was looking at her to judge hers. She tried for the rest of the day to make sure it did not happen again.

The next day, as she was ringing up a sale in the cash register, he made as if he were showing her something in the register, and he allowed his finger to run up her arm from her wrist to her elbow. She couldn't move her arm, it was against the cash register. He once again looked into her eyes. She avoided his glance.

These subtle moves began to happen more and more often. She now realized that he was beginning to make his move. She called Laverne on the phone. Yes, Laverne confirmed, that was his modus operandi. He had started the same way with her. "What shall I do? I need this job for now," she had lamented to Laverne.

"Rainey, honey, just don't go in the storeroom with him. There is just so much he can do in that public restaurant. Don't fall for his bullshit about having to see you in the storeroom."

"Well, okay. How 're you doing? Find anything, yet?"

"Oh, I've got a few irons in the fire. I can't make up my mind which one I want," she lied.

"Well, good luck."

"Thanks luv. Feel like going out for a drink after work tonight?"

She hesitated, then, "Yes, I'd like that."

"Meet me on the corner at 10:05."

"I'll be there."

She once again danced; several dances to be exact, and not with Tom. She held out for older men and they came. They had more experience than Tom and they held her tighter, much tighter-some, too tight, but she was learning how to handle that, too. With one particular man, she moved her arm a little more around his neck and he responded by bringing her in a little closer. She liked it, too, and when she felt she had been aroused just enough, she broke away and began to talk to him. It always worked, she found, especially if the subject was about him. She was learning how the game was played, and if she had questions she simply asked Laverne who could have easily satisfied all requirements for a Phd. in Social Relationships.

It had been nearly two weeks since Laverne had left and Bob Acker was getting bolder each and every day, probably due to natural causes, which most men address at home. He began the game of boy-girl, and she recognized it immediately. She was learning.

At 9:45 one night, when nearly everyone had gone, he stood near her at the register.

"So, how's it going with you?" he asked.

Without looking directly at him, "Just fine."

He hesitated. "I don't ever see any boys coming in here to pick you up around closing times. No boyfriends?"

"None to speak of," was her curt reply.

"Oh, don't you get lonesome? For male companionship, I mean?"

"No, not really."

"You don't like men?"

She felt brave. "Oh, I like men. It's boys I don't care for, especially those who haven't grown up, yet." She had meant the barb as a subtle reminder to him that he should grow up, but that is not how he interpreted it. He took it the opposite way.

As he assumed a manly pose, "Well, I can understand that. Most women prefer a mature and experienced man," and he ran his forefinger along her arm, smiling at her, blatanly.

She moved her arm. "That's not what I meant. I was referring to men who acted like men and behaved like men should," and before he could respond, she added, "and who accept the responsibilities of marriage and fatherhood like they should."

He grunted. "If you mean me. I think you'd better know that my wife and I have an understanding..."

"Oh, really? Is she aware of it?"

He returned his finger to her arm. "Oh, yes, she is well aware of it. She understands that I have my needs and she also knows she is not capable of taking care of them. Truth is, she really doesn't want to."

Rainey really did not want to pursue this matter with him, but she felt it may as well come to a head now as later. "So, you're telling me it is all right with her if you fool around?"

He continued his stroking of her arm. "That's right."

"Well, I'll make you a deal, Mr. Acker," and she hit the Mr. real hard. He smiled as if he had hit pay dirt.

"And what's that?"

"I'll go over to that phone and call Mrs. Acker, and if she says that I can take you to bed tonight, then, by God, I'll do it," and she smiled at him, demurely.

He removed his hand. "You're a real smart-ass, aren't you?"

"I wasn't born one, but men like you are making one out of me... real fast."

He shrugged. "I guess you must not like your job here very much. I'm sure you know I can fire your ass anytime I want to."

"I'm sure you can," and with more brovado then she really possessed, "and I don't really give a damn."

He was already short one waitress and Rainey knew it. He decided not to press the job issue any further. He moved away. "And I thought when you walked in here, you and I were going to have a lot of fun."

"Oh, I'm having fun right now."

He decided to give it one more try, a common trait of his type. "If you'd come with me in that storeroom for a half hour or so, I'd show you what fun really is."

"No, thanks, I have more fun by myself," and she picked up her sweater, saying as she walked to the door, "Lock up, huh."

As she entered the office of the attorney, she saw the land man sitting there, an unlighted long cigar clenched between his tobacco stained teeth. He grinned at

Lloyd J. Guillory

her. The attorney motioned her to a chair with, "Well, Rainey, my dear, I guess this is the day you've been waiting for. We have finally cleared everything up. The papers are all signed and recorded in the courthouse. It is all over."

She looked around the room, seeking her cousin. "Where's Elmer? Shouldn't he be here, also'"

"No, it's not really necessary," and nodding to the land man, "you remember Mr. Otis Hotard, don't you?"

She nodded in his direction. "Hell'o," and then took a chair as far from him as she could. He watched her move, changing his cigar from one side of his mouth to the other. They both waited for the attorney to speak.

"Rainey, I have gone over the offer which Mr. Hotard is prepared to make to you. He prefers that I pass on the offer to you so there will be no doubt that you understand it," and he shuffled several papers and selected one. He adjusted his glasses and cleared his throat as he continued: "You will recall that I told you, previously, that the offer would include two proposals- one an outright sale and the other a mineral lease, and you will also recall that I explained the differences to you. Is it necessary that I go through that again?"

She thought for a moment. "No, I remember and I understand the difference," and she waited, nervously.

The attorney continued as he glanced at the land man. "Well, let's go through the outright sale, first, since it is the simplest of the two. Mr. Hotard has made you an offer of twenty dollars an acre for your 160 acres. That means you would receive a check for three thousand, two hundred dollars, and in return, you would have no further ownership rights on the land."

To a young woman who had never had any real money, especially one who had never had more than two hundred dollars in her hand, and that was given to her by a man who had just raped her, this was an amount to make her suck in air, which she did. She tried to do it quietly. She tried to remain calm, but her heart began to beat more rapidly. She took a deep breath, then, "And the other part of the offer...?"

"This is the more complicated of the two. Mr. Hotard is prepared to offer you a mineral lease of five dollars an acre with a one-eight overriding royalty if they should discover any minerals on the property." He had been careful not to mention the word... oil. He looked up at her. "You will recall, Rainey, that I explained what a royalty is and how it works."

She nodded. She could feel moisture in her arm pits, and her hands became moist. "I'd like to ask some questions."

"Of course, my dear. Feel free to ask any and all questions you want to," and he looked at the land man who still had said nothing, just sitting there chomping on his long and unlit cigar.

The land man raised his hands. "Ask away little lady."

She still didn't like him, but she managed a tight-lipped smile in his direction, and turning to her attorney, "Do you consider twenty dollars an acre a fair price? I have no idea... I'm depending on you to..."

He nodded. "Yes, it is about as fair as you will get for that place. I checked with some real estate people. Some said it was not worth that much. It is hard scrabble land, as you well know, and your cousin, Elmer, pretty well confirmed it to you in this office."

She nodded, biting her nail as she placed a finger in her mouth. "And the mineral lease- is that a fair price?"

The land man started to respond, but the attorney raised his hand in his direction, and he ceased. The attorney continued: "I attempted to check on that, but there is no true market price on mineral leases. It depends on so many factors. For instance, is there oil on any adjoining sites? Have the seismographic logs indicated sub-structures favorable to the formation of oil reservoirs?"

"I'm not familiar with the term- seismographic logs..."

The attorney looked at the land man. "Would you be so kind as to explain that, Mr. Hotard, I have no expertise in that field."

He sat up in his chair, removing the cigar from his mouth. "Whal, you see, little lady," and he grinned his green-stained toothy grin.(She mentally wondered if any woman could stomach being kissed by him) as she gave him her attention, "a seismograph log is made when the crew shoots off some dynamite in holes in the ground, and then, this log, which ain't nuthin but a strip 'o paper, shows you a lot of zig-zag lines on it, and them petroleum engineers and geologists kin tell iffen they think there is oil down there." He laughed. "Hell, Ah don't unda stand how they kin do it, but they do."

"Have any logs been made on my site?"

He seemed offended. "Whal, no, honey, we cain't do that without your permission. We'd need a mineral lease with you 'fore we could go on yore land." He was lying through his green-stained teeth. They had, illegally, without anyone's permission, made some shots some months before, all in violation of existing laws.

In her innocence, and in the absence of any knowledge by her attorney, she was not given all the facts in the matter. She had no reason to believe that this land man was the crook that he was. She sighed as she turned her gaze to her attorney, "Well, let's see. Here are my two options: One, he will write me a check right now...", but the attorney interrupted. "Not at this meeting, Rainey, papers have to be drawn up."

She nodded. "Yes, I understand that, but, he will give me a check for three thousand, two hundred dollars, if I decide to sell outright?"

Both them men nodded their approval.

"And," she continued, "the other option is that if I decide on the mineral lease, he will give me eight hundred dollars, but I will still own the land... right? I am just giving them the right to drill for oil, Could the land still be farmed?"

The land man shifted in his seat. "Whal, nah, you'd betta understand that drillin fer oil is a messy thing when it is goin on." He chuckled. "You'd play hell tryin to farm anywhere around that well."

She looked at the attorney, preferring not to discuss this matter with the land man. She asked, "Can they mess up the propery that way? Is that legal, if the land still belongs to me?"

He nodded. "Yes, Rainey, that is part of the deal. It is common in the oil business. There are large trucks tearing up the ground, drilling mud all over the place... I have a cousin who went through that. It's a mess for a while, but they do have to restore your site when the drilling is finished, and then, all you see is the christmas tree."

She looked puzzled. "Christmas tree? I don't understand."

He smiled. "That's what they call that group of valves, etc. which terminates the well at the surface."

She nodded, then rose and walked to the window and looked out for a long and awkward moment. The men waited, then she turned to the land man. "If I went with the mineral lease and you did eventually drill on the land, how much time are we talking about?"

He scratched his head. "Whal, nah, that's hard to say, little lady. But, you could be talking in terms of years." Although this was true, it was also true that they could be talking in terms of months, but it was in his best interests to say years. He was shrewd. He had had Rainey investigated. He knew she was desperate for money. He also knew she was alone and had no family. He felt sure she would go with the fast money option. He counted on it.

She sighed as she looked at her attorney, and walking near his chair so she could whisper, "What should I do?"

He took her hand in his. He shook his head. "I can't make that decision for you, my dear. You will have to make it on you own."

She turned to the land man once more. "If I sold the mineral lease to you, and you drilled, and you hit oil, how much money are we talking about?"

"There ain't no body on God's green earth who kin tell you that. There's too many factors..."

"Such as?"

He was becoming irritated with her. She was too young to be asking all these questions, but a discerning look from the attorney calmed him down. He cleared his throat. "Whal, it depends on how good a well it is. Some wells pump hundreds 'o barrels 'o oil a day, and some only pump maybe five or ten. Nobody but Gawd knows fer shur in advance. Then, if there's natural gas in that well, whal, that's more money. And then, there's the price 'o oil at the wellhead. We don't neva know in advance what that will be."

It had, indeed, gotten too complicated for her uninformed mind, and her attorney had said he had no expertise in these matters. She felt helpless and trapped. She couldn't afford to wait for years. She had made her plans. She had to get on with her life. She wanted to leave Arkansas, and only money would allow that to happen. She was tired of struggling every day, not knowing what the morrow would bring. She was tired of being vulnerable, especially to the male of the species who seemed to control all the money. She was tired of having to accept some man's amorous advances, his touching her when she did not want to be touched, and why? Because he controlled her financial security. Without changes, she felt she would have to always trade her independence, her integrity, even her chastity, for financial security at the hands of some man.

She turned to her attorney "Let's go with the outright sale. I want to get this over with."

The land man had a difficult time suppressing his grin. He returned his cigar to his mouth. "Whal, Rainey, nah that's it over 'n you done made up yore mind, Ah think you don made the right decision," and he grinned.

She ignored him, and turning to the attorney, "What else do I have to do?"

He rose. "I'll have these papers drawn up in a day or two, then we'll have to get your cousin Elmer to come down here to receive the check, and then," and he smiled at her, "he is free to endorse the check over to you and the money is yours to spend," and anticipating her next question, "you should have money in your hand within a week."

She could not suppress a smile. "Thank God," and for some reason she probably could not have explained, she added, "and thank you, Grandma Orella," and she thought of her mother, and she fought back a tear and a sob.

The land man followed her out of the office and as they reached the stair going to the first floor, he grabbed her arm. "Could Ah talk to you fer a minute, Rainey?"

She really didn't want to talk to him. They were alone in the stairwell which was poorly lighted in the old building. She was sure he had something to add to the negotiations, so she stopped and turned. "Yes?"

He grinned at her, and placing his hand on her arm, "You know, Rainey, mah company gives us land men a lot 'o leeway in what price we kin offer folks. Nah, in your case, Ah could go anotha dollar ah acre... iffen" and he ran his hand over her arm, "... iffen you'd be a little bit more friendly towards me. Know what Ah mean?"

She regarded him with all the contempt she possessed, but she resolved to keep her cool. She gave him a bland look. "Now, let's see, Otis, if I understand you correctly. You'd give me another one hundred and sixty dollars if I... how did you say it... if I were just a little more friendly towards you. Is that right?"

Sensing she was interested. "Uh, huh, that's right. What the hell, that's more'n tha goin price but it's company money."

The words- going price- inflamed her, because it implied that she was a prostitute. Her thoughts raced to her mother and her imposed profession. Rainey had vowed that never in her life would she ever allow herself to be what he had just implied. She was furious. Her first impulse was to knee him in the groin. But, she did not have the check as yet, and he could kill the deal. He was standing on the stair tread below her. She looked down at his bald head, his beer belly, his green teeth, and his generally obnoxious demeanor. She shrugged, smiled, and patted him on the cheek. "You know something, Otis, it's worth a hundred and sixty dollars not to have to look at you in the nude," and passing him and proceeding down the stairs, she yelled back, "that has got to be a gruesome sight."

It would be a serious omission at this time not to comment on Rainey's decision. One cannot fault her logic in picking the outright sale option. In the context of her situation at the time and her desperate need for money, she really had no other choice, but, like she had on so many other times when she came to a fork in the road, she took the wrong path. Not only did they find oil under her hard scrabble acreage, they discovered a sizeable pool of it. Had she taken the other route, she would have ended up a very wealthy woman.

She gave Bob Acker her notice. Now, with visions of dollars dancing in her head, she felt a new confidence. She remembered her grandmother's advice..."don't take no crap from no man!", and now she didn't have to.

He had already hired another cute little thing. (That was the only kind he hired). Mabel had come with the place when it was bought, so she didn't count. Rainey looked her over, and in a tone more amusing than factual, told the new girl, "I think you're going to like it here."

"Uh, huh," she responded. "That Bob Acker is some cute, isn't he?"

Rainey smiled. "You just don't know how cute he can be. Are you married?"

"No," she responded, "not anymore. I'm divorced."

Rainey looked at the girl with womanly compassion. "I'll just give you one bit of advice and then, you're on your own."

"What's that?"

"He's got a sweet wife and two kids at home. I just thought you ought to know."

"Oh," and she lowered her eyes.

Laverne, who was still looking for employment, received the news of Rainey's luck with mixed emotions. They had moved in together, to save money, and now Laverne felt sure she was going to lose her roommate. Although she had not given her any figures on the amount, Rainey had told Laverne she now had enough money to leave town and start a new life.

As they sat in bed in their boarding house room, Laverne was doing her toe nails. She continued without looking up. "Where are going, luv? Have you decided?"

"Uh, huh, I'm going to New Orleans."

"Oh, how thrilling! What are you going to do there?"

"I'm going to enroll in a business school by the name of Spencer Business College. I want to take a secretarial course."

Laverne's head came up. "Oh, that is great! I always thought I was cut out to be an executive secretary, don't you think?" And she smiled as she started on another toe. "Why, I can see it now. My boss is handsome beyond belief. He heads a large corporation and he has to take business trips to all the great cities of the world and he would not think of going without me," and she grinned. "Sounds great, doesn't it, luv?"

Rainey smiled. "And, is he married?"

She shook her bronze tresses. "You sure know how to throw cold water on my dreams. When are you leaving town, anyway?"

"I'm not sure. It'll take a week or so to complete the sale."

Sadly, Laverne replied, "I guess I'll have to find another roommate." She giggled. "I wonder if our landlady will let me have a male roommate. I like you, Rainey, luv, but you're not much fun at night."

Rainey laughed. "Neither are you... love!" Then, after some deliberation, "Laverne, why don't you come with me to New Orleans? I hate to move there alone. You're so more experienced than I am. Come on, come with me."

Laverne said nothing for a while. "Do you really mean it? You really want me, or do you feel sorry for poor Laverne?"

"No, I really mean it. Come with me. We'll get a cute little apartment in the French Quarter. We'll meet a lot of new men. Come on. It'll be fun..."

Laverne became serious. "And what'll I use for money until I can find a job... and I'm not hinting, Rainey, I don't like charity. I've always paid my way."

"I don't like charity, either, but God knows I've had to accept a lot of it in my lifetime. No, I'll lend you the money until you can find a job and support yourself," and thinking of Verlie, "I've had to do that in my life, believe me."

Laverne gave it some serious thought. She had left her family and her native land to follow her soldier husband to this country, and now, like Rainey, she had no one. She looked up, smiling, "What the hell. I'll do it."

Hardly a week later, Rainey had once again, boarded a Greyhound bus. This time, it was not so traumatic. She was running away, again, that was true, but it was different. She wanted to. She looked forward to it.

Lloyd J. Guillory

    The bus headed out on US 65 and as it entered the state of Louisiana, a sign on the highway caught her eye. It read- OAK GROVE- TEN MILES. Something flashed in her mind. Verlie was from Oak Grove, and as the bus passed the sign, her eyes filled with tears. Laverne could not help but notice. "Rainey, luv, what is wrong? You're crying."

    "It's okay. I just remembered someone. Don't worry about it. I'm all right, now," and she smiled.

CHAPTER NINETEEN

1952

The New Orleans of 1952 was still a city to enchant the senses. Of all American cities, few could equal her in charm and ambience, the results of being a child of two cultures, French and Spanish, and like many children of mixed heritage, the results were stunning.

She owed her genesis to the mighty river which was her sole reason for being there, her "raison de etre", as the French would have so eloquently stated in their mellifluous tongue. As a great port city, she absorbed the cultures of many lands and many ethnic groups, and once again, like different seasonings in the pot, they added spice to the final product- a piguant flavor.

Along her miles of wharves, ships of many nations surrendered their products to the huge American market, from the beautiful white banana boats of the United Fruit Company to the less beautiful but still functional coffee boats from South American. Along Magazine Street and Julia Street, the sensory pleasing aroma of coffee permeated the air on any day, and on those days when the wind blew from the south, the odor was noticeable throughout most of the city.

Along St. Charles Avenue, that oak fringed street of stately mansions, little old ladies still waited at curb side to catch the St. Charles Avenue street cars which would take them to Canal Street, the main artery running north and south which connected the river and Lake Pontchartrain. The same little old ladies, still imbued with the genteel ways of the old south, would never venture out, even in the sweltering summer heat, without their white gloves, white hats, and a white lace parasol.

Around Jackson Square, the artist colony ventured forth each day, to paint and sell, hoping the latter would exceed the first.

On the corner by the Cafe DuMonde, a lone trumpet player could be heard producing sounds, as the song says, like the "wail of a down-hearted quail". If the tourist were appreciative enough to be generous and drop some coins in his hat, so be it. If they were not, he didn't mind- he kept on playing. It had to come out. On some days, he would be accompanied by a friend who tapped-danced to the rhythm of the trumpet, or to his natural rhythms. He didn't care. It had to come out.

The oil industry was booming in the bayous of south Louisiana, and since oil floats on water, some of it flowed to New Orleans. It was to New Orleans that the large "majors" as they are called, the largest oil corporations in the world, the "seven sisters" as they are also called, came to locate divisional headquarters. The city was rife with well educated young men, petroleum engineers, geologists, civil engineers, and MBA's to keep them on a straight financial course. And as sure as bees are attracted to honey, the young women of the south flocked to this cornucopia of men and jobs. What more could a young woman ask of a benevolent God?

It was to this world that Rainey Wether and Laverne Sutter had come.

They had taken a small two bedroom apartment just off Royal Street, towards the river. It was located on the second floor. An oyster shop and bar were located on the first floor so there was no lack of noise or excitement. For economy reasons, Rainey had suggested a one bedroom apartment, but Laverne had pouted at that: "Rainey, luv, I know it's your money and I'm being presumptuous and insensitive, but... oh, a one bedroom apartment is just not practical for me... if you know what I mean..."

Rainey smiled. "It's going to cramp your style, huh?"

"Well, yes, unless you don't mind going to a late movie or two at least once a week," she giggled.

Rainey had been transformed from a young girl to a mature woman in the past few years, and she knew the facts of life. Laverne, her tutor, had seen to it that she learned the tricks of the trade, as it were, and the older and more experienced woman delighted in teaching the younger woman what life was really all about, for, while teaching Rainey she continued to live it to the fullest.

Laverne had a greater capacity for love than did Rainey and she indulged in that emotion every time she had the opportunity as if she were shopping for it in a store and had to take the merchandise home on 30 day trial period. Although she did not love well, she loved often. Rainey, on the other hand, was more cautious. She had never fully trusted men due to her unusual upbringing and observations of the males she had encountered. Her relationships with men were more of the vertical kind while Laverne leaned more to the horizontal. It should not be construed that Rainey had remained in the virginal state all this time, for she had not. She had met several men who had charmed her into a more horizontal relationship, but, even though on some occasions she felt she could detect the faint sound of bells ringing, she was certain she had never heard the cathedral chimes Verlie had assured her she would some day hear if she ever met the right man.

In her private moments, she wondered, "Does he really exist? Is there someone out there for me, someone who can really set me on fire? Someone for whom I would do anything, go anywhere just to be with him for the rest of my life?"

She had completed her business course at Spencer Business college and she had talked Laverne into taking the course at the same time. They both became secretaries in the offices of a major oil company. Men were plentiful and they picked and chose as their fancies dictated, sometimes in such profusion, that they became bored with the game and longed for a weekend to themselves, away from the "studs", as they put it.

They had even purchased a second hand automobile and toured the surrounding countryside, including the bayou country to the west. They had fallen in love with Cajun cooking and had even attempted making seafood gumbo in their cramped apartment on some occasions, but preferred buying from the real source.

Rainey watched with interest as Laverne moved from one love affair to the other, marvelling at her capacity to do so.

"Geez, Laverne, I don't know how you do it. How can you fall in love every month with a different guy? How can you?"

They were sitting on the balcony of their second story apartment, enjoying their last cigarette and a bottle of Jax beer before retiring. The sounds of the Quarter wafted up from the street below- the raucous invitations of the strip joint barkers inviting the tourists to come in and see the worn out, tired, and bored women who gyrated through bumps and grinds each night, trying to convince some sexually deprived male that she was desireable- that she still had it. Some were so talented, and so well endowed by nature, that they were able to spin tassels attached to their pendulous breasts in counter rotation-quite a feat. The men, sipping their watered-down drinks, looked on in amazement, especially those with A cup wives.

Laverne pondered Rainey's question for a long time. She had asked herself the same question many times. She took a deep drag, and exhaling the smoke upward until it caught on the slight breeze coming in from the river. She shrugged. "I don't know. I can't decide if my desires far exceed my intellingence, or, if I am just plain horny. I don't know!" and she became pensive. Then, turning to Rainey, "On the other hand, luv, I can't understand how you can go so long without feeling some man's arms around you, whispering sweet nothings in your ear, caressing every inch of your body..." and she let her voice fade away.

Now, Rainey became pensive. She inhaled deeply. "Oh, I must admit I have those longings, too, and you know, Laverne, I do indulge now and then, but I guess I'm looking for more than you are."

Laverne shrugged. "Is there really more? Are you sure?"

She nodded her head, looking at the crowds down below them. "There's got to be more. Those sweet nothings you refer to... do you care if they're true or not?"

"No, I don't. I just want to hear them."

She shook her head. "No, I want them to be real. I want to hear them from a man who really means them... not just bullshit."

Laverne smiled. "Rainey, luv, I don't know if such a man exists... not for me, anyway. I hope you find one someday if that is what you really want. As for me,

I guess I'm just looking for a warm body with manly attributes, if you know what I mean, and when I am through with him, out he goes and I find another one."

"Did you ever think they're just using you?"

"Hell, yes! I'm using them, too. It takes two to tango you know. I'm way past that solo gratification bit. I'm a little too old to play games anymore."

Rainey nodded. "How about this Mark Berteau? You've been seeing a lot of that Cajun. Are you getting serious about him?"

She emptied the remainder of her beer over the rail, not looking to see if it had fallen on some tourists, or not.

She sighed deeply. "I could get serious over him. He rings my bells, as you like to say."

Rainey's eyebrows went up. "Really? Real bells or just a tinkle?"

"Real bells, I think," and looking off into the dark sky, "He's married, you know."

Rainey sat up, her head turning to her friend. "Dammit, Laverne, I thought we had an agreement when we came here. No married men! They're big trouble and you know it. Have you forgotten Bob Acker so soon?"

She drew her knees under her chin. "No, I haven't forgotten. I swear I didn't encourage it, Rainey. It just happened."

She snapped back. "Oh, bullshit, Laverne! Things like that just don't happen, especially to someone with your experience. You damn sure knew what was going on. You just didn't want it to stop."

This was the first real argument they had ever had. When they first came to New Orleans, they made a pact. They would never let a man come between them... never. Men just weren't worth it.

Laverne became defensive. "I couldn't help it. We work together, you know. How could I avoid him? He's my boss."

"You never told me he was your boss."

"You never asked me."

Rainey looked away without replying for a while. "Look, Laverne, I'm sorry if I snapped at you, but you know how I feel about you. Sometimes, I think I.."

Laverned placed her hand on her cheek. "I know, sweetie, and you know how I feel about you, too."

Rainey rose. "I'm going to bed."

Laverne rose also. "Me, too," and with some hesitation, then, "Rainey... can I come in your bed tonight? I need some company, luv."

She stood at the door for a minute, running her hand over the wood trim, thinking, and without looking back, "If you want to, Laverne... come on."

The next morning was Saturday and they both slept late. Rainey rose to go to the bathroom and she looked down at her sleeping roommate, still nude. She stood for a moment, admiring that still beautiful body on what was now a thirty-three year old woman. She thought: No wonder men won't leave her alone, and she doesn't do much to discourage them, so what can you expect. She reached down and pulled a sheet over her even though warm air was coming through the wood shutters which formed a visual screen for the open, full length windows, a holdover from the colonial architecture of past years when closed windows would have been unbearable.

She made her way to the kitchen and put on some coffee while she lit her first cigarette of the day. She walked out on the balcony. It was a different world, the French Quarter, between night and day. The raucous noises, the too loud music coming from the bars and strip joints were replaced by the sound of diesel trucks delivering merchandise or picking up garbage from the night before. She could see the usual allotment of drunks leaning against the buildings where they had fallen. Some proprietors, hosing their sidewalks down, would douse them along with the sidewalk. It would awaken some, and others, too far gone, would merely grunt and roll over.

Rainey smiled, thinking: There is just no place like it. I love it. Nobody gives a damn what you are and what you do. A hundred people would pass those drunks within the next hour and probably not one would stoop down to see if they were still breathing, or not. Only the police, if they saw them there by early afternoon, would nudge them with a billy club, telling them to move on or be arrested. After all, it made a bad impression on the tourists.

As she sauntered back into the kitchen, Laverne was coming from the bathroom. She could hear the toilet flushing. Laverne gave her a sheepish look as she went to the coffee pot. "I'm sorry about last night. I got carried away, I guess. I didn't intend for it to go that far."

Rainey sat in the chair, turning her coffee cup around with her fingers. "We agreed to quit, you know."

She looked down at the floor. "I know. I'm sorry."

She sighed. "It's okay. I'm a big girl. I could have said no."

"It won't happen again, I promise. I swear."

"Okay."

"What do you want to do today?"

"Nothing special. How about you?"

"Do you have a date for tonight?"

Rainey nodded. "Yes."

"Who with?"

You remember Harlan?"

"Harlan... who?"

"That civil engineer who has done some consulting work for the company. Harlan Kemper."

"Oh, yes. I thought you said you weren't interested in him."

She shrugged her shoulders. "Oh... I'm not real interested, but he is nice. Maybe, too nice."

Laverne looked up. "How can a man be too nice?"

"When he is so nice he is boring."

"What do you mean?"

"Geez, he drives me crazy trying to please me. He stands up when I get up, and he stands up when I come back, and he asks me every five minutes... do you want something?... can I get something else for you? What would you like to do, tonight?"

"So, is that bad? Sounds to me like the guy is crazy about you. That's the way they act, you know."

"Yes, I know," and she thought of the barnyard rooster with their posturing around the hens, and she smiled.

"Do you like him... even a little?"

She grinned. "Just a little, but I don't hear any bells ringing."

Laverne gave her an impish grin. "Have you bedded him down, yet?"

"Heavens, no! We're not even close to that?"

Rising, Laverne said, "If we're not going to do anything special today, I just may make some plans of my own."

"Would they include Mark Berteau?"

She smiled. "They might. His wife is visiting her mother in Baton Rouge, so he's available for the day," and she added without embarrassment, "and the night."

Curious, Rainey asked. "Since it's Saturday, why didn't he go to Baton Rouge with his wife?" These shenanigans always interested her.

Laverne grinned. "I can't imagine... can you?"

Rainey stood and looked at her friend and roommate "Laverne, you'd better be careful. You're playing with fire."

"That's where the warmth is, luv. You should know that."

She nodded as she went into the bathroom. "Uh, huh, and that's also where you get burned"

Sunday mornings are special in the French quarter. All the natives are still asleep and the streets are taken over by the tourists. Those with sense and experience know that this is by far the best time to walk Bourbon and Royal. The bars are open, that's true, for they never close, and the smell of stale smoke and stale liquor permeate the air coming through the open doors, but except for a few diehards, the places are empty. The strippers are asleep, whether alone or with some well-heeled tourist, or their bosses, or pimps, depends on the situation. These are the night people, and now, the Quarter is taken over by the day people.

Rainey rolled over in her bed and looked at her radio clock. It was 10:30. Her date with Harlan Kemper the night before was a quiet affair- a small supper at Tujaque's and a movie. Some ice cream in the Quarter, a walk home and a light goodnight kiss. He had asked her if he could come in. She had said..."No".

She could hear the bells of the St. Louis Cathedral peal as they beckoned the faithful to that mass. Her religious fervor had never taken root. She had been exposed to none when she lived with her mother and her grandmother. They had been immersed so deeply in their own misery that there was no room for God. With the Fosters, she had sat through those interminable Sunday harangues as the old Baptist preacher threatened the congregation with fire and brimstone, as if he were personally in charge of invoking them. With the school teachers, whose religious fervor had been dampened by too much education, she had only been required to sit through the services on Sunday, and having done that, the name of the Creator was hardly mentioned during the week, not even in vain.

She and Laverne had gone to mass at the St. Louis Cathedral on some occasions, especially Christmas and Easter. However, when the entire congregation had marched up to the communion rail for Holy Communion, not to be impolite or unappreciative, they, too, partook of the Sacrament. since they were both in a state of sin of varying degrees, ranging from fornication to adultery, it can be assumed that they committed an act of sacrilege. But, the church teaches that if a sin is committed in ignorance, then, it is not a sin.

She stretched and yawned. She arose and tip-toed to Laverne's door, and upon hearing no noises of any kind, she slowly opened the door. She had done this on previous occasions and in some cases, she had seen Laverne alone in bed- on others, she had seen Laverne and some male in bed- and on others, she had seen no one in bed. This morning, she saw no one. Laverne had not come home on this Saturday night. That, alone, did not alarm her because it was not an uncommon occurrence, especially as she recalled her previously announced tryst with Mark Berteau.

She closed the door and walked towards the kitchen. She heard a knock on the door- a loud knock.

As she peeked through the half-opened shutters, she could see two uniformed police officers standing there, clipboard in hand. She wrapped her bathrobe tightly around her body and went to the door. She stood there for a moment, not sure of what to do. There was another loud knock. She opened the door about six inches wide and peering through, said softly..."Yes?"

They removed their service caps. One was a sergeant and the other had no rank on his sleeve. He cocked his head at her to determine if there was anyone else behind the door.

"Excuse the intrusion, Ma'am, but we're trying to determine if a Laverne Sutter might live here."

At the sound of Laverne's name, she gasped. she knew this couldn't be good news. She was afraid Laverne had gotten herself in some trouble with Mark Berteau. She replied, weakly, "Yes, Laverne Sutter lives here, but she's not at home. Could I take a message?" Her voice was a little shaky.

The police nodded, as if they knew something she didn't. Looking around the balcony and seeing the couple next door on their balcony, cranning their necks and ears, they said, "Could we come in, Ma'am?"

She hesitated. She was not sure if she should let them in or not. She had read in the Times Picayune just recently that, right here in New Orleans, two men had gone around in stolen police uniforms and after gaining entrance to some woman's apartment, had gang raped her for several hours. She said in a shaky and unsure voice, "May I see your identification, please?"

They both nodded. "Yes, Ma'am, you can. We don't blame you. You can't be too safe these days, what with all the strangers and riff-raff in the city," and they both produced badges and photo identification. She carefully compared the faces with the badges, and being satisfied, opened the door. "Come in, please. The place is a mess, but..."

They entered and looked around, asking, "May we have your name, Miss?"

She nodded. "Yes, of course, my name is Rainey Wether."

They both gave her a quisical glance, with one saying, "Would you please spell your name?" She slowly did so.

He scribbled it down as he exchanged looks with his colleague.

She could wait no longer. "What is this all about? I think you owe me some explanation..."

They did not answer her question. Instead, "What is your relationship to Laverne Sutter, Miss Wether?"

She pulled her robe around her body even tighter. "Well, she is my best friend... and my roommate. We live here together," and she waved her hand around the apartment, and once again, she implored, "Has something happened to Laverne? Please... tell me!"

One of them took her by the arm and led her to the couch. "Perhaps, you'd better sit down, Ma'am."

Those words and his actions struck fear in her heart. She knew he would not be acting like this if something awful had not happened. She begin to shake with fear.

It was the sergeant who spoke: "Miss Wether, I'm afraid I have some bad news to tell you."

Her hands went to her throat. "Oh, my God! Something has happened to her... is that it?"

He nodded.

"What?"

Instead of answering directly, he inquired: "Miss Wether, do you know a Mark Berteau?" He had spelled the last name.

She shook her head, at first, and then nodded. "Well, I don't know him, but I know he and Laverne have been seeing each..." and she stopped. This was getting complicated. He was a married man. She corrected it to: "Laverne knows him.

He is her boss," and then in desperation, "For God's sake, tell me what this is all about."

He placed his hand on her arm in a gentle fashion. "I'm sorry to tell you they are both dead, Miss Wether..."

She gasped, then collapsed in his arms, screaming..."Oh, no, not another one. Oh, no, it can't be. Say it isn't so," and throwing her head back on the back of the couch, began to moan..."Oh, no! My God, say it isn't so..."

The sergeant, ever so solicitous, asked, "Can I get you something? A glass of water? A Coke?"

Her head came forward and she hunched over, her hands clasped in her lap. She shook her head. "No, thank you. I'll be okay," and trying to compose herself, "How did it happen?"

The sergeant turned to the other officer and nodding towards him, "Officer Commeaux, here, was the first on the scene. I'll let him tell you about it."

The young policeman moved his head from side to side. "Well, from what we can determine, they were coming back from Biloxi on Highway 90, and as they got close to the Rigolets, the road takes a turn... and they swerved to miss a bridge abutment," and he took a deep breath. "I guess the driver lost control and they went into the water." He added: "They must have been driving at a very fast rate. There is a sign warning drivers to slow down to 45 for that curve, but I guess..." and his voice dropped off

"Then," she suggested, "they drowned."

The sergeant responded. "Well, there will be an autopsy performed to determine the actual cause of death, but at first glance, we think they drowned."

Rainey moaned as she mentally picured her friend fighting for her life, trapped in that car, that beautiful face gasping for every breath, and she shuddered. She composed herself once again. "How do they know they had been to Biloxi?"

The younger officer responded. "We found some brochures from the Broadwater Beach Hotel, and we also found some whiskey bottles, one of them half empty. They had been doing some serious drinking," and he looked at his partner, adding, "we think drinking was the real cause of the accident."

Rainey nodded. She could believe that. She and Laverne had done their share of drinking in the past several years. Along with smoking, Rainey had developed a taste for alcohol, even scotch. Laverne had already had a taste when they met. She looked from one policeman to the other. "What is going to happen next? What am I supposed to do?" She dried her eyes on her robe, without shame, as one leg was exposed.

"We have some more questions that we have to ask you. Are you up to it, now?"

She nodded. "Go ahead."

"Well, for one thing, we need to know what the relationship was between the victims?"

Her head came up. "Why do you have to know that?"

"In going through Mr. Berteau's wallet, he listed his wife as the one to notify in case of an accident, so he was married, and quite obviously, not to Miss Sutter."

She didn't know how else to put it. "Yes, they were seeing each other," and thinking of the poor deceived wife, asked, "is it really necessary that the wife be informed of this?"

"I don't see how it can be avoided. The newspapers will certainly pick that up," and looking at his pad, "incidentally, we tried to call Mrs. Berteau but her phone went unanswered. Do you have any idea where she is?"

"Laverne said something about her going to Baton Rouge to visit her mother for the weekend."

One officer, the one with the clipboard, began to write on his pad. "Do you know the name of her mother?"

"No, of course not. I don't know them at all." She thought for a moment, then, "What will happen to the body? Where is she now?" She could not mention her name.

"Well, that's another thing we have to ask you. Did she have family hereabouts? Her wallet folder showed only you as the one to notify. We found that strange."

"She came here from England during the war. She was a war bride, but she divorced her husband right after getting here. She told me she was an orphan, like me," and she sobbed as she added, "I guess that's one more thing we had in common."

"Then, you know of no one that we can notify in her family."

She shook her head. "No, no one. You still haven't told me where she is now. I want to see her, even if..." and her words died off.

"The body is in the city morgue, and that's where it will stay until the coroner releases it, and he won't release it until he determines the cause of death. That's the law, Miss."

She could not help but notice that he now referred to Laverne as "it" and that hurt her deeply, but she realized they were only being realistic. Laverne, beautiful Laverne, was not a person anymore. "Then," she inquired, "what happens to the body after the coroner releases it?"

"It will be sent to the funeral home of the family's choosing," and he turned to her. "Who will make that decision, Miss Wether…you?"

She gave them an unsure look. "I can't think of anyone else who will do it."

Somewhat embarrassed, he asked, "Do you know if she has the money to pay for a funeral?"

"Why do you ask that?"

"Well," and he looked down at the floor, "if she doesn't, she will be buried in Potter's field"

Her eyebrows raised. "What is that?"

"It's the city graveyard for the poor and the indigents who have no family, or, no money... nothing. They have to be buried someplace..."

She stiffened. "No, that will not be necessary. Between her small savings and some money I have, she will have a decent burial."

The two officers rose, with the sergeant placing his arm on her shoulder. "I'm sorry, Miss Wether, that we had to bring you this sad news. Can we do anything else for you?"

She looked at him with vision blurred by tears. "No, thank you. You've been very kind. I know you're just doing your job. Will you call me when I can claim the remains'"

"I promise. I'll do it personally."

"Thank you. Now, if you don't mind, I'd like to be alone."

After showing them out, she barely made it back to the couch where she collapsed in a fetal position, moaning and sobbing, asking the usual questions of a God she had heretofore spoken to very little. "Why? why? For the second time in my life... why?"

For the remainder of the day and on into the night, she pondered her fate. Was she really star-crossed. Was she really a child of misfortune, destined to go from one heart breaking tragedy to the next? But, as she delved deeper into the two tragedies, she discovered a common thread. Verlie did not have to die. It was a result of her playing with fire, breaking the rules. And what of Laverne? She did not have to die on that particular day, at that particular time, either. No! She, too, had played with fire. She had flaunted the rules. As she lay in her bed that night, she made some hard decisions. She would take better control of her life. Although she had not flaunted the rules as they had, she watched as her friends did. Her thoughts went back to Martha Powell, who, in one of her many lectures to Rainey on morals and virtue, had intoned: If you play in the mud, you will get muddy, too.

CHAPTER TWENTY

It was a beautiful day for a funeral as the earthly remains of Laverne Sutter were lowered into the rich alluvial soil of the huge old cemetary at the north end of Canal Street where it turns into Canal Boulevard and continues its journey to Lake Pontchartrain.

Rainey stood, holding on to the supporting arm of Harlan Kemper. The tragedy had brought them closer together as she sought solace in his arms. In addition, there were three women from Laverne's office who felt it was their Christian duty to be there. The often discussed rumors of the affair had now been confirmed among their fellow workers. Some, the more moral of the group, had condemned them for it, while others, especially those who had previously sinned, understood the immorality.

In Baton Rouge just seventy miles to the north, in another cemetery, not too far from where she and her husband had attended L.S.U. together, a young widow stood with her two young children at the gravesite of the husband and father. They, too, were mesmerized by the tragdey. The wife, still young, attractive, and desireable, shook her head at the insanity of it all. She sobbed, squeezing the hands of her children, as she asked herself: Where did I fail? What did he want that I could not give him? Women have asked these questions for milennia, but no answers were forthcoming.

William Shakespeare, centuries before, wrote these profound and fitting words: OH WHAT TANGLED WEBS WE WEAVE, WHEN FIRST WE PRACTICE TO DECEIVE

* * *

It was Thursday of that fateful week before those unfortunate souls were laid to rest. Rainey had been shaken to her roots. Only a few days before, on Saturday, she had told Laverne goodbye as she had left to begin a weekend tryst with her lover, Mark Berteau, as she, Rainey, had made her plans to see Harlan Kemper that night. It had begun as a typical weekend for the fun loving and free living young women, and now...

She had taken the rest of the week off from work. She was in no shape to work and her bosses knew it. She had remained in her apartment... thinking... just thinking. Even Harlan Kemper, by repeated telephone calls, attempting to offer some diversion, was rebuffed in his attempts. She told him, simply, "I've got a lot of thinking to do." And she had. She began to search her life for the past five years, hers and Lavernes's. She was now twenty-three, officially and biologically, and Laverne had been thirty-three. They had had fun, it was true, but is that what life is all about. Other women her age were married and had children. They led

Rainey

stable lives, with a husband to give them protection and security... and comfort. Now, with Laverne gone, she had no one to comfort her, to give her solace, and with the safety of numbers, to afford some protection. She thought of Harlan Kemper, the mild mannered and boring man who was trying to make her his wife. She had never heard the bells chime as yet, and she wondered if he would ever do that to her... ring her chimes. Perhaps, she reasoned, she was living an impractical fantasy. Had not Martha Powell told her that most marriages were miserable and unhappy ones? But, how was she to know? She wasn't sure she was ready for marriage just yet, but she was sure of one thing; she wanted a change in her life.

Saturday morning after the funeral, still shaken from the tragedy, she remained in the apartment in spite of protests from Harlan Kemper. "Rainey, you have got to pull yourself together and get on with your life."

"I know... I know," was her soft reply.

She had retrieved her Times Picayune from the balcony where the paperboy threw it each morning from the street below. She walked back into the apartment and went to the kitchen for a cup of coffee. She withdrew a cigarette from the pack and beat it on the end table, then lighting it, she settled down to read. She opened it to the obituaries, and as she had expected, there was Laverne's notice. There wasn't much to say about her. She had no survivors, no family... nothing. And, said Rainey to herself, if I don't change my way of living I will end up the same way... no family... nothing.

As she swallowed some coffee, she drew hard on the cigarette, seeking some solace in that narcotic weed. She cocked her ear as she thought she heard someone come up the outside stair which served that apartment and the one next door. She did hear noise and she assumed it was her neighbor coming back from her grocery shopping which she did each Saturday morning. Then, she heard a key being inserted in her lock and she sat up, afraid, not sure what to do. She knew no one but Laverne and her landlord had keys to that door. She watched with eyes wide with fear as the door opened and a familiar voice yelled out, "Hi, luv, it's me. I'm back!" and the beautiful bronze tresses of Laverne could be seen followed by that still beautiful face.

Rainey screamed in horror, a blood-curdling scream as her coffee cup crashed to the floor and she fainted, slumping on the couch. Laverne ran to her "Jesus, luv, I expected you to be glad to see me, but, not this..."

Laverne ran to the prostrate woman, attempting to lift her, but she was limp and hard to hold. She looked up, bewildered, not sure what to do. She ran to the kitchen and wet a wash cloth and ran back to the still collapsed figure of her roommate. She applied the wet cloth to her forehead, then massaged her wrists, trying to increase the flow of blood. Rainey stirred and moaned, and with half-opened eyes, she looked at Laverne and screamed. "You're dead! We buried you two days ago..."

Laverne smiled "I admit I am dead tired, sweetie, but not dead... not hardly."

Rainey managed to sit up, shaking all over, still not able to grasp the fact that a real live Laverne was standing over her. She reached out to touch her, to ensure that she was really there in the flesh. Laverne gave her a strange look. "Rainey, what the hell is wrong with you? I go to Havana for a week and come back and find you a total wreck. What the hell happened?"

She tried to clear her head. "Havana? You've been in Havana?"

She shrugged. "Hell, sweetie, didn't you get my telegram?"

She shook her head. "What telegram?"

"Oh, shit. Those foreigners never get anything right. I sent you a telegram from the Hotel Nacional where Augie and I were staying for the week. I explained everything and I asked you to cover for me at the office."

Rainey tried to clear her head. "But, who is Augie? You died with Mark Berteau...""

"Really, Rainey, I wish you would drop all this dying crap. It makes me nervous."

Rainey managed to sit up. "Laverne, we buried you and Mark two days ago in..."

Laverne gasped. "Buried me and Mark? Is Mark dead?"

"Yes, you and Mark were killed in an automobile accident on your way back from Biloxi!" she practically screamed.

Laverne sat down, slumping in a chair. "Jesus, Mark dead?"

Rainey insisted, "And you, too!"

"Dammit, Rainey, I want you to quit saying I am dead. Look, luv, feel this flesh, put your hand on my boobs. This is the same old Laverne in the flesh. You may have buried some poor girl a few days ago but it damn sure was not Laverne."

The adrenaline was beginning to flow in Rainey "But, then, who did we bury? Who went to Biloxi with Mark?"

Laverned shrugged. "Hell, I don't know! He and I had a big fight in the car that morning when we were getting ready to go to Biloxi... a real bad fight. He called me a bitch and I threw my wallet at him. It was the only thing I had in my hands at the time. Some stuff flew out, but I gathered up what I could and got out the car. He yelled through the open window, "Go ahead, you crazy bitch, I can find another woman to replace you in five minutes, and he scratched off. That's the last I saw of him..."

"But... but, who did we bury?"

She rose to get some coffee while she lit a cigarette. "Probably some little trollop he picked up in the Monteleone bar. That's where he said he was going."

Rainey sat up, now in some control of her senses, and looking at Laverne: "How the hell did you get to Havana?"

She lit her cigarette. "Well, did I mention that I knew this fellow, Augie Medusa?"

Rainey shook her head, not answering.

"Well, I met him some time ago. I had a few dates with him, but I had never bedded him down. I was sitting in the Roosevelt bar trying to decide how to salvage the weekend when he came in. He's loaded with money, you know. I think he's connected with the Mafia. He lives in his boathouse at the marina at the Southern Yacht Club... real nice. Well, anyway, he sees me sitting at the bar, alone, and that always gets men excited for some reason." She dragged heavily on the weed. "Well, he came up and sat next to me asking the most profound question, and she smiled, "What's up, Laverne, baby?"

Rainey merely sat there, speechless, still trying to decide whether to kill her for real this time, or not.

Laverne continued her monologue. "Well, one thing led to another and he propositioned me, just like that," and she snapped her fingers. "He said, 'Laverne, honey, how'd you like to go to Havana for a week?' He must have seen my eyes light up. He said, 'some friends and I are leaving from Moisant in a few hours. Come on. Come with us. We'll have a ball.' I gave it some thought. I was still highly pissed off at Mark. I wanted to make him jealous. I decided to go... what the hell, and guess what, Rainey? When I told him I just had clothes enough for one night, he said, 'Don't worry about that, baby, we'll get you a new wardrobe in Havana.' Wasn't that sweet? So, I went."

Rainey sat up with fire in her eyes. "You crazy bitch! You are insane and you are driving me crazy," and before Laverne could respond, she continued her tirade, "you are completely irresponsible. I used to think it was cute when I was younger, but I am now convinced you are nuts."

Laverne opened her mouth as if to speak, but she was not able to as Rainey pointed her finger in her face. "Do you realize that I spent my last goddam dollar to buy you a casket? A nice one, too," she cried. As she wiped her eyes on her sleeve. "Jesus, I wish I had bought the cheaper one. That's all you deserve"

Laverne noticed that she was out of words for the moment. "I can understand, luv, how you might be upset, not having received the telegram and all, but, really, Rainey, luv, I think you are overreacting."

Rainey shook her head as she looked at her in amazement. "You know, Laverne, we have a mess on our hands, thanks to you."

In all innocence. "What mess?"

Rainey pointed in a direction which she mistakenly believed to be the graveyard. "There's some poor girl lying in a grave out there in that cemetery and it has your name on it. Who do you think is in that grave? Some poor soul. God knows who?" and she began to cry.

Laverne became solicitous. "Now, now, sweetie, we'll have all that straightened out next week. That poor girl is in no hurry, I'm sure," and she giggled. "Why don't we take a good hot bath and then put on some cute little dresses and go out for a good brunch at Brennan's... on me. I got lucky at the tables in Havana."

Rainey sat up with eyes ablaze. "No, Laverne, we will not go anywhere together... never again. I want you out of here and out of my life. I want to live a normal life for a change and I am convinced I can never do it with you."

Laverne sat up, stiffened. "Well, now if that is the way you want it, then, things might work out better than I thought. You see, Augie has asked me to move in with him in the boathouse, and I hesitated so as not to hurt your feelings, but..."

"The money, Laverne, I want the money back I spent on your casket. It was all I had."

Laverne took a deep breath, and reaching for her purse, extracted a large roll of hundred dollar bills. She smiled at Rainey. "Like I said, luv, I had good luck at the tables," and as she began to peel off the bills, "how much did you say it was? Twelve hundred? Here it is, sweetie."

Rainey, still shaking her head in disbelief, gathered the money and placed in her robe pocket.

Laverne stood looking down at her. "I wish we could have parted in a more friendly fashion, Rainey," and becoming more mellow, "we have had some tender moments together..."

Rainey raised her hands in protest. "Don't! Please."

"All right. What are you going to do, now, that I am gone? Are you going to stay here in this place?"

She started to answer, but she merely looked straight ahead, saying softly, "I don't know. I have a lot of thinking to do."

"Well, if you want to talk to me... if you need anything, you can find me at the marina... boathouse 95-B." She headed to the bedroom to pack, adding, "I told you Augie is loaded. As long as I can keep him happy, my money worries are over."

As she watched Laverne walk off, seemingly unconcerned at her part in the tragedy, Rainey noticed that pungent odor of marijuana followed her as she moved off. Rainey, herself, had tried it on several occasions, but when one episode had ended in a complete collapse of her morals and she woke up the next morning in bed with a man she did not even know, she never tried it again, but she knew the smell. There was no doubt of it, it was embedded in her clothing, she concluded. She nodded to herself. It all adds up. She is high on marijuana. She has been high on the stuff all week. Her system is soaked with it. Now, it makes sense. Augie Medusa is a Mafioso. It was a well known fact in New Orleans that the Mafia were bringing the weed in from Cuba. Some even suspected that Batista, the Cuban dictator, was part and parcel of the operation, although he had not been accused publicly.

Rainey

My God, she wondered as she thought about Laverne's latest whacky decision. What is that crazy woman getting herself into? It all made sense to her now. They wanted Laverne to be a courier for them. She had heard that the Mafia had recruited beautiful women to fly back and forth carrying packages of narcotics strapped between their legs, the last place a custom official would dare look. She shook her head in despair. She was still sitting there as Laverne came out with two bags packed. She came and stood in front of Rainey. Rainey noticed that she had dificulty in standing still and erect. She was high.

Through eyes half opened, Laverne managed a smile. "Rainey, I packed everything I could in these two bags, but I still have plenty of stuff left. Do you mind if I send someone back for the rest of it?" She shrugged. "Augie has all kinds of people around him all the time, just there to do his bidding."

She looked up with some compassion at this woman with whom she had shared the last five years. She felt she owed her this much. "Laverne... are you sure you know what you're doing? I don't think this is a good idea for you."

Laverne pondered that for a moment in her cloudy mind and she nearly sobbed. "Listen, sweetie, I've been looking all my life for some man to give me the luxuries of life, and I think I have found him. All I've got to do is keep him happy... nothing else. I did that all this week and it was not too unpleasant. He's Italian, you know!" she smiled. Those words struck home. Rainey's heart ached as she thought of Verlie and her admonition. "They make great lovers, but lousy husbands."

Rainey raised her hands in futility. "Well, Laverne, if that is what you want, I wish you well," and she smiled at her.

Laverne started to bend down to kiss her, but still shaky and not seeing any move on Rainey's part to meet her halfway, she threw her a kiss. "Bye, luv. Try to think a kind thought of Laverne every now and then, will you," and with tears in her eyes, "Life's a bitch, you know... especially for us girls."

Rainey watched as she made her way through the door, not looking back. She laid her head back on the couch, and she cried.

She stayed that way for quite some time, past lunch time and on into the afternoon. She finally fell asleep due to sheer exhaustion. As she awoke, she began to think again. She picked up the phone and called the Athletic Club of New Orleans. The black custodian coughed to clear his throat. "De Ath'letta Club. Jason speakin'."

"Is Mr. Harlan Kemper there in the club?" She knew his Saturday schedule, for he seldom departed from it.

The old porter took time to look around, then: "Yassum, he heah."

"Would you call him to the phone, please?"

"Yassum. Who's callin', pleeze?"

"Tell him Rainey.

"Jus Rainey? Lak in de weatha?"

"Yes."

Harlan, short of breath. "Rainey, I'm so glad you called."

"Hi, Harlan. I was just sitting here, thinking about you."

With some excitement. "Really?"

"Yes, you know you've been trying to get me to go out since the... the accident... you remember?"

"Of, course, I remember. I still think you should. You will have to forget Laverne someday, Rainey, and you might as well start now."

"I think you're right, Harlan."

"Well, do you want to go out tonight? Do you feel like it?"

"Uh, huh, I do."

"What do you feel like doing?"

"Oh, nothing exciting. Let's just go somewhere where we can talk. I have a lot to talk about. Some of it, you will have a hard time believing."

He paused. "Rainey, you sound funny. Are you all right?"

"I'm fine. I'll explain it all to you tonight. Goodbye, Harlan."

CHAPTER TWENTY-ONE

Audubon Park, which extends from St. Charles Avenue to the Mississippi River, dates back to the colonial period of New Orleans. It has seen floods when the great river was unable to contain the snow melt from the forty-one percent of the United States which it drains- it has seen duels, in earlier times, between men of passion when an apology was neither offered nor accepted- it has been a refuge from city life for the poor and middle class of the city who could not afford to seek those respites from more elite and private places, and under the moss-laden brances of the magnificent Live Oaks, countless lovers have exchanged those tender words of endearment meant to bind them together for life.

Rainey and Harlan had been in such a discussion for the past hour under those moss-laden limbs of the impressive trees. She had attempted, as best she could, to explain the Laverne Sutter saga to him, but other than shaking his head, saying, "Oh, my God, I can't believe what I'm hearing", he had difficulty in comprehending the story.

"Do you mean to tell me, Rainey, that that crazy woman went off to Cuba without telling you..."

"Well, she said she sent me a telegram from the Hotel Nacional in Havana, but..." and she, too, could only shake her head in disbelief.

Having gotten the Laverne thing out of the way Rainey now turned her attention to the main topic of the evening. She had given the matter much thought the night before as she tossed in her bed. She was confident that she could talk Harlan Kemper into marrying her because he had hinted at it on several occasions, and she knew that women held power over men because of their bodies. It was the way nature intended it. But, she was ambivalent in her own mind as to whether or not this was what she wanted. She was bored with her job, and in keeping with the modes of the times, she knew that if they married he would insist that she quit her job and become a wife and mother. She thought of children and her mind went back to her own unfortunate childhood. She had developed a deep-rooted compunction to bringing children into this world. Down deep in her soul, she really didn't want children, but she knew that men, especially family oriented men like Harlan, felt that children were a natural part of the marriage union. She made up her mind to skirt around the issue if it came up. She wondered if she might be taking advantage of the love-strickened man.

She was sitting to the far side of the car and he was to the far side of the driver's side. There had been no attempt at any degree of intimacy as yet. It was a warm night and the car windows were down. A slight breeze was coming off the river, a short distance away. She had purposely stayed on her side of the car, preferring not to confuse Harlan with intimacy, for his fires burned brightly-much more brightly than hers, but she had decided she needed to tone down her life and no one she knew was more toned down than Harlan. He came from a good solid Catholic family from the bayou country, and even though they were not Cajuns, his family had absorbed the Cajun virtues of family values. He believed in the sanctity of the family. Rainey, who had never had a family, longed for these same virtues in her life... as she understood them.

After she felt that he had absorbed the Laverne story as well as he ever would, she looked at him with female coyness and tickling the back of his neck, inquired, "Are you going to stay on that side of the car all night, Harlan?"

He swallowed hard. "Well, you told me you just wanted to talk, so..."

She nodded. "Well, I'm through talking about Laverne. I think it's time to talk about us, don't you?" and she slid over to his side.

He smiled both inwardly and outwardly. He had loved Rainey for some months, now, but every time he had broached the subject of marriage, she had demurred with, "I don't think I'm ready for that yet, Harlan," and being the low-keyed and gentlemanly person he was, he would reply, "I'm willing to wait, Rainey. I don't want to rush you. I want you to be sure."

The truth is that Rainey was not madly in love with Harlan. At first, this had bothered her, because she felt she should wait until the bells really chimed, but they never did. Now, with the pragmatism brought on by her nearing twenty-five and the desire to moderate her life style after the Laverne fiasco, she now viewed Harlan in a different light. Sure, there were other men who either worked with her or around her, but in some ways these men were sypmtomatic of her perception of what was wrong with men in general. They were boastful, deceitful, unfaithful, egotistical, unreliable, crude, uncultured, and downright obnoxious- she felt. This was based on her reference plane which was a result of her previous life. In other words, she had never met a really nice man even though some of the women she worked with said they had, on one occasion or another, but when questioned further by her, they all seemed to admit that they married something else. So, even though Harlan was not Mr. Magic she felt, quite erroneously, that she had to do something soon before her time ran out. She had made so many bad decisions in the past that she now lacked confidence in herself. And then, there was the matter of disclosure. She felt two people should bare their souls before taking the big step-a confession of sorts, so that the sacrament could be partaken with a pristine conscience. It was not the advice she had gleaned from Verlie and Laverne, but they were gone.

She snuggled close to him and ran her arm around his waist. He placed his arm around her neck and he began to breathe a little harder. For a while nothing was said. Harlan was reluctant to break this magic spell, then, without moving her head from his chest..."Harlan?"

"Yes..."

"You know, you've said on many occasions that you love me..." He nodded. "I do, too. I told you that."

She played with her forefinger on his chest. "I think I'm beginning to fall in love with you, too." This was basically a lie.

"Oh, Rainey," and he tilted her head back. "You've made me so happy by saying that," and he kissed her tenderly. She had closed her eyes waiting on at least a tinkle, but she heard none. Undeterred, she responded to his kiss.

He inquired. "When did you find out you loved me?"

She thought for a moment. "A few days ago, but, I've been thinking of it for a few weeks. I just wanted to be sure."

He held her close again, and she responded.

Harlan felt he should say something else to preserve the magic before it slipped away, and before she slipped away. "Don't you think we should talk about marriage, then?"

She smiled inwardly. It had been so easy that her conscience hurt her. But, still, the words jolted her. A psychologist, schooled in the arena of human emotions, would probably say her mental jolt was due to her reaction to the earlier disastrous venture in that field with Douglas Walker, incomplete though it was, and it was true. She had never observed, as yet, a happy marriage between any two people, so she had a natural compunction against that particular sacrament.

With complete coquetry, "What do you mean, Harlan?"

He held her close. "Well, when two people are in love, they usually think of marriage, Rainey."

"Do you mean you are really asking me to marry you, Harlan?"

"Uh, huh, that's what I mean."

"Oh, Harlan..." and she kissed him passionately. He was completely in her power after that as she resumed her plotting. "Well, when do you want to get married? This is so sudden. I haven't even given it any thought." That, too, was a lie.

"Well, whenever you want to," and drawing back, "I'll have to tell my mama and daddy about it, first."

"Of course. You should."

He sat up. "I guess we need to do some serious planning."

"You mean about the wedding?"

"Well, of course, Rainey. We need to decide where it will be and when and... about your bridesmaids and..."

She bolted upright. She had not expected the proposal this night and she was not ready with the answers. She had not actually thought of the wedding in detail. Her mind raced for answers. She felt she had to talk to him, now... about a lot of things.

She broke from his embrace. "Harlan, we need to talk."

"I thought we just did."

"No, I mean some serious talking... about us, but, mostly, about me."

"Oh, Rainey, I know as much about you as I need to..."

She shook her head. "No, you only think you do. I want to tell you about me, Harlan," and she breathed deeply, "when I'm finished, you might not want to marry me."

He tried to bring her to him. "Oh, Rainey..."

She drew back. "No, I mean it, Harlan... listen to what I have to say."

He sat up. "Okay. Go ahead."

"To begin with. I'm not a virgin."

"Oh, hell, Rainey, I'm not either."

She swallowed. "Well, it's not expected for a boy, but it is for a girl."

"I don't care about that. Uh, how many have there been?"

She tried to remember. "I'm not sure... maybe a dozen or so."

He blew air between his lips. "A dozen? I hadn't figured on that many, Rainey."

"That's not all, Harlan. I've been raped, too."

His head snaped back. "Raped? You've been raped?"

She fought back tears. "Yes," and she added, "maybe, I'd better start at the beginning. It's the only way it will make sense."

He lit a cigarette for himself and her, and placing it between her lips, "Maybe you'd better."

For the better part of two hours she tried to relate to him in some correct chronological order the dysfunctional drama of her life. He attempted to interrupt her on several occasions but she would place her fingers on his lips..."no, please let me finish... this is not easy for me."

Sometime in the middle of it, a park policemen came up and shined his flashlight on the couple, now sitting apart once again. "You folks know it's park closing time? You'll have to leave, now," and shining his light on the fully clothed couple, he smiled, adding, "you don't seem to be doing anything now you couldn't be doing somewhere else, so move on."

Harlan started the car and drove out the park and onto St. Charles Avenue. Turning to Rainey, "Go on. I'll drive out to the lakefront."

Before he had arrived at Lakeshore Drive, she had completed the narrative of her life until the time she and Laverne had arrived in New Orleans

He whistled. "That's some storey, Rainey."

She could not see his expression clearly in the dark car, but she asked, quietly, "You still want to marry me?"

He shrugged, attempting a smile. "Well, yeah, I guess so."

That was the wrong thing for him to say, and she took offense at it. "You guess so, Harlan? You guess so?"

"Well, what the hell, Rainey, what do you expect after what you just told me... Jesus, I'm still shook up a little."

She looked out the window. "Yeah, me too, Harlan... real shook up! I think I want to go home, now," she said between sobs.

"What's wrong, Rainey? Did I do something wrong?"

"No, Harlan, I did."

"What do you mean?"

"I told you the truth. I should have let you believe that I was an innocent little virgin. You'd have believed it, wouldn't you?"

He was truthful with her. "Yes, I wish you had," and starting the car up again, "Rainey, I want to do some thinking about this. Is that okay with you?"

She nodded. "Sure, Harlan... let's think about it."

As Rainey lay in bed that evening after returning to her apartment, she was depressed at the way things had gone with Harlan. She had tried to be honest with him, thinking that was the honorable thing to do, but it had backfired. In her mind she had made a mistake due to her inexperience. She knew she was old enough to be experienced, but, yet, there was a big gap in her learning. She reasoned, Verlie could have taught her a lot had she lived. She further reasoned that Laverne would have advised her differently on this matter, but she was gone. She knew what Laverne would have said, because she had expressed an opinion on many occasions when the suject had come up: "Don't volunteer anything and deny everything," would have been her advice. "I was stupid," she intoned to herself as she sat up in bed drinking a scotch and water and smoking her last cigarette for the day, "I was just plain stupid. I shouldn't have told him anything of my past. Hell, how would he know I was not a virgin He didn't seem too shocked by it anyway... just the number of times, that's all. Gee, men are strange. What difference does it make? I didn't ask him how many times. Who gives a damn?"

She thought of Laverne. It had been nearly two weeks since their breakup and she had not called her even though she was only a few miles away at the marina. Even though she had told her she wanted her out of her life, she knew she had not meant it, and Laverne knew it too. They had been too close for five years to allow the relationship to dissolve over one wild escapade.

To herself: I wonder what she is doing. I need to talk to someone. Hell, I think I'll call her, and she looked at the clock. It was 10:48. She knew Laverne was not an early sleeper. She was too hyper. She picked up the phone and dialed the number of the marina switchboard.

"Marina. How may I help you?"

"Are you able to give me the number of boathouse 95-B, please?"

"Hold on a moment, please. No, I'm afraid not. That is an unlisted number... sorry."

"Well, can you have her call me?"

Lloyd J. Guillory

"Who?"
"Laverne Sutter."
"I have no Laverne Sutter at that number..."
"That is the boathouse of Augie Medusa, isn't it?"
"I cannot give you that information."
"Look! Just leave a message at that number for Laverne Sutter to call Rainey Wether..."
"Is this a joke?"
"No, it is not a joke. That is my name."
She sighed. "All right, honey, I'll give them the message. Goodbye."

She got up and took two aspirins. She sauntered back to bed, and embracing her pillow, she went over the events of the evening. Her last words were..."Aw, shit!"

It was three days before Laverne called her back. She was breathless as she spoke: "Rainey, luv, I thought you'd never call me again, and I... I... made up my mind that if you didn't, then ..you simply did not want to talk to me, but... oh, honey, I'm glad you called. I miss you. How have you been?" using the British pronunciation... bean.

"Oh, okay, I guess," and she sighed. "No, that's a damn lie. I am miserable, Laverne."

"What's the matter, sweetie? Tell Laverne and I will make it well."

So, she related the unfortunate events of that night of disclosure as Laverne breathed into the phone, inhaling and exhaling as she listened. When there was a pause in the conversation, Laverne exhaled again. "Rainey, Rainey, Rainey. Haven't I taught you anything. Never, honey- I repeat, never, tell them anything about your past. Poor fools, they don't know the difference."

"I guess you're right. I really screwed that one up."

Laverne became concerned "Do you really love him? I thought you told me you were lukewarm about him."

"I am."

"Then, why the hell do you want to marry him? Just bed him down and get it out of your system. It works, believe me!"

"Oh, I don't know! I guess I'm just tired working. I want some man to take care of me. I thought in time, maybe, I could learn to love Harlan."

Laverne became serious. "Rainey, honey, you don't learn to love someone. It hits you like a ton of bricks. It just comes naturally. You don't have to work at it. You can't even make it go away if you try."

She sighed. "Then I guess I'm not in love."

If Rainey could have seen Laverne at that instant, she would have noticed her eyes light up. "Rainey, we need to talk, luv."

Still dejected: "What about?"

"I can't tell you over the phone. Meet me for lunch... some place where we can talk..."

"Where?"

"I'll pick you up in my car. That way, we can go to a drive-in and eat and we can talk in the car... in private."

"Why do we have to talk in private?"

"You'll see. I'll pick you up at 11:45. Okay?"

"Okay"

Laverne didn't say much as they drove out of the Quarter and headed out to the outskirts of town in Augie Medusa's Cadillac convertible. Rainey looked at her friend. "Gee, you look great, you wild and crazy bitch," she kidded. "I don't know what you've been doing, but you do look great."

Laverne smiled. "I'm getting it regularly," she teased. "It always helps my complexion when I get it regularly."

Rainey smiled. "Maybe, that's what's wrong with my skin. I'm breaking out."

Laverne looked at her, smiling. "Maybe, I can help you cure your problem."

Wistfully, Rainey responded, "I hope someone can. I'm not happy, Laverne."

"What's wrong?"

"I dunno! When I kicked you out, I thought I wanted to live a calmer life, and I do. I want to live a normal life, and that usually means a husband and a family and..."

Laverne interrupted her. "Are you feeling maternal?"

"Not exactly. It's different from that."

She grunted. "Thank goodness. I know I don't want any babies. I don't want any brats pulling on my boobs," as she looked at her, smiling. "Did you say you're tired of your job?"

"Yes, it's boring."

"Are you interested in a new line of work?"

They exchanged glances. "What kind?" she asked.

Laverne pulled into a curb service type of drive-in. "Let's order and get this little waitress out of the way. I want to talk to you in private."

As Rainey opened her purse to pay the usual dutch treat share which she and Laverne had always done, Laverne patted her on the arm. "It's on me, luv. I'm loaded."

Rainey laughed. "You were loaded the last time I saw you. You still in the chips from that one trip to Havana?"

Laverne became serious. "No, that was just one trip. I've made several trips since then," and she paused to let the waitress place the tray on the window. "I've made several trips to Havana since then." As she handed Rainey her food, "As a matter of fact, I average one trip a week."

"You do? Why do you go to Havana every week? That would get monotonous for me."

She looked her in the eye. "Not when you make the money I make doing it."

Rainey looked astounded. "What are you doing?" and with some consternation, "I hope it's not what I think it is?"

Laverne's eyes squinted. "And what do you think I am doing?"

"You tell me, Laverne."

She shrugged. "Oh, what the hell! You've probably figured it out anyway since I told you about Augie," and looking around, "Rainey, you've got to keep quiet about this. It could cost me my life..."

"Laverne, you're playing a dangerous game."

"Listen, luv, for the money I'm making, you'd do it, too."

"Oh, I don't know about that," and then, curious, "how much are you making?"

She once more looked around. "I make a thousand a trip."

Her eyes widened. "And you say you average a trip a week?"

She nodded. "Uh, huh, with no trouble."

"Holy shit! You've making a thousand dollars a week?" she asked louder than she intended.

"Sh'ssh! For God's sake, Rainey, you can get me killed."

"Geez, and I make a lousy two hundred and fifty dollars a month working eight hours a day," and she shook her head.

Laverne nodded. "That's what I want to talk to you about. I think I can talk Augie into taking you on. We can use another girl."

Rainey shrunk back in her seat. "What would I have to do?"

She took a deep breath. "All you have to do is strap some stuff between your legs and get on an airplane in Havana and fly back to New Orleans with it... that's all."

As if she were naive' "Why do I have to strap it between my legs?"

"Well, Rainey, don't be stupid. It's so you can get through customs without having to declare the stuff."

"What's... the stuff?"

"It's better if you don't know."

"It's dope, isn't it?"

"Oh, what the hell do you care? It could be a pack of mustard plaster for your sore leg. What's it matter?"

"Suppose they check between my legs in custom?"

"Oh, don't be foolish. No custom inspector is going to put his hand up your skirt with all those people around."

"But, suppose he does?"

"Well, then, you slap his face, and act insulted. That always stops them," she kidded.

"Suppose they hire some female inspectors?"

"Well, they haven't yet. Besides, no one has the legal right to put their hands up your skirt," and she giggled, "except maybe your date."

"It can't be that simple, Laverne."

"Well, hell, girl, I've been doing it for several trips and nothing has happened. It was a song, and I'm making money like mad, luv."

She pondered the matter for a while. "What else would I have to do for the money?"

"What do you mean?"

"You know damn well what I mean."

"Well, hell, Rainey, this organization is run by men, and you know how men are. Sure, some guy will probably make a move on you, but I'm sure you know how to handle that. If you like the guy, do it. If you don't, knee him in the balls."

She became serious. "I've been in situations when it wasn't quite that simple. I got raped. You know that."

"I know, luv. all I can tell you is that these guys might be persistent, but they are not rapists."

"Hell, Laverne, as far as I'm concerned, the line between persistence and rape is very thin."

Thinking it over, Laverne suggested "Well, I tell you what, luv. I think I can set it up to where you just pick up the stuff, strap in on, get on the plane, land here, go to the ladies rest room, unload, come out, and turn it over to the gorillas. You pick up your money and go home"

"You make it sound so simple"

"I'm telling you... it is! What do you say? Interested?"

She pondered it for a while. "I'm interested, but, I want to think it over for a few days."

"Okay, but don't take too long. There are a lot of girls out there who will jump at this thing."

"Are you sure you can swing this with Augie?"

She smiled. "Honey, Augie is the least of my worries. He's crazy about me," but her voice lacked confidence.

After Laverne had dropped her off at the apartment, Rainey, instead of going upstairs, started walking towards Jackson Square. She sauntered along for awhile, watching the artists around the square ply their trade, working on one painting while trying to entice some tourist to buy one of the completed ones. She entered the square itself and sat on one of the benches, avoiding pigeon poop as she sat on one of the steel grillework benches. The pigeons came to her with an air of expectation as they are programmed to do by habit. They cocked their heads up, looking up at her, waiting. She acted as if she had purposely insulted them by not feeding them: "I'm sorry," as she raised her hands, "I don't have anything to give you... I'm sorry," and not wanting to offend the birds anymore she rose and resumed her walking.

She was trying to think. She had to decide on Laverne's offer. She viewed it with much trepidation. She was afraid. She did not have Laverne's careless disregard for consequences. She noticed that several groups of tourists had looked at her strangely as they passed her, and then she realized she was talking to herself as she often did when she was in her apartment. It made her think clearer.

Her thoughts went out to Harlan Kemper. After her foolish disclosure to him of the lurid details of her life, could he ever view her as suitable material as a wife for himself and a mother for his children. No, she reasoned, not hardly. She felt the Harlan Kemper phase in her life was now over, and it had been so brief. She turned around and headed back to her apartment three blocks away. She had decided nothing.

Laverne waited nearly a week before calling Rainey. She had made another trip to Havana, without incident. The only thing that happened that had made her notice was the reaction of one of the custom inspectors. She had made the foolish mistake of getting into his lane on several previous occasions, and he had remembered her. "You must like Cuba, Miss Sutter?" It was more than just a casual comment, she reasoned, replying, smiling, "Yes, I can't decide if its the gambling or the latin men. I like both so much... I can't get my fill of it." He merely smiled and nodded as he looked at her passport and handed it back to her, making no response. The comment was not lost on her. She vowed to alternate her lines in the future, saying to herself: "You learn as you go."

Rainey was in the shower when the phone rang. She quickly threw a towel around her middle and rushed to the phone and breathlessly said, "Hello."

Laverne smiled at the other end. "Rainey, luv, you sound out of breath. I hope I didn't catch you in the middle of..."

"No," she interrupted, knowing full well what her earthy friend meant, "I just got out of the shower."

"Too bad," she teased, "I was hoping it was something else, for your sake..."

"I wish! Laverne, I'm' dripping wet. Can I call you back?"

A pause, talking to someone else. "No, Rainey, we're leaving now. Augie says he has to know what you've decided. He won't wait much longer. If you're interested, he wants to see you."

She sighed into the phone. "Okay, I'll talk to him, but I am not promising I'll do it. I just want to talk. Okay?"

"Of course, luv," and once more turning to talk to someone, "can I pick you up at four this afternoon?"

She nodded as if it could be seen. "Yes, four will be fine. Just toot the horn... I'll run down so you won't have to park."

"Fine. Bye, luv," and, "oh, Rainey?"

"Yes"."

"Wear something real cute, huh? You know that checkered blouse with the red skirt? How about that? You look great in that outfit."

"Okay, Laverne, red skirt it is." She shook her head as she hung up the phone. She knew damn well she looked great in that outfit. Many men had said so at the office, to the point that she quit wearing it to work.

Later, as she stood before her full length mirror in her bedroom, she regarded her image with mixed emotions. She was confident that she looked good. At twenty-five, she still had the lean but well rounded figure she had at sixteen. If anything, the added years had enhanced her appearance, giving her more of a womanly look. Even Laverne had remarked about that, but, as she continued to peruse herself, one word kept coming back to her mind, over and over, a word she had detested all her life. "I look like a whore in this dress," and her mind went to her mother. She wondered. Did she wear clothes like this? She was tempted to change into something else, but she heard the insistent honking of Laverne's automobile, so she sighed, gave herself one last look and walked out.

CHAPTER TWENTY-TWO

Augie was waiting for them in his boathouse, in the combination bar and office. After introductions, Laverne slumped in an overstuffed chair with her long legs hanging over the arm. She lit a cigarette and inhaled deeply. Rainey was left standing as Augie walked around her, more than once. She felt awkward as he looked her up and down, as if she were a show horse, but as she glanced in her direction, Laverne smiled and winked, and that bolstered her confidence.

Augie motioned her to a chair and directed his remarks to Laverne as if Rainey were not in the room. "Well, Cookie, she's everything you said she was... not bad at all."

Rainey had decided on the way over which of her two modes she would assume; the little girl demeanor, or, the tough-bitch one she and Laverne had developed in dealing with unwanted, obnoxious males. She decided on the latter.

She extracted a cigarette from her pack, knocked it on the coffee table with dramatic effect. Augie leaned over, and with a solid silver lighter, put the flame to the tip. She blew smoke in his direction and looked at him through half opened eyes. She had seen Bette Davis effect this in many films, and Bette would truly have been proud of her disciple. She took her first good look at Augie Medusa as she smiled, thanking him. He had the animal good looks so often found in Italian men, especially those who had a good tailor and a good barber. He was not too tall, less than her five-foot eight friend, Laverne, in heels, but rich and powerful men don't need height- they stand tall, anyway. He had a beautiful head of wavy hair, just beginning to turn grey at the temples, a testament to his forty-five years. His teeth were flawless, whether by nature or a good dentist, she was not sure.

One of his ever present "assistants", as he referred to them, moved a chair under him as he stood directly in front of Rainey, as if they could communicate without sound. Two other assistants stood near the bar, leaning on their elbows. He first smiled at Laverne and then, at Rainey. "So, Rainey, Laverne tells me you might be interested in going to work for us." It came out as a statement- not a question.

She looked hurriedly at Laverne who merely smiled at her. She gave him a nervous look. "Well, as I told Laverne, I'm willing to talk about it."

He nodded, which he did often. "Did Laverne tell you what this job entails?"

She was amazed at his articulation of the English language. She felt sure he would have the usual New Orleans-Irish Channel accent which resembles in sound the Brooklyn accent associated with that borough of New York. He would have had, had not his uneducated Sicilian father, who barely spoke discernible English, not insisted that he spend "atta leasta, two years" at Loyola University in New Orleans, so, as the old man put it, "so's you canna talka right".

She looked at Laverne for assistance, and receiving none, she replied. "Well, she didn't go into detail, but I think I got the picture."

He moved his gaze from Laverne back to her. "Oh, and what picture did you get?"

She shrugged, now assuming her little girl look. "All I know is that I would act as a courier for you... that's all I know."

He nodded, pausing for a while. "And, what do you think you'd be carrying? Got any ideas?"

She shook her head. "No, she didn't say. I don't know."

"It's better if you don't know. That way, if somebody should ask you, you can say you don't know and you won't be lying. Right?"

She felt his questioning had a childish quality to it, but she replied, "Yes, that's right."

He sensed her nervousness. "Are you scared of me, Rainey?"

She looked at Laverne who looked away. "Yes, I'm afraid of you." She knew this was the answer he wanted.

"Why are you afraid of me?"

She shrugged. "I don't know; I just am."

"It's good that you're scared of me," and he turned to look at the three goons standing near by "It would be better if you stayed that way," and he turned his gaze to Laverne as if to make a point. She smiled back at him, but her eyes showed that she understood the implication.

He stood up and begin to pace the length of the room. The goons moved back as he approached them and returned as he passed them. He turned to Laverne. "You're sure she can handle this?"

"I've already told you, Augie, she can do it. She's a lot tougher than she looks. She's been through the mill."

"She doesn't look like she's had it too hard."

"It's on the inside, Augie- not the outside- where she's been hurt"

He nodded, saying nothing for a long time. Rainey put out one cigarette and took another out of the pack. Augie, who was at the other end of the room, merely nodded to the goons, and one rushed to Rainey with a cigarette lighter. She looked in his eyes as he held the lighter. She saw nothing but a cold stare, and she shivered a bit, thanking him in a hardly audible whisper.

Augie walked back and stood in front of her. He took in a deep breath, as if the decision to hire her was a monumental one. "Are you sure you want to do this, kid?" and before she could answer, "I want you to understand, if you're caught, we don't know you- we don't lift a finger to save you- and if you open your mouth and say the wrong thing, we'll cut your tongue out. You understand what I'm saying?"

She shuddered, and she hoped he hadn't noticed it. She was scared, but they had not discussed the most important thing, the only reason she was here. She assumed her Bette Davis mode, as she exhaled. "We haven't talked about money."

He nodded. "Yeah, you're right," and giving Laverne a sideways glance, "we pay five hundred per trip."

Her heart sank in her bosom. She swallowed hard, determined to hold her own. She knew this was the way it was with men. They could not be trusted with anything. She swallowed, again, looking at Laverne for assistance, but none was coming. She looked directly at him: "Laverne told me she gets a thousand a trip. That's the only reason I'm here... for the money."

He smiled, showing his perfect teeth, and turning to Laverne: "You're right, baby, the kid's got moxey alright," and turning back to Rainey: "Well, now you have to understand, kid, that Laverne is special to me," and he put his hand on her exposed knee, rubbing it. He turned his gaze back to Rainey. "And, she is experienced. She's made a bunch of trips and she knows how to bullshit the custom inspections. She is good"

Rainey took on her best Bette Davis demeanor. "I can bullshit as good as Laverne. She taught me."

He laughed... a hardy laugh. "Hell, kid, I'm beginning to like you. I think you can cut it," and he put his hand on her knee. Her eyes moved from his hand to his eyes. He removed his hand. "Well, do you want to try it?"

She stood her ground. "We haven't settled the money, yet."

He grinned. "I'll make a deal with you, kid. Five hundred for the first trip, seven-fifty for the second, and if you're still alive and free after that, a thousand from then on."

"Can I get that in writing?"

He grinned. "Sure, but my spoken word is better than my written word. My written word is no good at all. Who you gonna complain to?" Laverne could not surpress a laugh. The goons all snickered. Rainey smiled and nodded, extending her hand. "It's a deal. When do I start?"

He turned to Laverne. "Baby, why don't you take Rainey in the bathroom and show her the procedures... you know- how to strap the stuff on. And, Laverne, show how to walk with the stuff between her legs, And, if she doesn't have a bunch of wide skirts and dresses, buy her some. You know what I mean. Get her what she needs."

Later that evening as she sat in bed thinking over the day, she was half-satisfied how things had gone. She had been pleasantly surprised with Augie Medusa. She had seen his photo in the Times Picayune when he had testified before the Kefauver committee which was investigating organized crime in the area, but the photos had not done him justice. She now understood Laverne's attraction to him. She had expected a gorilla, similar to the goons always at his side, not the educated man she had seen. But, there was no doubt he had a violent side. He had convinced her of that, whether purposely, to make her fear him, or not, she wasn't sure.

She viewed the job acceptance as a temporary thing, something to make some quick money, and then she would quit. It was too dangerous. She lacked Laverne's reckless nature. In order to keep her present job with the oil company as a hedge, she decided to ask for several weeks of medical leave. She would tell them that she needed minor surgery for a "female" problem.

The phone rang. She looked at the clock on her night table.

It was 10:15. Annoyed, thinking it was Laverne wanting to go over the day's events, she bruskly said, "Hello."

She recognized Harlan's voice. She had not heard from him since that night of disclosure. "Rainey, it's Harlan. I hope I'm not calling you too late..."

She paused to calm down a bit, then, softly: "No, Harlan, it's okay."

"Rainey... I want to talk to you... I..."

"What about, Harlan? It's kinda late."

She could hear him sigh deeply. "Rainey... I've tried to get you out of my mind, but... I can't."

"I thought this was all over, Harlan, that we were through."

"I thought so, too, but, I can't get over you..."

"What are trying to tell me?"

"I still want to marry you, Rainey, in spite of everything."

She shook her head. "In spite of everything, Harlan? You mean with all my deficiencies, you still want to marry me?"

"Well, I wish you wouldn't put it that way"

"There is no other way to put it, Harlan," and searching for the right words for she did not want to hurt this decent man, one of the few she had met, she continued, "you see... you're willing to overlook these drawbacks because you're in love. You want me because you've never had me, but, after..."

He tried to protest, but she cut him off with, "Maybe, the best thing I could do for you, Harlan, is to go to bed with you so you could get it out of your system." The tears began to flow as she continued, "then, you could go and find some pure little girl who could be a fit mother for your children."

He was silent for a long time. "No, I don't want you under those conditions, Rainey."

"Harlan, the truth is., you really don't want me as a wife under any conditions... period. Goodnight, Harlan. Don't call me again."

She was crying as she slammed down the phone. It was not that she viewed the loss of Harlan as any great tragedy. It was that, once again, she found she could not seem to develop any worthwhile relationship with a man- any man. Was it her fault, she wondered? The only mistake she felt she had made with him is that she was honest. She vowed that she would not make that mistake again. With men, honesty did not pay. She cuddled her pillow as she attempted sleep.

She met Laverne in the restaurant at Moisant Airport, nervous as a wet hen as she began her first trip to Havana. Laverne smiled as she watched her walk in in her new outfit with a wider than necessary skirt. "That looks good on you, luv. You could be eight months pregnant and no one would know it, but why are you wearing it for the trip over? Hell, on the trip to Havana, we're just plain tourists, two office girls on a week-end lark."

Dropping in the booth. "I just wanted to see how it looks on me Believe me, it doesn't do much for my figure. Not one guy turned around to look at my butt like they generally do," she giggled.

"That's the idea, honey. We're not trying to attract any male attention. At least, not with the body. Now, you and I are lucky that we've got both- body and face."

"So, just use the face to divert close scrutiny, huh?"

"That's right, just give the inspectors enough to keep their minds off their business."

She sighed. "Laverne, I'm scared and nervous. Does it show?"

"Well, yes, luv, but that's because I know you so well. Just relax. It's going to be okay. Oh," as she reached in her purse, "here's your ticket. Coach class."

Rainey looked disappointed. "Coach? I would have thought we'd go first class," she mocked.

Laverne became serious "No, these people don't miss a trick. We're supposed to be some New Orleans office girls going to Havana for a good time. Office girls don't travel first class."

Rainey nodded. "Good thinking."

Laverne rose. "Come on, sweetie, time to go to Havana and have a good time for two days."

Rainey grabbed her arm. "Can we really have a good time until we get ready to come back?"

Laverne smiled. "Just stay with me, kid, you'll see."

Rainey leaned towards her friend's ear. "Laverne, you don't play around on Augie in Havana, do you?"

"You want to get me killed? Hell, no!", but as she smiled, "that doesn't mean you can't, though"

Havana in 1953 was a city made for romance and excitement. The hotels and casinos of that beautiful tropical island had only two reasons for their existence: to ensure that you were having so good a time that you would return, and that you would not object to being separated from your money.

Rainey was in a state of exhilaration as she and Laverne went from one casino to the other, from one grand hotel to the other, sitting in on the picturesque Latin floor shows which were an integral part of any Havana evening. "Gee, those Latin girls have gorgeous bodies, Laverne," observed a fascinated Rainey.

"Yes, and look what they can do with them on that dance floor." She giggled. "They must be something in bed, huh?"

Rainey nodded. "Yeah, I bet. We don't stand a chance in this place, Laverne. We can't compete with them."

She shook her head. "No, that's not true, love. These Latinos go crazy over gringo women. They think we're all rich or we wouldn't be over here." She smiled. "They also think American men don't know how to make love, and they fancy themselves masters at it. That's the main reason we come over here, they think we're love-starved."

Rainey gave her a little girl look. "Hell, I am, Laverne."

Laverne gave her a motherly look. "That's your fault, Rainey. I've been telling you for years to..."

Rainey grabbed her arm. "Oh, don't be too obvious, but look at those two men at the bar staring at us. They're gorgeous."

Lavene dropped her napkin in practiced fashion, and she perused the bar on the way up. "Whewee, not bad at all."

"Oh, Laverne, they're corning this way. What shall we do?"

"Smile, baby, smile like mad and try to look love-starved.

They were not bashful one bit as they stood before the two women, with one saying with a decided Latin accent. "Ah, Senoritas, it ees a cr'rime against nature to see two beautiful women like you to sittin alone on a night like thees."

The other nodded, showing beautiful teeth. "Yes, ess true."

They were gentlemen, however, and neither made a move to sit until the first added, "Eeef you would like, eet would be our pleasure to show you Havana as you have never seen it before," and he flashed a beautiful smile as he added quietly, "and the price ees good, too. Only one hundred American dollars for the both," and he pointed to his friend.

Rainey, with eyes widened, now that she realized they were paid professional escorts, looked at Laverne who was not as surprised. Laverne looked at Rainey. "What do you think?"

It would be an untruth to say that Rainey was not titilated "She had truly, never in her young life, had a sexual experience that she had perceived to be satisfactory, based on what her friend Laverne had described as the expected results. She said, meekly, "I can't afford this, much as I'd like to try it."

Laverne patted her arm, "It's on me, luv. I want you to find out what it's all about. Okay?"

Rainey smiled and nodded.

Laverne turned to the leader of the two and nodded to the chairs. "Sit down, amigos, you're hired."

Rainey stirred in her bed, trying to remember where she was. She became aware of the heavy breathing next to her, and then she remembered. She looked over at the muscular and tanned back of the man lying at her side. She smiled as her mind went back to the evening and the night that had ensued. She stretched and yawned, reliving every joyous moment of the entire night, remembering the words of endearment whispered by a man with practiced expertise. She knew he had not really meant them, but he was so convincing, she did not mind. She lifted the sheet so she could slide in next to him and as she did, she saw that remarkably toned body, so bronzed, so... so...

He stirred, and turning to her, smiling a beautiful smile: "Oh, Raineee, my love. Did you sleep well?"

She giggled. "No, someone kept me awake half the night."

He embraced her. "Oh, Ah am so sorree. Perhaps, Ah can make up for that, now."

She snuggled to him. "Uh, huh, I bet you can."

As she explained the matter in response to Laverne's persistent questioning at lunch, "Well, I don't know if the Cathedral chimes rang, never having heard them before, but I'm sure of one thing; the bells damn sure rang," and she giggled, adding, "more than once, too." She looked at Laverne. "How about you?"

Laverne gave her a discerning look. "My bells always chime."

Two Cuban women came to the hotel at the appointed time and Laverne opened the door for them. They greeted her in broken English. They were carrying a leather satchel and were accompanied by two goons who looked around the room. Satisfied that no one else was in the room, the goons went to chairs and sat down, saying not a word. The women, known to Laverne from previous trips, placed the satchel on the coffee table. One went to the windows and closed the wooden slats. As she opened the satchel and began to remove the contents, Laverne looked at the two goons who were ready for what they considered a show. Laverne turned to the Cuban women. "Can't we do this in the bathrooms Do they have to watch?"

She shrugged and started towards the bathroom, asking Laverne, "Eees thees one the new girl?"

"Yes."

"She know what to do?"

"Yes, I've gone over it all with her."

She turned to Rainey. "Take off your dress, senorita. No, solamente la falda... onlee the skirt," she translated to English.

With Rainey standing there, embarrassed by another round of intimacy, having only a few hours before, experienced another type under different circumstances, the woman strapped the specially made leather pouches to her upper thighs. A strap extended to her waist to ensure that the pouches would not fall to the floor. Rainey glanced at Laverne who was suffering the same indignity. Laverne winked and smiled.

Making sure that the pouches were held in place securely, the women reached in the satchel and removed several small packages wrapped in plastic and inserted them in the leather pouches. Rainey shivered, for she knew the contents, and the matter jolted her sensitivities. She swallowed hard and took a deep breath.

Having completed their tasks in a practiced fashion, the women handed the skirts back to Laverne and Rainey, nodding. After the skirts were pulled down around their legs, the two Cuban women, once again, with a practiced hand, smoothed the material and rearranged it to their satisfaction. One looked at the other and they nodded. "Eeet eees feenished," and picking up the satchel, exited the bathroom. When they entered the bedroom, the goons arose. They looked at the room as if to ensure that no one had entered during the process and all four left, saying nothing more.

*   *   *

As the plane headed northwest on the route from Havana to New Orleans, the dark waters of the Gulf of Mexico could be seen through broken clouds. Rainey was at the window enjoying the view. Laverne tried to nap, but with Rainey continually shifting in her seat, she was constantly disturbed. She asked, with some consternation, "Rainey, what the hell is wrong with you? Why are you thrashing about so?"

She whispered. "I'm itching with those pouches between my legs. They bother me."

Laverne gave her a knowing smile. "Are you sure it's the pouches that are causing you your trouble?"

Rainey smiled in return. "Both, I guess."

Rainey's nerves really began to act up as they were shunted into the international passengers section of the terminal. She felt she was being herded like cattle, for once in that section, there is no escape except through customs. She began to perspire under her arms and between her legs and she was embarrassed. She continually grabbed Laverne's arm as they entered the line to the inspectors. Laverne sensed her nervousness. "Relax, for God's sake. You're sweating. I can see it," she whispered.

Rainey whispered in return. "I can't help it."

The inspector smiled as he saw Laverne. "Well, Miss Sutter, what a pleasant surprise. So, you've made another trip to your favorite island, huh?" Laverne felt he was getting too familiar. She decided to talk to Augie about this. Perhaps, a change had to be made.

She returned his smile "Uh, huh, I've been bragging so much about Cuba to my friend, here," and she nodded at Rainey, "that I just had to take her there to see for herself."

He looked at Rainey, and taking her custom declaration form, asked the usual question. "You ladies have anything you wish to declare?" Rainey swallowed hard.

Laverne shook her head "No, just what's on the form. We bought a few things but we're under the allowable, so we don't owe you any money today," she kidded.

Taking a last look at Rainey's passport, he nodded. "Okay, ladies, have a safe trip driving home."

Rainey's breath could be heard quite audibly as she exhaled the air she had been holding for nearly two minutes.

Laverne smiled at her. "Come on, baby, we're home free."

Augie handed the pouches to a goon as the girls exited the bathroom at the boathouse. He was pleased. He smiled at Rainey. "You did good, kid. I'm glad it worked out for both of us. You'll have a good future with the organization... if you know how to keep your mouth shut," and motioning the girls to chairs. "So, Rainey, this your first trip to Havana?"

She nodded. "Yes, Mr. Medusa, it was."

"Aw, call me Augie, honey. We'll be getting to know each other real good as this goes on."

Rainey could detect a slight flinch at the corners of Laverne's mouth as she looked at Augie.

Augie reached in his coat pocket and removing a thick wad of hundred dollar bills, he smiled at the women. "Payday, girls," and he handed each her share.

Rainey could not suppress a smile. "Thank You."

Laverne accepted hers without thanks, knowing full well she was not through earning her money.

"Well, girls, do you want to celebrate with a night on the town? Rainey, I'm sure I can get an escort for you."

Rainey gave Laverne a quick and questioning glance, which Laverne correctly read as, "My God, I've had all the excitement I need for a while." Laverne, ever resourceful, replied. "Augie, I hate to get this personal about Rainey's problem, but you see, well, she had the usual tourist problem in Cuba that most first time tourists get... know what I mean?"

He laughed. "Montezuma's revenge, huh? I understand. Poor kid, I feel sorry for you. Maybe, next trip, huh?"

Rainey nodded, thanking God and Laverne for her rescue from a night of what she was sure would result in her having to fend off advances neither warranted or desired.

"Can I drop you off at your apartment, Rainey?"

"Gee, I hate to make you drive all the way across town."

She looked at Augie. "You won't need me for a while, will you, sweetie?" and she kissed him on the mouth.

He smiled at her. "No, baby, just be here when the sun goes down, that's all."

She gave him a contrived and practiced look that would have melted steel. "Don't worry. That's all I've been looking forward to for three days."

He grinned. She had said the right thing.

As they went out the door, Rainey shook her head, and to herself: "My God... men! If only they knew."

As they headed down Canal Boulevard, Laverne kept smiling at Rainey who sat there with the wind blowing through her hair, thinking.

"Well, Rainey, luv, how was it?"

Rainey giggled. "Which part do you mean?"

The older woman smiled. "I guess... both of them."

Without answering her question, Rainey asked her own. "Laverne?"

"Yes, love?"

"You know those men we met in Havana? Remember?"

She grunted. "Hell, how can you forget them? They were great, weren't they?"

Rainey nodded, her eyes half-closed in memory of the night. "They sure were."

"I'm sure you realize they were professionals?"

Her eyes widened. "Professional what?"

"Anything you want, honey. They can supply it."

She was quiet for a while, then: "Do you think they have men like them in this country?"

"You mean... for hire?"

"Well, no! I mean men who are like that... you know... that good... but, not for hire. Just for real..."

Laverne smiled. "Sure, love. The Latins don't have a monoply on that. There are men all over the world who know what they're doing."

She said with some embarrassment. "I want one."

"I know, honey. You deserve one, too."

"Where can I find him?"

"I don't know. Be patient, you'll find him."

"Don't you want one, too?"

Laverne considered the matter for a long time. "No, it wouldn't work for me."

"Why not?"

"I'm not a one-man woman, Rainey. It's a serious defect in my makeup."

"Well, at least, you're smart enough to know that."

She grunted. "Hell, that's all I'm smart about."

Rainey patted her friend on the back. "I think you're smarter than you think you are, Laverne."

She grinned at her. "I wish I were half as smart as you think I am, Lovey," and opening her purse as she drove and taking a package of special cigarettes from it, continued, "I picked up some real good stuff in Cuba. Want one?"

Rainey looked at the dark cigarettes, shaking her head. "I've told you before, Laverne, that stuff doesn't agree with me. It makes me do things I don't really want to do..."

She laughed. "Hell, that's the idea, Rainey."

"No, thank you. I'll pass."

Taking one for herself and lighting it as she drove on, she replaced the pack. "Okay, sweetie, if that's how you want it."

"Why do you feel you need that stuff, Laverne?"

She pulled hard on the weed. "I guess you heard Augie, didn't you... about tonight?"

"Uh, huh, I heard. I guess you have a hard night ahead of you," as she regarded her friend with some sympathy.

"Why do you think I'm smoking the stuff? He'll be stoned on it by the time I get back. I need it to keep up with him."

"Laverne, do you really think it's worth it?"

"What, in particular, are you referring to, luv?"

"The whole Augie bit? The Cuba thing? All of it?"

"Rainey, where else can a nit-wit like me make that kind of money in this male-dominated society? Tell me."

She looked away. "I don't know, Laverne. I wish I did."

Laverne inhaled deeply and said nothing in reply.

CHAPTER TWENTY-THREE

Flushed with the easy success on her first trip to Cuba, Rainey could not have been more pleased when Laverne called her that evening. "Are you ready to make another one?"

"Uh, huh, if you're coming with me."

"I'll be making this one with you, but it's the last,for, me..."

Interrupting her, with some concern: "But, why is this one your last?"

"Augie feels that my face is now too recognizable in the custom line. He wants me to do something else for a while," and before Rainey could utter her protest, she added, "he says he's in love with me. He wants me to get out of this thing and just be there when he wants me, to be his woman."

She searched for the right words, the words Laverne could accept. "Is that what you really want?"

She paused for a moment. "Well, hell yes, Rainey. I will be living the life of luxury. It's what I've always wanted," she said with a lack of total commitment in her voice, which only a close friend would detect.

"Yeah, until he gets tired of you and wants something younger. You know how they are, Laverne."

She pondered the words for a moment. "Is it really all that different from marriage, Rainey. Don't husbands do the same thing when they get tired of the cute little girls they married, after the butt starts to spread from having their kids, and the belly starts to sag from having their kids, and the tits start to droop from their babies pulling on them, and..."

"Okay... okay, you've made your point! and I agree, it really is not all that different. Let's face it. Men are no good bastards! We agree on that, so what's new?"

"I'm sorry. I didn't mean to carry on so. I know you still retain some lofty notions about home and hearth and all that crap, but I don't. I have a jaundiced viewpoint of the whole human race." She laughed. "Maybe Augie is right..."

"About what?"

She giggled. "He says that with my attitude, he believes that I must have had surgery at one time and the doctor crossed my optic nerves with my rectal nerves and it gave me a shitty outlook on life."

Rainey laughed out loud. "Oh, Laverne, that is good. I'll have to remember that one. It explains so many people."

She laughed. "Doesn't it though?"

Getting serious: "When do we leave for the trip to that glorious island?"

"The day after tomorrow..."

"Laverne?"

"Yes, luv?"

"Do you think I can hire Julio again? You know what I mean?"

She laughed. "Yes, I know precisely what you mean. You like that Cuban lover, huh?"

Laverne could not see her nod over the phone, but she did, as she grinned. "Uh, huh, I figure I may as well have some real fun in Cuba. I'm not having much in this country."

"Is it worth that much money to you? He's kind of expensive for a passing pleasure. Next day it's gone."

"Oh, I don't know about that. It lasted a week last time."

"Well, that's up to you, luv. It's on you this time. I'm trying to be faithful to Augie from now on." She giggled. "Hell, I've got to start someday."

"Uh, huh. It's time you settled down, Laverne. You're getting old, you know."

"You're right. That's why I want this to be my last trip. I want to settle down, Rainey. I really do."

*   *   *

As the cool evening breezes blew through the open shutters on the tenth floor of the Hotel Nacional, Rainey and Laverne stood, having a post flight drink in their room. She walked out on the balcony and Laverne followed her. They could see the dark waters of the harbor with waves lashing out against the seawall. Rainey took in a deep breath, inhaling the incomparable scent of hibiscus and bougainvillea growing in the flower box which formed the railing of the balcony. She sipped her rum and coke, and crossing her arms, looked at her friend. "Why don't we just stay here forever, Laverne? Why go back at all?"

Laverne grunted a reply. "Because, luv, we get paid to go back... not stay here... that's why. Like this place, do you?"

She smiled and nodded. "Yes, I love it. I love the tropics," and turning back to glance at the sea, she was lost in her own thoughts for a while.

Rainey acted as though she were dressing for her senior prom, which she had missed anyway due to her ill-advised and tragically ended sojourn to California with Douglas Walker. She hummed a Latin tune as she stood before the bedroom mirror. Laverne, drying herself in the bathroom after stepping out the shower, cocked her head to see her friend. "In a good mood, huh?"

"Uh, huh, I'm looking forward to a night of rapture."

Laverne laughed. "So, that's what they call it nowadays?" and not waiting for a reply, "Don't get your heart set on Julio. He's a free lance operator, you know. He may already be taken by some other love-starved gringo woman."

"Why do you think I'm getting ready so early. I'm going down to the bar and see if he's there. Are you coming?"

"It'll take me a while. I'll be down later. Don't wait on me."

"Okay... I'll be down in the bar."

The strains of Maria Elena could be heard coming from the bar as she made her way across the hotel lobby. She ignored the stares of the single males sitting in the area. Most were young Cubans out on the make, selling their Latin charms to young American girls who, being away from the enforced morals of their own country, were ready to allow themselves to be led astray, at least for one night.

Not being brazen enough to sit at the bar- an almost open invitation to be picked up, she made her way to a small table in the rear. She quickly looked around but failed to see the handsome face of Julio Cardoza. She still had his business card from the last trip. She smiled to herself as she remembered the words: JULIO CARDOZA, ENTERTAINMENT CONSULTANT. When she had asked him what an entertainment consultant did, they were lying in bed. He had merely smiled, and bringing her closer to him, he whispered in her ear, "Eeet ees betta if I show you," and he did.

She ordered a rum and coke as her body began to weave back and forth to the rhythm of La Paloma. A young Latino, barely more than twenty made his way to her table. He bowed. "Senoreeta, do you need a escorrt forrr the evening?" He had dimples and a smile without equal. She smiled at him, thinking to herself, Oh, what a prize for a young college girl, but not for me. He's too young.

"No, thank you. I'm waiting for someone."

He sighed, and with Latin charm, "Then, eeet eees my loss, and another's man gain," and he started to walk off.

She grabbed his elbow, and, hesitantly, "Do you know Julio Cardoza?"

He grinned, showing both dimples. "But, of course, Julio is my beeeg brother."

Surprised as her hand went to her mouth. "Oh, my goodness! I should have noticed the resemblance," and looking around the bar, "is he here this evening?"

"No, not yet. He will be in later."

She was almost embarrassed. "Would you tell him that Rainey is looking for him?"

He smiled, knowingly. "Oh, so you are Raineee... no?"

"Yes."

"Julio spoke of you. He don't talk about most gringo girls, but he spoke of you," and turning to go, "I tell Julio you looking forrr him... okay?"

She nodded as she watched him walk off, thinking: God, I love Latin men.

She was on her third rum and coke. She had not heard the footsteps behind her as a man kissed her ear. "Raineee, my love. Eeet eees so good to see you again."

She recognized the voice. She quickly turned and saw the warm smile and white teeth of Julio above her. She placed her hand on his cheek. "Oh, Julio, it is good to see you again. Please sit down."

He gazed around the room, and waving to a table of four a short distance away, two American women with two Cubans, he yelled something in Spanish. He nodded at their reply and took his seat. "So, Raineee, my leetle brotherr tells me you are looking for Julio. Eees true?"

She didn't know how to begin. Here she was, a woman who had despised the word prostitute all her life because of her mother's role in it, getting ready to negotiate with a male one. She could only conclude that she, like most humans, was a hypocrite when it served her purposes. She smiled at him. "I'm just in town for a day or two, and I was wondering if you were available... to escort me around... you know... like last time."

He gave her a knowing smile, and then a frown. "Oh, Raineee, how come you don't call Julio earlier? I already make date for tonight..."

She was truly disappointed. "Oh, I guess I should have. I didn't know where to reach you..."

"But, the number, she eees on the card I give you."

"I didn't think. I guess I'm too late, then..."

He looked around the room. "How about Julio get you another man? Okay?"

She shook her head, and then, without shame, she looked in his eyes. "No, I want you... just you... no one else."

He was touched, deeply touched. There was not much sentiment in his business. It was just that. "You pay and we play", was the prevailing sentiment, but this love-starved woman triggered something in him. He placed his hand on hers, giving her a warm smile. She just noticed that, he too, had dimples; something she had not taken the time to appreciate before due to most of their time being spent in darkness. He thought for a while, and then, "Let Julio make phone call. Then, I come back, and then, Julio eees yours for the night... okay?"

She almost automatically agreed, but common sense took over. "Oh, Julio, what will this cost? I don't have much money..."

Visions of striking it rich quickly vanished, but in its stead, he could picture a night of amorous rapture with this love-stared young woman. He smiled. "Julio make you beeg bargain, Raineee. You pay all expenses... you know... drinks and food... and the rest eees on the house... like you gringos say."

She was about to grasp this bargain, and then she thought, the hotel room. Laverne would be in it. She needed another room and that would be more expense. Oh, what the hell. She'd do it. She would call the hotel and leave Laverne a note... and then, she saw Laverne coming through the door, smiling as she saw Rainey sitting with Julio.

"Well, I see you two have connected. Hi, Julio... good to see you again."

He stood, in practiced fashion. He reached for her hand and brought it slowly to his lips, kissing it. "Senoreeeta Sutter, eeet eees good to see you again."

Rainey

She withdrew her hand, slowly. Her pulse quickened, too, and then she thought of Augie. "It is good to see you, too, Julio," and turning to Rainey... "well?"

Rainey nearly blushed. She nodded. "I need a room for the night, Laverne. Do you think the hotel has a vacancy?"

Laverne rose. "You make your plans, luv. Leave the room to Laverne. My boss has some pull in this place." She winked. "I'll see if we can't get the company to pay for a suite," and as she walked off, she smiled. "A bridal suite."

Rainey would later recall that evening as one of the high points of her adult life. She was romanced as she had never been romanced before. What had added enhancement to the evening was the realization that she was only paying for "expenses" as Julio had termed it. The rest came from the heart. Laverne, in typical con artist style, had talked the hotel management into donating the bridal suite as a public relations gratuity to her boss and lover, after convincing them that Rainey was the granddaughter of a Chicago don. She had to register at the desk as Rainey Cantorella.

Julio, was inspired that evening. In matters such as these, one gives as one gets, and Rainey had plenty to give with some twenty-five years of pent up emotions now bursting forth in a torrent of passion. She and Julio had exchanged words they both knew were less than the truth, but what did it matter, as long as they both knew it. She had longed to hear the words, "I love you" said with some conviction, and she heard them.

She also heard a proposal of marriage from Julio, who longed to emigrate to the United States in search of a more permanent calling for the years when he would no longer be an adonis. Many young cubans of both sexes had used this ruse to gain admittance to what they believed was a better life in the north. She had wisely, although somewhat reluctantly, declined his marriage proposal- her first, since she could not remember if Douglas walker had proposed or suggested, or demanded. Her bells were heard to ring several times before a tired couple surrendered to sleep in the wee hours.

She was still asleep when the phone rang late the next morning. It was Laverne. "I hate to wake you, cinderella, but we do have work to do..."

She moaned into the phone as she looked over at the still sleeping Julio. "Oh, Laverne, I'm sleepy and tired..."

Laverne laughed. "Yes, I can understand both, luv, but I'm picking you up in an hour. The women are coming over with the merchandise. You know what I mean?"

She yawned. "Uh, huh, I know. Okay . I'll be ready," and hanging up the phone, she shook his shoulder... "Julio, come on... wake up... Julio... come on, love... wake up."

He grabbed for her. She sprang from the bed. "No ..no, I really don't have time... no... no!"

The flight from Cuba had been routine. The same procedures in Havana had been followed by the same people. Once aboard the plane, Rainey slept the whole way. Laverne would look at her with amusement and satisfaction, glad Rainey had found some excitement in her life, even some so tenuous. She smiled at the sleeping woman.

As they were once more herded into the lines leading to the customs area of Moisant Airport, Laverne had, as usual, led the way. A large family, obviously of South or Central American origin since they were all babbling at the same time in the Spanish tongue, had moved in the line behind Laverne and in front of Rainey, all nine of them. Rainey looked over their heads as Laverne looked back at her. Laverne had shrugged her shoulders, for now between the railings, there was nothing either could do to remedy the separation. Laverne moved up towards the custom inspector. Rainey noticed that there was a larger than usual crowd of men around the inspector, some in uniforms and others in civilian garb. She watched in horror as Laverne was being questioned by one of the men. She could see her friend's face become animated. Then, she was removed from the line and taken aside. Her heart leaped in her throat as she saw one of the men show Laverne a badge, and then, he pulled her aside. She saw a woman coming towards the group. She was in the uniform of a custom's officer. She saw the man with the badge motion to a room on the other side of the customs area and Laverne was led away. Rainey's heart began to pound in her chest. She knew- there was no doubt- that Laverne was being led away to be searched by the female inspector.

Rainey looked around. The Latin family was being beckoned to move up to the custom desk. She looked to the rear, and seeing some rest rooms just off to the right, she got out of the line, whispering to the woman behind her, "I think I have an emergency. I've got to get to the rest room." The woman nodded, knowlingly.

Rainey picked up her bag and headed for the restroom. She quickly entered the door, and seeing two other women at the wash counter, immediately made her way into a toilet booth, quickly closing the door and locking it. She grabbed the top edge of the booth for support. She was nearly hyperventilating, she knew that, and she gasped for breath. There was no doubt in her mind. Laverne would be arrested. She had the pouches between her legs. She had been caught cold, and now, she, Rainey, had the same thing between her legs.

She stood on her tip-toes, making sure no one was watching. She was afraid some custom officer would track her to the rest-room, but she saw none. She raised her skirt and quickly removed the pouches. She emptied the contents in the toilet and watched as the thousands of dollars worth of drugs went swirling down the sewer. She held the pouches in her hand. She knew the leather pouches would never go down the drain, so she wrapped them in her jacket and exited the booth, shaking quite noticeably. She made her way to the waste paper basket and quickly dumped the pouches into them, breathing a sigh as if she had gotten rid of something contagious. She leaned on the formica countertop, still weak from her near disaster. She thought of Laverne. Where was she? What would they do with her? Some other women came into the restroom, and without even giving her a glance, headed for the toilet stalls.

She tried to collect herself as she once again moved out into the large custom area. She paused to think. She looked around at the counter where Laverne had been taken. Things were routine. No one acted as if anything unusual had happened, except that the large Hispanic family were giving the inspector a hard time with their broken English. She moved to another line, as far removed from that line as she could. She knew she was perspiring. Her hands were moist and clammy, she could feel them. Her inner thighs itched where she had been carrying the pouches. She wanted to scratch, but she resisted. She breathed deeply as she entered the line. She was grateful that there were several parties ahead of her. It would give her time to settle down.

As she neared the desk, she made every attempt to calm down, but it was nearly impossible. She worried about Laverne. She thought of Julio, but her mind kept going back to Laverne. She knew her friend was in deep trouble, and not even Augie Medusa could save her. Would he? She wondered?

The inspector took her passport and her declaration, looking her up and down as he did. She thought he had looked at her groin area too long, but it could have been her imagination, she reasoned. She gave him as warm a smile as she could muster, hoping her face would do the job. It must have. He smiled back.

"Good afternoon, Miss Wether," as he perused the passport. "Do you have anything you want to declare?"

She shook her head. "No, I didn't have time to shop. I was too busy enjoying the local flavor," she smiled.

He nodded and returned her passport.

As she exited the airport terminal and proceeded to the taxi stand, she breathed more easily, but it was short lived. She could see the goons, the same ones who were always around Augie when she was in his presence. They nodded to her, and came forward, taking her by the arm, saying nothing. She allowed herself to be led. She didn't know what else to do. They led her to a large black automobile. One of the goons opened a rear door and practically shoved her in. She looked in and saw Augie Medusa sitting there. He was not smiling. He merely looked at her, and then he nodded to the driver as soon as the goons were in the car. As they drove off, he placed his hand between her thighs, and feeling nothing but legs, his mouth twisted as he demanded, "Where's the stuff?"

She was frightened. "I had to get rid of it, Augie. I saw them take Laverne out of the line. I knew they were there."

"Shit, all of it gone! The whole goddamn trip a waste, and Laverne is gone, too."

She gasped, no longer concerned about her own safety. "Where's Laverne?"

He hissed at her. "Where the hell do you think she is? The Feds have her. She's in deep shit."

"But... but... can't you get her out?"

"Are you nuts? If I run down there and post bail, they'll tie the whole thing into me."

She attempted to be brave. "But, she loves you, Augie... she told me so..."

"Hell, kid, you think I don't love her... why..." and he never finished.

Near tears, she pressed on: "But, if you love her, surely, you won't let them..."

He cut her off. "Shut up. I'm trying to think." After a moment, "You know, kid, you might have done the smart thing, flushing the stuff down the toilet. If they had caught you, too, I'd have twice as much trouble as I've got... yeah."

She made no reply.

He laughed. "I bet that's the most expensive pile that's ever been flushed down a toilet, huh, boys'" They all laughed in unison. He turned to Rainey. "Did Laverne tell you this was her last trip?"

"Yes, she told me. I was so glad when she told me she just wanted to be with you... that's all she wanted, Augie." It was obvious she was appealing to his better nature.

He was quiet for a while. "Damn, the first time I meet a broad who could set me on fire and, now this..."

Rainey kept working on him, trying to secure some help for her friend. She knew if Augie wouldn't help her, then who?

"She loved you so much, Augie..."

"Oh, shut up. I'm trying to think. I've got to decide what to do about you and Laverne."

She shuddered. Her voice quivered. "Me? What do you intend to do with me?"

He looked at her with cold eyes, the kind of look she had always felt he could effect. "My first impulse is to tie some concrete to your feet and dump you in Lake Pontchartrain, but with my crappy luck some shrimper would drag you up in his net and I'd be in bigger trouble."

His words stabbed her in the heart. She had no idea he had even thought of killing her. She moaned, saying nothing.

"But," he continued, "I've got a job for you to do..."

"Oh, Augie, I don't think I want to go back to Cuba..."

"I didn't say anything about Cuba, kid. I've got something else in mind."

Her mind raced through all kinds of eventualities he might have in mind for her. She knew the mob was into prostitution and she was afraid it might be that. "What?" she asked softly.

"I'll talk about it later... not now. I've got too much on my mind right now."

After reaching the boathouse, she was practically dragged into the living area by one of the goons. She was shoved in a chair and left there for a long time, with no one saying anything to her even though there was a lot of conversation in the room. Augie was making phone calls all over the country, she knew that. He was highly animated in his calls, his hands waving in the air as if they could be seen on the other end.

After some time, he came and sat opposite her. "Now, listen to me, kid. Here's what I want you to do. Go to your apartment and pack up... everything... you understand. They're gonna be looking for you, I'm sure. Bring all your stuff back here until I decide where you're going. You can move into that bedroom on the upper floor, in the loft," and he nodded to it.

She was afraid of what might happen to her, but she felt this was not the time to protest. He sensed her fear. He touched her arm. "Don't worry, kid, you're not going to be molested by me, and damn sure not by these guys, either. I might have my faults, but my mama, God rest her soul," as he looked heavenly, "raised me right. I've got three sisters. We don't rough up nice girls... just whores." The words tore at her heart, but she said nothing, just nodded.

He beckoned to one of the goons. "Salvadore, you take her to the apartment, and if you touch her, I'll make a soprano outta you, understand?" The man nodded without smiling.

Augie rose. The meeting was over, but she walked to him, standing close: "Augie, what's going to happen to Laverne? I have to know."

He took on a nearly soft look. "I don't know. That's what I have to look into. Now, get the hell outta here."

She had been at the boathouse for two days, now, and just as Augie had promised, no one had laid a hand on her. She was brought her meals on a tray, and other than that, the only person she talked to was the colored maid who cleaned the place every day. She wondered, she fretted, she paced the floor. The suspense was killing her, but no one would tell her a thing. She had been instructed to tell her previous landlord that she was leaving the city and had no forwarding address. She had closed her bank account, withdrawing her small savings, and had been instructed to tell them the same thing- no forwarding address.

On the third day, she could hear Augie's voice on the lower level. He yelled up to her. "Rainey, I want to talk to you. Come down when you can." He was not usually that solicitous. She was encouraged. She made an extra effort to look good, feeling it never hurt a woman to do so if she had to negotiate with a man. She was now sure he would not force her to do anything of a personal nature if she did not want to.

He was sitting on the couch. He motioned for her to sit next to him. He spoke softly. "I think I got his thing under control, somewhat," and he shook his head. "It took every trick I could turn to get her out on bond..."

She interrpted him. "Oh, is Laverne out? I want to talk to her... please, Augie. She needs me..."

He once again shook his head. "No, kid, that's not possible, she's gone, already."

She gasped. "Gone? Gone where?"

"She's in South America... in a place where I sent her. She's okay, so don't worry about her. She has everything she wants for the time being."

"But, how long will she have to stay there?"

He breathed deeply. "For quite a while... until this thing blows over."

She pondered that, and knowing she could do no more for her friend, she asked softly, "And what of me?"

"Your case is a little easier to solve. They didn't catch you with anything. As a matter of fact, they don't even know about you, but, they knew about Laverne. They were waiting for her."

"Will she have to stand trial?"

He laughed. "Well, they'll play hell even finding her, much less bringing her back for trial."

"And me, what of me?" she persisted.

He didn't reply to her question, directly. "We don't need that phase of the operation anymore. That was small time. We've found a better way of bringing the stuff into the country. South Lousiana has so many ports with the oil industry that we can bring it in on boats to places like Morgan City, Houma, and Grand Isle. It's safer and bigger."

She shuddered. She didn't want to know this. "Why are you telling me all this? I don't want to know it."

He nodded. "Yeah, you're right. Why am I telling you all this, huh?"

She didn't reply.

"That brings me to the business at hand," and he put his hand on her knee in an impersonal manner. She looked into his eyes and he didn't have that look that men have in such a circumstance. "Look, kid, I like you, and I trust you. You been square with us, and we're gonna be square with you." He laughed. "For a bunch of crooks, we have honor, too. We take good care of people who have treated us right." She felt he was conning her. She knew that he knew that she knew a lot about the operation. He had two choices. He could kill her or he could keep her happy. He had obviously chosen the latter.

"I've got one more job for you to do and then," he laughed, "then, I'm laying you off... retiring you, so to speak."

She squirmed in her seat. "What kind of job?"

"I have a package I want you to deliver to Chicago. That's all, and after you do that, you're off the hook."

"What's in the package? Couldn't you just mail it?"

He smiled. "Well, you know, there's this thing about postal inspectors and all that. We want a personal delivery to be made. Anything wrong with that?"

"Couldn't you send one of them?" and she nodded to the goons.

He laughed. "I need them down here, and besides, they couldn't find their butts with both hands." He laughed and the goons laughed. "Well, what do you say?"

She attempted some brovado. "What does it pay?"

"Like I said, Rainey, we treat people right. We're gonna give you a damn good termination bonus, and taking an envelope from one of the goons, he withdrew some bills. "We owe you seven-fifty for the last trip... right?"

She nodded. In the excitement, she had not been paid. She looked at the huge pile of bills. She knew it was much more than the money he owed her.

"Then," and he began to count the bills, all in hundreds, "there is the pay for this job. We're gonna give you five grand for this trip. Not bad, huh?"

She swallowed hard. As much as she would have liked the money, she knew she was being much over paid. "That's a lot of money for one trip."

He nodded. "Yes, it is, but like I said, sweetheart, we treat people right. Are you interested?"

"All I have to do is deliver this package to Chicago, and that's it?"

He nodded again. "That's it," spreading his hands.

Her mind began to play with the amount. A total of five thousand, seven hundred and fifty dollars- more money than she had ever had in her lifetime. She swallowed hard, trying to remain calm. "I'll do it, but that's it. I quit after that."

He smiled, patting her knee. "Sure, kid, if that's what you want."

"When do I leave?"

"How about tomorrow morning. We'll have a rental car waiting for you..."

Surprised that she was driving, "Oh, I thought I'd be flying."

He stammered a little, not ready for her rebuttle. "Well, you see, the man you're gonna give the package to... well, he's outa town and won't be in Chicago for a few days, so you can take your time... see the country... know what I mean?"

She felt that his words were hollow, but she decided not to push it. The money was too good. She rose. "Well, I guess I'll go and pack. Then, I have to go and do some shopping..."

He cut her off. "No, Rainey!" and then softening his tone, "I'd prefer you not go out before you leave... for your own safety... know what I mean? You tell us what you need and one of the boys will pick it up," and he nodded to the goons.

"Well, some of it is of a personal nature."

He smiled. "It can't be too personal for them to handle it, believe me." The goons chuckled and so did Augie.

She shrugged. "Okay, then I guess I'll go and pack."

CHAPTER TWENTY-FOUR

Rainey spent a restless night on, this, her last one before she undertook her trip to Chicago. She had locked her loft bedroom door in spite of Augie's assurances that she was safe. She didn't trust any man that much.

She was awakened in the middle of the night by loud talking coming from the kitchen area of the boathouse apartment. The area over the living room was two story, and her bedroom balcony overlooked it, but the kitchen, which is where the loud talking was coming from, was back out of sight. Unable to sleep because of the loud voices, she opened her bedroom door and walked softly out on the balcony, hoping to see who was making the noise, but she couldn't- they were in the kitchen.

She could hear Augie's voice, the only one she recognized:

"Jesus, be careful with the damn stuff. Are you sure you know what you're doing?"

"Yeah, I'm sure. I done this before... many times."

"Well, hurry, I want to go to bed."

"Go on. I don't need you to watch me."

There was no more talking for a while, so she tip-toed back into her bedroom and locked the door. She went to the bathroom and took two aspirins and returned to her bed, lying on her back for a while, then, she rolled on her side, attempting sleep.

Augie was waiting for her in the living room when she descended the stairs in the morning. He was smiling a broad smile. "Well, good morning, Rainey. Sleep well?" He was too solicitous, and that bothered her. He was not the type.

She stifled a yawn. "No, I didn't sleep well. I could hear you people talking half the night..."

He gave her an embarrassed look. "Geez, I tried to tell those goons to be quiet. They were, uh... mixing some new drinks or something like that. I went to bed."

"Oh, so that was it."

"Uh, huh. Are you ready to travel? Is your luggage ready?"

She turned to go up the stairs to fetch it.

"No, don't bother," and he nodded to one of the goons who immediately went up the stairs to retrieve her luggage. He went to the coffee table and picked up a package the size of a shoe box. He motioned her over, holding it out to her.

"Now, this is what I want you to take to Chicago for me. The address of the man is on the outside. Just take it to his office and leave it with his secretary if he is not there. Okay?"

She reached for it, but he kept it from her, saying, "The boys will take care of it until you leave," and motioning her to be seated, he continued, "I want to make sure you understand how to handle this thing. It's very valuable and it's delicate, too, so be careful how you handle it. Understand so far?"

She nodded.

He continued: "Now, listen carefully, Rainey. This is important. You take this box with you at all times. If you go into a restaurant to eat, have it with you. If you check into a motel, have it with you. Don't leave it alone. It's too valuable."

She looked apprehensive. "Gee, Augie, you sure you want to trust this thing to me. I'm scared of it."

He put his hand on her shoulder. "No, honey, I know you can do it. I have faith in you. That's why we're paying you so much money to do this. I know you can do it. Are you ready?"

She nodded, bending to pick up her two bags.

"No, we'll take care of your luggage," and he nodded to the assistants. One picked up the two large suitcases and the other picked up the box.

She started to walk out.

He caught her arm and with an overly warm smile. "Ain't you gonna give old Augie a goodbye kiss? You may never see me again."

She hesitated, and then, leaned over to kiss him on the cheek, and as she drew back, "Augie, please let me know where Laverne is. I want to contact her..."

He patted her on the shoulder. "Don't worry, honey, you call me in a week and I'll give you her address."

"You promise?"

He smiled. "Hey, have I ever lied to you?"

She shook her head, and then walked out to the car. He followed her out, opening the door for her. He nearly stuck his head in the open window. "How do you like the rental? I told the boys to get you a nice car. Look, an Olds Ninety Eight ain't bad, is it?" as he waved at the car.

"No, it's nice. What do I do with it when I am finished?"

He was caught unaware. He thought for a moment. "Well, it's prepaid, so just take it to a Hertz rental place and leave it there. That's all."

She picked up the rental papers to look at them, but he waved her off with: "Don't worry about the difference in names. It's registered to one of our secretaries who rented it. You know those damn people... they never get anything straight."

She nodded and smiled. "Well, I guess this is goodbye, Augie."

He backed away. "Yeah, kid, be careful. Remember what I told you about the package," and he waved her off.

She headed out to the Airline Highway and passed the airport on the way out. Her mind went out to Laverne. Where was she? Was she really safe as he had assured her. He was too sweet this morning. That bothered her. He was not really a sweet man.

It was late autumn when she headed north to Chicago. In those post-war days, U.S. Highway 61 was the best route to take to Memphis. Although she considered herself a fairly good driver, she had never undertaken a long trip alone and she was apprehensive. She had decided, since Augie had told her she did not have to hurry, that she would stop before dark and check into a motel each night. She had never lived alone, either, and that scared her. She realized she was really not sophisticated for her age.

As she drove through Natchez she slowed to admire the magnificent old antebellum homes which lined the streets. She would have liked to stop but she wanted to make Vicksburg before dark, so she didn't. As she looked at the homes, she realized just how dysfunctional a life she had led so far. She had really done nothing to improve her cultural side- absolutely nothing. To herself: Rainey, honey, you're still nothing but a country hick with a cute face and a good figure. Take that away and what have you got? You're still nothing that would make an ambitious man, headed for success, want as his wife and the mother of his children. No, men on the way up pick their wives like horse people pick their horses. Who was their mama and who was their daddy? What have you got to offer? Your mama was a whore and your daddy is unknown. What a record to run on? She indulged in this self flagellation for the better part of an hour, sometimes in tears. Then, she sniffed and said aloud, as if to someone in the car: "Oh, what the hell? I've got good health and nearly six thousand dollars in my purse," and with that, she lit up a Camel.

She looked at the gas gauge. It was nearly empty. She was hungry and she had to tinkle. She saw a combination gas station and restaurant at an intersection and she pulled in.

"Fill up and check the oil, please," she instructed the young attendant as he came up with a broad smile and a thick Mississippi accent.

"Yes, Ma'am. Ah shur will. Nice day, ain't it?"

She returned his smile. His front teeth had a wide space, she noticed. "How far to Vicksburg?" she inquired.

As he leaned against the car, scratching his head, "Whal, nah, it ain't too far, Ma'am. You kin make it 'fore sundown, fer shur."

"Thank goodness. Is the food good in that restaurant?"

"Oh, yassum, mah ma cooks in thar," and he laughed, "it's just like home."

"Where should I park while I eat?" she inquired.

He nodded to an oak tree over in the distance near the edge of the shelled parking area. "Why, you jus park ova unda that thar tree, Ma'am. It'll be okay," and looking the car over, "it shur is a nice car... shur is."

After moving the car to the secluded spot. She started to get out, and she remembered the box. "Oh, God, I nearly forgot the damn thing. Augie would kill me if he knew."

She picked it up and proceeded to the restaurant. She picked a booth and as an old waitress walked over with the ever present glass of water and the menu, she could not help but smile. The waitress waddled just like Mabel had so many years before in the Pine Cone Cafe in Pine Bluff.

The waitress adjusted the bra under her pendulous breasts without shame. She grunted. "Geez, Ah wish we could have these damn things cut off after our babies and our husbands git through playing with 'em," and looking at Rainey with a practiced eye, added, "Ah guess you still having fun with yourn, though."

Rainey smiled, not wanting to encourage her any further.

"You know what you want, honey?"

She nodded. "I just want a club sandwich and a cup of coffee, and oh, yes, a slice of apple pie with ice cream."

She grunted and waddled off.

Leaving half her pie and ice cream, and anxious to get under way again, she picked up the box and rose to leave. She searched her purse for some change to leave a tip, but seeing nothing but large bills, she made her way to the counter. After engaging in small talk with the manager, she exited the restaurant and made her way to the car. As she reached it and opened the door to enter, she realized that she had forgotten to leave the waitress a tip.

"Oh, hell," she shook her head, and remembering her own waitressing days, she placed the box on the seat and walked back some fifty yards to the restaurant with her purse in hand. She had to give her a generous tip. The old waitress smiled as she saw her coming with a dollar bill in her hand, and taking it, she said, "You know, honey, I had you pegged as one of them rich bitches who don't give a damn about us working girls, but, Ah see Ah was wrong. Thanks," as she pocketed the bill.

The explosion could be heard for a mile around as the time bomb went off in the car. The entire front wall of the restaurant was wracked by the blast. Rainey and the waitress were thrown to the floor. The patrons began to scream as they tried to figure out what had happened. Rainey got to her feet, her purse still in her hand. She ran her hand through her hair, trying to compose herself, and looking at the waitress: "Are you all right?"

"Shit... what happened?" she responded.

"I'm not sure. Something exploded, I guess," and then Rainey looked at her car, or, where her car was. It was a fireball, what was left of it. She could not believe her eyes. The box was in the car, she thought to herself, and then, the whole thing came together in her mind. "The godamm box was a bomb. That no good bastard, Augie Medusa, had intended to kill me."

She staggered to a booth and sat down, trying to sort the thing out. She looked up as a man came running into the restaurant, asking the still shocked waitress, "Rita, whar's Miz Clara? Her boy's dead. He went with the car. He's all blowed up... it's pitiful."

The waitress began to wail "Oh, Lord Jesus, help us. Tha world's comin' to the end."

Rainey now realized that the young boy who had filled her car was dead, an innocent victim of Augie's twisted mind. She wanted to cry but she decided she could not afford to cry. She had to think, and fast. She looked again at the car. It was gone and all her clothing with it, including her mother's old shoe box which she had kept all these years. The silver locket was around her neck. Thank God, she thought, I still have it.

As her mind cleared, she realized she could be in big trouble if she had to explain how her car exploded and killed a local boy. She shook her head as if to clear it. She reasoned, he was the only one who could really connect her with the car and he could no longer do that. She felt her purse. She opened it and glanced in. She had to be reassured that the money was still there. It was all she had in the world. She had been reduced to nothing, thanks, once again, to the perfidy of a man. He had been too sweet- too kind. She should have suspected something. Martha Powell's words came back to haunt her. "They will say anything, do anything, to get you to do what they want."

She stood and looked around her. The place was in chaos with everyone running, but not sure where to. She saw a fire truck coming up, siren screaming; then, a police car. She began to breathe hard. She knew they would be inside in a minute, asking questions. She had to get out. She looked towards the kitchen and seeing no one coming from that door, she made her way to it. She realize that she was bleeding from a cut on her arm from flying glass. She grabbed a kitchen dish cloth, a dirty one, and wrapped her arm under the elbow. She saw a rear door and made her way to it. She saw no one. Everyone had gone to the front where the explosion had occured. She went out the door and walked out into a rear alley. She proceeded to a side street and started walking.

She remembered her arm. She removed the dirty cloth, giving it one last wipe, and then threw it in a bush. She looked up, not knowing where to go, and then she saw a motel sign a few blocks away. She headed in that direction. She knew she had to be alone... to think. She had to get off the street. She was still shaking, badly. If she had to answer a policeman's questions just now, she would appear guilty as homemade sin-she knew that.

The clerk looked her up and down, suspiciously, when she requested a single room. "For how long, Miss?"

"Just tonight," she stammered.

He looked over the counter. "You have no luggage?" His eyebrows raised.

Jesus she thought, he thinks I'm a whore.

"No," she lied, "my luggage was put on the wrong bus," as she breathed deeply. "They're trying to track it down now."

"I see. That'll be ten dollars, in advance."

She threw herself on the bed after locking the door behind her, and lay on her back, her hands over her face, as she tried to fathom what had really happened. As the pieces of the puzzle came together, she was sure she had it all figured out. There was no package to be delivered. It was a time bomb! Thinking of the noise in the kitchen the night before, she now realized they were putting the lethal thing together. She remembered, it was near 3:00 o'clock when she had awakened that morning. She looked at her watch. It was now 3:25. The bomb had gone off about 12 hours after they had finished it. It had been timed to go off after she was on the road, alone. She remembered Augie's words. "Don't ever leave it alone. Take it with you at all times." She now realized that if she had not gone back without the box to leave the waitress a tip... she would have been blown to bits along with that poor unfortunate young boy. She cried, but her tears were tears of anger and outrage. "That sonofabitch, Augie, wanted me dead!" She thought of Laverne. Was she really in south America, or was she also dead? She shook her head in desperation.

She began to ponder her predicament. She had lost all her clothing, which was really all she had accumulated the past few years. Several small pieces of jewelry were in her bags, but that was all. She thought of the money. Would they really have wasted five thousand dollars of real money knowing full well that it would be blown to bits. She knew they were involved in counterfeiting, also. She panicked. If that money was no good, then... she was broke. She reached for her bag. She withdrew the bills and went to the light on the night table. She scrutinized the bills, holding them up to the light. They looked real to her, but then, she was no expert on fake bills. She had to know. She thought for a while. Tomorrow, she would go to the bank and ask for one to be changed to smaller bills.

She felt she needed a bath, as if the water would cleanse her body and soul of Augie Medusa and his perfidious act. She realized she had no change of clothing. She went to the tub and began to draw her bath water. She rinsed out her bra and underpants, hanging them on the shower curtain bar. She eased into the soapy water and lay back on the reclining end. Her head eased back and she closed her eyes. Her head moved back and forth in total disbelief. She opened her eyes and looked at the peeling plaster above the tub. She said, aloud: "Rainey, honey, you've got to have the worst goddamn luck of any human being on the face of this miserable earth. What did I ever do to deserve this?"

She had no sleeping aids, no aspirin- nothing, but in spite of that, she slept the sleep of the dead. It was mid-morning before she awoke with a start. She looked around the dingy room. Strange, it looked better the night before when she was more than happy to have it. She sighed, remembering her predicament. She knew she had to make plans, and fast. She needed to get out of town as fast as she could. There was bound to be an investigation- police asking questions at all motels- going over the registrations. She remembered. She had registered as

Shirley Brown, the first name that came to her in her state of panic. She needed clothing. She needed transportation. She jumped out of bed. Her underclothes were still damp in that moist southern climate. She cursed under her breath as she put on the damp undergarments and completed her dressing. Thank God for small favors- her cosmetics were in her purse. She jabbed on the lipstick as if she were angry with her mouth, then, taking one last look at the finished job, and being unhappy with what she saw, shrugged and left.

She asked the daytime motel clerk locations of banks and clothing stores. He perused her, looking at her suspiciously as he checked the registration book. "You will find banks and department stores about three blocks that way, and two blocks over to the right. May I call you a cab? Your luggage will be heavy to carry that far."

She related the same story concerning her lack of luggage as she had the night before. He nodded. "Then, you will also want to know the location of the bus station. They're all within a few blocks of each other," and he explained.

As she left the motel, she peered around the streets as if she were a criminal bent on evading the police, for in her mind, she might just as well have been. She was tempted to walk back towards the restaurant to see what was left of her car, but she thought better of it and headed for the bank.

She tried to calm her nerves. She plotted her strategy. She had to know for sure if the money was real or not. She had a plan. It would involve a lie, but in her predicament, she really didn't care. It was a fight for survival. She walked up to the bank teller area. She saw two female tellers and one male. She selected the male after looking in her makeup mirror for some reassurance.

She smiled, nervously. "Good morning. I wonder if you could do me a favor," and showing him one of the hundred dollar bills, "I've been reading so much lately about counterfeit bills, and I want to be a good citizen. You see this bill? I was given it when I cashed a check at a hotel in Vicksburg, and well, it looks so nice and new... I just wondered if it was real." She gave him her little girl look. "You, know, us girls just can't be too careful these days. You just never know..."

She had appealed to his southern manly compulsion to aid any female in distress. "Why, shur, Ma'am, I'll take a look at it. I can spot one a mile off. We're trained to detect them, you know..."

She smiled, her eyelashes batting, as she ran her tongue over her lips, nervously. He handed it back to her. "No, Miss, this thing is good as gold. Ah wish Ah had a bunch of them."

If he had been listening instead of looking at her heaving breasts, he would have heard air being exhaled in sheer relief. She thank him profusely, and to his query, "Will you be in town for a while?", she shook her head. "No, I'm leaving within the hour," and she could see the look of disappointment on his face.

Now, feeling relieved that she had real money in her purse, she had a new lease on life. She bought a modest wardrobe and a piece of nice luggage. Laverne had instructed her that it was permissible to have cheap underclothes in a bag as long as the bag, itself, was impressive. "Ater all," she had intoned, "how many people see your underclothes, but everyone sees your bags." She thought of Laverne.

Now, looking as if she were really a traveling woman, she went to a restaurant for lunch. She had to make plans and her brain functioned better on a full stomach. She viewed herself in the glass storefront as she paused for a moment. She had chosen a feminine looking business suit, something a girl would wear to the office. It had a small pin stripe pattern with a white silk looking blouse and a hankerchief in the pocket. The whole shopping spree had cost her nearly two hundred and fifty dollars, but, as she sighed looking in the glass, "It was worth it."

When she had inquired about a rental car at the restaurant, she was told there was no rental agency in the small town. "No, Ma'am, the nearest one is in Vicksburg. Where you headed?"

She hesitated. Where was she headed? She had no idea. "Well, I'm on vacation. I'm like a leaf in the wind, heading wherever the wind blows," she had responded in little girl fashion.

Upon being seated in the restaurant, she saw a pile of newspapers on the counter. She inquired: "Are these papers for sale?"

"No, they're complimentary, honey, help yourself," from the waitress.

She took one and returned to her booth. There it was on the front page, complete with photos of the wrecked car. She read hurriedly, as if time were a factor. Yes, the police were looking for the owner of the car. No corpse other than the unfortunate young man had been found. The waitresses in the restaurant had all been questioned. Yes, most all the patrons were locals and could be accounted for. Yes, there was this nice young woman who had been in the restaurant. The police were trying to locate her, to question her. Her heart sank. She was not out of the woods yet. She began to breathe faster. Her heart pounded in her bosom. She knew they would be covering the bus and train stations. She had to think of an alternate plan.

She could hear two men talking in the next booth, obviously traveling salemen. One was headed to New Orleans and the other on his way to Vicksburg and then Memphis. She rose to go to the restroom. She had to see what they looked like. She gave them a sideways glance as she left, hoping they would still be there when she returned. They were. She could tell who was who by their voices. She knew her only hope of getting out of town without being detected was in a private automobile.

The New Orleans salesman bid his goodbyes. The other, the one headed for Vicksburg was still in the booth. She swallowed hard, knowing she was playing a dangerous game, but she had no choice. It was this or nothing.

She rose and turned to face him, her best little girl demeanor came to the fore. "Excuse me, Sir, but I couldn't help but overhear you tell the other gentleman that you were headed for Vicksburg."

He came to his feet. He was of the old south. His mama has taught him that you rose when a lady came to your table. He was in his fifties, with prematurely white hair. He had a nice pink complexion, and he wore rimless spectacles. He half-bowed. "Why, yes, I'm headed that way. May I be of some help to you Miss?"

She looked around, as if helpless. "Well, I do have a big problem. You see, I just got word that my mama has had a stroke in Memphis and... and... I just have to get there before she... she.." and she let the words settle in his conscience.

"Well, I am leaving in a moment, and... and... I would be happy to give you a ride, but..." He was a family man, a deacon in the Blue Ridge Baptist Church, and he viewed this very attractive and well-built young woman as the devil incarnate... in the flesh.

She pressed further. "I could take the bus, but the next one doesn't leave for over an hour, and... it might be too late by then..." She suppressed a sob, satisfied with her performance as she read his eyes.

He patted her shoulder. "Now, don't you fret, my dear, I'll do what I can to help you, but... you see... I'm a married man, and I... I could be compromised if the wrong person saw you in my car as we leave town."

"Oh, the last thing I would want, Sir, is to compromise you, or me. I'll just lie down on the back seat... if that will help."

He cleared his throat. "Well, I hate to resort to subterfuge but, it might be the best if you do until we get out of town."

She nodded. "I think so, too." And as an after thought, "I'll be happy to pay for the gas..."

He interuppted her. "No, my dear, that will not be necessary. I will offer this up like the Good Samaritan."

Rainey, whose religious education had been sadly neglected, was not sure what he meant, but she nodded, picking up her luggage and following him to the checkout counter.

As she settled down in the back seat, she felt foolish. like a child, but if this is what it took, she was ready to suffer the indignity. From time to time, she would look up as he carried on a one way conversation, extolling the virtues of doing God's work in the vineyard of life. She, from time to time, intoned, "How true... how true."

She could not resist looking up as she heard him say, "Oh, oh, a police checkpoint. It must have something to do with that terrible tragedy at the restaurant. I'm sure you heard about that. Now, I know they will see you in the back seat," and looking back at her, "do you mind throwing my topcoat over you for just a while?"

"No ..I think that would be a good idea."

She could hear the car slowing down, and then, a voice coming from the outside. "Goodmornin' Mr. Ashbrough, Sir. We're looking for someone, but you shur ain't her... you go on." She heard the car accelerate. She breathed more easily, but only for a while. He looked back, saying, "I think you can come up for good now. We're out of town," but having said that, she could feel the car slowing as he pulled off the road. Her eyes widened with fear. Surely, this kindly gentleman would not attempt to take advantage of her in this situation. "Why are we stopping?" her voice quivered.

He looked in the back seat, not smiling. "I think we need to have a little talk. Would you get in the front seat, now?"

She reluctantly moved to the front. "What do you want to talk about?"

He gave her a fatherly smile. "You. I think we need to talk about you, young lady. You could have gotten me in a lot of trouble back there if that policeman didn't know me extremely well. I want to know- are you the young woman they're looking for back there?"

Her eyes widened. "I don't know what you're talking about." She hated to lie to this kindly gentleman, but she felt she had no choice.

He was not convinced. "You know, an innocent young man was killed yesterday, a fine young man. If you had anything to do with that, then, you're guilty of manslaughter. I'm convinced it was an accident, so it's not murder."

She looked genuinely remorseful. "I swear to you, Sir, I had nothing to do with that explosion yesterday. I read about it in the morning paper, but that is all I know." She felt this was a half-truth she could live with.

He regarded her for a long time, trying to evaluate her. He had been a salesman all his life and he prided himself on being able to read people. That's the mark of a true salesman. They could read people and plan accordingly.

"Is your mother really sick?"

She hung her head in shame. "No, that was a lie. I'm running away from a man who wants to kill me." She looked him directly in the eye. "That's the truth, so help me God."

"Where is this man?"

"In New Orleans."

"Why don't you go to the police?"

She shook her head. "It would do no good. They'd never believe my side of it. That's the truth."

He started up the car, and looking in her direction, "I'm not sure I completely believe you, either, but..." and he shook his head at the machinations of the young generation.

Lloyd J. Guillory

It was only after the plane had taken off from the Memphis airport that she could feel really free of the horrible trauma of the attempt on her life. She was still incredulous at the insanity of it all. She was only a very small cog in the entire operation. She did not consider herself important enough to be assassinated. And what of Laverne? was she still alive as he had maintained? Could she ever believe anything that Augie Medusa had to say. Not hardly! She looked out the window at the disappearing landscape as the plane climbed.

She reviewed her options. She saw none that she considered viable. She knew she had money enough for the time being, but that wouldn't last forever. She had to settle in some place while she still had money and then get a job. She thought of Arkansas and Martha Powell- her cousin Elmer- the kindly old attorney, Justin Holstead, and she wondered if she should go back to her roots. No, she shook her head, defiantly. There was nothing there for her to go back to-nothing. She did not have one pleasant memory of the place, except for meeting Laverne there. Laverne. Laverne. She shook her head as she thought of her. Where was she? Beautiful, sensual, desireable Laverne. If only you had had the brains to go with the rest of you, there would have been no stopping you, but...

Thinking of Laverne and her wild and eratic life only impressed her more with her own predicament. She was nearly twenty-six, and what did she have to show for twenty-six years of living on the planet? Somewhere near fifty-five hundred dollars- that's all! She took out a piece of paper and pencil and divided the money by the years and came up with $211.53 per year. To herself: "That's all you're worth, Rainey, honey, is $211.53 for each and every year you've lived." She chuckled. "Hell, even the worst of whores make more than that in one week," and she sobbed to herself, "excepting my poor mama. She would have considered that a damn good week."

She sighed deeply as she told the flight attendant she was not hungry. She had to think some more. She had to settle down, she knew that, and the only way for a woman to settle down in this society was to settle down with a husband, in a little vine-covered cottage with a mortgage and kids. Wasn't that the way Hollywood pictured it? Wasn't that the way June Allyson and Jimmy Stewart did it? Kids? Did she really want any? She was not sure, but if that's what the men want, then, that's the way it had to be. It was a man's world. If you gave them what they wanted, then, they'd give you what you wanted. That's the way the game is played. She was tired way down deep. She let her head go back on the cushion as she closed her eyes.

Her ticket had been purchased to St. Louis. She had no idea why St. Louis. She felt she would stay there for a day or two while she decided where to go. Her ticket had been coach class. She wanted to conserve her money.

CHAPTER TWENTY-FIVE

She arrived in St. Louis with one large piece of luggage, something near five thousand dollars in her purse, and trepidation in her heart. As she checked into a large motel near the airport (to conserve on taxi fares) she knew she had to make some plans. She had to restore some semblance of order to her unsettled life.

After signing in and freshening up in the room, she went down to the lobby, having nothing else of a substantive nature to do. She went into the gift shop and purchased two packs of Camel cigarettes and a Life magazine. She started to go to the coffee shop, but her stomach, still churning from the recent trauma in her life, rebelled at the idea. Instead, she bought a roll of Tums and proceeded to the lobby. She selected a chair in the remote corner, not wishing to talk to any other human being at the moment. Several men gave her solicitous glances which she returned with a disinterested lowering of the eyes.

She lit the Camel, drawing hard on the weed, feeling the warm narcotic vapor filling her lungs. She allowed her head to go back on the high back chair for a moment, then she lowered her eyes to the cover on the magazine. The cover photo was of an attractive young woman climbing the steps of the U.S. Capital, and the caption read: WASHINGTON WOMEN. She slowly turned the pages until she reached the cover story. It was an account of how thousands of young women, after the war, had flocked to the nation's capital in search of men and jobs, not in that particular order. The story went on to say that these young women had various reasons for this migration. For some, the men they had loved failed to return home. For others, the men they had waited for were not the same men they had kissed goodbye- they were different. (Her mind went to Verlie. She had explained that many times)

To others, having been mired down in the drab lives of small town America, they craved a new life- excitement. Many believed, quite correctly, that the new breed of men flocking to the capital to man the ever growing bureaucracy, were better educated and better mannered, and yes, even more handsome than the hicks in their home towns. The grass is always greener.

As she read on, her head nodded in agreement, quite unconsciously, as the written words entered her brain. She inhaled deeply, tilted her head back, and looked out at the darkening sky. A winter storm was comings she had heard at the desk when she checked in. She breathed deeply as she pondered the words in the article. Why not? She had no other plans, and her mind began to play with the scenario. She would move to Washington. She would get a cute little apartment in some quaint section of that great city. She would get a job as a secretary to some important man- a handsome and eligible man. He would fall madly in love with her to the point that he could not live without her. Even his job was suffering. He would beg her to marry him... She didn't notice that she was smiling to herself.

After supper that evening in the motel, she sauntered down to the bar during the last portion of the Happy Hour. She selected a table in the back corner. She really didn't want to be noticed. She was not in the mood for men- any man. She watched the interaction of the sexes. She had no difficulty in determining who was trying to achieve what. She could even detect those who were married and cheating. They had that look in their eyes, glancing toward the door ever so often. The human conscience is a troublesome thing, a burden to man's pleasures.

Several men came by. "Interested in some company?" was the most often heard opening statement, followed by a raised eyebrow look. She was firm, but not resentful: "No, thank you, I'm waiting for someone." In truth, she was. She was truly waiting for someone- someone who could make her chimes ring like the greatest of medieval cathedrals. She saw no such person in this bar, and tiring of the spectacle, she went up to her room, alone.

Lying in bed that night, she made up her mind. She would go to Washington to find a job and hopefully, eventually settle down with the man of her dreams. What else could she hope for? There were no other options open to a young woman in the year 1956. Dwight Eisenhower was president, and he had a nice smile. He had ended the Korean stalemate, and the nation was at peace.

She sat in the coffee shop the next morning, once again being able to stomach the acidic brew. She refined her plans. If she were going to Washington to compete in the market place of American politics, she knew the competition would be formidable. The magazine article made no bones about that. The girls were mostly young, twenty to thirty, well dressed, many quite pretty, and many more, quite shapely. Some were college graduates. That didn't bother her too much. Between Martha Powell's insistence on her speaking English correctly and Laverne Sutter's clipped articulation of the King's English, she spoke well. She knew that. Unless someone pressed the issue, they could not tell she had not gone to college... if they didn't delve too deeply into the classics. She had her limitations, she was aware, but a pretty face and a long lean figure could cover up many less evident shortcomings, and she had those.

She thought of her physical attributes. They could be enhanced, she knew that, also. Since those days when aboriginal women first put a bone through their pierced lips and smeared fine powder on their faces, they knew the female countenance could be made to look like something it really was not.

She entered the beauty salon of the motel. She was impressed. It was a lot larger than she had expected, testifying to the vanity of the female of the species as they planned and plotted to capture their prey- the unspecting and willing male.

An employee came forward, smiling a toothy smile. "Hi, can I help you?" She was a hard blond who had gone to excess with her hair too many times.

Rainey smiled. "Yes, I want the works. Make me gorgeous."

The hard blond looked her up and down with some envy. "Well, you've got the raw material, honey- it shouldn't be too difficult. Anything particular in mind?"

"Uh, huh, you can begin with a bleach."

"How blond do you want to be?"

She pondered the question. "Well, Marilyn Monroe is too blond for me, but Grace Kelly is just about right."

She took her by the elbow. "Grace Kelly it is, then."

Nearly three hours later, she emerged. She gave herself one last look in the full length mirror at the checkout corner. It was a mirror of high quality glass, without distortion, and the lighting was soft- designed by an expert in the field.

The operator who had peformed the bulk of the transformation stood beside her. "Well, Rainey, what do you think?"

She smiled with complete satisfaction. "I think I look great. What do you think?"

She grunted. "Honey, if you can't drive them nuts, then, there's something wrong with them."

She sighed. "I hope so. That's my intent," and she giggled as she reached in her purse to pay the bill.

She had decided to splurge on one more thing. She felt she deserved it. Her ticket to Washington was first class. She had never flown in that pampered forward section where egoes ruled supreme. She had often wondered why any sane person would be willing to pay an exhorbitant extra to ride on the same plane just to have a wider seat and be pampered by a flight attendant who bothered you so much you could not take a nap. But, now, she wanted to be counted among that number.

She sat in the bar next to her boarding gate, having "one for the road" as she justified it. She stirred her gin and tonic as she watched the men in the bar. She was the main attraction among the males, and even the envious females nodded in her direction as they whispered to one another.

She lit a cigarette, blowing the smoke in her best Bette Davis fashion as she reviewed the scene. She looked across the terminal corridor which harrowed in this area of bars and gift shops. She saw a door which struck envy and desire in her heart. It had a sign to the side. PRIVATE- VIP LOUNGE. She breathed deeply. What would it be like to enter that over-indulged domain of the rich and powerful?

The door opened and two men exited. They paused for a moment, and then they shook hands, and the older man walked off. The younger one turned to cross the corridor. She gasped as she saw him, She licked her lips, then gently bit them until they hurt. She had never in her entire life ever seen a man whose outward appearance so caught her attention. He was extremely well-dressed, near six feet in height. He was in his middle thirties, she guessed, noticing that his hair was greying at the temples. He was lean. His open jacket showed a flat stomach. He carried a briefcase. He looked in both directions and then walked towards the bar, looking at his watch as he did.

She began to breathe harder and she could feel her nostrils dilating. He passed near her table, so close she could have touched him. She could smell his cologne. He walked to a table to the other side of the crowded bar and sat at a two person table. A shapely young waitress in a too short and too tight hot pants outfit came to take his order. He gave the waitress a warm smile and jealousy raged in Rainey's heart. She could not take her eyes off him and she was embarrassed. She forced herself to turn away as any lady should do, but her eyes returned to him time and time again. She was mesmerized by him, and she didn't care.

Two other women sitting at a table near her began to nod in his direction, their heads together in animated whispers. To her horror and dismay one of them got up and walked over to his table. She leaned over, showing an impressive clevage. Her effrontery made Rainey furious. What right had she? He looked up in response to her words, then, he smiled, shook his head. The woman shrugged and said something, and then returned to her table.

Good for him, thought Rainey. He turned her down. He should have. The nerve of her trying to pick him up. And two of them. What would they do? Share him?

She pondered these thoughts and then, he looked in her direction... and he smiled. She was sure of it. She managed just a slight smile... her little girl smile. He turned back to his drink and her heart sank.

The P.A. announcer called for her flight to board at Gate 32. She rose and gave him one last look. She knew she would never see him again, and it burned in her. She was almost tempted to introduce herself. Hadn't he smiled at her? But, her inhibited nature came to the fore. She sighed, giving him one more look. He was glancing at his gold watch. He didn't notice her. She walked out into the millieu of people in the passage and she became lost in the crowd.

She took her seat in 4D, a window seat. She loved to look out the windows. She had read that a person's first look at Washington as the plane came in for a landing at Washington National was inspiring, with the capital dome and the Washington monument there below you- all the things you had studied in school there before your very eyes.

She squirmed in her seat, looking around, hoping that some interesting person would sit next to her- perhaps a Congressman, or even a Senator. That was one of the reasons she had splurged on a first class ticket. She believed that first class people traveled first class- another one of her many misconceptions.

Then, she saw him coming through the cabin door. He had to lean to enter. The stewardess examined his ticket and she pointed towards Rainey. Her heart skipped a beat. Could it really be true? Fate had never been kind to her. Why would she be now?

He paused in the aisle, examining the numbers on the seats. He smiled as he sat next to her, placing his brief case under the forward seat. She smelled the cologne again. She loved his scent. She became nervous as a high school girl at her Junior-Senior Prom. She was not sure which demeanor to use- the little girl or Bette Davis, and before she could decide, he turned to her: "Didn't I see you in the bar a minute or so ago?" His teeth were white and even, and his voice was modulated like honey flowing off a hot spoon.

She almost choked with nervousness, nodding, her eye lashes flicking nervously. "Yes, I think I saw you, too." Oh, what an outright lie?

He opened his brief case and extracted some papers which he began to shuffle. He turned to her. "I have to do some paper work. Will that bother you?"

She was sorely disappointed, for she had visions of having his complete attention for two hours or so. She smiled, shaking her newly coiffeured tresses. "No, of course not." But to herself: Damn, I spend a small fortune on myself and the one man I meet that I want to attract, and I can't even get his attention... damn! What a waste of money!

She tried to think of something she could do to remedy the situation, but in the confines of an airplane, the options were limited. She thought of going to the restroom. She knew she would have to sqeeze past him and that thought titilated her, but she had just gotten on the plane. He would surely think: Why the hell didn't she do that before she left. She would look silly and childish. She shrugged, looking out the window as the plane roared down the runway and climbed into the darkening sky. That was it... the weather. People always talked about the weather. It was generally accepted. She looked out the window, and then turning to him. "Oh, my gosh, look at that sky. It's turning black."

He turned to look. "Yes, there's a winter storm coming through here, from the midwest to the Atlantic coast. I got a weather report just before I left the office." He turned back to his work.

She glanced at him sideways. The only other man she had ever met who caught her attention like this was Julio Cordoba. She knew Julio had come very close to ringing her chimes- bells, yes, but no chimes. She mentally attempted to compare the men. They were both magnificent animals as Laverne would have described them. Julio was a diamond in the rough, unpolished and uncultured, through no fault of his own. In a different place and under different circumstances, he could be like this man next to her. But, this man, who had all that Julio had and more, was undoubtedly as polished a stone as one could find. His demeanor and his ambience told her that. His modulated voice came from a childhood in which a strict mother probably admonished him in his younger days: "Don't shout, please. Speak softly, and your words will carry more weight." She could picture his mother, a refined and cultured woman, over-indulging him with love and encouragement- everything she never had in her youth.

The pilot's voice broke her reverie: "Ladies and Gentlemen, please make sure that your seat belts are fastened. We anticipate some rough weather between here and Washington, but we think we can get through. We'll keep you posted."

Her eyebrows went up and she gasped: "Oh, did you hear that?" and she gave him the look of a frightened and nervous female. He gave her a reassuring smile. "I don't think it will be too bad. Are you afraid?"

Her voice quivered a little. "Yes, I am."

The plane did begin to shake a little as the turbulence increased and she became truly scared now. She did not have much flying experience and the two trips to Cuba had been relatively smooth.

He returned his papers to their case. He couldn't read, anyway, due to the vibration. His eyes could not focus. He looked at the frightened woman next to him. "Are you afraid, Miss?"

She nodded. "Yes... I am."

He thought for a while, not wanting to be too forward, but he truly believed she was scared. "Please don't misconstrue my offer, but would it help if I held your hand? They tell me it helps."

She offered her hand. "Oh, yes, would you?"

He took her hand in hers. She sighed deeper than she had wanted to. His hand was warm- not moist- just warm, which indicated he was not afraid. Her's was moist. She was embarrassed and she could not help commenting, "I'm sorry. My hand is moist."

He laughed. "Mine is dry. It'll make a good combination."

She wanted to say..."Oh, yes, I think we make a great combination," but she just smiled and sank in her seat. She was in heaven. Never before in her life had she been so grateful for a disruption of nature's forces.

Much later, he looked past her towards the window. "Those are snow clouds down there. I can tell."

"Have you flown before?"

He laughed. "Quite a bit. I was a pilot during the war."

She ooo'hed at him. "What did you fly?"

He replied somewhat reluctantly, "I was a bomber pilot in the Pacific."

"Did you see much action?"

He smirked. "As much as I cared to see."

She felt she had to add something to the conversation. "I had a friend killed in the war." She felt that would impress him and invoke sympathy.

"Yes, most people did," he replied without looking at her.

She noticed he had turned back from her. I guess he's tired talking to me, she thought, and she turned to the window. She would have been happy if this flight had gone on for days, but the pilot's voice came over the P.A. "This is your captain. We will be descending into Washington National in a few minutes. You have about ten minutes before I turn the seat belt sign on. I thought you'd like to know."

"Oh," she exclaimed as if she had a good idea, and rising, she turned to him, "would you excuse me please?" but as she tried to get to her feet, the plane lurched and she was thrown in his lap. She was embarrassed. It's true she wanted to brush past him, but she was not ready for this degree of intimacy in front of others. She turned to look at him as she struggled to her feet. "Oh, I'm so sorry. I couldn't help it."

He placed his hands on her hips, trying to aid her. Be smiled at her. "I enjoyed every minute of it."

She was too embarrassed to reply, but that was one happy and titillated young woman who made her way back to the toilets.

To herself: Oh, my God, he held me about the hips.

She rearranged her clothing as well as she could in the cramped confines of the small airplane restroom. She looked in the mirror and repaired what damage had been done in the past two hours. She gave herself a last look, still pleased with the image she saw in the mirror. She made her plans as she returned to her seat. He moved his long legs sideways to allow her to past and he automatically placed his hands on her hips to steady her, saying, "I hope you don't mind. I don't want you to lose your balance again."

"No, thank you. I appreciate your help. "And to herself: If you only knew how much I enjoyed it.

Settled in her seat, strapping her belt, she looked at him, not quite sure she should ask. "Are you going to Washington, or going on somewhere else?" She had to know.

"No, I'm scheduled to go on to New York."

"Oh." She was truly disappointed. Her heart sank.

The captain's voice came over the loud speaker. "This is the captain. Those passengers who are going on to New York, please raise your hands as the flight attendants go through your section. We have some news you need to know."

He waved his hand. A truly attractive stewardess came towards him, and leaning over. "Sir, if you planned on going through to New York, I have bad news for you. All flights out of National are being cancelled after we land. They're closing the airport. A blizzard is coming. There's a lot of snow on the ground now. I'm afraid you'll have to make arrangements to stay in Washington for a while."

He sighed deeply, shaking his head. "Damn... what luck?"

She felt she had to say something. "Gee, I'm sorry."

He nodded. "Yeah, me too. I have to make some arrangements to stay in Washington until this thing blows over, I guess."

She nodded her head. "I guess so."

The airport was a bedlam of activity as stranded passengers went to and fro, from ticket counters to transportation desks, trying to make arrangements in that busy city while Congress was in session. The town was full of the ubiquitous lobbyists and consultants all trying to influence a not too recalcitrant Congress to sway from the path of righteousness.

She saw him at the transportation desk, his hands waving in the air, trying to impress some young attendant in the midst of many attempting the same thing. He turned away shaking his head.

She saw a driver with a Marriott cap on. She went to him.

"I have reservations at the Marriott for three nights. Are you taking us there?"

He nodded towards an area with several people standing. "Yes, Ma'am, just wait over there a minute. Things are a little hectic right now. We'll be leaving as soon as I collect all of you."

She saw him coming towards her. He smiled, shrugging his shoulders. "I guess I'll go to the Marriott and see if I can find something there." He looked around. "It's kind of wild, isn't it? They tell me the Hilton is booked solid and the Holiday Inn is too far away. The buses are about to quit running, I'm told."

She became concerned for him. "Suppose the Marriott doesn't have anything open?"

"Then," he smiled, "I'm in big trouble."

She nodded, but her brain was running full speed. She could not help but feel that fate was finally on her side, after all these years. She moved close to him in a proprietary fashion, fearing that some other predatory female might move in on this unbelievably desireable man. He smiled at her.

The Marriott driver yelled out. "Come on folks. Let's see if we can get through. It's the last trip tonight. It's getting mean out there."

She signed in. Thank God, she thought as she watched the melee, that I called ahead for reservations or I'd be out on the streets tonight, or, at least, trying to sleep in this lobby.

She watched him arguing with another clerk down the line, and the clerk was shaking his head. He was waving his hands in protest. She could hear him say. "What the hell do you expect me to do? Sleep outside? I own stock in this damn chain. Doesn't that mean anything to you people?"

"Sir, I couldn't find a room tonight for Mr. Marriott, himself. I'm sorry."

He shrugged and walked off. She picked up her bag and went to him. She had already made up her mind. Perhaps, he would think her cheap, making him an offer like this, but she percieved herself a humanitarian, trying to help another human being. It is interesting to wonder if she would have made the same offer to a fat old man with bad teeth and a bald pate, suffering from high blood pressure.

She slowly went to him. She smiled at him and he smiled at her. She was hesitant. This had to be presented properly, or it might be misconstrued. She gave him a sheepish little girl look. "I couldn't help but overhear your conversation with the clerk."

He nodded. "Yeah, that's the pits. Nothing! Absolutely nothing."

"I hope you won't get the wrong idea about this offer, but, but... well, since you have no place to stay... and you do look like a nice decent man... well... if you want... you can share my room with me." She was quick to add as she saw his surprised look, "It has two beds. You can have one... and I will take the other," as if she had to explain.

He laughed at her. A quiet laugh. "Didn't your mama teach you not to make offers like that to a strange man?"

She smiled. "No, my mama died before I was old enough to make such offers."

He thought for a while, and realizing he had no other viable options, he asked, softly, "Are you sure you want to do this? People might get the wrong idea..."

She looked around. "What people?"

"You're right. What people?"

She touched his arm. "I just want to know one thing."

"Yes?"

"Are you married?"

He shook his head. "Not at the moment. We're separated."

She tried to explain. "Not that I expect anything to happen, but, if you were married, well..." and she didn't finish.

As they made their way to the elevators, her heart began to beat faster. She could not have planned it any better she thought, not that this would be a night of rapture for she felt down deep in her heart it would not work out that way. She had to be very careful and not overplay her hand. The wrong word-the wrong move- the wrong body language, and he might bolt like a scared animal. She had to be careful. He was no pool hall type. He was not used to wild and reckless women who could and would jump into bed with a stranger at less than a minute's notice. He had not been brought up in that world, she was sure. Still, he was a man- a young and virile man, and a common thread of desire ran through all of them.

There were several other people in the elevator; two couples and a single woman. She moved closer to him to establish her turf. The single woman looked at him, and then at her. She could read her mind. "Lucky girl."

When she reached the room, he put his hand out for the key. She had seen Cary Grant do that in the movies. That, alone, indicated his suave manners. He smiled at her as he slipped the key in the lock, and opening the door, he waved her in, with, "After you, Mademoiselle," and turning to her. "It is Mademoiselle, I presume, and not Madame."

She smiled. "If it were Madame, I don't think you'd be here."

As he closed the door and latched it, the sound of the lock snapping gave her a feeling of intimacy. Whereas, they had always been in the company of others, she now had him alone in a hotel room. She felt a warm feeling come over her. Her emotions were stirred. She wondered if he felt the same.

"Oh," he exclaimed, "before we go any further, I want to thank you for coming to my rescue tonight. I insist on paying for the room. That's the least I can do."

She shook her head. "No, I'm afraid I can't let you do that." She grinned. "I'd feel like a kept woman." She said this with all the female innocence she could muster. "But," she added coquetishly, "I'm willing to go dutch treat." she was proud that she has said that. It sent the correct message to him. Some cheap floozy might have quickly agreed, willing to be bought, so to speak.

He nodded, placing his bag on the floor and throwing the brief case on the bed. "Okay, dutch treat it is, Miss... miss... Do you realize we're sharing a hotel room and I don't even know your name."

She gave him an impish look. "That's only fair. I don't know yours, and I'm locked in a hotel room with you."

He laughed, an easy and warm laugh. "I guess it is time we introduced oursleves. My name is Jordan McNair," and he extended his hand.

She came forward to meet him. "My name is Rainey..."

He looked up, waiting for her to finish it, and when she didn't, he asked, "Rainey? Rainey, what?"

She intended to have some fun with it. "Guess."

He waved his hands. "I don't know."

She moved her hands as if they were playing a guessing game. "Come on... Rainey... Rainey... what?"

He laughed. "Uh, Rainey Day?"

She shook her head in little girl fashion. "No."

"Oh... Rainey Week?"

"Uh, uh."

He was enjoying this, too. "Rainey Month?"

She sat on her bed, smiling. "No."

"Aw, come on, give me a hint."

"It's not that hard... just think... we're having Rainey what?"

His eyes lit up. "I've got it! Rainey Weather?"

"Well, maybe. How did you spell it?"

"W-E-A-T-H-E-R"

She laughed. "No, leave the A out and you've got it."

He sat on his bed, looking at her with amusement. "Is it always that tough to get anything out of you?"

The question titilated her senses. She knew it was a double entendre question. Had he intended it that way?

She gave him a sideways glance. "It depends. Sometimes, it is and sometimes it isn't."

His mind played with her answer. He, too, knew he had asked a question with some latitude of interpretations, and he felt he had gone far enough. He stood up. "You know we haven't eaten yet. Are you hungry. Dinner is on me."

She noticed he called it dinner. She had always called it supper. She nodded. "Yes, I'm famished."

"Then, come on. Let's get washed up and go eat. It is on me. I owe you that much."

"No, we'll go dutch treat."

He touched her arm. "Now, look, Rainey, are you going to go through that every time I want to do something for you?"

She smiled and nodded. "Yes, Jordan, I am."

He made no reply. "You go ahead and take the bathroom first. I'll wait."

"No, you go first. I may be a while. You know women."

As he disappeared in the bath, she looked heavenly. Oh, God, you really are up there. Thank you so much. Please let it snow for at least a week. She threw her bag on the bed and opened it. She took out a new wool dress, the kind that clings. She wondered it she should take a coat in this weather. She placed the dress in front of her as she looked in the mirror. No, since they were condemned to the hotel, she decided on no coat. It would be a crime to deny him that view, she reasoned.

He was lying in bed going over some of the papers from his brief case when she came out of the bath. He laid the papers down on his bed as he watched her. She could see him out of the corner of her eye. She could read his desires.

He started to whistle, but he caught himself. He didn't know her well enough for that. She might be offended. But, he did say. "You look very lovely, Rainey. You're a very pretty woman. I hope you're not offended by that remark. I simply meant it as an abstract compliment... nothing more."

She smiled. "No, I'm not offended. It was nice of you to say so. Ready?" Her heart pounded in her chest.

As they entered the elevator on their floor, there were several people already in the crowded contrivance, one, an elderly couple who smiled at Rainey and Jordan as they entered. The woman, a grandmotherly type, looked them over in great depth, and being the grandmotherly type, could not resist a comment: "You're such a good looking couple; you were made for each other. How long have you been married?"

Jordan smiled at Rainey as he replied, "Oh, we're not, but we are comtemplating marriage... for the sake of the children."

Rainey, truly embarrassed, whispered to the woman. "He's just kidding you," and to Jordan, "you devil. I'll deal with you later."

He smiled. She had now seen another side of him. He had a sense of humor, too. She moved closer to him, instinctively, as the elevator began to move.

CHAPTER TWENTY-SIX

As they exited the elevator she gently slapped his arm, admonishing him, "Oh, Jordan, how could you tell that poor woman such an outrageous lie about us?"

He laughed. "It served the old bitty right to get so personal."

"She was only trying to be nice..."

"I know, but suppose we had been an adulterous couple trying to have a snowy weekend tryst while attempting to deceive our spouses?

"Hm 'mmm, that does sound interesting, and I see what you mean, but still, you should not have said it."

As he led her into the dining room he smiled at her. "If I embarrassed you, I'm sorry."

Demurely, "You're forgiven."

Conversation during the meal was more formal and impersonal than either would have preferred, but there was a reason for it. They each, subconsciously, knew they had a delicate hurdle before them as they, two complete strangers, had to return to the intimacy of a small hotel room and spend the night within six feet of one another.

It was this thought that forced Rainey to make a decision contrary to the deep desires which burned within her. After dinner, he nodded towards the bar/lounge across the way. The strains of big band music could be heard coming across the passageway. "Would you like to go to the lounge for an after dinner drink... and maybe a dance or two?"

She swallowed hard. She wanted to, but she knew if he held her in close embrace, she may make a serious mistake in her intentions and her plan. She realized that if the snow subsided during the night and he was able to get a flight out in the morning, she would probably never see him again. But, if she allowed nature to take its course, she felt sure she knew where they would end up. After all, he was a man. He would undoubtedly have taken advantage of the situation; most men would, but, would he still respect her in the morning? No, she thought not! Men, hypocrites that they are, are unforgiving in these matters, though they are the instigators of the perfidy. She knew men that well. She had to be careful if she had any chance with this man, slim though it was. He had told her he was separated from his wife, and that made him eligible.

She replied: "As much as I would like to, I think I'll say no. I'm a little tired. It's been a hard day."

He nodded. "Yes, you're right, and tomorrow could be a trying day for me if I can get out of here. Shall we go?"

Upon returning to the room, each was aware that the anticipated moment of enforced intimacy had arrived. He went to the far side of the room and looked out at the swirling snow.

Turning to her, standing by her bed, not sure what to do, he said, "You want the bathroom first? I'm in no hurry."

"No... you go ahead. I want to straighten out my clothes. I have reservations for three days, so I'll put my clothes in the dresser and the closet."

He went to his luggage. "Okay, I'll take a fast shower. I won't be too long."

"Take your time. I'm in no hurry."

After he closed the bathroom door and she could hear the shower running, her mind began to picture him in the shower, nude, and her desires deepened. She longed to join him there, there was no denying that. She turned her attention to her night clothes. She had one pair of pajamas and one revealing night gown. She thought for a while and against her desires, she chose the pajamas. She laid out the night clothes and the robe which she would take in the bathroom. She walked to the window and sat in one of the two chairs, crossing her legs. She had noticed that he didn't smoke. She wanted a cigarette, but decided to wait and smoke in the bath which had an exhaust fan.

He opened the bathroom door and steam poured out. He was dressed in a beautiful matched set of pajamas and dressing gown. She had never been in the presence before of what she referred to as a "first class man" and she was not accustomed to them. Julio had worn no robe or pajamas in her presence- just nudity or Jockey shorts. She was tempted to tell Jordan how pretty his night clothes were, but she demurred. She picked her clothing up, saying, "If you're asleep when I come out, I'll try to be quiet as I can."

"Oh, don't bother. I won't be asleep. I have some paper work to do. I'll just sit here at the table by the window and try to do some work while I look at the snow falling."

She was delighted at his words. She wanted to talk. It may be the last chance if he left in the morning. She entered the bathroom and going to the toilet to tinkle, she, instead, turned on the faucet so he would not hear her as she had heard him. She generally took a bath, but she indulged in a shower, allowing the warm water and soap to relax her body as she ran her hands over her anatomy. The shower only added to her desires. She smiled to herself as she thought: Perhaps, I'd be better off if I turn the water to cold. But, she didn't. She dried off and went to the lavatory to brush her teeth. Her expensive coiffeur was now in disarray, but she felt it lent an air of sensuality. She put on more than her usual amount of cologne in places she didn't usually apply any at all. She put on the pajamas and robe and taking one last look in the mirror and forcing one more strand of hair to disarray, she open the door.

He was at the chair at the window with his feet up on the table, just looking at the snow falling. But, his work papers were not in sight.

"Oh, my goodness, it's still coming down, isn't it?" she asked, trying to see if he wanted to talk.

"Yes," he replied softly, "as much as I want to get out of here, tomorrow, it is beautiful to watch, isn't it?"

She came to the window and stood near him. "Yes, it is beautiful to see."

He motioned to the other chair. "Why don't you sit for awhile so we can talk. Tell me all about Rainey Wether."

She was afraid he'd get to that sooner or later. She hated to attempt to tell anyone about her disjointed and dysfunctional life. She slumped in the chair, also placing her legs up on the table, making sure her robe covered her legs, as if it really mattered since she was wearing pajamas. "Oh, my life is too dull to spend any time telling of it."

He was persistent. "Where were you born?"

She felt he would not let up. What else was there to do on this snowy night except... . She took a deep breath. She decided to make it a long monologue, without stopping so he could not interrupt with questions. She cleared her throat, still husky from the long smoke in the bathroom. "Well, let's see. I was born in rural Arkansas during the bottom of the depression. My family was very poor. When my mother died, I went to live with a foster family," and she laughed, "named Foster, believe it or not, and then... . She adjusted the words and events to conform to her wishes, with a smattering of truth.

He had listened without interruption, alternating his glance from her to the snowy exterior. "What was your mother like?"

She gave him a sad look. "I don't know. She died when I was five. I don't remember her."

He smiled, looking at her, "And who gave you that marvelous name of Rainey?"

She returned his smile. "I'm not sure. I think it was my grandmother."

"She must have been a character."

"I don't remember too much about her, but, yes, she was a character, from what I have heard."

He started to ask more questions, but she held up her hand. "Oh, no... that's enough about me. Let's talk about Jordan McNair for a change."

He raised his hands. "What do you want to know?"

"You say you're separated. How long have you been separated?"

"I don't want to talk about that..."

She pouted. "That's not fair. I didn't tell you one time that I didn't want to talk about me.*"*

He shrugged. "Okay, you're right," and he looked out at the swirling snow with half closed eyes. "I've been separated about five... no, six... months."

"Are you legally separated?"

"No, I just moved out."

"Why did you move out?"

He laughed. "She asked me to."

"If I'm getting too personal, then, tell me to stop..."

"Stop!"

"That's not fair."

"Okay."

"Why did she ask you to move out?"

"I guess I'm hard to live with."

She hesitated to ask this for it was very personal. "Are you still in love with her?"

He pondered the question for a long time. His mouth flinched at the corners. "Hell, I guess I was never really in love with her."

"I'm afraid I don't understand. Why would you marry a woman you never loved?" This was a hypocritical question. She almost married Harlan Kemper under the same circumstances.

"Well, you see. We were practically raised together as children. We lived next door to each other... the families did." He paused, wondering how much detail to go into. "Our fathers went into business together in St. Louis before the war. The business became very successful. They were 50-50 partners and very close friends. When the children came, Nancy and I, who were born at almost the same time, we became close... very close friends... they just assumed we were meant for each other, and they decided we should marry some day."

Her eyebrows went up. "They decided you should marry? A pre-arranged marriage?"

"Well, it was not exactly like that, but, I guess," and he laughed and shrugged, "it's hard to call it anything else."

"And, Nancy, is she in love with you... still?"

It was difficult for him to answer. "She says she is."

"Do you have children?"

He nodded, his eyes lighting up. "Yes, I have two daughters, one almost seven and the baby four."

"Oh... that's nice. Then, you should try to make your marriage work." Those were the most difficult words she had said all evening. She was not sure she meant them, but, she felt she had to say them.

He shrugged. "I know we should, but it's easier to say than do."

She was really getting to the meat of the matter. She felt she was treading on really thin ice, but she had to know. "Have you been seeing any other women during your separation?"

He grinned at her. "You're getting a little personal, aren't you?"

Without shame. "Yes, I am. If you don't want to answer that, then... don't. You won't hurt my feelings." That was a lie. She had to know.

"Ah, what the hell? Since we're baring our souls- no, Rainey, I have not been out with another woman in six months," and smiling at her, "perhaps you might want to call hotel security to protect you for the rest of the night."

She re-crossed her legs and returned his smile. "I don't think that will be necessary. You're not the type, Jordan, to force yourself on some innocent little girl... are you?"

He grunted. "No, unfortunatley, I'm not," and looking at her, "even though I am tempted to try."

She rose. "In that case, then, perhaps it would be better if I retired for the night."

He watched her walk to her bed, and as she turned the covers back, he said, softly... "Rainey?"

She could tell by the inflection in his voice. Women can always tell. She did not turn back. She looked at the wall as she replied, "Yes, Jordan?"

"If I were to ask your permission to climb into your bed tonight... what would your answer be?"

She continued to look at the wall. "I'm afraid I would have to say... no. I'm sorry."

"Then, please consider the question unasked, will you?"

"Yes, Jordan, I will," and she pulled the covers back and slid in under them. She turned her back to him so he could not see the tears. Those were, indeed, the most difficult words she had ever uttered in her entire life, for they were so contrary to what her desires were demanding. Never, had she wanted the touch and feel of another human being as she did this man, and she had refused him. She knew that if the snow subsided and the airport reopened the next day, he would go out of her life. It would have been a one night stand- something she did not want. She wanted him permanently for her own.

She was still awake when he turned down his bed and climbed in. She could hear him turning, trying to find the right position for sleep. She heard him sigh and it pained her. She could easily imagine the same desires burning in him, perhaps even deeper, for she knew and understood men. She caressed her pillow.

During the night, in response to one of nature's urgent calls, she got up to go to the bathroom. There was enough light in the darkened room for her to see his outline in bed. She stood there for a moment. He was emitting a low snore... almost a pleasant sound to her. She smiled and went to the bathroom. Upon returning, she once again looked down at him. She was tempted to go to his bed, to pull down the covers and to move in next to him. She knew he would not object. He would have, without question, responded to her initiative and it would have resulted in a night of sheer rapture, she was sure. But, she merely shook her head and returned to her bed. She was adamant. She would not be one of his easy conquests. It was not in her long term best interests.

If only she had known as she lay still asleep the next morning that he stood by her bed, watching her sleep. Her pajamas had been twisted to one side during the night and one breast was partially exposed. He, too, was greatly tempted to pull back the covers and move in next to her, but, she had told him, no, the night before, and he was a gentleman. He shook his head and proceeded to the bathroom, his desires burning within him.

When she awoke, she could hear him on the phone and she lay there listening. He had called the airport only to learn that it was still closed and would be so for all that day. It had been a record snowfall for so early in the season and they were not prepared for it. She had heard him curse several times. Then, he called New York. She could understand only part of it, but the substance of it was that he would not be able to make the conference and they would have to proceed without him, only to be told that New York, also, was mired in deep snow and the conference had been cancelled, "Really? Well, that helps," she heard him say, "then I don't have to bust my butt trying to get there, do I?" He hung up the phone. She had attempted to get out of bed before he turned around to look at her.

She pulled the sheet over her head. "No, Jordan, don't look at me. I look terrible in the morning... please don't look."

He laughed. "Aw come on. I can't believe you'd ever look bad, Rainey. You're a good looking woman."

She peered above the edge of the sheets. "Jordan, no woman is pretty in the morning... believe me. Now you turn your head. I have to go to the bathroom... really bad."

He laughed. "Okay, go ahead. I won't look. And don't take too long. I'm starving. Let's go eat. The airport is closed. You're stuck with me for another day."

As she ran to the bathroom, she thanked a merciful God for granting her wish with regard to the snow. She would have him for one more day. She felt she might have to adjust her plans.

As they walked out the elevator on the lobby level, he took her arm. "Look, since I am stuck in Washington for another night, at least, perhaps I had better see if I can get a room for tonight. What do you think?" He was not really sincere.

She stopped. She had not planned on that. "Oh, well... I don't know... do you think you can get one?"

He pulled her aside near a potted palm. He took her hand in his and looked in her eyes. "Rainey, do you really want me to get a separate room tonight? I need to know, but before you answer, I can't promise you that you won't have more trouble with me tonight than you had last night."

Her eyebrows went up. "What do you mean?" she asked with innocence, but without much conviction.

"You know damn well what I mean. We're adults. Let's not play boy-girl games, huh?"

She breathed deeply. Oh, how she had longed for those vrords, said without reservation or hesitation. He wanted her as much as she wanted him, yet, a definite yes would still give the wrong impression. She had to offer some resistance. It was in the manual of instructions all girls read.

"Well, like you say. We are adults, aren't we? Shouldn't two adults be able to share a room witout indulging in... in..."

He gave her a Clark Gable smirk. "Not this adult, Rainey. You're too desireable a female for me to resist. I won't promise not to even try."

She sucked in air. "Whew... you don't beat around the bush, do you?"

"Not after last night. You tested me to the limit."

She sighed a deep sigh as she looked him in the eyes. "Did it ever occur to you that I might have been tested too?"

Another Clark Gable grin: "I certainly hope so."

She laughed out loud. "And I thought you were such a nice man when I first met you."

"I was... when you first met me. I always am. Well, what shall it be? Shall I try for a room, or not?"

"It seems like such a waste of money and I'm sure many other poor people will be trying to find some place to stay. It just seems like the humanitarian thing to do... to... share a room, under the circumstances..."

He took her arm. "Let's go eat." They were both grinning internally.

As they exited the coffee shop, he grabbed her elbow.

"Do you have things to do for an hour or so?"

Confused. "Why?"

"I've got to do about an hour or so of phoning up in the room, and it would be boring to you if you had to sit there and listen to it."

She gave him a mischievous smile. "Are you trying to evict me from my own room?"

He laughed. "For only a short while."

"Oh, well, I could do some shopping, I guess. I do need some things."

He hesitated. "Do you need any money?"

She gave him a hard look. "No, thank you. I do not," and she walked off, slightly miffed, saying to herself, "Damn men and their money thing. They think we can't do without it."

Alone now, she sauntered down the boutique-lined passage, examining each show window, without much interest. Then, at an exclusive ladies' shop, she saw a stunning dress in the window. It was a dinner dress, marked down 25% for winter clearance. The merchants were already thinking of spring and winter was hardly here. She stood, picturing herself in the dress. As a female clerk would tell her about ten minutes later, "This dress was made for you, and believe me, dear, you were made for this dress." She agreed as she viewed herself in the full length mirror. It was expensive, more than she wanted to spend, but to her, this was working equipment. She intended to get Jordan to take her out to eat this evening in the hotel's more exclusive dining room than they had eaten in the night before- the one the big band played in. She was tempted to pay another visit to the beauty salon, but having been only two days before, she felt that was overkill.

Having done all the shopping she could afford for one day, she walked through the lobby. It was still a melee of anxious people trying to adjust to the weather induced crisis in both lodgings and transportation. She looked at her watch. It had only been an hour since he left her. She decided to give him more time. She went to the gift shop and bought a copy of the Washington Post and proceeded to the lobby. She selected a wing-back chair which was in a seating circle around a huge coffee table. Several paunchy men, all smoking large cigars watched as she sat and crossed her legs. She removed a cigarette from her pack and lit it in true Bette Davis style. She blew smoke in their direction and lowered her eyes to the paper.

She was only interested in the want ads section. She knew she had to find a job if she wanted to stay in this town. Her money, which was going fast, would not last forever. She read in column after column- WANTED-SECRETARIES- and she read the qualifications- must be neat in appearance- pleasing personality- able to meet the public- and oh, yes- must be able to type 65 words a minute with only two mistakes. Not bad, she thought. I can do that. She glanced at the front page, mostly about the weather. Washington was shut down. Even Federal employees had been dismissed or told not to come in. She smiled. There was no doubt about it. Jordan McNair was her's for another day and night. What would she do with him? What would he do to her?

She had almost made up her mind to return to the room, but she saw his impressive figure coming towards her, smiling that incomparable smile. She put her cigarette out. She wondered if he could smell her cigarette breath.

With animation, he exclaimed. "Do you know they have a swimming pool in this place? A heated pool, of course."

She gave him a blank look. "Who cares? I'm not going swimming in this kind of weather. I'm from the south. Are you serious?"

"Oh, come on! It will be invigorating. Let's do it. We have nothing better to do."

She pouted. "Oh, Jordan, I don't want to go swimming. You go. I'll find something to do..." She pouted further. "It will mess up my hair for tonight." (You will note the presumptive phrase- "for tonight")

He either didn't get the phrase or it mattered not, so he countered with: "If you go swimming with me, I'll pay for a visit to the beauty salon before tonight... tonight? What about tonight?"

She looked at him coyly. "I just bought a gorgeous new dress just in case you might want to take me out to the supper club tonight," and she nodded to the beautiful ballroom across the way.

Taking the chair next to her, he looked at her with considerable amusement. "You know something, Rainey, I under estimated you. I really did."

She uncrossed and recrossed her legs. "What do you mean?" as she saw the same old men watch her leg crossing.

"I must confess to you. I had you pegged as some innocent little cornpone from Arkansas, but you're not."

"No, I'm not, Jordan, and don't you forget it."

"You're as manipulative as I am."

"Perhaps even more so. I'm a woman. We have tools you men don't have," and she gave him a sly look.

He swallowed hard, nodding. "Yes, you do, Rainey. I must admit that you have a formidable array of assets."

"Well? What'll it be?"

"I'll make a deal with you. If you come swimming with me for one hour, then, I will pay for two hours in a beauty salon and take you out tonight for a memorable evening in that room," and he nodded in the right direction.

"But, I don't have a swimsuit."

"Aw, what the hell! I'll buy you a new swimsuit, too. Come on."

She rose, grinning, taking his hand. "Let's go." She smiled inwardly as they returned to the ladies' shop to purchase her bathing suit.

She had been in the bathroom for over an hour. He had paced the floor and then, went down to the lobby, and then returned. She was still in front of the mirror, touching up her makeup.

He stood at the door, watching her. She closed the door. "I don't allow men to watch me dress. Find something to do, Jordan."

"Hell, what do you think I've been doing for an hour. Come on, Rainey, I'm starving." He walked to the window seat and sat down. The snow had slacked but was still falling.

She emerged, standing in the middle of the room. "Well, I'm ready,"

He turned to look. He whistled. He had not last night because he didn't know her well enough, but now, he did. Hadn't he seen her in a bathing suit? The sight of her in one had only added fuel to a fire already burning. "Oh, Rainey, you look great. You really do. You're really a beautiful woman." He rose and went to her. "I can't decide if you look better in that dress or in the bathing suit."

"Well, when you decide, let me know. Then, I'll know where to spend my money."

Many eyes followed the handsome couple as they made their way into the crowded supper club. With nothing much else for the well-heeled crowd to do on a snowy evening, the room was packed. Reservations had been hard to come by, but Jordan had considerable experience in persuading recalcitrant maitre 'd's to find one more opening.

She felt proud as she marched by his side. She knew they made a striking couple. She inhaled deeply as she walked, her shoulders back and her head held high. After the swim, she had gone to the beauty salon, as promised, and a very expensive coiffeur job had resulted in her hair being piled high on her head, accentuating her long and graceful neck. She looked elegant. She had learned some charm secrets in the past few years, mostly from Laverne. With all her other faults, Laverne still had inherent class in every fiber of her being.

When they sat at the table a vast array of silverware confronted her, but, thanks to the teachings of Martha Powell, she was not intimidated in the least. When she first saw the menu printed in French, however, she was alarmed and her raised eyebrows showed it. Jordan sensed it. He laughed. "Hell, I don't speak it either," and he requested an English menu. The waiter sniffed his disappointment. "Mai oui, an liste de manger dans l'anglais. Oui... certainement, Monsieur." He could have replied in English which he spoke fairly well, but in a French restaurant, one is not impressed by an English speaking waiter.

With the meal settled by two after dinner drinks, the couple looked at each other dreamily. They knew the moment of truth was at hand. He placed his hand on hers, the first time, really, that he had touched her... not counting the swimming pool when wet flesh met wet flesh. "Care to dance?"

"I don't dance very well. It's one of my shortcomings."

He rose and went to her chair. "I was not aware that you had any."

She stood. "I don't boast about them, but I do."

The dance floor was small and crowded, barely room for them to sqeeze in. She laughed. "We're going to get bruised out here."

He brought her in close. "I'll protect you."

She allowed herself to be held close. It was the moment she had lived for since she first saw him. She cooed softly. "You promise to protect me from all harm, Jordan?"

He nodded. "On this dance floor... I sure do."

She did not reply. Her arm went around his neck and she nestled her face next to his. In high heels she was five feet eleven. Her face was almost level with his.

"You're a tall gal, Rainey."

She laughed. "I know. I think I'm still growing at twenty-six..."

"So, that's how old you are."

She kept her face near his as she replied. "Almost twenty-seven."

"How did something like you stay single all this time?"

"I've been waiting for the right man."

"You've never met him?"

"No... not yet?"

"Maybe, you're too particular."

She nodded. "Maybe." She moved her hand and touched his neck and he responded by holding her closer. She breathed harder and so did he. There was chemistry going on. They both knew it. She had never been so contented in her life. She knew where the evening was headed. There was no doubt about it. It was not a matter of if she would surrender, it was just a matter of time... and how it would be done.

Dancing was impossible. They were buffeted from one pair of hips to the other. She moved her head back to look at him.

"I don't know about you, but I'm getting bruised."

He led her off the dance floor. "We can't have that body getting bruised."

The reference to her body caught her attention. As they reached their table and he reached for her chair, "Do we really want to fight this crowd anymore?"

She shook her head. "No, I'm ready to go."

He removed a sheaf of bills from his wallet and with a nod to the waiting waiter, they left the crowded room.

CHAPTER TWENTY-SEVEN

Her pulse began to quicken as they entered the elevator. She stood apart from him as her middle-class morality began to take hold. She was ambivalent as she had never been before about her expected intimacy with this man. It was not due to any lack of desire, for it burned brightly in her. No, it was the knowledge that this night was to be the memory of her he would take with him when he left. He would either recall it as a night to remember with a lovely and desireable woman- a lady- or, a one-night stand in a snowed-in hotel with a floozy. That was what bothered her, and she reasoned that regardless of the outcome, which she viewed as inevitable, it was the events leading to the surrender which would shape his recollection.

He moved closer to her as the elevator began to move. They were alone in it. As his arm went around her waist, she moved in closer to him. He bent his head to kiss her, softly, on the cheek. She, in anticipation, offered her cheek to him, closing her eyes as she did.

He grinned. "Our first kiss."

She blushed. "Yes," smiling at him.

When they entered the room, they both felt awkward. These are always awkward moments when even two experienced, yet, sensitive adults, don't want to make any move that the other would construe as too much... too soon. He turned to her. "Want the bathroom first?"

"Yes, I won't be long." She went to her bureau and withdrew the nightgown she had rejected as too revealing the night before. She looked to see if he was watching her, and he was. She smiled at him as she went into the bathroom.

When she came out, she was wearing the gown under her robe. She felt she was dressed modestly enough. As she came into the room, she instinctively pulled the robe tighter around her.

He moved to his luggage. He looked back at her. "I see you have new clothing for tonight." He shrugged. "I don't. I guess you'll have to look at me in the same pajamas and robe."

"I don't mind. They're very pretty."

"I won't be long," and he headed for the bathroom.

She was standing at the window when he came out. She was watching the snow fall, the flakes reflecting the lights of the city, like butterflies in a breeze. She could see his reflection in the glass. He came behind her and standing close, his arms went around her waist. She placed her arms on his and she nestled her head in his neck. Now that she had no heels, this was possible. Encouraged by her actions, he moved his hands up, cupping her breasts in each. She placed her hands on his as if to discourage any further movement.

Her mind began to race. Even though she had no intentions of resisting him, there were things she wanted to say... things she wanted him to know before the final surrender. She wanted to tell him of the trauma and sadness in her life, some of it so recent that it still burned in her. She wanted to tell him that she was a vulnerable woman who could come out of this with a broken heart, for she truly believed he had no serious or honorable intentions towards her. To him, it would be the satisfying of passionate desires. To her, it would be the realization of her dreams and fantasies of all these years. She wanted to tell him she had suffered enough in her life; she didn't need any more. She wanted to be loved and cared for, not used to satisfy some temporary and passing desire. She wanted to tell him that she was surrendering to him the most sacred gift a woman can bestow on a man. And having taken that, she had nothing else to offer him. Yes, she wanted to say all these things, but she didn't. She knew if she had, the magic of the moment might have died, and she wanted it to live... at least for tonight.

He released his hold on her and took her hand, leading her toward the bed. She held back for a moment. She looked up into his eyes. "Jordan... you have a wife and two children back in St. Louis, who love you. Are you sure you want to do this?"

He thought for a moment, and he took her hand again. "Yes, Rainey, I'm sure. Perhaps, I'm trying to find out something about me."

She felt she had cleared her conscience. She had always vowed that she would never get involved with a married man. She remembered Verlie's admonition. "There are men out there who are so smooth, so charming, so smart, so desireable, that the average woman doesn't stand a chance of resisting them." And one more sentence in that conversation burned in her. "They are always married. Nothing like that is ever running around loose." She remembered those words, but like so many women over the ages, she remembered them when it was too late. The battle was already lost.

She would remember that night, later, as the culmination and realization of all her sensual dreams and fantasies. She had always believed that someday, some man, somewhere, would cause her chimes to ring like those of the greatest cathedrals, and chime they did... many times. When morning came, a PLEASE DO DOT DISTURB sign was hung on the door knob. The couple were not seen until much later in the afternoon. Breakfast and lunch were by room service only, and the food was mostly uneaten.

This time, they showered together. When he attempted to soap her back, she admonished. "Please keep your hands above the waist."

He laughed. "Oh, how soon they forget."

She turned to face him, laughing. "Oh, no... you're wrong! I will never forget. It's your memory I'm worried about."

As they stepped out the tub, he asked, "What do you mean by that?"

She took the towel from him. "I mean, Jordan, that I hope you will remember this next week, or, next month, or whatever."

He rubbed her back. "Do you expect me to forget you?"

She turned to face him. "I don't know. That's what worries me."

Having dressed and enjoying a newly delivered pot of coffee in the room, she asked, jokingly, "What'll we do for excitement now?"

He beckoned to her with crooked finger. "Come over here. Let's talk for a while."

She grinned. "Talk? Now, that'll be different."

"Come on. Sit by me. I want to talk to you."

She took a chair and crossed her legs on the table. "Okay, let's talk."

"You know, you've never told me what you're doing in Washington."

She giggled. "Well, you never asked. You were too busy doing other things."

"Yes, I guess so, but I'm asking now... what are you doing here?"

She sighed deeply, wanting a cigarette, but holding off. "I came here to go to work."

"Do you have a job?"

"No... not yet.'

"Do you know anyone in this town?"

She laughed. "The only person I've heard of in this town is President Eisenhower, but I doubt he's heard of me."

He shook his head. "So, you're unemployed?"

"Well, I think they refer to it as between jobs."

"For an unemployed girl, you don't seem to be short of money."

She was offended. "What do you mean by that?"

"Well, you fly first class, and you stay at a Marriott instead of a Holiday Inn, and you buy nice clothes..."

"You're getting a little personal, aren't you?" she teased.

"I thought, Rainey, dear, that you and I have been as personal as two people can be."

She blushed. "That's different, and you know it."

"I was just wondering if you had a rich uncle somewhere?"

She looked at him in Bette Davis style as she recrossed her legs. "No, that's not what you mean, Jordan. What you want to know is... am I a kept woman? Do I have a sugar daddy out there somewhere?"

He nodded. "Yes, that is what I'd like to know."

"Would it really matter to you?"

He gave her a tender look. "Yes, it would upset me very much."

"Why? You have no claims on me, and I don't have any on you."

It was difficult for him to say. "Perhaps, I'd like to have some claim on you..."

Her eyebrows went up. "Are you asking me to marry you, Jordan?" She asked it in a joking manner.

He shrugged his shoulders, shaking his head. "No, I'm afraid that is not possible, even though it is an interesting idea."

Her eyes ablaze, "An interesting idea? Is that what I am to you? An interesting idea?" (He is finding out as men have for ages that it is difficult to talk to a woman who is post-coital. Their emotions have not settled. It would have been better if they had gone out for a long walk.)

"No, Rainey, you are much more to me than that..."

She wanted to know. "How much more?"

"So much so that I want to see more of you."

"H'mmm, that's interesting. You want to see more of me here, in Washington, or... St. Louis?"

"It would be kind of awkward here in Washington, don't you think, since I live in St. Louis?"

"Do you want to see more of me in St. Louis, then?"

"Well, yes. That would work out better, don't you think?"

"Then, you have no intention of trying to get back with your wife? Is that correct?"

He paused for a long time. "No, that is not so. I have to get back with my wife," and he looked out the window, "whether I want to or not."

These words were like a spike in her heart. She thought she was making headway, but, obviously, she was wrong. "I'm afraid I'm a little confused, Jordan. You tell me you want to see more of me in St. Louis, but you have to get back with your wife. Is that correct? Am I hearing it right?"

He knew he had painted himself into a corner. He looked exasperated. "I know it sounds strange, but I do have to get back with her. My future depends on it."

She sighed deeply. She was tempted to cut the conversation off at this moment, but, she couldn't. "Jordan, please look me in the eye, and if there is an honest bone in your body, tell me the truth. What the hell do you mean by this double-talk?"

"When I told you about me last night, I didn't give you the whole story..."

She interrupted him. "Did you lie to me about your wife?"

"No, everything I told you was the truth. I simply didn't tell you everything. I had no reason to the other night, but, now..."

"I think you owe me the truth, now, don't you?"

"Yes, I do," and he stood, looking out the window. The snow had stopped and the sun was making some effort to shine. He sighed deeply as if this pained him. "When I told you about my dad and his partner owning the company fifty-fifty, that was correct and true. What I didn't tell you was that the two fathers are dead, both Nancy's and mine."

He returned to his chair. "The stock in the company was divided like this- the widows got half and the children got half. I am an only child so I own one-fourth of the company stock. Nancy is an only child so she and her mother control one half of the outstanding shares, so..."

Rainey, who had been following the math, interrupted him. "You don't have to explain it any further. The three women control three-fourths of the company and poor Jordan only has one-fourth to call his own."

He nodded, saying nothing, but holding out his hands.

"Which means," she continued, smiling, "that poor Jordan has to keep three women happy in order to have things his way in the corporation. Right?"

He nodded.

She laughed. "Oh, my God, I love it. At last, the women have some power over you men. I love it."

"I don't think it's so damn funny, Rainey."

"No, I would think not," and she patted his hand as if in sympathy, "and that's why poor Jordan can't leave his little wife he doesn't love. My, my, this is interesting."

(She made light of this but her heart was sinking while she spoke the words. This confronted her with an almost impossible situation, if she had any serious designs on this man.)

"Is this that funny to you, Rainey?"

She became serious. "No, Jordan, my dear, it is not your situation that strikes me as funny. It's mine."

His eyebrows went up. "I don't follow you."

"No, that's because you're a man. I'm a woman. I have different brain lobes where logic is concerned."

"I still don't follow you."

"No, then let me draw a picture for you. You just stated that you wanted to see more of me in St. Louis. Right?" and not waiting for his reply, continued, "and you just pontificated as to why you cannot leave your wife, and I must admit you have damn good reasons since she has you by the balls, Jordan."

He flinched at her earthy language. He was not accustomed to women who cursed.

She continued. "So, where does that leave poor little Rainey. Let me see. The only conclusion I can come to is that if sweet little Rainey is to be available for Jordan to play with when he is in the mood, she must be ensconced in some convenient place in St. Louis, to make it expedient and economical. Am I getting close, Jordan?"

He avoided her gaze.

"Why can't men look you in the eye when you have them dead to right? Oh, well, let me finish the picture. If I will be in St. Louis, available to you upon demand, while you are securely guarded from all legal recourse by a faithful wife, what does that make me?" She waited for an answer, but none came. "Since the cat has your tongue, Jordan, allow me to give it a name. I will be your mistress- your concubine- your whore!" She broke down at the sound of this word, a word she had always detested, not in generality, but only if it could be applied to her. She would never forget her mother's role in the profession. She began to sob and she hated herself for breaking down.

How could things have deteriorated so quickly. Only a few hours before, they were locked in embrace, whispering tender terms to one another as if it would never end, and now, this...

He tried to touch her, but she recoiled, "No, don't touch me. Not now, anyway. I'm pissed off, Jordan. I expected better from you... I really did."

"You misunderstood my intentions, Rainey..."

"Really? Well, then, explain them to me if there is another interpretation. I'll listen, Jordan. You don't know how much I want to hear them."

"I have hopes of perhaps working out some arrangement with my wife. I hope to convince her that there is no real chance for us to live as man and wife..."

"Oh, Jordan, don't be a fool. You don't understand women. You men generally hold the power over us. She has you where she wants you. She is not going to let you go. She has your name. You will be at her side when your little girls graduate from kindergarten, elementary, and high school. It is you and she who will stand side by side in the wedding reception line when your daughters get married, and you and she will share the joy when those girls present you with grandchildren." She took a deep breath. "And where will poor little Rainey be? Sucking hind titty, as they say out on the farm... that's where." Her shoulders sagged. She was worn out. It had been an emotional exchange and it had drained her.

He sat, saying nothing, for the conversation had turned sour so fast, he was not sure he knew this woman with whom he had just been so intimate. He rose. "Well, I guess I'll find some other place to stay tonight. I have reservations on a flight out of here tomorrow."

The words startled her. She bolted up. "You're leaving tomorrow?"

"I've got to leave some day, don't I? I'll try to find some place for tonight."

She went to him. "Oh, Jordan, don't do that. This will be the last night we'll ever spend together. Let's... let's try to recapture what we had last night."

"I thought you were through with me after the talk we just had."

She smiled. "Jordan, we had to have that talk. I didn't enjoy it, but we had to have an understanding. I now know where I fit in your life," and she grunted. "There's no place for me. It's that simple."

"Rainey?"

"Yes, Jordan?"

"I'm not sure I want to let you go. I'm not sure I can."

"Unless things change, Jordan, you have no choice in the matter. I will not be your plaything. Yours, or any man's."

He would not give up. "Well, maybe, if you moved to St. Louis, we could at least see each other from time to time..."

She laughed, shaking her head from side to side. "Vertically, or horizontally, Jordan?"

"Do you have to put it that way?"

"What would I do? Sit by the phone waiting for you to call?""

"We could see each other from time to time."

She knew how to put him to the ultimate test. Men were territorial animals. They had to have control over their turf.

"And what would I be allowed to do between your visits? Could I date other men?"

She watched his eyes narrow and his mouth twitched. "I don't think I could live with that."

"You men are really something. I would have to share you with your wife, but you cannot stand to think of sharing me with another man. Is that right?"

"There would be nothing going on between me and my wife. I told you I don't love her."

"Jordan, men don't have to be in love to do that. Women, yes, but not men. Men are driven by different forces."

He looked up at that. "How do you know so much about men?"

She shook her head at him. "Not by doing what you think, Jordan, but I had some damn good teachers who were women, not men, as you suspect."

He stood, smiling. "Are we still friends?"

She went to him, kissing him passionately. "Does that answer your question?"

Wiping his lips. "You continually surprise me, Rainey. "

"Before you get the wrong idea about me, wondering how I can turn it off and on so fast, let me explain it to you. I now know that tomorrow you're going to get on that airplane and fly out of my life. I will have no more control over you, but for now, and for tonight, Jordan, you are under my spell, and I intend to make sure you never forget me."

"You're one hell of a woman, Rainey. I thought you'd never let me touch you again."

She laughed, looking at her watch. "You only have about twelve more hours. You'd better enjoy it while you can, and if you're wondering how I can do this after the talk we just had, let me explain it to you some more. Women are very resilient in their emotions. Nature made us that way. If we were not that resilient in dealing with men the human race would have died off long ago, because, Jordan, you men really piss us off."

He was hesitant as he saw her go to her bed. He hung back, not sure what his reception would be from this upset woman. She lay there for a while watching him standing next to his bed and she was inwardly amused. She thought: How like little boys they are.

Moving over to one side and turning back the covers, she smiled, beckoning him with a crooked finger. "Come on, Jordan, I won't bite you, I promise."

As her eyes opened the next morning, she instinctively moved her arm over to his side of the bed, to feel his presence, but she felt only an empty bed. She sat up, looking around the room, searching for him, but he wasn't there. She was aghast. Would he dare to leave without telling her goodbye. She knew he had an early flight out this morning, but, would he really leave without so much as a goodbye kiss. Then, she saw his bags all packed against the wall near the bathroom. She breathed easier.

She looked at his place in bed, at his pillow, reliving the moments of the night. Then, she saw the note lying on his pillow.

GONE TO CHECK OUT. BACK IN A MINUTE
J. M.

She bolted out of bed and dashed in the bathroom. She could not let him see her like this in daylight, and what if he tried to kiss her. She had not even brushed her teeth. She needed a cigarette.

She closed the bathroom door. She reached in her purse and extracted a cigarette and lighter. She fired up and proceeded to the toilet, lifting her nightgown and sitting in one motion. While she tinkled, she inhaled deeply on the weed- three or four times, then, she spread her legs and dropped it in the commode, reaching for the toilet tissue with her left hand and flushing the commode with her right. She went to the lavatory counter, and after dabbing his toothpaste on her brush, she vigorously cleaned her teeth. She gargled with his mouthwash and disposed of the liquid in the lavatory. She ran the cold water faucet, and slapped some cold liquid on her face. She looked at herself as she dried with a face cloth. She ran her brush through her hair, and then, debated whether to apply lipstick or not. She shook her head, thinking: Hell, he's been looking at me all night in the buff, why the hell do I need lipstick?

She rushed back to bed, climbed in, and leaned against her pillow just as she heard the lock in the door. He smiled as he entered. She feigned a yawn with her shoulders back and her breasts thrust forward. "Oh, Jordan, I just woke up. I was wondering where you were," and coyly, "I was afraid you'd gone without saying goodbye."

He sat on the bed as she moved over. He leaned over to kiss her lightly on the lips. "Good morning to you, too."

She seemed embarrassed "Oh, good morning," she cooed as her arms went around his neck.

He sat up, grinning at her. She noticed he had on a beautiful suit, one she had not seen before. "Do you really think I would have gone without telling you goodbye?"

She regarded him warmly. "You'd better not." She allowed her arms to fall to her lap.

He was quiet for a while. "Rainey, I have to know where to get in touch with you after you get settled here in Washington."

"Why?"

He gave her a quisical look. "Why? Because I might want to talk to you... that's why."

"What do we have to talk about? We said it all last night."

"I have to see you again," and pausing for a long time as if he wanted not to say the words, "I think I'm falling in love with you."

She moved her head from side to side. "You think, huh? Well, when you know for sure, then, you call me, Jordan."

With all seriousness, he replied, "I won't know where to call you."

She took his hands in hers. "Jordan, until your situation changes, and I really don't believe it will, I don't want you to find me. I'm heading for a broken heart and I don't need that in my life just now. I'm trying to make a new life for myself..."

"Rainey... what are you running from?"

She shrugged. "I wish I knew."

"Let me help you. Come to St. Louis where I can take care of you..."

"Oh, Jordan, we went through all that last night. I am not going to be your mistress. You can forget that."

"Suppose I can find a way to change my... situation " He had to search for the right word.

She looked at him, wistfully. "When you do that, then, you call me and I'll come running."

"How will I find you?"

"I'll find you... don't worry."

"When?"

"I don't know."

He rose and went to the dresser. He removed his business card case from his coat pocket. He turned to her. "I'm leaving my business card here on the dresser. You'll know where to find me. I have to go now, Rainey."

She made no reply. She got out of bed and went to him. She was wearing only her nightgown. He looked at her and he swallowed hard. He put out his arms and she went to him. They held each other closely for a while. He looked down at her. "Rainey, do you think you can learn to love me?"

She looked in his eyes, softly. "It all depends, Jordan... it all depends. I've waited all my life to meet you, and when I do, I can't have you for my very own." she turned and walked to the window, sobbing. But, she never turned around as she looked out the window at the sunny skies. "Goodbye, Jordan, and thank you for a wonderful weekend. I'll never forget it."

He started to say something, but, instead, he picked up his bags and left quietly. She made her way back to the bed and laid there for a while. She got up, reached for her cigarettes. Then, she made her way to the telephone and dialed room service.

"Hell 'o. Room service? This is room 1416. could you send up a bottle of gin, please? Oh, any kind will do. And, four bottles of tonic water. Thank you."

CHAPTER TWENTY-EIGHT

Her arm hung lifelessy over the edge of the bed, her hand resting near the empty gin bottle. Only one of the four tonic bottles had been emptied, a testament to her lack of need to dilute the liquid as she attempted to drown her sorrows. The liquor, along with two packs of cigarettes, had overburdened her system to the point that two trips to the bathroom were necessary in the middle of the night to empty her stomach's contents.

She attempted to raise her head. She groaned and let it fall back on the pillow. She did manage to roll over on her back as she attempted to focus her eyes on the ceiling. Her hand went to her forehead and she groaned again. She was badly hungover. She squinted her eyes as she directed them to her Big Ben alarm clock on the dresser. It was 10:48 and checkout time in the hotel was 12:00 noon. She laboriously sat up and ran her fingers through her hair, shaking her head. "Jesus, why did I do that? Why the hell didn't I just fill the damn bathtub and let my head sink below the water?"

She thought of Jordan McNair and she half-groaned, half-spoke: "Oh, Jordan... you bastard. Why did you have to come into my life? I don't need this, but," and she began to sob, "but, I do need you. Oh, God, how I need you."

She staggered to the bathroom and stood at the lavatory, looking at the bedraggled spectacle in the mirror. She shook her head as she once more ran her hand through her hair. She ran some cold water and splashed it on her face. Feeling that that small amount of water would not suffice, she slipped her nightgown over her shoulders and let it slip to the floor. She turn the shower knob to COLD and taking a deep breath, stepped into the tub.

Her head throbbed as she completed packing, She looked around the room to see if she had forgotten anything. She saw one of Jordan's hankerchiefs on the floor. He had evidently dropped it from his pocket as he changed clothes. She picked it up and brought it to her nose. The scent of his cologne was still on it. She suppressed tears as she inserted it in her purse. She picked up her bags, looked once more around the room, and proceeded to the lobby.

The desk clerk smiled as he saw her coming. He had come to recognize her in the past three days. "Goodmorning, Miss Wether. Beautiful day isn't it?"

She managed a smile with great difficulty. She wanted to tell him that, no, it was not a beautiful day. On the contrary, it was a shitty day, but she returned his greeting, faintly, while she reached in her purse for her money. "I'm checking out. I'd like my bill, please."

He once again smiled. "That won't be necessary. The gentleman who shared your room," and he could not hide a smirk as he said it, "has taken care of the entire bill. He insisted on having us bill his corporation, and," and he broadened his smile, "when we checked him in Dun & Bradstreet, we were more than happy to do that."

She started to protest, but to whom? Her argument was with Jordan McNair, not this nice man. She nodded, and in an attempt to salve her conscience, at least with the desk clerk, she replied, "Oh, well, then, I'll send him a check when I get settled." He nodded and turned to another guest.

She placed her bags in the corner near the bell captain's stand, asking him to watch them for a few moments. She went to the gift shop and purchased the Monday morning's edition of the WASHINGTON POST. She proceeded to the coffee shop and ordered coffee and a roll. She knew her stomach needed some attention. She had badly mistreated it for the past twelve hours.

She turned to the real estate section and perused the rental units. She needed a place to stay, badly. She could not afford the hotel much longer. She secretly, though reluctantly, thanked Jordan for taking care of the bill. It helped. But, it was the least he could do. Wasn't it he who spent hours on the long distance phone? Wasn't it he who ordered lavish trays from room service- only to remain uneaten due to other pressing matters? She felt better about his paying the bill. It was the least he could have done after all she did for him, but, those words burned in her as she pondered the implication of them. Oh, hell, how can a woman win? She is damned if she does and she is damned if she doesn't.

Her eyes caught a nice unit: ONE BEDROOM, SITTING AREA AND KITCHENETTE. NICE BATH, COMPLETELY FURNISHED NEAR GEORGETOWN. She was not sure where Georgetown was, but if they boasted about being near it, it had to be nice. That was logical.

She surreptitiously opened her purse and counted her money. She had just a little over forty-five hundred left. She, once again, silently thanked Jordan for his generosity in paying the hotel bill. The bastard!

She liked the place, she told the agent, "It's cute. Just what I was looking for. I'll take it. Does all the furniture stay with it?"

"Yes," she nodded, "except the linen and stuff like that."

"How much is the deposit?"

The agent hesitated. "It's high. The batchelor who owns this pad is proud of it. He wants it returned in good shape. You don't have children, do you?"

She shook her head. "I'm not married."

It didn't take her long to get settled. She went to the nearest department store and purchased as little linen as she felt she could live with. The deposit and first month's rent had torn a nice-sized hole in her reserves. She had to go to work and soon, she intoned to herself as she spread the mayonaise on her ham and cheese later that day. She opened a bottle of coke, having sworn off intoxication beverages- for life, she maintained- and proceeded to the small seating area. She wished she had a television set, but, that was not practical for the time being. She sat in a large chair and brought her legs up under her as she bit into the sandwich. She looked around her small apartment. She shurugged her shoulders. What the hell?

Having satisfied her hunger and with the throbbing in her head now down to a tolerable level, she lay on the couch on her back, with her hand on her forehead. Then, she began to relive the past three days with Jordan. They had been the most satisfying hours she had ever spent, from a purely physical standpoint. Of that, she was sure. If it got any more satisfying than that, she doubted she could have stood it. But, the physical side is not all sides of a human's emotions. There is that hidden side- the more powerful of the two- the emotional side. For every physical thrill that racked her being, a greater one racked her brain. After his disclosure that he had no intention of leaving his wife- he could not afford it- she knew she was what millions of other women before her have been- the other woman. She had no claim on him other than the intangible one of desire. She was sure of one thing. She could do something for him that his wife, evidently, could not. That was the only card she held.

She sat up and began to sob. She was lonely, and if she didn't do something to change her life, she would remain lonely. She got up, went to the bathroom, took two sleeping pills out of a recently purchased bottle, swallowed them and went to her purse. She extracted Jordan's handkerchief and took it to bed. She brought the handkerchief close to her nose as she lay there, tears running down her cheek. She eventually achieved sleep, but her head was on a wet pillow.

The office manager looked her up and down as she stood before his desk in the State Department building. She could read his mind, especially as his eyes lingered on her breast area. He motioned her to a chair to the side of his desk. She ceremoniously crossed her legs, taking longer than she usually did, which was not wasted on him.

"Well, Miss Wether, it is fortunate that we lost a girl the same day you called."

Her eyebrow went up. "You lost her? What happened to her?"

He chuckled, his hand running through a thinning remnant of hair. "She got married. Most girls in Washington get married within six months of hitting this town. I guess it goes with the territory," as he waved towards the window. He became business-like. "I hope you're not ready to get married? Quite frankly, if you are, I would not be interested in hiring you. We're looking for someone on a permanent basis."

"No... no... I'm not even seeing anyone. I just got to town."

His eyes lit up. "Oh, that's nice," and she could see his wheels turning.

His questioning went on for thirty minutes. Longer than she felt necessary, but, she concluded, he must be enjoying it. He rose, extending his hand, "well,

Miss Wether, welcome aboard. We'll have everything ready for you to start by tomorrow morning. Is that too soon for you?"

"No, I'm anxious to get started. Thank You."

As he walked her to the door, "Do you have a car? Parking is real tight in this town..."

She had not thought about that. "No, I have no car. What is the best way to get to work?"

"Well, it depends on where you live."

"I live in Georgetown."

He was impressed. "Georgetown... h'mmmm. Well, the city transit buses run right down Virginia Avenue. You get off at 21st. St. and you're here," he announced proudly.

As she got off the city transit two days later, she was at least partially satisfied. She had a place of her own to call home and she had a good job with an employer who would always be in business. There was no doubt about that. The only disappointment was the caliber of men in her immediate office. She was not impressed. There was not one adonis in the bunch. She grinned as she thought: How the hell can I even begin to forget Jordan McNair with that sorry bunch?

She had fallen into a routine since she first moved in the apartment. She had returned to her place at or near six o'clock each evening, unless she stopped to shop. She had gone nowhere at night. She knew no one. She trusted no one. She wanted to see no one, especially men.

But, the evenings were lonely. She had purchased a small black and white ten inch television out of desperation, and she derived what pleasure she could from the live programs of the future television greats who performed in that period. Even as she looked at the small set her mind was not on the show, it was on Jordan McNair. She tried to forget him, but she couldn't. She tried to convince herself that her attraction to him was purely physical. Except for Julio Cardoza, no other man had rung her chimes and she had to admit that Julio ran a far second to Jordan. No, try as she might, her thoughts each and every night were of him. She wondered what he was doing at that moment? Had he returned to his wife as he suggested he might have to do? Was he, even now, lying in her arms, pretending passion to ensure his hold on the company. The mere thought of it pained her and she closed her eyes and mind to it.

This soul searching had gone on for over three weeks now. She wanted to allow her mind and her passions the latitude to determine if it was a passing fancy. After all, it had happened so fast. But, she knew the minute she saw him in that St. Louis airport terminal that he was the man of her dreams. Many women feel that way about certain men, especially movie stars whom they have never met and probably never will. But, he had proved to her in two nights of unparalleled passion that he was, indeed, what she had been seeking for all her twenty-six years- nearly twenty-seven, as she had whispered in his ear while they were dancing.

Now, weeks later, she was sure. She was hopelessly in love with Jordan McNair. She didn't know what to do about it. She didn't know if there was anything she could do about it. She had promised him that she would call him. Perhaps she should.

Perhaps she should tell him where she was. She felt sure he would come to her. But, for how long? Another weekend? And then, she would have kissed him goodbye as he returned to his wife. She shook her head. No, that was not the answer.

In desperation, she had even accepted a date with a man from her office. It was not that she wanted male companionship. She didn't. Jordan's touch still burned in her. She merely wanted to see if she could even be responsive to another man's talk, his touch, if they even touched hands, for that was all she intended to touch. He was nice. He was gentlemanly. He was kind, but as he held her on the small dance floor of the supper club, she held her distance. He was not Jordan McNair, and he never would be. At the door to her apartment, he offered his hand, hoping she would offer more, but a tepid hand shake was all he got.

As she sat at her desk the next morning, shuffling papers she had to type for her immediate boss, she glanced at her calendar. It was a desk type which the department had given all employees for a writing pad. She looked at the date. She knew it was nearly time for her menstrual period. She took a note pad out of her purse and turned the pages. She remembered her last one had ended just before the trip to Cuba and her liason there with Julio. She began to count days as she checked them off on the calendar. She remembered that neither she nor Jordan had even mentioned any birth control as they pursued their passions. Like most men, he assumed that was her problem. She had not been concerned because, according to her mental notes, she was safe- at least, as little as she understood the so called "rhythm method" , she was safe.

She began to doodle with her pencil on the date she calculated she was due to begin, but she hadn't. She peered off into space, looking at the ceiling, then, out the window. Her shoulders sagged as the thought sank in her brain. Was she pregnant with Jordan's baby? At first, the thought thrilled her, but upon deeper reflection, she wondered, and asked herself, "What the hell do you have to be happy about if it is true?"

As her mind explored all possibilities, she thought of her liason with Julio Cardoza. Yes, he was a chronological possibility, but she quickly discounted him. Julio was a professional and with his promiscuous lifestyle, protection was a way of life with him. It was he who had insisted on it as she suggested it. No, there could be only one and that was Jordan McNair.

She had difficulty in concentrating on her work the rest of the day. Her boss, sensing her preoccupation, asked: "Rainey, are you okay? Do you feel alright?"

She snapped her head back, embarrassed. "Oh, yes, I'm fine. I was just preoccupied with a minor problem I might have."

He smiled and nodded, and handed her some more papers.

She got naked in the bathroom that night after she had eaten a troubled supper. She had toyed with her food, her mind completely preoccupied with her "problem". She stood before the mirror and ran her hand over her stomach. She turned side ways and looked again. She could detect no increase in her flat stomach. She put her nightgown on and returned to the couch in the sitting area. She lay back, thinking.

What if she were pregnant? What would she do? Would she tell Jordan? What would he do? What could he do? He was certainly not going to marry her. How could he?

As the probability sank into her brain, she shook her head, talking aloud to herself, "Rainey, honey, if you are pregnant, you're in deep shit."

She had never had a gynecological exam before, at least, not one performed by a real doctor. She lay there, somewhat embarrassed as he poked and probed. Her eyes went from his to the nurse standing by. He finished his probing, and removing his gloves, he said to her softly, "You may put your clothes back on now, Miss... miss," and he picked up her chart to reexamine it, not wanting to mistakenly further embarrass her. "It is Miss, is it not?"

She lowered her eyes. "Yes, it is, Miss, doctor."

He had seen it often in this large city with it's thousands of young girls willing to surrender their bodies to either capture or hold a man. In both cases, generally, they ended up as futile efforts. He beckoned her to a chair. "Miss Wether, there is no doubt about it, you are pregnant. All three tests which we use to verify the condition confirm it."

It did not suprise her. With her luck, it had to be. She breathed deeply, nodding. "What should I do about this?"

She really didn't know why she asked that, but the truth is, she really didn't know what to do about it?"

He understood her dilemma. He gave her a fatherly smile as he shuffled papers on his desk. "Well, my dear, there are only two things a woman can do when she is in this situation. She can bring the baby to term, and deliver it, or, and he lost his smile, "she can have an abortion and terminate her pregnancy." Before she could reply, for her lips were parted, he continued, "I do not perform abortions, but, you might find someone who does. I don't even make recommendations along that line. I am a Catholic, you see"

"I see." she looked around the room as if to seek counsel from someone. "Is there anything I should do? To ensure the baby's health, that is?"

He interpreted her response as not even considering an abortion, and he was pleased. He gave her a warm smile. "May I call you, Rainey? It's such a pretty name."

She nodded. He continued. "Of course, you should remain under the care of a doctor until you deliver. There are prenatal considerations to be observed if you want to have a healthy baby and a safe delivery." And as he always did in these cases, "You don't have to stay with me, there are many doctors in this town who..."

"Oh, no, I would want you to..." She gave him a meek look, "It's just that I don't know if I will stay in Washington. I may return to my family," she lied with a broken heart. Poor soul! She had absolutely no one to turn to, and she knew it.

He rose. "Well, whatever you decide, Rainey, I'll be here if you need me. In the meantime, take it easy and eat correctly. Do you smoke?"

She nodded. "Well, my dear, that is your perogative, but I suggest you refrain from smoking during your pregnancy. When you smoke, your baby smokes, too."

She warmly took his hand. "Thank you, doctor."

He nodded, holding the door open for her."

That night, after she had eaten a well-balanced meal of a lettuce, carrots, and tomato salad, she sat watching the small televison, not really interested in what was on. She was preoccupied with her problem. She placed her hand on her stomach and she thought she could feel the baby move, which was not true. It was merely the gas from the coke churning in her belly.

She thought of Jordan, the man who had impregnated her. Most women, at this time, think about the "bastards" who impregnate them. It's only natural. She wondered. Should she tell him?

What would he do? He certainly could not deny this child, or could he? What did he really think of her? She had surrendered to him on the second night. was that enough time, or, would he wonder, as so many men have... "how do I know it's mine?"

She pondered these thoughts and many more. If he did acknowledge the child, what would he do about it? He would certainly not leave one wife with whom he had two children and thousands of shares of company stock to take another wife who could only offer him another child, but, no stock. No, she concluded, he would not marry her even with his child in her belly. She had very little bargaining power over this man.

But, her mind would not cease it's searching. If she stayed in Washington and continued to work, what would she do when her time drew near. She could remember the women in the New Orleans office she worked in, waddling around the office in their eighth month of pregancy, with hideous veins protruding from their legs, their bellies so swollen they could not get close enough to their desks to be functional in their work.

And when the time came to deliver... who would be there for her? No one, that's who! And when she returned from the hospital with a new baby, how could she work? Who would support her and her child? And the medical bills; who would pay for them? She had been in some tight spots in her lifetime, but, never had she been in as much trouble as she found herself now.

In moments of despair, she considered an abortion as a viable option, but when she thought of a part of her being flushed down the drain, she sobbed, "No, I can't do that."

After a few days of soul searching, she came to a conclusion. "No, by God, it's his baby and he will take care of it. I didn't make this baby by myself and I won't have it by myself. He had his fun and it's time to pay the piper."

But, how to do that? She had two options as she played with the plan. She could notify Jordan and have him come to Washington for a showdown, or she could go to St. Louis and have the showdown there. But, in St. Louis, he had all kinds of excuses and the moral advantage would be on his side. He was legally married to another woman. He could tell her to go to hell, if he chose. What could she do about it?

She searched in her purse for his card. She looked at the clock. It was 11:38 Washington time, so it would be an hour earlier in St. Louis. She hesitated as she dialed the number. How could she be shaking just thinking of talking to a man with whom she had shared the most sacred of intimacies?

The secretary had a crisp and flat mid-western drawl. "Good morning. McNair Consulting. How may I help you?"

"Jordan McNair, please."

"Mr. NcNair is busy. May I tell him who's calling. Perhaps he can squeeze in a return before lunch. He has a luncheon engagement, I know," and Rainey could hear her shuffling papers.

"Just tell him that Washington is calling? He'll understand, I'm sure"

The secretary was puzzled. "Just Washington, Miss? No name at all?"

"No, just Washington... that's all."

"Very well, I'll see Mr. McNair gets the message."

It was nearly thirty minutes before he called back. His voice was nervous. Although he knew many people in the nation's capital, they all left names. This could only be one person, and he felt sure he knew who. He was nervous as he dialed the number she had left with the secretary. She had never seen any reason to go through the expense of a phone since she didn't know anyone to call, but with the pregnancy, she had had one installed in case of an emergency.

She breathed harder as she answered the ring and the deep modulated voice replied to her hell'o. "Miss Wether, is that really you? It's so good to hear from you. How is your boss doing... the old reprobate. Look, I'm tied up, now. Please give me your numbers again and I'll call you back when I'm not busy. I have people in the office now. Okay?"

She could detect some pleading in his voice. She felt he was telling the truth. He probably did have some people in this office. She would give him the benefit of the doubt.

But, it was after five o'clock that day before he called her back and she was irritated. Wasn't that just like a man?

When she answered the phone with a soft hell 'o, he paused for a moment. "Oh, Rainey, is it really you? I've waited for weeks for you to call. How have you been?"

"Yes, I can tell how anxious you are to talk to me since you waited over six hours to call me back." She was peeved and her preganancy did not help it. She had begun her morning sickness only a few days before.

"Aw, come on, sweetheart, don't be angry with poor Jordan. I wanted to wait until we could be alone. Oh, Rainey, I miss you. I want to see you."

She took hold of her anger, knowing this was not the time. She cooed into the phone "I want to see you, too, Jordan. Do you think you could come to Washington for a visit?"

"Well, why don't I send you an airline ticket and you fly to St. Louis?"

She expected that and she was ready "No'ooo, Jordan, I want you to take me back to the Marriott... in the same room if we can get it. I have such pleasant memories of that room." Her voice was dripping with sweetness, and it was not lost on him.

"H'mmm, I know what you mean. Well, if you insist. Let me see if I can get away this weekend."

She cooed in her best little girl mode. "Oh, do you think you can get away... what with all your distractions?"

"Yes, they want to go to the lake this weekend; the whole family, but I can tell them something came up."

She grinned. "I can promise you, Jordan, something will come up."

"Yeah, I know what you mean. Look, let me make some plans on this end. I'll call you back to confirm. Okay?"

"That'll be fine. Goodbye, Jordan."

There was no denying it. She was excited about seeing him again. She only wished her stomach was more settled, but since her sickness was confined to mornings, she felt they could work it out. He had told her to meet him in the lobby of the Marriott on Friday morning. He would land at National at 11:48. She wanted to go to the gate to meet him, but he talked her out of it.

The desk clerk smiled as he saw them approach the desk. He recognized them. "Goodmorning, Mr. McNair, it's good to see you again, and Miss Wether, you, too." He was not surprised at the adulterous couple. It was a major industry in that cosmopolitan city supplying rooms for weekend trysts among the rich and powerful. Confidentiality was part of the staff's training, for many famous faces seen on the six o'clock news were often seen at the desk. The truly famous, however, stood back as the females registered.

He held her close in the elevator in spite of several other people. He felt confidant of his turf. She merely allowed herself to he held. She did not move closer to him.

They had, indeed, been able to reserve the same room. That meant a lot to her in spite of the fact that she had experienced both rapture and hangover in it.

He placed their bags on the counter, and he went to take her in his arms. Sensing he intended to have her at this early hour and still feeling weak from the morning sickness of only an hour before leaving the apartment, she moved away. He was surprised and he gave her a surprised look. She patted his cheek and went to the chair by the window. "We just got in the room, Jordan, and I haven't seen you in weeks. Tell, me, dear, what have you been doing?"

He knew it was a diversionary tactic. She was not ready to hop into bed with him. No, there had to be some talk, first-a lot of talk.

He realized he had been gently rebuffed, but it was the women who controlled these things. He knew that. He smiled and went to the chair next to her. "Well, I've been working like mad since I last saw you. We're trying to open an office in Europe in the next year or so..."

She seemed interested. "You know, Jordan, I don't even know what you do. What does your company make?"

"We don't make anything. We're a consulting company. We're consulting industrial engineers. We set up factories for large corporations all over the world."

"I see. And what are you?"

He seemed offended. "I'm the president of the company..."

She smiled. "No silly! I assumed that. But, what are you? Your education, I mean?"

"Oh! I'm an industrial engineer. I graduated from MIT."

She looked curious. "What's an MIT?"

He shook his head at her. "MIT means the Massachusetts Institute of Technology. It's one of the best engineering schools in the country," he added, proudly.

"My... my, I am impressed."

He looked at her with half closed eyes. "Do I detect some cynicism in your voice that I must have missed before?"

She realized she might have allowed her latent anger and resentment to show, and this was not the time. "I'm sorry if I seem that way. I didn't feel well this morning..."

He looked at her. "I noticed you look a little pale. Do you feel alright now" He seemed genuinely concerned as he looked at her more deeply.

She forced a hearty laugh. "Oh, I feel fine, Jordan. I don't want a little upset stomach to spoil your fun this weekend."

He smiled at that remark. They always do.

Lloyd J. Guillory

Since the conversation had peeked and he was sure it was too early for anything else, he rose. "How about a nice long lunch in the Palm Room?"

She rose, too. Smiling. "Okay." Food was the last thing she wanted at the moment, but...

CHAPTER TWENTY-NINE

As they exited the dining room, she was still anxious to keep from spending the afternoon in the hotel room with him. It was not that she lacked desires. She didn't. But, her plan of disclosure to him of her pregnancy was already outlined in her head and she intended to follow it. She gave him a vivacious smile as she took his arm. "Jordan, it's such a beautiful sunny afternoon; let's take a long walk in the sunshine and fresh air." And then she applied some psychology. "I'm sure it will make me feel better... for tonight."

He could not argue with her logic. "But, we'll need our top-coats. The're up in the room. We'll have to go up and get them."

"Oh, that's true. Why don't you run up and get them. I'll rest in this comfortable looking chair while you do that."

What could he say? He grinned. "Why do I feel like I am being ordered around?"

"Because you are, sweetie. You're not used to it and you need more of it." She smiled as he sauntered off after a shrug of the shoulders.

As they exited the building, he took her arm. "Where would you like to go, Madam?"

Her eyes lit up. "Let's go to the Smithsonian. I've never been there. Have you?"

"Many times."

"Oh."

"But, if you want to go, why, then, the Smithsonian it is, but we'll have to hail a cab for that"

"Oooh, that's expensive. I ride buses."

"Well, I don't. I ride cabs."

"Must be nice."

He flagged a Yellow. "Come on, Princess, I'll show you the Smithsonian," and he laughed, "at least a part of it."

She snuggled up to him in the cab, smiling as she looked at him. "You keep looking at me like that and I'll have the driver ride around for an hour or so. Know what I mean?"

The driver, who barely understood English, smiled. She gave Jordan an impish look. "You wouldn't dare..."

"Uh, Driver, would you..."

"Okay... okay... I believe you. Now behave yourself, Jordan. We're on a tourist trip right now."

As she stood before the display of inauguration gowns worn by the president's wives, she ooh'd and aah'd. "Oh, look, Jordan. They're so beautiful.

Lloyd J. Guillory

How proud those ladies must have been on those nights. Just think, their husbands were just elected President of the United States."

"Uh, huh."

"Are you bored?"

"Let's go to the Technology Building. That's interesting."

As she perused her program map. "No, not yet, I want to see the jewelry collection, first. Come on, Jordan," and she gave him the kind of smile he could not resist.

They exited the Technology Building and started to the Museum of Natural History, at her insistance. He gave in, but not without this: "Rainey, you're going to owe me tonight after all this."

She placed her hand in his coat pocket, holding his. She looked up at him. "Jordan, I promise you. This will be a night you will never forget as long as you live."

He could feel his emotions churning. "You promise?"

"Uh, huh, I promise, Jordan, I swear."

After finishing "her" tour, she welcomed the cab ride back to the hotel. He looked at her. "I think the afternoon out did you a lot of good. Your cheeks are pink again. I was worried about you."

She savored the words. "Were you really worried about me, Jordan?"

"Of, course, I care about you. You know that."

"How much?"

He thought for a while. "Probably more than I should."

"We'll see, Jordan, my love, we'll see."

After dinner, he suggested an after dinner drink, The thought of hard liquor still did not set well in her memory. She had not had a hard drink since that ill-fated night in that same room. She had never forgotten it. "I don't care for one, but if you do, I'll have some Tia Maria and cream."

"Well, why don't we just have some sent up to the room. Sounds good to me, too."

As they entered the room, she felt it was time to begin her plan in correct order, so things would either fall in place, or, they'd come crashing down. She went to him, kissing him lightly on the lips. "I'll jump into the shower while the drinks are on the way up. I won't be long, sweetie."

As she showered, she became apprehensive of the coming moments. She had no idea how he would take the announcement of her pregnancy. She was sure of one thing. She had to tell him in the cool light of dawn, as the saying goes; before they got enmeshed in the whirlpool of passion. She wanted his reaction to be rational and truthful, not clouded by emotions. Men would agree to anything at the right time and under the right conditions. They would virtually agree to poison their mothers if it meant the satisfying of their animal desires. Laverne had told her so.

She wore only a nightgown when she exited the room. She planned it that way. If he cast her aside, she wanted him to be sure he knew what he was throwing away, because if his answer was not to her liking, a look would be all he'd get for the rest of his life. He nodded, approvingly, as he watched her cross the room. "You are still a lovely woman, Rainey, and I am still in love with you."

She took the chair next to him. "Is it love, or desire, Jordan? Do You know for sure?"

"It's love, Rainey. I've been thinking only of you for the past few weeks. I swear... it's true."

She nodded. "I believe you, Jordan. Why don't you slip into something comfortable and we'll talk for a while."

He rose, not quite being able to figure her mood, but he knew one thing for sure; it was different.

She wanted a cigarette while she waited for him to return, but she had cut down to five a day, and she had already had four. She looked out at the skylight of the nation's capital.

He came out, smelling good as usual. Her desires were still there when she saw him. She guessed they'd always be there, no matter what happened tonight. He smiled at her as he made his way to his chair. "Am I going to get a lecture on morality, tonight?"

She shook her head, smiling, and replying softly. "No, Jordan, tonight you get a lecture on biology"

"Biology? I haven't studied that since high school." He didn't have the slightest idea what this was all about.

She chuckled as she looked out the window. "I guess I was five- maybe six- I'm not sure, when I had my first lecture on the birds and the bees. You remember I told you about this family I went to live with, the Fosters?"

He nodded. He really didn't.

"Well, that sweet little lady, Nell Foster, instructed me and her daughter, Cora, one day on the facts of life." She giggled. "She had to, after a revealing episode which I will not go into details on at this time... maybe later, 'cause it's funny."

He looked at her, wondering if she had been drinkng, but he had been with her the past several hours and she hadn't touched a drop. She held the Tia Maria in her hand, but, lordy, one small glass of that wouldn't make a child tipsy. He waited as she continued. "You know how babies are made, Jordan?"

"Uh, huh, I think so. Two people just..."

She shook her head. "No'ooo, that's not what I mean. Do you really know the technical stuff?"

"Oh, Rainey, really! Where is this going? What the hell are you up to?"

She ignored his protest. "Women have eggs in their bodies, Jordan, lots and lots of eggs, but those eggs will not produce babies until some man," and she put her finger in his chest, "like you... fertilizes those eggs with his sperm. You know where sperm comes from, don't you, Jordan?"

"Yes, Rainey, I think so."

She grinned at him. "Well, Jordan, you have been careless with your sperm," and she looked him in the eye with a cold stare. "I'm pregnant!"

He took the news move calmly than she had expected. He flinched, that's true, but some men would have gone through the ceiling. He thought for a while, giving her a soft look.

"Are you sure?"

She nodded. "Yes, Jordan, I'm sure. I'm been to the doctor."

"That wasn't what I meant, Rainey. Are you sure it's mine?"

She had expected this and she was ready for it. She had resolved not to overreact. She looked at him without smiling and he looked at her solemnly, too. "Jordan, I don't know for sure what you think of me considering I willingly jumped into bed with you just forty-eight hours after meeting you, but I assure you...I am not tramp. I admit I was not a virgin, not harldy at my age, but you'd be amazed how infrequent have been my sexual experiences." She had learned her lesson with Harlan Kemper. There would be no details, but she continued. "But, I can tell you one thing, Jordan. No man, not one man, ever had the love and warmth and tenderness I gave to you, because no man deserved them. I saved them for you," and she surpressed a sob. "Whether you care to believe it or not, this is your baby in my womb."

He looked out the window for a long time and she felt if a judge were debating her fate in his mind. He turned to her, taking her hand. "I believe you, Rainey."

"Do you really, really, believe me, Jordan? Luke warm won't do it."

"No, I believe you, and I still love you. It won't change a thing."

She was incredulous. "What do you mean? It won't change a thing? Hell, I'm pregnant," and pointing to her abdomen, "my belly is going to get big, and in about seven and a half months, I am going to deliver a baby." And here is where she intended to separate the wheat from the chaff. "Unless I decide to have an abortion."

He bolted. His mouth opened. "An abortion? You can't have an abortion. I want this baby."

She heard what she wanted to hear. He wanted the baby. Many men would have said. "Yes, I think an abortion would be the best thing to do," but he didn't.

"You really want me to have this baby, Jordan?"

"I really do. I wanted more kids, but Janice had her tubes tied after the last one. When things turned sour with us, she said she..." and he let the words die, but she understood.

"Jordan, do you realize what you're saying? You want the baby. What about me? Where do I fit into this plan?"

He shook his head. "I don't know. I haven't figured that out, yet. Have you?"

She shook her head in desperation. "No, I haven't. I don't see any solution to my problem... just yours. I will present you with a baby and you will say... gee, thanks, Rainey. That was nice of you to do this for me and Janice..." and the tears began to flow in spasmodic sobs. She tried to stop, but...

He brought her to him, setting her on his lap. He began to console her. "No, sweetheart, don't cry. We'll work this out. I'll take care of you, I swear I will. You'll have the best of..."

"Oh, Jordan, that is not the problem. The problem is me...after the baby... what happens to poor Rainey... the brood mare?" She put her face in his shoulder and the tears flowed in profusion. He patted her back and caressed her hair, whispering consoling thoughts in her ear, but nothing seemed to help. She got up and went to the bed and lay on it without turning the covers down. Her shoulders shook uncontrollably. He went to her and sat on the bed near her. They stayed that way for several minutes as he continued to run his hand down her back, through her hair, patting her cheek.

She rose, saying, "Excuse me, I have to go to the bathroom. I always have to pee when I get upset," and she closed the door. As he heard the toilet flush, she came out putting on her robe.

As he watched her, he assumed that romance was dead for this evening.

She sat up in bed as she placed her pillow against the headboard. "We have to talk, Jordan," and she took the other pillow and placed it between them, as if to form a barrier to intimacy. He noticed the intention.

She wiped a tear with the back of her hand. "Jordan, we have to make plans for this baby."

"I'll do anything you want, Rainey. Just tell me what you want me to do."

She was quiet for a long time, trying to sort out the mixed feelings in her own mind. "Jordan, I had a screwed up childhood, I guess you know. My own mother gave me away when I was five, and then it seemed that no one else wanted me. Do you have any idea what that does to a child's self image?"

"I can only imagine," as he took her hand. She withdrew it.

"I want to make sure that that never happens to this child," and she patted her belly. He said nothing as she continued: "I've given this a lot of thought, Jordan. It's not a hasty decision."

He waited for her announcement.

"I've come to the conclusion that I'm not a fit mother to raise a child."

"Oh, Rainey..."

"No, I'm really not! I have never lived in a stable home. I don't even know what it's like, so... how can I provide one for this baby?" She sniffed. "So, that's why I'm going to let you have him, to raise... without me."

This was what he wanted. He had hinted it, but he felt she would never agree, the maternal bond being as powerful as it is.

"Are you sure this is what you want, Rainey?"

She shook her head, once again, wiping a tear and sniffing: "No, it's not what I want, but, it's what is best for him."

"Do you think you can live with this, not being able to see him grow up?"

She began to cry profusely. "That's the hardest part. The mere thought of it tears at my heart."

He removed the pillow separating them, and she didn't protest as he took her in his arms. "Well, we can arrange for you to see him from time to time..."

She drew back, her eyes wide. "Oh, no, Jordan! That would be a fate worse than death. What would we do? Meet on a street corner for a few minutes, or, on a park bench, and you'd say, here is a nice lady I want you to meet..."and she broke down completely, sobbing in his arms.

He went to the bathroom and came back with a Kleenex. She wiped and blew, handing the soiled tissue to him without even thinking. He put his hand under her chin, and looked deeply in the eyes of this woman he now knew he loved very much. "Then, my dear, what do you want me to do?"

"I never want to see him, Jordan. I never want to set eyes on him. I couldn't give him up if I ever saw him."

He swallowed hard. He knew she was probably right.

She continued. "I have some demands to make on you, Jordan, in exchange for this child."

He nodded. "Just tell me what."

She sat up, proudly. "I want you to legally adopt him. I want you to name him Jordan... what is your middle name?

"William."

"Oh, okay. I want you to christen him Jordan William NcNair, Jr. Okay?"

He nodded.

"And I want him to be a full heir to all that your daughters have coming to them. How rich are you people, anyway?"

He shrugged his shoulders. "We're not filthy rich, Rainey. A few million... maybe six or seven"

"That's enough. I want a trust fund set up for him. Do you have them for your daughters?"

He nodded. "Yes."

"I want to make sure he is never poor... you understand?"

He grinned at her. "You keep saying him... him. How do you know it won't be a girl?"

"Because, Jordan, I refuse to bring a female into this miserable world. Females have it too hard. No, he will be a boy, I promise you"

He breathed deeply. "Rainey, I agree to everything you've asked."

"Your wife? Will she agree?"

"I'll take care of that... I promise."

"Then, I guess we've settled everything..
"No, we have not. What of you. What do you want out of this arrangement?"
"I want only to be cared for during the pregnancy. I want the best prenatal care available during my pregnancy, and I want the best doctors in St. Louis at my delivery, and once I bring him into this world and hand him to you, then, I want to go out of your life and his."
"But, I intend to care for you for the rest of your life. Why, I thought that you and I..."
She shook her head. "No, Jordan. It's not going to be like that. I am still not going to be your concubine... brood mare, yes, but concubine... no!"
His face fell. "You mean it's all over between us?"
She managed a grin. "No, not quite. We still have a weekend ahead of us," and as she drew him near she whispered in his ear, "but, you had damn well better enjoy this one, Jordan, because it will be your last."
The rest of the weekend was more of a family affair. Instead of lovers, hell bent on extracting from their bodies, all that nature and physiology could provide, they were more like mom and pop on a trip to a resort. He was very attentive and solicitous of her in every way. She was warm and tender, more like a wife than a lover. They both knew the passion they had shared that one weekend when they created another life, was, one in a lifetime, and would not be experienced again.

*   *   *

She was happy with her commodious apartment he had rented for her in a fashionable section of St. Louis. It was more than she expected or needed, but he brushed aside her protests. When she inquired, "And how will all these expenses be handled in your office? I don't want to make trouble in your marriage"
"There won't be any. My father left me some real estate in my own name. I sold some of it. No one knows about it but me and the lawyer who handled the sale, and he is not our company attorney."
She smiled. "Oh, you men are devious. No wonder we have such a hard time keeping tabs on you. I feel sorry for women who are married to them."
He took her hand. "Will you ever marry, Rainey?"
"Would it matter to you, Jordan, if I did?"
"I wouldn't like it, but, you are deserving of your happiness."
She thought about his question for a moment. "Are you and your wife now living together as man and wife?"
He seemed embarrassed. "Yes, I've moved back in. I thought it was best if our plan is to succeed."

"That's true. I don't want my son going into a divorced situation," and giving him a quisical look, "how are you going to get your wife... Nancy... isn't it... to go alone with this plan?"

"I've already begun to plant the seed in her mind. I told her I had talked to a lawyer who had asked me if I knew of some couple who might be interested in adopting a child in a few months." He gave her a sheepish look as he continued. "It seems this young lady got involved with a married man and she became pregnant..."

His words pained her, but she knew he had to have a plan. She shrugged. "Like they say, art imitates life, or something like that."

He tried to hold her, but she moved back. "No, Jordan. I meant what I said in Washington. You've had all the fun you'll ever have with me. It's all over."

"But, what'll you do when you want... you know?"

She gave him a cruel laugh. "Oh, men! Can it be true that God made them in his own image?" She looked in his eyes. "Without going into details, Jordan, I will tell you this much, if only to convince you that the mother of your child is no tramp. No man will violate me during my pregnancy. That, I can assure you."

He had to ask. "And... after?"

She gave him a hard look-a Bette Davis look: "After, is none of your business. I will not owe you a thing... especially fidelity."

"Where will you go?"

"You will never know, Jordan."

"But, I promised you that I would take care of you for the rest of your life..."

"I appreciate your offer, but I didn't agree to it."

He rose to leave. "If you need anything, you know where to find me."

She looked around the lovely apartment. "Thank you, but you've been overly generous with me already. I don't need anything else."

"May I come over to see you every now and then? To see if you're all right?"

"Of course. Drop in for coffee from time to time, but, remember, always call first."

He nodded. He knew he had lost her. It was only a matter of time before he would lose her completely.

*   *   *

It was not an easy delivery for her. She was long and lean, with a narrow frame, and the baby boy had a large head. She screamed as women are prone to do in these situatons, and she cursed the man who was responsible for her misery. This, also, women are prone to do, but she had to be careful not to mention him by name. When the nurse asked her, "well, are you ready to see that fine young man you've brought into the world?" she shook her head and turned away. The nurse, who was privy to the matter of the adoption, blinked back a tear of her own, patting Rainey on the head, saying softy, "All right, dear, if that is what you want."

There was much joy in the McNair household as the newest member was brought home. Both grandmothers, wealthy women in their own rights, tried to outdo each other in gift giving to the new arrival. "Oh, he's beautiful, Jordan," exclaimed his own mother, and as she perused the infant further, "You know, it's strange how the imagination can play tricks on one's eyes, especially at my age."

"What do you mean, Mother?" asked Jordan as they stood at the crib.

"Well, if you look at him from a certain angle, he seems to have your dear father's eyes and nose."

He smiled at his mother. "Yes, it is strange how these things happen."

The grandmother moved away and the new "mother" came up and took her husband's hand. "He's beautiful, Jordan. I'm so glad you talked me into this adoption. Perhaps, this child is all we need to cement our relationship into what it once was."

He nodded. He truly hoped so, too, but his thoughts went out to the woman with whom he had shared this miracle of life.

The wife continued. "I still don't understand how a woman can give up a baby like this as if he were a sack of potatoes."

He sighed. "Well, Nancy, some women have it hard in this world. They don't all have the advantages you and I were fortunate enough to have."

She nodded. "I guess so, but it is still sad. And she never saw the child. .not once?"

"No. That was the way she wanted it."

The new foster mother fought back a tear.

In another part of town, in a lovely apartment, the real mother, just delivered by hospital van to her home, sat in a chair by the window. She was suffering badly from post-partum syndrome. She tried to bring her legs up under her but pain in her groin changed her mind about that. She took out her cigarette pack she had purchased just before going to the hospital. She had discontinued her smoking completely when she moved to St. Louis. She was determined to deliver a healthy baby. She was equally determined to see that he had all the advantages in life she had never had. She lit her cigarette. Her thoughts went out to her mother, her grandmother, and her early life- what she could remember of it. She began to cry as she came to the realization that she had just done the very same thing she had condemned her mother for all her life, she had given her baby away. She shrugged as she inhaled deeply on the cigarette, and then exhaling, she smiled. "It must be in the genes."

CHAPTER THIRTY

In the weeks following the delivery and surrendering of her child to its natural father, she had lots of time to ponder her future. She had already made her decision. She did not want to see the child, believing that each time she did- if she did-would only tear a larger hole in her heart than now existed. But, the bond between mother and child is such that it is easier to control the tides than to breech that bilogical attraction. Nature planned it that way.

Succumbing to that attraction, she toyed with the idea of, perhaps, from time to time, devising some devious plan to see him. She felt sure Jordan would cooperate with her in that regard. But, a life of misfortune and unhappiness had made her a cynical pragmatist, if nothing else. She viewed life, not as a challenge to eventual success, but as a pain-in-the-ass which one endured until fate or God decided to end it. And with that pragmatism, she finally decided that seeing the child, now and then, would be a disaster for her, which would only add to her already unhappy state. She now accepted her situation: She had loved and lost.

When she had agreed to come to St. Louis in accordance with the terms she had imposed on Jordan, especially the financial one, she was able to retain her savings still left over from the money Augie Medusa had given her as a "termination" bonus. She had had about thirty-five hundred left at the time, and with the money on interest in a St. Louis Savings and Loan during her pregnancy, it now amounted to slightly more than thirty-seven hundred dollars. It was all that divided her from poverty because she had made the decision that she would not accept Jordan's offer to support her "for the rest of your life." She did not trust his offer. What if he died? Certainly, the support would stop immediately And then, there was the matter of being a kept woman. She could not abide even the thought of it.

But, still, she was curious. She had never even seen where Jordan lived, and now, where her child resided. She gave the matter much thought. What would it hurt if she drove by the address she had found in the telephone book as long as no one knew she was doing it?

The second hand car salesman had guaranteed her that it had had only one owner and that was a little old gray-haired lady who only drove it to church on Sunday. Since the odometer had been rolled back, he had little difficulty in convincing of this lie. She gave him seven hundred and fifty dollars in cash, and drove away, the proud owner of her second automobile.

She glanced at the city map as she read the street signs on each corner of the exclusive neighborhood. The yards were wide and deep in order to accommodate the large and impressive homes their owners had imposed on them. Some house numbers could be easily read from the street and others were hidden by shadows and shrubs. She squinted in the sunlight as she read the numbers. The phone book had shown his address as No. 7, Meadowlark Lane. Children were riding bikes on the sidewalks. They watched as she went by at a speed slower than they were going on their bikes. Strangers were always viewed as suspect in this neighborhood. Then, there it was- No. 7. She stopped the car and looked. Her mouth opened slightly and air rushed in as she viewed the impressive two and a half story house of brick and native Missouri limestone, designed in an eclectic style- a little of this and a little of that. Her mind went back to the hovel she had shared with her mother and grandmother. Although she could not remember the particulars of it, she could imagine what it looked like. She had seen many others like it as she was growing up.

She sighed deeply, inwardly satisfied, and proud, that her child was living in such style. She felt she had done her duty by him, no matter the cost. Then, she gasped! She saw the front door open and a woman emerged with two small girls in tow. The woman looked back in the house and another woman was standing there holding a baby in her arms. The baby was wrapped in blankets and no features could be seen, but the magic of the moment seized her. This was her child. She knew that. The pain in her heart burned deeply. Oh, how she longed to see him, to hold him, to feel his little fingers grasp hers. The tears came as she pressed on the accelerator, wanting only to get distance between her and this baby. She realized she had made a mistake. The pain was too great.

The episode had shaken her. She knew this would never work. She had to get away from St. Louis. As long as she was within a few miles of her child, the temptation to see him would be there, and she couldn't handle it. Motherly love had given in to pragmatism. On the way home she stopped at a drug store to buy some sundry items and cigarettes. She needed a smoke. On the way out she stopped by a newspaper vending machine and extracted a copy of the St. Louis Post-Dispatch.

Having arrived home, she lit the cigarette, intending to curl up in a chair and read the paper. She was not a regular reader of the daily papers, depending instead, on the television and radio to keep her informed. As she inhaled deeply, she perused the front page. She casually looked at the large photo on the front page, the kind that editors use to attract passersby to purchase the paper. It was the photo of a bloody-faced man lying next to a table in a restaurant. Then, her eyes widened, and she gasped, nearly hyperventilating in her delicate post-partum condition. She could not recognize the face, but the words under the photo caught her eye.

MAFIA MEMBER VICTIM OF GANG WARFARE
AUGIE MEDUSA WAS ALLEGED BOSS OF THE NEW ORLEANS MAFIA FAMILY.

Her mouth sagged as she continued to read: Female companion also victim of the attack. She was identified as Laverne Sutter, who police maintained, had just been extradited from South America to testify on drug dealings in the New Orleans...

The newspaper dropped from her hand as her head went back on the chair. Laverne was dead. No doubt this time. And Augie Medusa was dead. Good riddance to the vermin, she thought, but Laverne...

She believed that Laverne had been killed to prevent her from testifying- but Augie? Why was he killed? How was he able to be seen in the presence of Laverne if she had been extradited by the government? She felt she would never know the answers, and she really didn't want to. She feared for her own safety if they knew where she was.

After her nerves had settled a bit, she picked the paper up again and resumed her perusing. She opened to the business section, but only in passing through, for she had no interests in that section, but another photo caught her attention. She knew that face. She would never forget that face; a face she had held in her hands, caressing it, loving it. She read the caption: LOCAL EXECUTIVE TO MOVE TO EUROPE. Jordan McNair to head new office in Stuggart, Germany. McNair International is a locally owned family business which...

Her shoulders sagged and she emitted a groan. It was really all over now. He would move to Europe and take her child with him. She would never see her child again, whether she wanted to or not. She sat in the chair a long time, moving only to extinguish one cigarette and light another. The warm smoke in her lungs helped to settle her rattled nerves. She moved her head from side to side, and the only audible words she emitted were..."Aw shit!"

*   *   *

There is a decided advantage to not having much in the way of wordly goods, it is much easier to move. Except for an impressive and costly collection of maternity clothing which Jordan had insisted she buy, she had accumulated very little additional belongings since she left Washington. The expensive collection of maternity clothes, which she felt sure she would never need again in her lifetime, she sold to a young expectant mother in the apartment complex for a goodly sum which was added to her bank account, thereby adding to her security.

She had tossed and turned most of the night. She knew she had to leave St. Louis, but for where? She was persona non grata on the west coast and the gulf coast. Washington had too many bitter memories. She had even considered Cuba, but the winds of revolution were blowing across that beautiful island and she didn't need any more upheaval in her life.

She had once again come to a fork in the road of life and in keeping with the laws of least resistance, she decided to go back to her roots. She would, for reasons of nostalgia, visit her birthplace and then, go to northern Arkansas and lose herself in the wild hills of the Ozarks. She had read that some of the most desolate areas of the country were in those beautiful and rugged hills. She laughed as she thought of it: "Rainey, honey, you started out as a hillbilly and now you are going back to being one again. There must be a story there somewhere."

She had no idea where her birthplace actually was. She would begin by visiting Pine Bluff. She clearly remembered that town since she was seventeen when she had first arrived there, and it had only been... what?... ten years since then. Ten years? How could so much shit happen in just ten years, she wondered?

The town had grown. She could see the difference. She drove by the bus station where a frightened little girl had gotten off after experiencing deep trauma in California. She thought of Verlie and her eyes watered. She thought of Douglas Walker, who had so brutally deflowered her. She forgave him. Poor Douglas. How many Douglas Walkers were left in foreign soil from that great war? She thought of Mario Culotta and her mouth twitched in anger and resentment.

She parked her car and walked toward the place she had remembered as the Pine Cone Cafe. It was now a washateria. It was here she had first met Laverne. Her eyes watered once again. She had loved Laverne, wild as she was, as she would have loved the sister she never had.

She moved on to the building which had housed the offices of Justin P. Holstead, one of the few men she had encountered in her life of whom she had warm memories. He had been kind to her. The old secretary/receptionist was still at her desk. She had aged, but then, who hadn't. Rainey refreshed her memory, and she smiled: "Oh, Ah do remember you, dear. My... my, but you have turned into a beautiful woman, Rainey." But, in response to her next inquiry, she became sad. "No, dear, Mr. Holstead died just after he handled your case," and she, too, surpressed a tear, wiping her eyes with a tissue. "We miss him so much."

"I'm so sorry to hear that. I wanted to get some information from him."

"Perhaps Ah can help you. All his files are still here with the firm."

"Oh, I hope so. I'm trying to find the address of my cousin, Elmer Ritter... you remember him?"

"Ah sure do. Ah have a good memory," and she smiled, "in spite of mah age."

"Do you think you could check my files and find the address of my cousin... and the land I inherited. I want to visit my birthplace."

"Well, Ah think so. You just sit there for awhile. You want some coffee, dear?"

"No, thank you."

"Ah'll be back in a moment."

With a state map on her lap, she went deeper into the country side, to the place where she entered this life. She became emotional as she neared "her farm". Even though she had very few memories of her days there, emotions are funny things. Sometimes, even those imagined are as vivid as those actually lived. When she had identified the property as the 160 acres her grandmother had left her, she was amazed. It was still in a rural area, but all she could see were pumper wells going up and down like a bunch of chickens pecking at corn. Steel tanks were everywhere. It was hideously ugly in her mind. She could see nothing here that she would have missed. Surely, it must have been more attractive than this at one time, but, who knows?

A pickup truck stopped next to her car which she had parked along the main road leading into the property. The man alighted. He was wearing a hard hat and a warm smile. "Mornin', Ma'am. Are you having trouble. Can Ah be of any help? Ah'm the foreman here in this field- the Wether Field."

At the sound of her family name, she was astounded. "What did you say the name of this place was?"

He removed his hat and mopped his brow. "This is the Wether Oil Field, Ma'am. They alway name a field after the family who owned the land at the time of the exploration."

She swallowed hard. "My name is Wether. My family used to own this land."

He looked at her decrepit old car, and his eyebrows went up. "Well, Ah guess you and your family have seen a lot 'o dollars come out of this heer ground."

She could not suppress a grunt. "No, I'm afraid not. I sold this land for thirty-two hundred dollars about ten years ago."

He shook his head from side to side in amazement. "If you don't mind mah saying so, Ma'am, you made a bad deal."

She nodded. "That's the story of my life. How bad a deal was it?"

"Oh, Ma'am, this heer field done pumped millions of dollars of oil outa that no good ground in the past ten years."

Her heart sank in her chest. She had surrendered a fortune. She remembered the words of the old attorney: "I hope you realize you might be trading a comparatively small amount of money up front for a potentially large amount, if you are willing to risk and wait." she thought to herself: Well, Rainey, honey, you've done it again.

She smiled at the foreman. "Like they say... easy come, easy go," and she looked around. "The old house... is it still standing?"

"Oh, no, Ma'am, that old place is long gone."

She grinned. "You might say, GONE WITH THE OIL... huh?"

He got the analogy. He smiled. "Yassum, you could say that."

She thanked him for his time. She turned away, but turned back. "Do you know how I can find the farm of Elmer Ritter? He's my cousin."

He nodded. "Ah shur can. Ah used to know Elmer... real good."

"You used to know him? Is he dead?"

"Yassum, Elmer died last year."

She became sad. "Oh, I'm sorry to hear that." She now realized she had no immediate family left. His children would not even know who she was. She got in the car, feeling it was not worth the trip to his farm.

There was only one more place in this part of the country which had any interest in her memories. The Powell house was the only place that even resembled a family home life for her during that period. She had spent her formative years with these school teachers. It was in that house that she made her passage from a little girl to womanhood, if menstrual periods were any indication of such a transformation.

She had no trouble finding the town. It had grown to what was considered a "big town" in that rural area, now having 3,786 souls living there, according to the sign on the highway at the city limits. She passed a small doctor's clinic. She could remember having a to go to a doctor in the county seat, and now... their own doctor.

Her pulse quickened as she neared the area where the Powell home had stood. She wondered what kind of reception she would receive from Martha Powell. She didn't really care. It had been over ten years, now. She was a grown woman, not a child. It was time Martha Powell realized that and forgave her for her foolish mistake.

Whereas the home had stood alone on a large lot with no other houses near it for hundreds of feet, it now stood on the corner of a subdivision lot. It was still a large lot, but there were houses next to it, and across the street.

She had no difficulty in recognizing the place. It had not changed all that much. It had been well kept. It was recently painted and the lawn and shrubs were well cared for. She was nervous as she parked her car in the street. She had been tempted to pull into the porte cochere as Cornelia Powell used to do, but she thought that would have been presumptious.

She was somewhat startled as she read the name on the mailbox. It was Hunter...not Powell. So, the ownership had changed. She now realized her trip had been in vain. Martha Powell was gone from here. She was tempted to return to her car and leave, but nostalgia overcame her. She walked slowly to the front porch and climbed the steps she had climbed so many times. Martha Powell's admonitions still rang in her ears. "Rainey, for goodness sake; can't you go up and down stairs like a lady? Do you have to bound up them like a wild animal?" She smiled in warm recollection. She didn't know why, but she wanted to ring the doorbell, and when it was answered, to say, "Excuse me, but I used to live in this house, and I..."

As if driven by unknown forces, she did ring it. She could hear noises coming through the screen door. The sound of children- more than one child. She smiled. That was nice, she thought. This magnificent old house needed children to bring it the life it never had. An attractive black woman came to the door; two small black children holding on to her skirts.

She smiled a warm smile. "May I help you?"

Rainey was embarrassed. "This is probably an imposition, but... you see... I used to live in this house, and I..."

The black woman came out on the porch, a curious look on her face. "You say you used to live here?"

She nodded. "Yes, that's true... for eight years."

"But, the Powells lived here. Could you be mistaken? Perhaps you have the wrong house."

Rainey smiled. "No, I'm sure. I have the right house. I lived here with the Powells.."

The black woman came close to Rainey, squinting her eyes as she looked directly in her face. She grinned. "Are you Rainey?"

Rainey's mouth opened in surprise at being recognized by this woman. Her hands went to her chin. "Why, yes, I am Rainey. But, how do you know me?"

The black woman smiled a broad and beautiful smile, her hands wide at her side. "Rainey, it's me, Magnolia! Don't you remember me? My papa found you on the side of the road when you were a little girl."

Rainey's mouth opened wide. Her jaw dropped. Her eyes lit up as if she were seeing a miracle. "Magnolia, I remember you. Yes, I do," as her brain recalled the events. The two women embraced warmly, as old friends would. Rainey held her back to look at her again.

"Why, you used to come here to pick up and drop off laundry. But... what are you doing here, now?"

Magnolia gave her an embarrassed look. "I own this house, now, Rainey. At least, my husband and I do."

Rainey laughed. "You own it?"

Magnolia nodded and laughed. "Yes, things have changed in the past ten years, and especially since the 1954 decision, but," and she shrugged, "they still have a long way to go."

Rainey nodded. "And for the best, thank God, but, Magnolia..."

The black woman interrupted her. "And one more thing has changed, Rainey. I shortened my name to Maggie. I hate the name of Magnolia." She shrugged. "It's so stereotyped."

Rainey smiled. "I know what you mean. I've had to fight this name of mine all my life."

"Oh, but Rainey, you have a beautiful name." And taking her by the arm, "oh, my God, Rainey, forgive my bad manners. Come on in. I'll make us some coffee and we'll catch up on the past twenty years, and she chuckled.

Rainey's eyes widened as she entered the house, and standing in the large foyer, she looked up at the stairs which had fascinated her so much as a child. The house had not changed all that much- some new wallpaper in the parlor and dining room.

Maggie Hunter watched, smiling, as Rainey's brain raced in reverie, remembering this one particular instance here and another there. Rainey took the black woman's hand, squeezing it: "Oh, Maggie, this house has such memories for me. I didn't realize how much. How long have you lived here and what happened to the Powells?"

Maggie pulled her hand in the direction of the kitchen. "Come on in and make yourself at home and I'll bring you up to date." It took two pots of coffee, some pie and ice cream, but eventually, the story was told. Rainey was amazed as she viewed her new-found friend. "But, your cornpone accent, Maggie, the one we all had in those days... what happened to it?"

Maggie smiled, nodding her head. "I was determined to lose that awful accent, Rainey, and when I left here to go to Xavier in New Orleans, I had lost most of it, to my parents dismay."

"Oh, your parents, Maggie, are they still alive?"

She chuckled. "Oh, yes, they're fine except for some rheumatism in most joints. I know they'd love to see you..."

"Oh, do you think we could see them?"

"I'm sure we can."

Rainey's eyes misted. "You know, Maggie, I was eight at the time, almost, so I can still remember the morning your papa stopped for me on that road."

"Rainey, that was unbelievable, your running away like that."

"I'm still running, Maggie," she said solemnly.

"Want to tell me about it?"

"Not now... perhaps later. Now, I want to hear how you got this house for your own."

Maggie looked sad for a moment. "It was not easy, Rainey, and if my husband was not a doctor, and this rural area had not needed one so badly, I don't think they would have let us live here."

"Your husband is a doctor?" she asked with incredulity.

"Uh, huh. He and I met when we both attended Xavier. I was in nursing and he was in pre-med, I fell madly in love with him, and," as she waved her hand, "the rest is history."

Rainey's eyes misted, again. "Oh, Maggie, you've done so well with your life." She sniffed. "I wish I could say the same."

Maggie's eyes were sad. "Where are you headed?"

She shrugged her shoulders. "Nowhere. I have no place in particular to go. I'm just a gypsy."

"Oh, Rainey, why don't you spend a few days with us. We have plenty of room. Then, you can meet my husband, Calvin, and we can have my folks over, and..."

Rainey's eyes widened. "That sounds so nice..."

Maggie slapped Rainey's hand. "Then, do it. Come on, we'll have some fun."

"If you really want me to... okay, I'll do it."

Maggie rose, excited. "Come on, let's get your bags and take them upstairs. Oh, I'm so excited about this. I'm gonna call mama and papa and invite them over for supper tonight. We'll surprise them. I won't tell them who is here."

As the old black couple came into the parlor later that evening, Maggie went to her father and mother, holding Rainey by the hand. "Mama... Papa... I want you to try to remember something that happened a long time ago," as they perused this white woman closely, wondering what this had to do with them. Turning to her father, "Papa, you remember that little white girl you picked up along the road about twenty years or so ago?"

He looked at Rainey over his spectacles. "Ah shur do. Why she weren't nothing but a litt'l thing..."

"Mama... Papa... here is that little girl, Rainey Wether."

Rufus' face broke into a broad grin, still showing a good set of white teeth. "Nah, you tell me. Is that you, Chile?"

Rainey went to him, hugging him, while she held the hand of a surprised Clarissa, also grinning from ear to ear. Rainey brought both of them to her, hugging them warmly. "Yes, it's me, the same crazy white girl you picked up," and as she squeezed his hand, "I don't know what would have happened to me if you hadn't come along."

Clarissa laughed. "You was a gutsy litt'l thing to do something lak that... you know that, Chile."

Rainey nodded. "Like they say... more guts than sense."

Maggie made an attempt to gather them all up at the same time. "Come on in the dining room. I hear Calvin's car in the driveway. He'll be ready to eat soon's he gets washed up. Come on, Papa... come on Mama. You have all night to talk to Rainey.

As Rufus walked next to her, he could not take his eyes off her. He kept repeating his favorite phrase. "Nah, you tell me. Ah cain't bleeve it... You shur grow'd up pretty, Chile."

Rainey extended her stay, at Maggie's insistence, to nearly a week. In that time she had told Maggie virtually everything. She felt she had nothing to hide from this woman with whom she had shared such common roots at one time. There were no reasons for pretenions on either side. They held nothing back. They shared secrets as if they were sisters.

Maggie could only shake her head in disbelief as Rainey told her of her unfortunate love affair, the surrendering of her child- a child she would never see again. "I couldn't have done that, Rainey... I just couldn't!" she insisted.

"It was not easy, Maggie. It tore my heart out, believe me."

Maggie rubbed her hand across Rainey's, as if to give her support and solace. "What are you going to do now? Where will you go?"

"I don't know. I guess I'll go to northern Arkansas and get lost in the Ozazks, somewhere."

Her eyes lit up. "You know, Rainey, if you want to stay here, I'm sure Calvin could find you a job... maybe at the clinic. You said you were a secretary..."

She pondered the offer for a monent. "No... I'm not sure I'd want to stay here. This place holds no particular attraction for me."

Maggie studied her for a long time. "Well, you do what you want, but I want you to know one thing. You alway have a home with us, here. If you ever need a roof over your head, come back to Maggie... promise?"

Rainey fought back tears, nodding. "Thank you, Maggie, I appreciate that," and they hugged.

As she headed north towards Little Rock, she was despondent. Except for seeing Maggie and her parents, the visit to her roots had not lifted her spirits. She secretly envied Maggie's success. Why had she failed when Maggie had succeeded so well. She just couldn't understand it.

She had just lit another cigarette when she glanced up at the rear view mirror. The flashing lights on the state trooper's car filled the glass. "Aw shit! I must be speeding." She pulled over and looked in the mirror to check her appearance. She had heard that an attractive woman could usually talk her way out of a ticket, especially if the trooper was young and horny. She watched in dismay as the gray haired man with a paunch stepped out of the patrol car. He had to be in his fifties' at least, she reckoned.

Be tipped his hat. "Good mornin', Ma'am. May I see your driver's license, please?"

She mangaged a smile, but her heart was not in it. She felt this was a lost cause. She would get a ticket. He took the driver's license, looking at it, and then at her.

In a little girl's voice. "What is the problem, officer? I'm sure I wasn't speeding. Why this old car can't go..."

He was all business. "Yes, Ma'am, you were doing nearly seventy. The speed limit is fifty-five in this area."

"I'm so sorry. I just looked down for a minute and..."

He still did not smile. "Are you aware that your license plate is expired, Ma'am?"

She was truly surprised. "Oh, no, I didn't know that. You see, I just bought this car a little over a week ago from a dealer in St. Louis and... and... he told me they would take care of everything... the registration and all..."

"May I see your papers, please?"

She nervously searched the glove compartment and retrieved the papers, which she proudly handed him. He looked at them for a moment. He turned to her and crooking his finger, said, "Would you please get out of you car, Miss, and come with me?"

He led her to the passenger side of the patrol car. Her eyes now widened with fear, "What's the problem, officer? What have I done wrong?"

"I don't know that you've done anything wrong, Miss, but we have had notices to check cars from this car lot. They deal in a lot of stolen cars. I want to call headquarters and have them run a check." He didn't tell her that the check would also include the name of Rainey Wether. It was a routine procedure.

She waited nervously as she stood along the highway, the noise of the large trucks in her ears. She puffed on her cigarette with a vengeance. She could hear him talking on the radio with some staccato sounds coming back, but she could not follow it.

He gave her a solemn look. He pointed to her car. "Get in your car, Miss, and follow me. In the meantime, I'll hold your purse with me in this car just in case you get any funny ideas, so don't."

She began to panic. "But, what have I done? Please tell me what is wrong..."

He didn't reply. "Just do as you're told, Miss."

She was shaking with fear as she followed him into the headquarters of the Arkansas State Police on the outskirts of Little Rock. She swallowed hard. She had no idea what this was all about. She could only assume it was all a misunderstanding. It would all soon be ironed out. She wanted a cigarette badly, but she saw the NO SMOKING sign. Her heart beat loudly in her heart. She could hear and feel it. She felt all alone and helpless in the male-dominated room. Some men were on the phone and others were huddled to one side of the room. She was near panic. She had no one to turn to for help if she were in trouble.

CHAPTER THIRTY-ONE

She sat alone at a table in the center of the room. It reminded her of the movie version of an interrogation room with the bare light bulb shining down on the victim, but there was no bare light bulb, just flourescent bulbs humming on the ceiling. Several men stood to one side in animated conversation, looking in her direction from time to time. She was terrified. She had no idea what she had done to warrant this kind of treatment. She had been speeding, true, but that usually involved the simple issuance of a ticket, not this.

She raised her hand as if she were a child in school. One of the men walked over. "Yes?"

She was embarrassed. "I have to go to the bathroom. I always do when I get upset." He nodded and walked off. He walked to the door and motioned to someone. A very large female officer, in uniform came in. He whispered to her, and she beckoned to Rainey to come forward.

As they entered the ladies' restroom, Rainey touched the officer's arm and with a pleading look, "Please... tell me what this is all about."

The officer shook her head. "I'm sorry. I can't discuss the matter with you," and nodding towards the toilet, "you go ahead and do your business so we can go back."

When they returned to the room, Rainey noticed that two more men had come into the room. They were well dressed, in business suits. She returned to the chair and sat there with her arms crossed in her lap. She could feel the moisture rolling down her back. Her hands were moist. She was afraid.

Finally, the men moved in her direction. One of the two well-dressed men spoke to her first. He nodded, attempting a slight smile. "Miss Wether? Is that correct?"

She nodded and replied softly. "Yes."

"Is that your real name?"

"Of course," and she softened it to... "yes."

"Do you have any idea why you're here?"

She shivered. "No."

"My name is Robert Turner," and pointing to the other man who came in with him, "and this is Tom Fraser. We're with the F.B.I. here in the Little Rock office.

At the sound of those words, she shuddered. Why would the F.B.I. be interested in her?

He continued. "We're going to ask you some questions, Miss Wether. It would be better if you told the truth. We feel sure we already know the correct answers."

She nodded. She had no idea what he was referring to.

"Did you ever hear of a man by the name of Augie Medusa?"

Her mouth opened and her eyes widened. Now, she knew why she was here. But, how could a simple speeding ticket have triggered this? She still had no idea. Her mind raced to come up with an answer that would not sound incriminating for her.

"Well, I met a man by that name when I lived in New Orleans."

"When was that? How long ago?"

She thought. "Well, let's see. It must have been almost a year ago." One man looked at the other and he nodded.

"And the name of Laverne Sutter- does that ring a bell with you?"

She knew down deep in her heart that they had all the answers. They were testing her to see if she would lie about it.

"Yes, Laverne and I roomed together in New Orleans. We knew each other... yes." She decided she would volunteer nothing.

"How well did you know Augie Medusa?"

Her shoulders moved. "Oh, I didn't know him for very long," and she searched her memory. "Perhaps, a month or two."

"Do you have any idea what he did for a living?"

That question shattered her. They knew. They were playing games with her. She shrugged. Fear had gripped her. She was trembling. The men noticed it, too. One touched her shoulder. "Try to remain calm, Miss Wether. We're not going to hurt you. We're only trying to get at the facts in this matter."

"What matter?" she stammered. She knew.

He ignored her question. "You didn't tell me if you knew what Mr. Medusa did for a living."

"I'm not sure. I really am not. He never told me."

"Are you aware that he is dead?"

"Yes."

"And how did you find that out?"

"I... I... read it in the newspaper... in St. Louis."

"Then, you must be aware that Miss Sutter is also dead?"

She nodded. "The article said she was."

"When was the last time you saw Miss Sutter?"

She had seen enough crime movies to know she was in big trouble. She had often heard this line at this stage of the questioning in gangster movies: "I want an attorney. I'm not saying anything else until I have an attorney present."

He sighed. "That's your legal right, Miss Wether. Can you afford to pay an attorney. If not, we'll have the judge appoint one for you?"

She made a tactical error. "No, I can't afford one."

He pondered her remark for a moment and pointing to her purse, he asked, "May I see the contents of your purse and wallet?"

She had heard and read about the fourth amendment to the constitution to know better. "Am I required to do that?"

"No, you're not, but, it's simply a matter of a telephone call to a judge and we'll then have the legal right. The harder you make it on us, the harder we make it on you." That was probably an illegal statement to make, but it is a common one.

She nodded and handed him her purse. He slowly emptied the contents on the table. It held the usual female articles: make-up, handkerchief, note pad with calendar for counting days, but the thing that caught his eye was an envelope- a plain white envelope with the address of the St. Louis Savings and Loan in the upper left hand corner. He slowly dumped the contents on the table and all the cash she had in the world fell out.

She saw the eyebrows of the men go up as the nearly three thousand dollars in hundred dollar bills fell out. He moved the bills around with his index finger. He grinned at her. "Well, Miss Wether, I thought sure I just heard you say you could not afford an attorney... is that right?"

She knew she was getting in deeper all the time, but she felt she had to explain. She fought back a sob "That's all the money I have in the world. If I pay it to an attorney..." and she didn't complete the sentence. She didn't have to.

"Where did you get this money, Miss Wether?"

Her mind raced for an answer. "My boyfriend gave it to me."

"Why would your boyfriend give you this kind of money? What did you do to earn this?" he grinned at her.

She hated to say this, but..."I had a baby for him... and this was part of the settlement money."

He gave her a non-believing look. "And I'm sure he will be willing to testify to that?"

"He's gone to Europe. He's not in this country."

With some sarcasm, "Now, isn't that convenient." And with a glance at his cohorts: "Now, Miss Wether, where did you really get this money?"

She shook her head. "I'm not saying anything else. I want an attorney and I don't care who pays for it."

The F.B.I. man sighed. "Okay, if that's how you want it," and turning to the other men, "We'll have to book her until the judge decides what to do with her."

The state troopers came up. "In that case, this will be a federal charge, won't it?"

The F.B.I. man nodded. "Yes, the charge will be transportation of illegal drugs into this country. That's a federal crime." At the sound of these words, she shuddered. Her heart began to beat fast and she could hardly breathe.

"Then, replied the state troopers, "This is over our heads. We give her to you. She's all yours."

"Well, wait a minute. We'd like to have you folks lock her up for the night. We can't take care of her until we see a Federal Judge and it's too late in the day for that. Can't you put her up for tonight?"

"Well, yes, I guess so, but we don't want her too long. This is too heavy for us."

The large female office came and took her arm. "Come on with me, please."

Once again, her movie experiences came to light. "I thought I was entitled to a phone call," she said meekly.

He stopped. "You are," and turning to the female office, "let her make her call and then lock her up."

She didn't know whom to call. She had no one, but she had to let someone know of her predicament. She thought of Maggie Hunter. She nervously dialed the number Maggie had given her only that morning as she left her with these words: "Here, Rainey, is my phone number in case you ever need me. Please don't hesitate to call on me."

It seemed like ages before she heard the familiar voice. She stammered into the phone, "Oh, Maggie! I..." and she blurted out the tragic events of the day.

She was booked with all the usual trappings- photographs, fingerprints, and the rest. She moved as if in a stupor. She merely did what she was told and went where they pointed.

She thought of Jordan. Oh, how she wished he would know. He would do something for her, she was sure of that, but, he was not even in the country. All her hopes for any kind of aid or support lay with her newfound friend, Maggie Hunter.

But, she pondered further. What could Maggie do for her? She was a black woman in a southern state. She had her own problems in just coping with a white dominated society. She felt hopeless. She felt her life was coming to an end, and she didn't give a damn. But, it was the strip search that humiliated her the most. To have absolute strangers move their hands over the most private parts of your body, and even to examine the anus, was more than she could accept, but she had to.

She lay in a dark cell that night, caged like an animal, she thought. She had never imagined the horror of being locked up, the thought that she could not walk to that cell door and go out into the fresh air. She was traumatized badly. She shook and shuddered as if she had difficulty in breathing, for she did. She began to cry as if she were a child. She was as helpless as one. Children, at least most of them, can cry and someone who loves them will come to their aid, but she could cry her heart out, which she did, but no one came.

She was taken to a small interrogation room the next day and led to a table with two chairs. She waited. She didn't know what was supposed to happen. Then, the door opened and a young man in a suit came in. He was smiling. He had a nice face, she thought. He came up to her and extended his hand. "Miss Wether, I'm Don Cooksley, your court appointed attorney."

At the sound of these words, she felt a little better. At least, she thought, I have someone on my side. She attempted a smile, but it was difficult. She shook his hand, saying nothing.

He pulled back a chair after placing his brief case on the floor while he placed a note pad on the table. He adjusted his body in the chair. "Well, now. Where shall we begin?"

She looked into his young face, thinking: My God, he looks like he should be in high school! Can he really have finished law school? She asked: "Mr. Cooksley, how many cases have you tried?"

He answered proudly. "You're my third."

She answered his questions as best she could, but, a feeling of confidence never developed between them. He simply didn't know the correct questions to ask. She told him what she thought she was guilty of, but, she added plaintively, "it was so little-just two trips, and I flushed the stuff down the commode on the second trip, so..."

Little would be gained in relating the particulars of the trial, for it was, indeed, a farce if ever there was one, but some recounting of the incident must be made for the sake of continuity of the narrative:

Rainey was only a small cog in the heinous crimes committed by Augie Medusa and his gang of criminals. Under ordinary circumstances, she might have been found guilty of stupidity, only, and sent to a minumum security federal incarceration center for a short period of time. But, these were not ordinary circumstance as shall be related.

It was the intent of the federal government to not only put a stop to the practice of smuggling drugs into the country in the manner already described, but to put behind bars for a long time, the real culprits who had masterminded the practice, such as Augie Medusa.

It must be explained here, as it was at the preliminary hearing, how Laverne Sutter, who had been extradited to this country from Columbia by the government of the United States, in order to testify against the same Augie Medusa, could have been in his company at the time of their demise. Even the judge trying the case was perplexed about this, and he demanded an explanation of the D.E.A and the F.B.I. people. The F.B.I. man, under oath, had to tell the embarrassing story truthfully:

"Well, your honor, I guess we goofed on that. You see, we had bargained with Miss Sutter to testify against Mr. Medusa in exchange for immunity from prosecution."

"She had agreed to this?" asked an incredulous judge.

"Yes, your honor."

The judge scratched his bald pate. "But, if I have my facts straight, you did not have Mr. Medusa in custody during that period. Is that correct?"

"No, Sir, we did not. That was part of the plan. We had been informed that Mr. Medusa was a one time lover of Miss Sutter, and that he still loved her. That was why he had her sent to South America after her arrest in the airport in New Orleans."

The judge shook his head. "I'm not sure I follow you, but, do go on."

"Well, Sir, our plan was to bring Miss Sutter back to this country after one of our informants in Columbia had told us where she was. We felt, if he still was in love with her, he could be talked into a meeting with her in a neutral area, not in New Orleans. She knew where to find him. We were right about that. He had gone underground after the arrest of Miss Sutter and the stupid attempt on Miss Wether's life in that car bombing."

Rainey sat listening with wonderment. They had pieced it all together- the whole plan, including the attempt on her life.

The F.B.I. man continued his testimony: "We were right about Mr. Medusa. He wanted to see Miss Sutter in the worst way, and he agreed to meet her in Chicago as we had suggested to her. As you know, Your Honor, most all crime families are interconnected. We thought we might also get some Chicago big-wheels in the trap."

The judge raised his hands. "Then, what went wrong?"

The F.B.I. man lowered his head as if embarrassed to answer: "It appears that they had a pipeline into our conversations. They found out what we had in mind."

"How did this happen?" asked an enraged judge.

"We don't know at this time, Sir, but we'll find out."

"You had damn well better. But, I'm still confused. Why were Mr. Medusa and Miss Sutter killed and by whom?... the mob?"

"Yes, Sir, there is no doubt in our minds that their killing was done by the mob."

"Why would they kill one of their own Dons? He was a Don, was he not?"

"Yes, Sir, he was, but that is not hard to explain, Your Honor. This is not the first time a Don has been killed by the mob in an intrafamily dispute."

"So, you're telling me he was killed by another mob family. Is that correct?"

"Yes, Sir, that's the way we see it."

When Rainey finally appeared in court, all her unanswered questions about the affair were answered. She listened to testimony from paper boys, bartenders, waiters in the restaurants of their apartment neighborhood. They had interviewed the people at the Hotel Nacional in Havanna, including Juio Cardoza. They had subpoenaed everyone and anyone connected with the case, but the trail had turned completely cold after the car bombing near Natchez. They knew Rainey had survived the bombing due to a complete lack of remains, but the trail died there. The old salesman who had carried her to Vicksburg had died of a heart attack shortly thereafter and the trail had died with him.

She discovered during the trial the link that tied her to the case. They had not pursued her with any vigor, knowing full well of her very minor part in the scheme. She was a small fish, not worthy of too much manpower expended in looking for her, but computers had entered the law enforcement arena and her name was listed as a fugitive wanted only for questioning, but the speeding infraction on that lonely stretch of Arkansas highway was her undoing, for when the computer was asked of it knew anything of one Rainey Wether, the computer, honest and infallible things that they are, said... YES.

When the federals were finished, she and Laverne had been tied together and Laverne and Augie had been tied together, and the entire scheme had been brought into the light of day.

It is safe to assume that, had the federal scheme to "get" Augie Medusa, succeeded, Rainey, if she had been dragged in, would have gotten off with a slap on the wrist. She was simply not that important. But, the federal agencies, especially the F.B.I., do not like to be caught in an embarrassing mistake and their anger was vented on that poor unfortunate creature sittting in that courtroom.

It is the perogative of prosecutors to choose from a wide range of choices in charging any arrestee who has been charged with a violation of the law. For instance, a person caught jay walking is not only guilty of jay walking, he could be charged with public endangerment, for by jay walking, he might run into an automobile driven by a little old gray-haired lady who is easily rattled and she could run her car into the plate glass window of the local drug store and hit a mother and child who were at the checkout counter. The possibilities are endless. It all depends on how the prosecutor feels that day or how well he slept the night before. Such is our justice system.

But, poor, unfortunate Rainey, who was in the wrong place at the wrong time, bore the brunt of their wrath. As she had suspected, her attorney, although well meaning, was as green as grass. He didn't even recognize some of the legal jargon he heard in the courtroom, and he was too polite to inquire.

The judge, whose own young daughter had just been involved with drugs, was on a one man crusade to "clean up the mess" as he put it, and he took his wrath out on Rainey. She was sentenced to from ten to twenty years in a minimum security prison near Little Rock to serve out her sentence.

Needless to say, she was devastated. she had given serious consideration to ending her own life. She had even asked Maggie Hunter, who had sat in that courtroom everyday without fail, to bring her some razor blades to perform the act, but Maggie refused to even discuss it.

"No! Absolutely not, Rainey. I don't want to even talk about it," and she placed. her hand an Rainey's. "I know things look bad, now, but you're only...

what... twenty-eight? You have many years ahead of you. This will be over same day and .." but the words died out as she watched Rainey shake her head in depair.

Maggie continued as she rubbed the back of Rainey's hand. "You know, I feel kind of responsible for you. Why if my papa hadn't picked you up along side that road, we'd never have met, but, maybe, fate decided that you would need me some day, and believe me, girl, I will be here for you 'til hell freezes over. You understand that?"

Rainey smiled a very weak smile as she nodded, replying, "Maybe so, Maggie. Thank God I have you. There is no one else," and rising to go off to her incarceration, she added: "Well, I guess you won't see me for about ten years, if I'm good, and twenty... if I'm bad, huh?"

Maggie grabbed her hand. "Oh, no, Rainey, honey, that's not how it's gonna be! It's just a little over an hour's drive from my house to that prison. You're gonna see ole Maggie once a week whether you want to or not, and I don't want to see you with red eyes when I come. .you're too pretty for that...hear?"

Rainey sniffed and wiped her eyes with the back of her hand, attempting a smile, looked at her friend. "Aw, Maggie, you don't have to come that often, but... but...I would like to see you every now and then."

"Suppose you just let me decide if its too often or not. My kids are grown and my husband is a doctor," she giggled. "Ah ain't gotta work fo a livin', you know," as she mocked her childhood jargon.

Rainey grabbed her hand. "Whatever you say, Maggie," and they embraced like sisters, both crying as they broke away. Maggie paused at the door, and blowing her a kiss, turned and left Rainey to her misery.

CHAPTER THIRTY-TWO

When she heard the steel door to her cell clang shut, the sound of the heavy metal ran through her brain like a death knell. Never had she felt so alone, so God-forsaken, so helpless and forlorn. She had turned around to watch the two female guards exit her cell, hoping for at least some words or support like, "good luck, honey", but the hardened and cynical women did not even look back. But then, one returned, handing her a sheet of paper, saying in a flat monotone, "Here, Ah forgot to hand you this list of regulations. Make damn shur you read them and make damn shur you obey them," and with that they were gone.

She looked around the small cell, six by nine feet. It had concrete walls with peeling whitewash paint. There were two steel bunks with wire springs on which lay a thin mattress covered in striped ticking with a pillow to match. Both were badly stained. Some of the stains appeared be blood. Across from the bunks was a stainless steel lavatory and toilet. A grill-enclosed light bulb of very small wattage gave the cubicle barely enough light to read by.

A stainless steel mirror was anchored to the wall above the lavatory. She walked to the mirror and looked at herself for quite some time. She had always considered herself pretty because many people had told her so, both men and women. Laverne had even told her she was beautiful. She looked in the mirror for confirmation but found none. Her eyes had dark circles beneath them. Her hair was straggly. Her mouth was drawn tight at the edges. She had always felt that her eyes and her mouth, with its full lips, were her best features, but now...

She was surprised to see that her cellmate was not in. Then, she glanced at the regulation sheet which included a schedule and realized that it was exercise time. She could see the cellmate's meager belongings in a cardboard box under the bottom bunk. Her own were in a paper bag, and this caused her to shake her head in misery as she remembered the paper bag she had carried with her to the Fosters so many years ago, as a frightened child. She thought for a moment. "You've really come a long way, Rainey, baby, but it's been in a circle. You're no better off now than you were in 1935."

Her reverie was broken by the sound of the cell door locks being thrown and then the doors being opened by the electrical operating system. She stood with mouth open as the huge black woman came in shouting some obscenties towards the white guards, with her head looking back into the cell corridor as she entered.

With her hand on the cell door, she continued to curse the guards as they exited the cell corridor.

She turned and looked at Rainey, saying nothing as she walked around her, hands on hips, inspecting her as if she were a horse at an auction. Rainey stood still, standing erect, with her hands folded in front of her, not knowing what she should do or say. She looked straight ahead while the other woman circled her.

The black woman returned to Rainey's front, and while grunting and smiling, remarked, "Well, nah, if you ain't the cutest little piece of ass Ah seen in a long time... you shur is. What's yore name, sweetie?"

Rainey took in a deep breath. She would have preferred not to answer her at all, but she knew better than that. If this large and powerful woman was to be her roommate, she knew she had to establish some type of realtionship with her. She replied, softly: "My name is Rainey."

"Rainey? You joshin' me girl? What kind 'o name is Rainey? .You mean like de' weather?"

Rainey nodded. "Yes, like the weather."

The woman went over to the bottom bunk and sat down. Rainey, not knowing what to do, remained standing. "Whatcha in for?"

"I'm not sure. I really do not know for sure," she replied softly.

The woman grunted and then laughed. "Just like the rest of us, huh? Ain't none of us know fer shur what we in fer, but we know one thing fer shur. We damn shur in. How long you in fer?"

"I was sentenced to ten to twenty years..."

The black woman cut her off. "Ten to twenty? Oh, baby, you done somethin' bad... you shur did. Ah had you figured for a whore, but you done somethin' worse than whorin'. Now, you sit yore little ass down on this bunk and you tell me fer shur what you in fer. Ah don't like no bull shit. Ah wants the truth."

Rainey nervously and fearfully complied with her order to sit. She placed her hands in her lap, shrugged her shoulders, and began to tell her story, interrupted only now and then with the black woman repeating... "Nah, you tell me. No shit."

When Rainey had completed a condensed version of her misfortune, her cellmate stood up to her full five foot ten height, shaking her head of close-cropped hair. "Woo'eee, baby, you shur got yoresef in deep shit... you shur does," and lightinq a Camel cigarette as Rainey looked on in silence, she inhaled deeply as she leaned against the opposite wall. "That jus proves what Ah say 'bout men. They ain't no damn good." She chuckled as she looked at Rainey..."Whal, dey is good far one thing... dat's fer shur. Whew, Ah could shur use me a good man 'bout nah," and she returned to the bunk, slapping Rainey on the thigh. as she gave her a lascivious grin. "How 'bout you, sweetie?"

Rainey drew back, shaking her head gently. "I really am not in the mood to talk about that right now."

"No? whal... in time you will, sweetie... dat's fer shur," and as a bell rang out, she started for the cell door, beckoning to the scared woman who had no idea what the bells meant. "Come on, baby, dat means chow time. Let's go eat."

Much later that night as they returned to the cell for the evening, the black woman pointed to the top bunk. "That's yore bunk, Rainey. Ah got the bottom, and Ah don't want you waking me up at night if you got to climb down to pee. You understand?"

Rainey nodded, still not sure how to take the black woman. She seemed to vacillate between friendly and menacing as if she was fighting a constant battle within herself as to how to react to the world.

Rainey went to the lavatory and washed her hands and face and brushed her teeth. She could see the black woman watching her in the mirror as she performed her toiletries. She had brought pajamas with her to prison and felt she should wear them, but she noticed that her cellmate had merely brushed her teeth and flopped in bed in her prison uniform. She felt reluctant to undress in order to put on her sleeping clothes.

She turned to the black woman, somewhat embarrassed. "I don't even know your name. What do you like to be called?"

The woman hesitated a moment. "Ah like to be called by mah name. Mah name is Ora Lee. Ora Lee Wilson. You didn't tell me yore last name."

She was always embarrassed when she had to say it. "It's Wether... Rainey Wether."

The black woman let out a raucous laugh... half laugh... half cough... as the effects of many years of smoking took hold of her body. "No shit... Weather?... Rainey Wether?"

She nodded. "Yes, but it's spelled W E T H E R."

The woman continued to chuckle. "It don't matter how you spell it. Somebody had a sense of humor to name you Rainey Wether. Who done that to you, girl... yore mama?"

"No, I think it was my grandmother."

Rainey sat next to the black woman on the lower bunk, and with some hesitancy, inquired, "Ora Lee, what are you in for, and how long?"

She waited a while before answering until Rainey had regretted asking the question, but finally, "Ah kilt a man... dat's what Ah'm in for, but it was self defense my lawyer proved so Ah got off with manslaughter. Ah got to serve ten more years. Ah done served ten."

"This man you killed. Did you know him?"

The woman grunted. "Know him? Ah was married to the bastard."

Rainey's hands went to her cheeks. "Oh, my God"! You killed your husband?"

She replied with a mixture of pride and defiance. "Uh, huh, Ah sure did. If ever a bastard deserved to die, he did."

"What did he do to you to make you do that?"

Without replying, she began to unbutton her blouse on her prison uniform. She had removed her bra for the night so her breasts were readily visible. Rainey started to turn her head as the woman exposed her very ample breasts. The black woman, holding a breast in each hand, said, "Don't turn your head away, girl. You wanted to know what he did to deserve it and Ah'm showing you... now look... see for yoresef."

Lloyd J. Guillory

Rainey slowly gazed at her breasts and could see horrible scars running across each one. The scars, which were now nearly ten years old showed white scar tissue on the darker background.

The black woman fondled her breasts, lifting them up for Rainey's inspection. Rainey looked and shook her head and turned away. The black woman rebuttoned her blouse, adding, "And that ain't all. I got more scars." She chuckled. "You 'll git to see all mah scars before you git outa here, and Ah' ll git to see yours... that's fer shur."

After a moment of reflection, Rainey asked, "How did you do it? Did you shoot him?"

She grunted once again. "No, that woulda been too quick and easy fer him."

"Then, how did you do it?"

"You ever go deer huntin' when you was a kid?"

She shook her head. "No. Why?"

"Cause if you had, you'd know how to field dress a deer. That's what Ah did to him. Ah field dressed him right there in mah kitchen."

She hated to ask. "What is field dressing?"

She grinned as if she was enjoying the retelling of it. "Whal, as soon as you kill a deer you got to open him up and let his guts spill out to keep the meat from spoiling."

Rainey cringed and asked, "How do you do that?'

Ora Lee motioned with her hands. "You take a good sharp knife and start at his crotch and slit his belly up to his rib cage."

Rainey drew her legs up under her and moved back until her shoulders were resting against the wall."You did that to him?"

She nodded. "Ah shur did," and she made a clucking sound with her tongue as she ran through the motion again.

"But, I don't understand. How would he let you do that without a fierce struggle. I know you're a big woman. How big was he?"

"Oh, he was a big stud. He was six foot four and weighed two hundred and fifty pounds. He was a big one, he was."

"But, didn't he put up a fight?"

"No... not a bit. He was already dead. I stabbed him in the heart four or five times while he was sleeping in his rocking chair with his wine bottle in his lap. He died happy. He was drunk. He was always drunk... or screwing. That's all he ever did."

Rainey was now more fearful than ever of what her future held in stare. Her cellmate was a cold blooded killer. No matter that she was prevoked. To field dress another human being, even one who deserved it, was more than her basically genteel mind could fathom, or accept.

She rose and looking at the black woman who was looking at her with no expression at all, just judging her reaction to this grisly tale, she said, meekly, "If you don't mind, Ora Lee, I think I'll go to sleep."

Ora Lee turned to the wall as if to also go to sleep. "Yeah, you do that, sweetie. Ah know it's yore first day in this place and you kinda nervous and scared, so you go on and go to sleep, but you and Ora Lee gonna have some pillow talk tomorra night."

Not knowing what she meant and not really wanting to find out tonight, Rainey made no response as she climbed up to her bunk.

She lay on her back in the darkened room. Lights had been dimmed in the cell corridor, but some light filtered in through the open cell fronts. The sounds of some snoring and whispers came through, also. Some whispers were those issued in passion. She could tell, and since there were no men in that cell block, she could arrive at no other conclusion than it was female to female passion. She shuddered and she began to tremble, wringing her hands and shaking her head.

Where had she gone so wrong in her life she wondered. She had tried to be a decent person. She thought she had been. Her sins, as she related them to herself, were minor enough, but, her minor sins had induced traumatic events.

She thought of her childhood... the Foster family. The school teachers who had made a "lady" of her... of Douglas Walker, and her tragic relationship with him. Of Verlie... of her rape at the hands of a deranged Mario Cullotta. The loss of a small fortune when she "gave" her land away. And, Laverne! Her thought went to that wild and beautiful creature who had led her into the trouble which finally put her where she was this very night.

But, could she really blame Laverene? No, she was an adult when she agreed to become a drug runner. It was the lure of easy money which caused her downfall.

Her final thoughts vere reserved for Jordan McNair, the only man she had ever loved. The only man she would ever love. She relived those estatics moments in that hotel in Washington and the passion which produced her son. Her son? Where was he now? How old was he? Let's see. He was born... when was it? In 1957? He'd be about two years old now. What did he look like? What was he like? Her heart ached for her child and the man she loved.

She began to cry, at. first, softly, and then more audibly. The black .woman in the lower bunk shook her head. They always cry the first night, she remembered. She tolerated it for as long as her cynical nature would allow. "Rainey, girl, quit that damn crying... you hear me! It ain't gonna git you otta here no how. Now, go to sleep before I crawl in that damn bed with you and really give you something to cry about."

She placed her hands over her mouth to stifle her sobs. Her body shuddered. Her head throbbed. She had never been so miserable in her entire life. Never had she felt so God-forsaken, so forlorn, so helpless.

The next night she found out what Ora Lee had meant by her offhand comment the night before. As they lay in bed after lights out, Ora Lee called out softly, "Rainey, come on down here, baby, let's talk."

Skeptical, but not wanting to agitate the woman, she replied even more softly, "I'm sleepy, Ora Lee. I want to go to sleep. I'm tired."

In a more agitated voice. "Rainey, git yore white ass down here and git it now. This ain't gonna be no free ride fer you while you in this place. Now, goddamit, git down here."

Fearful of what would happen if she resisted and even more fearful of what would happen if she didn't, she slid off the top bunk and stood by the lower one. Ora Lee was strip naked, lying on her side, close to the wall. Taking Rainey by the hand, she said, once again, softly, "Come on, baby, you be nice to Ora Lee and Ora Lee will be nice to you. Ora Lee will see to it that you ain't gonna be bothered by them bull-dykes they got in this place. You betta be thankful that Ora Lee likes men more than women. But, when you ain't got... you make do with what you got. Now, climb in this bunk."

Rainey, still being held by Ora Lee's powerful grip, shook her head in desperation. She slowly and gently sat on the edge of the bed. The black woman put a hand on her shoulder, forcing her down on the bed. "Nah, that's betta, baby. You just relax and try to have some fun yoresef. You'll git use to it."

* * *

As she had promised, Maggie did, indeed, visit Rainey each and every week during her incarceration period of ten years. She had made up her mind to be a good girl and cause no trouble. She was determined to serve no more than her minimum sentence.

It had only been three weeks into her imprisonment when Maggie, holding both of Rainey's hands as they sat across from each other at the bare table, asked, "How are they treating you, honey?"

She didn't reply far a long time. Maggie could tell this was a painful question to answer for she felt she knew the answer. Rainey lowered her eyes and sighed. "Well, if you like being fondled by a male guard every time you pass them, and you like being forcibly seduced by your cellmate several times a week, then, you'd just love this place," and she began to fight back tears.

Maggie's eyes widened and then narrowed with anger. "Rainey, you don't have to tolerate this. Why, I'll write to the..."

Rainey placed her hand on her friend's. "No... please, Maggie, don't do anything... don't say anything about this..."

"But.," she protested. She was cut off again.

"No, I mean it. You know what those indignities buy you?"

The black woman shook her head. Her eyes narrowed as Rainey continued. "They buy peace and quiet and a degree of protection, that's what."

Maggie gave her a sympathetic look. "But, is it worth it'?"

Rainey looked off into space, not wanting to look in her friend's eyes. "Well, the male guards can only grope and fondle. They don't have access to us, if you're careful to stay out of their way, but," and she sighed, "there's not much you can do about a cellmate who is bigger and stronger than you are."

Maggie shook her head in disgust. She could only imagine how a beautiful and shapely woman like Rainey would be desired in a place like this, even among her own gender. She placed her hand on Rainey's cheek, tears in her eyes.

"Please don't cry for me, Maggie. At least my cellmate is tender and sensitive at times. It could be worse."

Maggie rose to leave. "Do you need anything, honey?"

She was embarrassed. "I would like some cigarettes, but you know they kept all my money for evidence. I don't have any money to pay for them..."

"Rainey, as long as I'm alive and Calvin is still working, you don't need money. I'll get you some, sweetheart." Turning to move towards the door, she said, "Your cellmate? You haven't told me what she's like. Is she white or black?"

Rainey hesitated. "She's black. I didn't want to bring it up. Her color makes no difference to me... you know that."

Maggie nodded as she moved back closer to Rainey. "But, it makes a big difference to me. What's her name?"

"Ora Lee... Ora Lee Wilson."

Maggie pondered her reply far a moment. "Rainey, I want you to do something for me. I know that you prisoners have to place the visitors on a list for the prison authorities to check out. I want you to ask Ora Lee Wilson to request a time for Magnolia Hunter to visit her."

Rainey's eyebrows went up at the mention of her real name, Magnolia. "Magnolia... Magnolia Hunter? Why Magnolia? You told me you haven't used that name in yesrs."

"That's right, and I told you because it was stereotyped. You remember?"

"I remember."

She giggled. "I want that black woman to know there is a black woman coming to see her... that's why."

"But, what on earth will you say to her?"

"Now, Rainey, honey, thats gonna be between two black women. You wouldn't understand if I told you. Just set it up, okay?"

She shrugged. "I'll try, but what if she doesn't want to see you."

"Just tell her my husband is a doctor and I'm concerned about her health and her future. That's all."

305

As her cellmate took in the words of Maggie's request to see her, Rainey waited for a response. Ora Lee pondered the strange request for a moment. Ever cynical, ever suspicious, she turned it over in her mind, looking for ramifications.

"What she want with me? How come that woman... that Magnolia, wants to visit me. Ah don't know her even if she is a black woman... what she want?"

"She wouldn't tell me, Ora Lee, I swear."

"You say her husband is a doctor?"

"Uh, huh."

Oral Lee pondered the matter for a long time, then grabbing Rainey by the hand and jerking her around to face her, "You ain't told her 'bout us... did you?"

"What... what... do you mean?"

"Bout us foolin' around at night... you know. You ain't told her 'bout that... did you?"

Rainey chose her words carefully in view of her menacing stance. "Well, no, Ora Lee, I certainly did not go into any details... no."

"And you say she wants to talk to me 'bout mah health and mah future?"

"That's what she said," and Rainey shrugged her shoulders.

"Whal, what kin it hurt? Ah 'll have her put on the list, but that woman betta not try to pull no crap on me... black or not!"

It was nearly two weeks before the visit between Maggie Hunter and Ora Lee Wilson took place. It was a short visit. It lasted only fifteen minutes. The ever present guards could overhear raised voices at the beginning, but then, the conversation became nearly muted with hand waving and finger pointing, and finally, a hand shake between the two women. The guards assumed a family dispute had been settled amicably.

Later that night, as they lay in their cell bunks, neither woman said anything for a long time. Rainey was just dying to know what had transpired between the two black women, but she was afraid to bring it up. Finally, it was Ora Lee who broke the silence. "You know, Rainey, that Magnolia Hunter is the nicest li'l woman Ah eva met. She's sweet... and some smart, too. She talks like a college professor. She shur do."

Rainey waited for Ora Lee to expand on her comments but none was forthcoming. Curiousity ate at her until she could contain it no longer. "Well, what did she want with you, Ora Lee?"

"Oh, she didn't want nothin' special. Like she said, she wanted to talk 'bout mah health and mah future."

"Well, what did she say about your health and your future."

Ora Lee giggled. "Well, all Ah kin say is mah health is good and mah future looks brighter than it did before, when Ah gits out in a few years. That's all Ah got to say, Rainey. Nah, you go on and go to sleep. Ora Lee's got some thinkin' to do. Goodnight, sweetie."

Rainey often, in weeks and months to come, wondered what Maggie had done or said to change Ora Lee's actions towards her. She wasn't sure, but there was a definite change in their relationship. There were no more nocturnal visits between bunks-never again, and Ora Lee took on a more protective attitude towards her white cellmate which even extended to the other prisoners. On one occasion, when several women were in the gang shower together, where considerable groping and fondling took place, much to the amusement of the female guards, another prisoner, a white woman, began to soap Ralney's back, without invitation, and her hands gradually made their way to her pelvic area. Ora Lee, soaping herself nearby, saw the transgression and the perpetrator was rewarded with a bar of soap in her mouth and an admonition: "Keep yore hands to yoreself, bitch, this li'l white ass belongs to Ora Lee," with a wink and a grin towards Rainey.

* * *

Maggie was as excited as a child on the day they were scheduled to pick Rainey up, the day on which she was to be discharged from prison. "Come on, Calvin. We gonna be late if you don't hurry, and I know Rainey is anxious to get out of that place."

He chuckled. He was used to his high strung wife after nearly twenty years of marriage. "Now, now, Maggie, I don't know who will be the happiest today; you or Rainey."

As she gave herself one final look in the mirror: "Well, if you had been in that place for the past ten years, you'd be happy to get out. I feel like I served time with her."

He took his wife's hands in his. "Are you sure you're not too involved with this thing?"

She was adamant. "No! Rainey and I go back a long ways, Calvin, and I'm the only friend she's got in this world."

He chuckled. "Okay, baby, if that makes you happy."

Rainey's eyes were moist as she met her friends in the small area set aside for the meeting of families at discharge time. She warmly embraced Maggie, and then, Calvin. Maggie gave her despondent friend a discerning look as she held both her hands. "Now, you listen to me, girl. When you walk out that door, I want you to put all this behind you. It's all over... like a bad dream."

Rainey nodded. "Uh, huh, a ten year dream."

Maggie was persistent. "I don't care. It's still all over. Now, when you walk out in that sunshine, I want to see the blue of the sky reflected in the blue of those eyes, and I want to see a smile on that beautiful face. You hear me?"

Rainey tightened her grip on her friend's hands. "I hear you, Maggie," and turning to Calvin, "How can you live with this domineering woman?"

Calvin chuckled. "It ain't easy, Rainey, honey, it ain't easy."

In spite of Maggie's admonition, Rainey's spirit lacked ebullience after the first days of euphoria had worn off. She began to spend a great deal of time sitting alone on the same old back yard swing she had sat on so many years ago, under the same old two hundred year old oak. Maggie could see her from the kitchen window just as Martha Powell had so my years before.

Maggie, trained as a nurse, with some courses in psychology, stood looking at her friend on many occasions, merely shaking her head. She had discussed the matter with Calvin, who, trained as a general practitioner and family physician, had more insight and objectivity in the matter than did his wife. He counseled Maggie. "Be patient, baby. It has to run its course."

"Suppose it doesn't?"

"Then, I'll try to arrange some counseling for her, but, first, let mother nature go to work."

Rainey, with some justification, was highly resentful of the ten years which had been extracted from her life by a vengeful society. She, in moments of reflection, realized that she should share some responsibility for her actions. Her agreement to work with Laverne as a courier had been an act of stupidity. She knew that, although it had seemed like a good idea at the time- more like a sorority initiation prank.

She continued this review of her past life, to come up with some explanation as to why she had failed so often when others like Maggie, had pulled their lives together with happy results. Martha Powell and Verlie had both been wrong. There were happy marriages- many of them. She realized she had been looking in the wrong places. Martha Powell was right about one admonition-IF YOU PLAY IN THE MUD, YOU WILL GET MUDDY.

Most of her thoughts were about Jordan McNair. Where had she gone wrong with him? She had not agreed to any intimacy until she was assured that he was not living with his wife. He had assured her he did not love his wife. She truly believed that, too. (It is so easy to believe what you want to be true to begin with) Yet, her liason with Jordan had ended in a disaster for her. She shook her head as she suppressed tears in recalling it. She had conducted herself as a "nice girl" should. She had tried all her life to be a "nice girl" since her mother had not been one. She felt she owed it to her mother to be a "nice girl".

Then, her thoughts went to her child, that unfortunate result of her night of unparalleled passion with the father. But, he was not a baby anymore. No! He was... what?... now- over ten years old, as she mentally calculated the years and the months. What did he look like? Whom did he looked like. She would not have minded if he looked more like Jordan than her. After all, Jordan was an extremely handsome man. But, of course, she admitted in a moment of non-modesty, "I'm kinda pretty, too."

In time, her despondency faded as Calvin had predicted to Maggie it would. If time did not heal, then humans, who have the most retentive memory of all mammals, would live lives composed mostly of regrets. Nature is neither harsh nor cruel. She is merely indifferent.

After she had spent the first two months of her newly won freedom with Maggie and Calvin Hunter, her conscience began to bother her. She had freeloaded all that time, at their insistence. But, she remembered reading in school the wise words of that wise man, Benjamin Franklin, who maintained that "fish and company both began to turn bad after three days".

"No, Maggie, no matter what you and Calvin say, it's time I move on. It's time I get on with this miserable life of mine," she said in jest, managing a smile, but she felt that way about her life.

Maggie stood her ground. "Where're you gonna go, girl? You don't have any money..."

"That's another thing. No, it's the main thing, Maggie! How do you think I feel about you having to buy my cigarettes and giving me money to buy my necessities..."

Maggie grinned. "So, that's it, huh? The poor little white girl has her feelings hurt that this little black girl has to give her money" She laughed. "Hell, that's what's been going on in reverse order for the past two hundred years in the south. You gonna deny me my pleasures, Rainey?"

They hugged, both giggling like children.

"In spite of what you say, Maggie, I have my pride."

Maggie was no fool. She recognized an opportunity when one stared her in the face. "You know something, Rainey, you are right. I do think it's time you quit free loading and went to work," and before a surprised Rainey could reply, Maggie added, "I'm gonna have Calvin find you a job in the clinic. You got to be good for something, girl."

CHAPTER THIRTY THREE

"You're just being stubborn, Rainey! There is no logic to your moving to some boarding house place just so you can say you're not dependent of us anymore. There's just no sense to it."

"She's right, Rainey," piped in Calvin Hunter as he looked up from the daily paper.

"Look," added Maggie, "the kids are off to college and Calvin and I are alone in this big house. We'd be glad to have your company. Besides," as she winked at her husband, "maybe that old goat would quit chasing me around the house at night if there was someone else around."

Calvin winked towards Rainey. "Oh, I don't know about that, sugar. Rainey's been here for some weeks now and I ain't slowed down one bit, yet."

Rainey smiled at her friend. "And you love every minute of it, Maggie."

"I sure do," she chuckled, "but, to get back to the suject at hand, Rainey. If you have to salve your conscience now that you're making money again with your job at the clinic, why, then, pay us some room and board money. Would that make you happy?"

"It would make it more acceptable to me."

"Well, then do it, girl. Huh, Calvin?" as she looked at her husband.

He smiled at both. "You girls leave me out of those high-leveled negotiations," and turning to Rainey, "you know it is not necessary that you pay anything, but, if it makes you feel better..."

"How much do you want me to pay?" she inquired.

"Hell, Rainey, whatever you want. We're not gonna starve no matter what you pay. This is for your benefit, not ours."

She pondered the matter for a moment. "Well, let's see. I make about four hundred a month, so, if I paid you two hundred for room and board, that would leave me two hundred to spend, so..."

"No, interrupted Maggie, "that's too much. One hundred a month would suffice, I think... huh, Calvin?"

"Whatever you say, baby."

"No," protested Rainey, "that's not enough. Let's compromise at one hundred and fifty."

Maggie got up and went to her, patting her on the head. "Okay, Rainey, one hundred and fifty a month, and grinning at her, "and I expect to be paid on time. I don't want to have to dun you for it."

Rainy smiled. "I promise."

And so, in the year 1968, Rainey was once again ensconced in the very same house she had lived in for eight years beginning about thirty years before. As they say, what goes around comes around. But, for the first time in her life she now lived with a functional family; one with a mama and a papa and with children, although they were now grown and gone to college. They still came home two weekends a month and the old house came alive. Maggie and Calvin both had siblings- in Maggie's case, plenty of siblings. On weekends, when the siblings came over for the usual barbeque yard party, people abounded everywhere. Of course, Rainey's was the only white face in the crowd, and at first, it was a little awkward for the black faces to accept her, but in time it made little or no difference to any of them. She was just one of the family.

The bitterness and resentment of her long incarceration still ate at her and if one looked carefully at her at these family gatherings one could detect a sad expression on her countenance from time to time, and then, she would shake her head and smile once again to whomever she was speaking.

As to her social life, it was virtually nil. She went to movies from time to time, alone. For even in those days, especially in rural areas, blacks were confined to the balconies in the old movie houses. She could not accept this practice in spite of her friend's protests: "Oh, go ahead, Rainey. We don't mind. We're used to this."

And as to men and male companionship, she still had a problem with that. Like any woman of thirty-eight, she was still young and vibrant and her emotions churned like they had since reaching maturity. But, whenever she had consented to go out with men she had met at the clinic or those Maggie and Calvin had steered towards her, she was still awkward with them. If they attempted any degree of intimacy, even to the simple holding of hands in a movie, or helping her down some steps, she stiffened. She could not explain it herself, but it was there.

There was one man in particular who had aroused some interest in her- nothing spectacular, but something. She had even, after his persistent pleadings, decided to make an attempt at the ultimate intimacy, more as an experiment than the satisfying of desire. As she later explained it to Maggie: "To see if it was really just in my mind... like a mental block."

"And," asked a wide-eyed Maggie. "How was it?"

She shook her head, making no audible reply. Maggie, four years older than Rainey, and a very perceptive woman, sensed her problem. "As long as you believe that Jordan McNair is the only man for you, you're gonna have that problem, honey."

She knew what Maggie was right, but, she also felt that these things could not be forced. They had to come from the heart, not the loins. To the lusty forty-two year old Maggie, this was more than she could fathom. She had not disguised her feelings in dealing with the subject on some occasions: "Rainey, baby, you might just as well be a nun. You ain't having no fun," she teased in the black dialect of her youth.

Rainey sighed. "I know, Maggie, but, I just don't want them, not yet, anyway..."

"But, Rainey, Jordan is gone, honey. You don't have him and you probably never will."

She nodded. "Yes, I know, but, he's the only one I want, and if I can't have him, then, I don't want any of them."

Maggie shook her head. "I don't understand women like you, Rainey," and she chuckled. "As much as I love that Calvin, if anything happened to him, well, I'd find me another man, I swear to you, I would. It isn't natural to live like you live, Rainey. It just ain't natural!"

But, for the time being, that was the way she wanted it. She was not happy with it, but she would not have been happy with the alternative, either.

This went on for several years and there was nothing Maggie could do to change her feelings, try as she might.

The winter of 1974-75 was coming to an end, and although winters are not severe in southern Arkansas, the advent of spring is always welcomed. Maggie was especially happy and excited as she discussed the matter with Rainey.

"Guess what, Rainey? Calvin is going to attend a meeting of The General Practicioners Association and he's agreed to take me with him, and guess where it is?"

Rainey smiled at her as she sipped her coffee. "I have no idea... where?"

"St. Louis! I always wanted to go there," and she began to sway as she sang: "St. Louie woman... with her diamond rings..."

The sound of the name of the town where she had given birth and abandoned her baby jolted her, as it always did, but she smiled at her friend's good fortune. "I'm so happy for you. I know you'll enjoy it. St. Louis is a beautiful city. Be sure you go to Forest Park."

Maggie placed her hands on Rainey's. "Come with us. It was Calvin's idea... no kidding. He wants you to come."

She shook her head. "Oh, no, Maggie. You and Calvin should go alone," and she smiled. "You two can make it a second honeymoon," she cooed.

"Huh, that old rooster doesn't need a hotel room for that. He thinks he's on one every week in this house."

"You're a lucky woman, Maggie, to still have your man wanting you after all these years."

Maggie became serious. "You have to work at it, honey. It doesn't happen on its own, believe me. You have to keep a man interested," and she laughed. "They're not monogamous by nature. They're born philanderers, you know. Nature made them that way."

Rainey sighed and chuckled. "I wouldn't know. I haven't had one of my own long enough to tell."

Maggie started to say: That's your fault, honey, but she didn't. There was no sense in hurting the poor woman's feelings.

"Are you sure you won't come, Rainey?"

"I'm sure, Maggie, but I thank you and Calvin for asking me. It was very unselfish of you to do so. Besides, who's going to house-sit for you while you're gone if I don't?"

"Good point," replied Maggie.

* * *

Maggie could hardly refrain from issuing gushy reports on St. Louis for weeks after the trip. No matter what the subject was under discussions, she found some way to tie it into her trip.

"What did you do with your time when Calvin was in his meetings?" asked Rainey.

"Oh, I had no difficulty in finding something to do in that town, believe me."

"Like what?"

She gave both Calvin and Rainey a coquettish look. "Well, really, Rainey, you surely don't expect me to tell you what I did every minute. I do have my secrets, you know..."

Calvin gave her a bemused look, shaking his head, and returning to his paper.

"Did you go to Forest Park like I suggested?"

"Uh, huh."

"And did you go to the zoo?"

"Uh, huh."

"What did you see in the zoo?"

"Animals... plenty of animals."

"Did you see Marlin Perkins?"

Maggie giggled. "Are you making fun of me?"

"Uh, huh."

Rainey had noticed a nervousness in Maggie since her return from St. Louis, and to some extent, also in Calvin. She could not put her finger an it, but it was there.

As they sat in the kitchen that morning, on April 17, 1975, Maggie was more nervous than usual. She had always been sort of hyper, but this was different. She had been cleaning the house for the past three days, in places that had not been cleaned since last spring. Rainey watched her for some telltale signs. "Do you feel alright, Maggie?"

Her eyes widened. "Of course, I do. Why do you ask?"

"You seem to be more hyper than usual," she smiled.

"Oh, it's springtime. I just love springtime. I guess my sap is rising," she grinned, and then, "Rainey, do you know what the date is today?"

"Yes, Maggie, it's April the seventeenth."

"That's right. And what is tomorrow, Rainey?" as if she were speaking to a child.

So that was it. Rainey smiled. "Tomorrow is my birthday, and I'm sure you know that. You don't have to hear it from me."

Maggie would not be denied. "And how old will you be tomorrow?"

Rainey decided to humor her. "I will be forty-five, tomorrow, and you damn sure don't have to remind me of it," she smiled.

Maggie took her hands. "Rainey... Calvin and I want to take you out for a fabulous supper tomorrow night..."

"Oh, Maggie, you and Calvin have done so much for me, already, save your money..."

"No, we will not be denied," and she chuckled as she continued, "especially since they have just admitted Calvin to Pine Crest golf club. We are now full-fledged members. We can eat in the dining room just "lak white foks," she mimicked.

"Oh, I'm so happy for you two. It's about time."

"Oh, bullshit, Rainey. If Calvin wasn't a doctor, he'd never have made it, believe me."

"Well, what the hell? You made it and that's all that counts."

"But," as Maggie raised her hand, "that is not all we want to do for you."

Her eyes widened. Maggie was acting strangely, she could tell it. Like a high school girl with a secret as she continued.

"And, also, we want to send you to the beauty salon in the morning far a complete overhall..."

Rainey started to protest."

Maggie raised both hands. "Believe me, Rainey, it's a purely selfish act on our part."

"What do you mean? Selfish? Don't you mean selfless?"

She giggled. "No, I meant what I said," and she smiled, shaking her head. "Rainey, honey, you look like shit these days. Look in the mirror. You're a beautiful woman... you still are, too, but you don't do a damn thing for yourself. Your self image must be terrible. You have stringy hair which badly needs some coloring to hide those grey streaks coming in profusion these days and you don't use the right makeup, and you..."

Rainey raised her hands this time. "Okay... okay... I get the picture. I look like hell..."

"No." Maggie shook her head. "I said you look like shit. You have gone beyond hell, and Calvin and I have taken all we're going to take. Before we take you out tomorrow night, you have to do something with yourself."

Rainey looked deep in her friend's eyes. "Isn't this a little overkill? Do I really look that bad?"

Maggie gave her an embarrassed look. "No... but if I hadn't laid it on the line, you'd have given me some backtalk. Now, are you going to let me and Calvin do this for you?"

"That's going to cost a lot of money..."

"We can afford it, Rainey. How about it?"

She shrugged her shoulders. "If you really want to."

Not since the foray in that beauty salon in St. Louis so many years before had she had the complete works done to her-a complete overhaul- an automobile mechanic would have called it. Her hair was bleached to a nice blond color and cut fairly short as middle-aged woman are prone to wear it. She had a mud pack and a massage which brought color to her cheeks. The beautician, who had just come back from an update course at a school in Chicago, showed her the kind of makeup she needed to fit her bone structure and coloring.

As she perused herself in the mirror with Maggie looking over her shoulder, she turned around to her friend. "Was it worth the money?"

Maggie grinned. "Well, honey, my sexual preference is males, but if I stretch a point, you do look great," and she poked her in the ribs..."even sexy."

Rainey shook her head. "Sexy? Oh, my God. I never expected to look like that again... never."

Maggie became serious. "Don't sell yourself short, Rainey. You still have it, girl. You just don't know what the hell to do with it."

When they had returned home, Rainey stood before Calvin as he looked her up and down, walking around her.

She smiled at him, waiting for a comment which she felt sure was coming. He grinned. He whistled. "Whew, Rainey, baby, if only you were black."

Maggie shook her head at her husband, "At least, Calvin, you know what color your bread is buttered with."

Rainey held her arms wide as they all came together and hugged. "I want to thank you for it all. I really do appreciate it," and as she stepped back, "but we did this too early. we're not going out until tonight. What'll I do all afternoon all made up and no place to go?"

Maggie and Calvin exchanged glances, and Maggie looked at the clock on the mantle. "Why don't you go outside and sit on the swing. It's so pretty out there, today. I'll fix us a light salad lunch since we're going out tonight for a big meal. I'll call you when it's ready. Okay?"

Rainey's eyebrows went up and she shrugged. "Gee, it's great to have a birthday. Why don't you treat me like this every day?"

Maggie grunted. "Because, everyday is not your birthday."

The black couple watched from the kitchen window as she sauntered to the old swing in the back yard. They smiled as she dusted the swing off, making sure as she sat that she did not fold her dress under her. She crossed her legs and raised her head as if to test the air for fragrances.

Rainey watched as the expensive late model automobile came to a halt in the street in front of the house. The oak tree and the swing were off to the side in the rear yard. It was from this vantage point that she had watched the traffic go by many years ago, as a young girl. She saw the man in the car look at the house and then down in the car. He pulled in the driveway leading to the porte cochere.

How presumptious of him, she thought, as she had always considered the porte cochere the private entrance of the home's owner. She watched as he got out of the car and stood there looking at the house for same time. He was tall, over six feet. He was also very young, not quite twenty, she concluded. She strained to see him better. He was probably some young friend of Calvins's- from the clinic, maybe. He saw her sitting on the swing and he headed in her direction. This surprised her. She became somewhat suspicious. He looked like he might be a salesman- an insurance salesman, she guessed.

Calvin and Maggie watched from the kitchen window, their arms around each other. Maggie looked up at her husband. "Should we go to her?"

"No, let her handle it."

As he came closer, he was smiling. She could not help but think there was something about him- his smile- his walk- the way he carried himself. He walked directly up to her. She waited for him to speak. "Excuse me, Ma'am, but I was wondering if you could help me." His voice was low-pitched and well modulated for one so young, she thought.

She returned his smile. She felt she had never seen a young man so handsome as this in all her life, as she responded. "How may I help you?"

"Well, I'm looking for someone."

"What is his name? Perhaps I might know him."

He was still standing, looking down at her. "It's a she. "I'm not sure what her name is these days."

She smiled, feeling he was playing games with her. "How can you find her if you don't know her name." He reminded her of someone, but she could not be sure.

He pointed to the swing. "May I sit down? I find it difficult to speak to you from up here?"

She felt he was being a little presumptuous for a stranger, but she moved over. "Please do... sit down." She looked into eyes as blue as hers. Her heart beat faster. She didn't understand what was happening to her, but something about this young man stirred her emotions.

He said softly. "I hope I'm not being too forward, or, personal, but you see... I'm trying to find my mother. I was told she might reside here in this house."

Her mouth opened. She could not believe her ears or her eyes, as he continued. "Did you by any chance give birth to a baby boy in St. Louis on October 17, 1957, in St. Ignatius' Hospital?"

She stared in disbelief. Her mouth opened and her eyes went wide. She breathed hard. "Oh, my God... my son," and she collapsed in his arms. He said nothing as he patted her back, attempting to soothe her. She would move her head back to look at him, and then hold him close. She finally regained some composure. She wiped her eyes with the hankerchief he handed her. It had the same scent as his father. He sat smiling at her, also fighting back tears. Between sobs: "How did you find me?"

He nodded towards the house as he saw Calvin and Maggie coming forward, grinning from ear to ear. "I could never have done it if it hadn't been for your friends, here," and he nodded to them.

Rainey looked up at the couple. "Maggie... Calvin... do you have any idea who this is. He is my baby... my son."

Maggie could no longer hold the tears, and she, too, began to cry as she hugged Rainey. "I know, honey. We met him in St. Louis when we went to the convention."

Calvin just stood there smiling. He knew there wasn't much he could say that would interest anyone at this time.

"But, how did you find him?" Rainey persisted, as she ran her fingers over his cheeks, as if to be assured he was really there in the flesh.

Maggie now wiped her eyes with Calvin's handkerchief. She sniffed. "It wasn't really all that hard. I just looked up the name of the company in the phone book, and... I figured it was time someone had a talk with Jordan McNair... that's all."

Rainey gasped. "Jordan? He's back in this country?"

The son smiled. "Oh, Mother, we've been back in this country for years..."

She grabbed his arm. "Your father? How is he?"

The boy nodded towards the car, and waving his hand. "Why don't you ask him for yourself? Here he is, coming this way."

Rainey looked up in that direction. She could not believe her eyes, but there he was. She'd know that walk anywhere. She broke loose from their grasp and ran to him. He stopped- his arms outstretched as she ran into his grasp. They stood for a long time, simply holding each other, not even looking at the eyes. Then, she moved back and held him at arms length.

"Oh, Jordan, I thought I'd never set eyes on you, again. I can't believe it even now," and she held him close.

He caressed her back, her hair, as he said soft words like these. "I've never forgotten you, Rainey. I just didn't know where to find you. I tried, but the people I hired told me you were in..." and he could not finish it.

She nodded. This was not the time. She had to know something more important. "And, Nancy, how is she... and the girls?"

"The girls are fine. They're both married, now, and with children." Then, he became serious. "Nancy has been dead for almost five years. She had cancer..."

"Oh, Jordan, I'm sorry... I really am... so sorry."

Be nodded. He took her by the hand and returned to the others, and taking their son by the hand, he brought him forward. "Well, Rainey, what do you think of this young man you brought into the world?"

She sniffed as she held them both close. "He's beautiful. I'm so proud of him."

Maggie reviewed. the scene for a long time, then: "My goodness, what kind of hostess am I? Let's all go in the house and have some refreshments."

Jordan, the father, took her hand. "Maggie, I can't thank you enough for all you've done... getting us back together again. I'll never be able to repay you for this."

"Sure you can, Jordan. Just take that woman off my hands. That's all I ask. I just can't stand that moping around like she does all the time. For God's sake, take her with you."

Rainey was embarrassed at her friend's crass request that he take her with him. "Really, Maggie, must you be so presumptuous? Jordan doesn't... he's not required... he might not..."

"Let the woman talk, Rainey. She knows what she's doing," Jordan interrupted as he smiled at them.

Maggie looked at her. "You know me, Rainey. I don't believe in beating around the bush, girl. When I talked to him in St. Louis and found he was as moonstruck as you and he was single... well, that's all it takes for old Maggie to go to work."

Rainey grabbed Maggie's hand, holding her back. "Have you and Calvin been planning this since you came back from St. Louis?"

"We sure have."

"And all that baloney about taking me out for dinner tonight at the country club was just that... simply baloney?"

Calvin chimed in. "Oh, no, that invitation still stands, but what I didn't tell you is that I made reservations for five, not three people."

After entering the house, Rainey pulled Maggie aside. "Oh, Maggie, thank you so much for making me go to the beauty parlor. Why, if he had seen me like I was... well... I just don't know..."

Maggie chuckled. "Oh, I don't know about that, honey. The way that man feels about you, he'll take you any way he can get you, but, it don't hurt to fudge a little, does it?"

As they danced later that evening at the country club, Jordan held her close-not at first, because he treated her like a porcelain doll, not sure of her reaction.

But, as she moved her fingers on his neck, he brought her in. He wispered in her ear: "You remember that room in that hotel in Washington?"

She cuddled her face in his neck. "Oh, yes, I'll never forget it, Jordan," and turning her head to look at their son who was dancing with Maggie, she whispered back, "That's when we made him... you remember'?"

"Uh, huh, I remember. But, you know, Rainey, we still have unfinished business between us..."

She moved her head back. "We do?"

He brought her in close again. "That boy needs a mother."

She nodded. "I think all children should have mothers." These words burned in her for they had special meaning to her.

He nodded. "You know, I just happen to have reservations at that same hotel for this coming week, in the same room.

Are you interested?"

"Oh, yes, Jordan," and she moved her head back to look at him. "You know, you never did finish showing me the Smithsonian."

THE END

9 780759 621268